Thomas B. Johnston, James A. Robertson

**Historical Geography of the Clans of Scotland**

Thomas B. Johnston, James A. Robertson

**Historical Geography of the Clans of Scotland**

ISBN/EAN: 9783337391645

Printed in Europe, USA, Canada, Australia, Japan

Cover: Foto ©Andreas Hilbeck / pixelio.de

More available books at **www.hansebooks.com**

# HISTORICAL GEOGRAPHY

## OF THE

# CLANS OF SCOTLAND

BY

T. B. JOHNSTON, F.R.G.S.

AND

Colonel JAMES A. ROBERTSON

*THIRD EDITION*

EDITED WITH

## A NARRATIVE OF THE HIGHLAND CAMPAIGNS

BY

WILLIAM KIRK DICKSON

W. & A. K. JOHNSTON

EDINBURGH AND LONDON

MDCCCXCIX

# PREFACE TO THE FIRST EDITION.

1358155

THE following publication was suggested by the frequent applications made to the Publishers for information as to the limits and positions of the districts occupied by the CLANS OF SCOTLAND, and as to the correct line of separation between the Highlands and the Lowlands. At first nothing more was intended than a reproduction of one of the old maps, which have now become scarce, but a little investigation showed that the best of them were very imperfect and inaccurate, and not worth reproducing. In these circumstances it was found necessary to commence the work from the beginning, taking as a basis the Acts of Parliament of 1587 and 1594, for the reason given in the note explanatory of the Map. After having produced the Map, it was thought that some interesting additions could be made to the publication by combining with it, in a convenient form, several articles connected with the Highlands not of easy access to the general public—such as the Roll of the Clans, Strength of the Highland Forces, their War Cries, Badges, etc. Having gone so far, it followed, almost as a matter of course, to introduce the last appearance of the Clans as an Army, when they rallied round the standard of the unfortunate Prince Charles, an interest in whose adventures, and those of his gallant followers, can never cease to be felt so long as the exquisite songs and ballads in which they are narrated maintain their place as "household words," not only in every house in this country, but also in every distant land in which the Scottish emigrant has found a home. This led to the Map of the Prince's Wanderings, the Plans and Descriptions of his Battles, and, as a sequel, the Act of Parliament of 1746 for disarming the Highlands and restricting the Use of the Highland Dress.

It will thus be seen that the work is not in any sense a history of the Clans, although it is hoped that it may be found a useful companion to any history of Scotland, or of the Highlands.

*August 1872.*

# PREFACE TO THE THIRD EDITION.[1]

T HE foregoing Preface sufficiently indicates the original plan of the present work. The First Edition was received with much favour by the public, and a Second Edition was soon called for. It has been out of print for many years, and a Third Edition has now been prepared in response to numerous inquiries.

In the present Edition the general plan of the book has been adhered to, but has been considerably modified in detail. The "Roll of the Landislordis and Baillies," Roll of the Clans, etc., have been retained, the appended notes having been revised and corrected. The Lists of Badges and War Cries of the Clans have been revised and added to. Two documents have been added which afford much interesting information as to the state of the Highlands between 1715 and 1745. General Wade's Report of 1724, and an extract from a "Memorial anent the True State of the Highlands," attributed to Lord President Forbes. The Disarming Act of 1746 is again printed at length, as illustrating the policy by which the Government ultimately succeeded in breaking up the old militant clan system. The itineraries of Prince Charles and descriptions of his battles have been omitted, and their substance has been incorporated in a continuous narrative of the Highland campaigns, from the time of Montrose down to the end of the Forty-five, which now forms Part II. of the work.

The Maps and Plans have been revised, and a new Map, to illustrate the rising of 1715, has been added. The former Plan of the Battle of Culloden has been replaced by a new one, based on Home's plan and description. A few illustrations have also been added. The portraits are reproduced from engravings kindly lent for the purpose by Mr James Bruce, W.S.

The historical narrative does not profess to be more than the brief recapitulation of an oft-told tale.

[1] Both the authors are now dead. Mr T. B. Johnston, Geographer to the Queen for Scotland, died in 1897 ; Colonel James Alexander Robertson, sometime of the 82nd Regiment, died in 1874. He was a son of General William Robertson of Lude, and was the last representative of that ancient family. He was the author of *Comitatus de Atholia, the Earldom of Atholl* (privately printed, 1860 : *Concise Historical Proofs respecting the Gael of Alban* 1865), and *The Gaelic Topography of Scotland* 1869).

*December 1898.*

# NOTE ON THE MAP.

THE large Map is constructed and coloured to show the situation and possessions of the Clans, and the properties of the landlords, in the Highlands and Islands of Scotland.

The Clans are enumerated in two Acts of the Scots Parliament, passed in 1587 and 1594 respectively, as to which see pages 3 and 7. The names of the landlords are appended to the Act of 1587. There is thus historical authority for the names and possessions of the persons occupying all the north of Scotland at the end of the sixteenth century.

This early date was selected, because then most of the Highland tribes were still in occupation of the lands which they had inherited from their forefathers. During the troubles of the following century some of the weaker clans were deprived of their possessions by their stronger neighbours.[1]

In compiling the Map Mr Johnston and Colonel Robertson made every effort to secure accuracy. It will be understood, however, that in most cases the boundaries of clan territories can be only approximately indicated.

The rotation and numbering of the Clans and Landlords have been made as they occur in the Acts of Parliament (see page 9).

On the Map the residences of the chiefs and heads of families are marked in black, having the number of the clan below in upright print, while the possessions of the landlords are named in italics with Roman numerals.

---

[1] General Stewart of Garth's well-known map shows the clan territories as in 1745. Mr W. B. Blaikie's *Itinerary of Prince Charles Edward Stuart* (Scottish History Society, 1897) contains a fine map, based, as regards the clan boundaries, on General Stewart's, with some necessary modifications.

# CONTENTS.

# MAPS AND ILLUSTRATIONS.

# PART I.

## CLAN LISTS, Etc.

# ROLL OF THE LANDISLORDIS AND BAILLIES.

THE ROLL OF THE NAMES OF THE LANDISLORDIS AND BAILLIES OF LANDIS IN THE HIELANDIS, QUHAIR BROKEN MEN HES DUELT AND PRESENTLIE DUELLIS, 1587.

[This and the following Roll of Clans are appended to the Act "For the quieting and keping in obedience of the disorderit subjectis inhabitantis of the Bordouris, Hielandis, and Ilis" (1587, c. 59, Acts of the Parliaments of Scotland, Record edition, vol. iii., p. 461). As to the working of this important Act, and the "General Band" or agreement of all landlords over the kingdom to be held responsible for the good behaviour of their tenants and adherents, see the Register of the Privy Council, vol. iv., pp. liii.-lv, and 781 *et seq.*]

## *Landislordis and Baillies.*

The Duke of Lennox.[1]

The Laird of Buchanane.[2]

The Laird of M'Farlane of the Arroquhar.[3]

The Laird of Luss.[4]

The Laird M'Cawla of Ardincaple.[5]

The Laird of Marchinstoun.[6]

The Laird of Glennegyis.[7]

The Erle of Glencarne.[8]

The Laird of Drumquhassil.[9]

[1] Ludovick, second Duke of Lennox, son of Esme Stuart, Lord of Aubigny in France. Born 1574. Had a charter under the Great Seal, July 31, 1583, of the Earldom of Lennox and various other lands, which had been erected into a dukedom. Was Great Chamberlain and High Admiral of Scotland ; attended James VI. to England, created Earl of Newcastle, Duke of Richmond, and K.G. Died 1624.

[2] Sir George Buchanan of that ilk, second of that name, and, according to Auchmar, nineteenth Laird of Buchanan. The lands of this family lay chiefly in the districts of Menteith and the Lennox, and are now possessed by the Duke of Montrose.

[3] Andrew Macfarlane of that ilk, descended, in the male line, from Gilchrist, a younger son of Alwyn, second Earl of Lennox, of the old family.

[4] Humphrey Colquhoun of Luss, who acquired the heritable coronership of Dumbartonshire from Robert Graham of Knockdollian, confirmed by charter under the Great Seal, 1583. Slain by the Macgregors after the battle of Glenfruin, 1604.

[5] Awlay, afterwards Sir Awlay Macawlay of Ardincaple, one of the principal vassals of the Duke of Lennox.

[6] Sir Archibald Napier of Merchiston and Edinbellie, father of John Napier of Merchiston, the inventor of Logarithms. He possessed lands in the earldoms of Menteith and Lennox, and likewise at Ardownane (or Ardeonaig), on the south side of Loch Tay, in virtue of his descent from Elizabeth, daughter of Murdoch Menteth, and sister and one of the co-heiresses of Patrick Menteth of Rusky.

[7] John Haldane of Glenegeis (now called Gleneagles), descended from Agnes, the other co-heiress of the above-mentioned Patrick Menteth of Rusky, through whom he possessed lands in the districts mentioned in the preceding note.

[8] James, seventh Earl of Glencairn. Perhaps only brought here as answerable for his kinsman, Drumquhassill (*see next note*). Glencairn was also connected with the Highlands by marriage, his first wife being eldest daughter (by the second marriage) of Sir Colin Campbell of Glenurchy.

[9] John Cunningham of Drumquhassill was served heir to his father, John Cunningham, in the £5 lands of old extent of Portnellan, Galbraith, and Tullochan, with the Islands of Loch Lomond, adjacent to the same, in the Dukedom of Lennox, 1613.—(*Dumbarton Retours, No.* 15.)—This family descended from Andrew Cunninghame, said to have been a younger son of Sir Robert Cunningham of Kilmaurs, and to have lived in the reign of David II.

The Laird of Kilcreuch.[10]
The Tutour of Menteith.[11]
The Laird of Knokhill.[12]
Hary Schaw of Cambusmoir.
The Laird of Kippanross.[13]
The Laird of Burley.[14]
The Laird of Keir.[15]
The Master of Levingstoun.[16]
The Lord of Down.[17]
The Lord Drummound.[18]
The Laird of Tullibardin.[19]
The Laird of Glenorquhy.[20]
The Laird of Lawaris.[21]
The Laird of Weyme.[22]

The Abbot of Inchaffray.[23]
Coline Campbell of Ardbeich.[24]
The Laird of Glenlyoun.[25]
The Erle of Athoill.[26]
The Laird of Grantullie.[27]
The Laird of Strowane-Robertsone.[28]
The Laird of Strowane-Murray.[29]
The Laird of Wester Wemyss.[30]
The Laird of Abbotishall.[31]
The Laird of Teling.[32]
The Laird of Inchmartine.[33]
The Laird of Purie-Fothringhame.[34]
The Laird of Moncreiff.[35]
The Laird of Balleachane.[36]

[10] James Galbraith of Kilcreuch. His name frequently appears in the Privy Council Register as a Commissioner for executing the laws against Papists, and in other similar capacities.--*Register of the Privy Council*, vol. iv.

[11] George Graham, tutor or guardian to John, sixth Earl of Menteith, of the Graham line, who succeeded to the earldom in 1587 and died in the following year.

[12] William Shaw of Knockhill, in Menteith.

[13] James Kinros of Kippenross, in Perthshire, had a charter under the Great Seal, Dec. 6, 1584, erecting Kippenross into a barony.—*Reg. Mag. Sig.*, 1580-1593, *Charter No.* 764. His daughter Katherine married in 1586 George Shaw, son of William Shaw of Knockhill. *Ib., Charter No.* 1528.

[14] Sir Michael Balfour of Burleigh, who was superior at this time of the lands of Mochaster, etc., in Menteith.

[15] Sir James Stirling of Keir.

[16] Alexander, afterwards seventh Lord Livingston, created first Earl of Linlithgow. He possessed the lands of Callander, Corriechrombie in Menteith, and other lands in Perthshire.

[17] James Stewart, first Lord Doune, father of the "bonnie Earl of Moray."

[18] Patrick, third Lord Drummond.

[19] Sir John Murray of Tullibardine, in Strathearn. He also possessed lands in Balquhidder.

[20] Duncan, afterwards Sir Duncan Campbell of Glenurchy.

[21] John, afterwards Sir John, Campbell of Lawers (whose ancestor was a cadet of the family of Glenurchy). He possessed considerable lands both in Breadalbane and Strathearn.

[22] James Menzies of that ilk, or of Weym, proprietor of extensive lands in Breadalbane, Strathtay, and Rannoch.

[23] James Drummond, Commendator of Inchaffray, and laird of Innerpeffry, possessor also of lands in Balquhidder.

He was brother of Patrick Lord Drummond, and was created, in 1609, Lord Maderty. His grandson, William, fourth Lord Maderty, was created Viscount Strathallan in 1686.

[24] Brother to Sir Duncan Campbell of Glenurchy. His lands lay in the vicinity of Lochearnhead.

[25] Colin Campbell of Glenlyon, descended from the house of Glenurchy.

[26] John, fifth Earl of Atholl, of the Innermeath line.

[27] Sir Thomas Stewart of Grandtully, descended likewise from the house of Innermeath, proprietor of lands in Strathtay.

[28] Donald Robertson of Strowan, in Atholl.

[29] John Murray of Strowan, in Strathearn. His daughter was married after this period to Eoin dubh Macgregor (killed at Glenfruin), brother to Allaster Macgregor of Glenstrae, chief of the Clan Gregor.

[30] [31] There were two families in Fife, Wemyss of Wester Wemyss, and Scott of Abbotshall, the heads of which are probably meant here. The family of Wemyss acquired right to an estate in Atholl, called Kinnaird, by marriage of the heiress of Inchmartine, Perthshire. They sold the property of Kinnaird to Stewart of Rosyth, but retained the superiority, and a younger son of Rosyth was the ancestor of the Stewarts of Kinnaird. (Robertson's *Concise Historical Proofs*.)

[32] Sir David Maxwell of Teling, in Forfarshire.

[33] Patrick Ogilvie of Inchmartine; proprietor of lands in the south-eastern Highlands of Perthshire.

[34] Thomas Fothringham of Powrie, a proprietor in the Brae of Angus.

[35] William Moncreiff of that ilk, proprietor of the lands of Culdares and Tenaiffis in Breadalbane, which he afterwards sold to Sir Duncan Campbell of Glenurchy. These lands had been possessed by the family of Moncreiff for several centuries.

[36] Sir James Stewart of Ballechin in Atholl.

The Barroun of Fandowie.[27]
The Erle of Erroll.[28]
The Erle of Gowry.[39]
The Laird of Cultybragane.[40]
The Lord Ogilvy.[41]
The Laird of Clovay.[42]
The Laird of Fintray.[43]
The Laird of Edyell.[44]
The Erle of Mar.[45]
The Master of Elphingstoun.[46]
The Erle Huntlie.[47]
The Master of Forbes.[48]
The Laird of Grant.[49]
Makintosche.[50]
The Lord and Tutour of Lovate.[51]

Cheisholme of Cummer.[52]
The Larde of Glengarry.[53]
Mackanyie.[54]
The Laird of Fowlis.[55]
The Laird of Balnagown.[56]
The Tutour of Cromartie.[57]
The Erle of Suthirland.[58]
The Laird of Duffus.[59]
James Innes of Touchis.[60]
The Erle of Caithness.[61]
The Erle Merschall.[62]
The Lord Oliphant.[63]
The Laird of Boquhowy.[64]
The Laird of Dunnybeyth.[65]
Macky of Far.[66]

---

[27] John Macduff, alias Ferguson, Baron of Fandowie, in Atholl, executed for his accession to Gowrie's Conspiracy, 1600.

[28] Francis, eighth Earl of Errol, proprietor of Logie-almond, part of Inchmartine, and other lands on or near the Highland line.

[39] James Ruthven, second Earl of Gowrie, and fifth Lord Ruthven, possessed lands in Strathardle and Strathbran, in the south-eastern Highlands of Perthshire. He died in 1588, in his fourteenth year.

[40] Alexander Reidheuch of Cultebragan. His lands lay in and near Glenleidnoch, in Strathearn. Edward Reidheuch, fiar of Cultebragan, is frequently mentioned in the records at this period.

[41] James, sixth Lord Ogilvie of Airlie. He had large possessions in Glen-Isla and other parts of the Brae of Angus.

[42] Alexander Ogilvie of Clova was alive in 1557. James Ogilvie was served heir to James Ogilvie of Clova, his father, in the lands of Clova, etc., 1623. The lands of this family lay principally in the Brae of Angus.

[43] Sir David Graham of Fintry, knight, a considerable proprietor in Forfarshire, was alive 1577. This family descended, it is said, from a younger son of the Grahams of Kincardine, afterwards Earls of Montrose.

[44] Sir David Lindsay of Edyell, proprietor of Glenesk, and other lands in Forfarshire.

[45] John Erskine, seventh Earl of Mar, proprietor of Braemar, etc.

[46] Alexander, afterwards fourth Lord Elphinstone, proprietor of lands in Banffshire.

[47] George, sixth Earl, and afterwards first Marquis of Huntly, Lord of Badenoch and Lochaber.

[48] John, afterwards eighth Lord Forbes, proprietor of estates near the sources of the Don, in Aberdeenshire.

[49] John Grant of Freuchie.

[50] Lauchlan Macintosh of Dunauchton, Captain of the Clanchattan.

[51] Simon, eighth Lord Lovat, and Thomas Fraser of Knockie and Strichen, his uncle and tutor.

[52] Alexander Chisholm of Strathglass was alive in 1578. John Chisholm of Comer is mentioned in 1613.

[53] Donald Macdonald, eighth of Glengarry. He had a charter under the Great Seal of the lands of Glengarry, July 19, 1574, in which he is described as "Donaldus M'Angus M'Allestare, filius et heres apparens Angusii M'Allestare de Glengarrie."

[54] Colin Mackenzie of Kintail.

[55] Robert More Munro, fifteenth baron of Foulis.

[56] Alexander Ross of Balnagown, descended in a direct line from Hugh Ross of Rarichies, second son of Hugh, fifth Earl of Ross.

[57] John Urquhart of Craigfintry and Culbo, tutor to his grand-nephew Thomas, afterwards Sir Thomas Urquhart of Cromarty.

[58] Alexander, eleventh Earl of Sutherland.

[59] William Sutherland of Duffus.

[60] Not known what lands in the Highlands he possessed.

[61] George Sinclair, fifth Earl of Caithness.

[62] George Keith, fifth Earl Marischal.

[63] Lawrence, fourth Lord Oliphant. He possessed among other lands, Berriedale in Caithness, on account of which he appears to be included in this Roll.

[64] Patrick Mount of Boquhally, a considerable proprietor in Caithness.

[65] William Sinclair of Dunbeath, in Caithness.

[66] Hugh Mackay of Farr, father of Donald, first Lord Reay.

Torquill M'Cloyd of Cogoych.[67]
The Laird of Garloch.[68]
Makgillichallum of Raarsay.[69]
M'Cloid of the Harrich.[70]
M'Kynnoun of Strathodell.[71]
M'Cleud of the Lewes.[72]
M'Neill of Barrey.[73]
M'Kane of Ardnamurchin.[74]
Allane M'Kane of Handterum.
The Laird of Knoydert.[75]
M'Clane of Dowart.[76]
The Laird of Ardgowir.[77]
Johnne Stewart of the Appin.
M'Coull of Lorne.[78]
M'Coull of Roray.[79]
The Laird of Lochynnell.[80]
The Laird of Caddell.[81]
The Laird of Skermourlie, for Rauchry.[82]
M'Condoquhy of Innerraw.[83]

Angus M'Coneil of Dunyveg and Glennis.
The Laird of Lowip.[84]
The Schiref of Bute.[85]
The Laird of Camys.[86]
Erle of Ergile.[87]
Laird of Auchinbrek.[88]
The Laird of Ardkinglass.[89]
M'Nauchtane.[90]
M'Lauchlane.[91]
The Laird of Lawmont.[92]
The Laird of Perbrak.[93]
The Laird of Duntrune.[94]
Constable of Dundy, Laird of Glastry.[95]
The Laird of Elanegreg.[96]
The Laird of Otter.[97]
The Laird of Coll.[98]
Makclayne of Lochbuy.[99]
M'Fee of Colowsay.[100]
The Lord Hamiltoun.[101]

---

[67] Torquil Macleod was the eldest son of Roderick Macleod of the Lewis, by that Baron's second marriage with a daughter of Mackenzie of Kintail. During his father's lifetime he held the estate of Cogeache, and was known by that title; but on his father's death he claimed the estates and style of Macleod of Lewis, his title to which was disputed.

[68] John Mackenzie of Gairloch.

[69] Malcolm Macleod, or Macgillechallum of Rasay, nearest heir male at this time of the Macleods of Lewis, after the descendants of the body of Roderick Macleod of Lewis.

[70] William Macleod of Harris, Dunvegan, and Glenelg, chief of the Siol Tormaid.

[71] Lauchlan Mackinnon of Strathwardill in Skye, and of Mishnish in Mull.

[72] Roderick Macleod of the Lewis, Cogeache and Assint, chief of the Siol Torcuil.

[73] Roderick Macneill of Barra.

[74] John Maccoin, or Macian, of Ardnamurchan, chief of a tribe sprung from the family of the Isles.

[75] Alexander Macranald of Knoydart, chieftain of a branch of the Clanranald.

[76] Lauchlan, afterwards Sir Lauchlan Maclean of Duart.

[77] Ewin Maclean of Ardgour, representative of an ancient branch of the family of Duart.

[78] Dougal Macdougal of Dunolly.

[79] Allan Macdougal of Raray.

[80] Archibald Campbell, second Laird of Lochnell, killed at the battle of Glenlivat, 1594.

[81] John Campbell of Calder or Cadder, frequently written Caddell.

[82] Sir Robert Montgomery of Skelmorlie, who seems, at this time, to have possessed the small island of Rachry, or Rachrin, lying near the coast of Antrim.

[83] Dougal Macconachy (Campbell) of Inverawe, head of an ancient sept of the Campbells.

[84] Alexander Macallaster of Loupe, in Kintyre.

[85] John Stewart, Sheriff of Bute.

[86] Hector Bannatyne of Kames, in Bute.

[87] Archibald, seventh Earl of Argyll, then a minor. His principal guardian was John Campbell of Calder.

[88] Duncan Campbell of Auchinbreck.

[89] Sir James Campbell of Ardkinglas.

[90] Malcolm Macnaughtan of Dunderawe.

[91] Archibald Maclachlan of Strathlachlan, or of that ilk.

[92] James Lamont of Inveryne, or of that ilk.

[93] Colin Campbell of Barbreck.

[94] John Campbell of Duntrune.

[95] James, afterwards Sir James, Scrymgeour of Dudhope, constable of Dundee, and proprietor of the barony of Glassary in Argyllshire.

[96] Colin Campbell of Elangreg.

[97] Archibald Campbell of Otter.

[98] Hector Maclean of Coll.

[99] John Moir Maclean of Lochbuy.

[100] Murdoch Macfie of Colonsay.

[101] Lord John Hamilton, afterwards Marquis of Hamilton, proprietor of the Isle of Arran.

THE ROLL OF THE CLANNIS [IN THE HIELANDIS AND ILES] THAT HES CAPITANES, CHEIFFIS, AND CHIFTANES QUHOME ON THAY DEPEND, OFT TYMES AGANIS THE WILLIS OF THAIR LANDISLORDIS: AND OF SUM SPECIALE PERSONIS OF BRANCHIS OF THE SAIDIS CLANNIS, 1587.

Buchananis.
M'Ferlanis, Arroquhar.
M'Knabbis.
Grahmes of Menteth.
Stewartis of Buchquhidder.
Clangregour.
Clanlawren.
Campbellis of Lochnell.
Campbellis of Innerraw.
Clandowill of Lorne.
Stewartis of Lorne, or of Appin.
Clane M'Kane of Avricht.[102]
Stewartis of Athoill, and pairtis adiacent.
Clandonoquhy, in Athoill, and pairtis adiacent.
Menyessis, in Athoill and Apnadull.
Clan M'Thomas in Glensche.
Fergussonis.

Spaldingis.
Makintoscheis, in Athoill.
Clancamroun.
Clanrannald, in Lochquhaber.[103]
Clanrannald of Knoydert, Modert, and Glengarry.
Clanlewid of the Lewis.
Clanlewyd of Harray.
Clanneil.
Clankynnoun.
Clan Ieane.[104]
Clanquhattan.
Grantis.
Frasseris.
Clankanye.
Clanandreis.[105]
Monrois.
Murrayis, in Suthirland.

LIST OF CLANS AND BROKEN MEN CONTAINED IN ACT OF 1594.

Another statute was passed in 1594. "For Punisement of thift, reif, oppressioun, and sorning" (1594, c. 37, *Act. Parl. Scot.*, vol. iv., p. 71). The preamble, so far as relating to the Highlands, is as follows :—

Oure Soverane Lord and his estaitis in this present Parliament, considering that, nochtwithstanding the sindrie actis maid be his Hienes, and his maist nobill progenitouris, for punischment of the authoris of thift, reiff, oppressioun, and sorning, and masteris and sustenaries of thevis ; yet sic hes bene, and presentlie is, the barbarous

---

[102] The Clan Eoin, or Macdonalds of Glencoe, whose chief was patronymically styled "*Mac Eoin Abrach.*"
[103] The Macdonalds in the Braes of Lochaber, commonly called the Macdonalds of Keppoch.

[104] The Clan Eoin of Ardnamurchan.
[105] The Rosses, of whom Balnagown was the chief.

cruelties and daylie heirschippis of the wickit thevis and lymmaris of the clannis and surenames following, inhabiting the Hielands and Iles ; Thay ar to say :

Clangregour.[106]
Clanfarlane.
Clankawren.
Clandowill.
Clandonochie.
Clanchattane.[107]
Clanchewill.[108]
Clanchamron.
Clanronald, in Lochaber.
Clanranald, in Knoydert, Modert, and Glengarie.
Clanleyid of the Lewis.

Clanlewid of Harriche.
Clandonald, south and north.[109]
Clangillane.
Clanayioun.[110]
Clankynnoun.
Clanneil.
Clankenyie.
Clanandreis.
Clanmorgan.[111]
Clangun.
Cheilphale.[112]

*And als many brokin men of the surnames of*

Stewartis, in Athoill, Lorne, and Balquhedder.
Campbellis.
Grahames, in Menteith.
Buchannanis.
M'Cawlis.
Galbraithis.
M'Nabbis.
M'Nabrichis.[113]
Menzeis.
Fergussonis.

Spadingis.
M'Intoscheis, in Athoill.
M'Thomas, in Glensche.
Ferquharsonis, in Bra of Mar.
M'Inphersonis.[114]
Grantis.
Rossis.
Frasseris.
Monrois.
Neilsonis.[115]

And utheris inhabiting the Schirefdomes of Ergyle, Bute, Dunbartane, Striviling, Perth, Forfar, Aberdene, Banf, Elgin, Forres, Narne, Inuernes, and Cromertie, Stewartries of Stratherne and Menteith, etc.

---

[106] An undesirable precedence seems to be assigned to the Clan Gregor in this Roll. See the Acts of the Privy Council against the Clangregour, printed in the *Miscellany of the Maitland Club*, vol. iii., pp. 11-44.

[107] It will be observed that the Clanchattan and Macphersons are distinguished from each other in this Roll.

[108] Probably the Shaws of Rothiemurchus, but the "Clan Quhele" has never been identified with certainty. They are named in 1392 as followers of the De Athelia family, the ancestors of the Robertsons of Atholl (*Act. Parl. Scot.*, vol. i, p. 579). See Hill Burton's note on the subject, *History of Scotland*, vol. ii., p. 371.

[109] The Clandonald South were the Clan Eoin-mhor of Isla and Kintyre. The Clandonald North were the Clan Huistein of Skye and North Uist.

[110] Clan Eoin of Ardnamurchan, probably.

[111] The Mackays of Strathnaver.

[112] A sept of the Mackays, descended from one Paul Macneil Mackay.

[113] *M'Nabrichis*, a contraction probably for *Mac Eoin-abrichis*, the Glencoe Macdonalds.

[114] See Note 107.

[115] *Neilsonis*, probably another sept of the Mackays, called by Sir Robert Gordon *Sclil Neill*.

ROTATION OF THE HIGHLAND CLANS AS MENTIONED IN TWO ACTS OF
PARLIAMENT, 1587 AND 1594.

[The numbers correspond with those given on the Map of the Clans.]

1. Buchanans.
2. MacFarlanes.
3. MacNabs.
4. Grahams of Menteith.
5. Stewarts of Balquhidder.
6. Clan Gregor, the MacGregors.
7. Clan Lauren, the M'Larens.
8. Campbells of Lochnell.
9. Campbells of Inverawe.
10. Clan Dougal, M'Dougals.
11. Stewarts of Appin.
12. Clan Ian Abrach, or Macdonalds of Glencoe.
13. Stewarts in Atholl, and parts adjacent.
14. Clan Donachy, or Robertsons of Atholl, and parts adjacent.
15. Menzies.
16. Clan M'Thomas, in Glenshee.
17. Fergusons, in Glenshee.
18. Spaldings, in Glenshee.
19. M'Intoshes of Glentilt.
20. Clan Cameron.
21. Clan Ranald of Lochaber, or Macdonalds of Keppoch.
22. Clan Ranald of Moydart, Knoydart, Arasaig, Morar, and Glengarry, all Macdonalds.

23. MacLeods of Lewis.
24. MacLeods of Harris.
25. Clan Neil, or MacNeils.
26. Clan Kinnon, or MacKinnons.
27. Clan Macian, or Macdonalds of Ardnamurchan and Sunart.
28. Clan Chattan, Macphersons and Mackintoshes.
29. Grants.
30. Frasers.
31. Clan Kenzie, or Mackenzies.
32. Clan Anrias, or Ross's.
33. Munroes.
34. Murrays, or Sutherlands.
35. Clanquhele, or Shaws of Rothiemurchus.
36. Clan Donald, north and south, Macdonalds.
37. Clan Gillean, or MacLeans.
38. Clan Morgan, or Mackays.
39. Clan Gunn.
40. Macaulays.
41. Galbraiths.
42. Farquharsons.

B

NAMES OF HIGHLAND CHIEFS AND LANDLORDS IN THE

HIGHLANDS AND ISLES IN 1587,

CONTAINED IN THE ACT OF PARLIAMENT OF THAT DATE, AND NOT
NAMED IN THE ROLL OF THE CLANS.

| | | | |
|---|---|---|---|
| IV. | Humphrey Colquhoun of Luss. | LXXXV. | John Stewart, Sheriff of Bute. |
| XVII. | James, Earl of Moray.[1] | | |
| XVIII. | Patrick, third Lord Drummond. | LXXXVII. | Archibald, seventh Earl of Argyll. |
| XX. | Sir Duncan Campbell of Glenorchy. | | |
| | | LXXXVIII. | Duncan Campbell of Auchinbreck. |
| XXI. | Sir John Campbell of Lawers. | | |
| XXIV. | Colin Campbell of Ardveck, brother of Sir Duncan Campbell of Glenorchy. | LXXXIX. | Sir James Campbell of Ardkinglas. |
| | | XC. | Malcolm Macnaughtan of Dundaraw. |
| XXV. | Colin Campbell of Glenlyon. | | |
| XXVI. | John, fifth Earl of Atholl of the Innermeath line. | XCI. | Archibald Maclachlan of Strathlachlan. |
| XXIX. | John Murray of Strowan, in Strathern. | XCII. | James Lamont of that ilk, Inveryne. |
| XXXIX. | James, second Earl of Gowrie, and fifth Lord Ruthven. | XCIII. | Colin Campbell of Barbreck. |
| | | XCIV. | John Campbell of Duntrune. |
| XLI. | James, sixth Lord Ogilvie of Airlie. | XCV. | Sir James Scrymgeour of Dudhope and Glassary. |
| XLVII. | George, sixth Earl, and first Marquis of Huntly. | XCVII. | Archibald Campbell of Otter. |
| | | C. | Murdoch Macfie of Colonsay. |
| LII. | Alexander Chisholm of that ilk, and Strathglass. | CI. | John, first Marquis of Hamilton. |
| LXI. | George, fifth Earl of Caithness. | | |

[1] James Stewart, son of Sir James Stewart of Doune, assumed the title of Earl of Moray in 1580, on his marriage to Lady Elizabeth Stuart, daughter of the Regent Moray. He was called the "Bonnie Earl."

# BADGES OF THE CLANS.

SUAICHEANTAS[1] NAN GAEL; OR, THE BADGES OF THE CLANS,
IN GAELIC AND ENGLISH.[2]

| CLANS. | GAELIC. | ENGLISH. |
|---|---|---|
| Buchanan. | Lus nam Braoileag ; an Darach | The Bilberry ; the Oak. |
| Cameron | An Dearc-fithich | The Cranberry. |
| Campbell | Roid. . . . | Wild Myrtle. |
| Do. | Garbhag an t-sléibhe | Fir Club Moss. |
| Chisholm | Raineach . . . | The Fern. |
| Colquhoun . | Braoileag nan con . | Dogberry, Bear-whortle. |
| Cumin | Lus Mhic Chuimein . . | Cumin Plant. |
| Drummond . | Lus nam Macraidh (Lus) Mhic Righ Bhreatuinn) | Wild Thyme. |
| Do. . . . . | Cuilionn . . | Holly. |
| Fergusson, MacFarquhar, and Farquharson . | Rós-gréine ; Lus nam ban-sith . | Little Sunflower ; Foxglove. |
| Forbes and Mackay . | Bealaidh . | Broom. |
| Fraser . . . | Iubhar | Yew. |
| Grant, MacGregor, Mac-Kinnon, MacNab, and MacQuarrie . . | Giuthas | Scotch Fir. |
| Gordon | Iadh-shlat Eidheann . . | Rock-Ivy. |
| Graham | Buaidh Chraobh, no Laibh-reas . | Laurel, or Tree of Victory. |
| Hay . | Uile-ic | Mistletoe. |
| Johnston . . . | | Red Hawthorn. |
| MacAulay and MacFarlane | A'Muileag | Cranberry. |
| MacDonald, MacAlastair, and MacNab . . | Fraoch | Common Heath. |
| MacDougal | Fraoch Dearg . | Bell Heath. |

[1] *Aodach-suaicheantais* means the national costume or dress complete, with the badge, etc.
[2] The Gaelic in the lists of 'Badges' and 'War Cries' has been revised by Mr Duncan MacIsaac, Oban.

| CLANS. | GAELIC. | ENGLISH. |
|---|---|---|
| MacIntyre . . . | Fraoch Geal | White Heath. |
| Mackenzie and MacLean | Cuilionn . . | Holly. |
| MacLaren . | Labhras Fiadhaich | Wild Laurel. |
| MacLachlan . . | Uinnseann | Ash Tree. |
| Murray, MacLeod, Gunn, and Ross . | Aiteann | Juniper. |
| MacNaughton . . | Lus Albanach . . | Trailing Azalea. |
| MacNeill and Lamont | Luibh nan Tri-beann | Trefoil. |
| MacKay . . . . | Luachair . | Bulrushes. |
| MacPherson, MacIntosh, MacDuff, MacBean, Shaw, Farquharson, MacQueen, and many others, as belonging to Clanchattan . . . | Buesa | Box-tree. This is said to be the oldest badge. |
| Do.    Do . . | Lus nan Cnaimsheag; Braoileag . . | Red Whortleberry. |
| Menzies . . | Fraoch nam Meinearach . | The Menzies Heath. |
| Munro . . . | Garbhag nan Gleann | Common Club Moss. |
| Murray and Sutherland | Bealaidh . | Broom; Butcher's Broom. |
| Ogilvie . . | Boglus | Ox-tongue; Evergreen Alkanet. |
| Oliphant | Luachair . . | The Bulrush. |
| Robertson . | Dlùth Fhraoch . | Fine-leaved Heath. |
| Do. | Frith-raineach . . | Dwarf Fern. |
| Rose . | Ròs-Màiri Fiadhaich | Wild Rosemary. |
| Sinclair | Conusg | Whin, or Gorse. |
| Stewart Do. | An Darach . An Cluaran . | The Oak; also the Thistle, the present national badge. That of the Pictish Kings was Rudh (Rue), which is joined with the Thistle in the Collar of the Order. |
| Urquhart . | Lus Leth-an-t-Samhraidh. | Gillyflower, Wallflower. |

# WAR=CRIES;

## OR, RALLYING WORDS OF SOME OF THE CLANS.

| CLANS. | GAELIC. | ENGLISH. |
|---|---|---|
| Buchanan | "Clàr Innis" | An island in Loch Lomond. |
| Campbell | "Siol Dhiarmaid an Tuire" | "The Clan of Diarmid of the Boar." |
| Do. | "Cruachan" | A mountain in Argyllshire. |
| Farquharson | "Càrn na Cuimhne" | "The Cairn of Remembrance' in Strathdee. |
| Forbes | "Lonach" | A hill in Strathdon. |
| Fraser | "A' Mhòr-fhaiche" | "The Great Field." |
| Do. (later) | | "Castle Downie." |
| Grant | "Creag Ealachaidh" | A hill in Strathspey. Some of the Grants have "Creag Rabhach" ("The Warning Rock,") and add "Stand Sure." |
| MacAlpine | "Cuimhnich Bàs Ailpein" | "Remember the death of Alpin." |
| MacDonald | "Fraoch-Eilean" | "Heather Island." |
| Do. (Clanranald) | "Dh'aindheoin cò theireadh e" | "In spite of who would say it." |
| MacDonnell (Glengarry) | "Creag-an-fhithich" | "The Raven's Rock." |
| MacDougal | "Buaidh no Bàs" | "Victory or Death." |
| MacFarlane | "Loch Slòigh" | "The Loch of the Host." |
| MacGillivray | "Loch Moidh." | |
| MacGregor | "Ard-Choille" | "The High Wood." |
| MacIntosh | "Loch Moidheidh" (Loch Moy) | "The Loch of Threatening," a lake near the seat of the Chieftain. |
| MacIntyre | "Cruachan." | |
| MacKenzie | "Tulach Ard" | A mountain near Castle Donan, anciently the stronghold of the clan. |

| CLANS. | GAELIC. | ENGLISH. |
|---|---|---|
| MacKinnon | "Cuimhnich Bàs Ailpein" | |
| MacLaren . | "Creag Tuirc" . | "The Boar's Rock." |
| MacNaughton | " Fraoch-Eilean " | {" Heather Island," Loch Awe, Argyllshire. |
| MacNeill | " Buaidh no Bàs" . | |
| MacPherson | {"Creag Dhubh Chloinn Chatain " | {"The Black Craig of Clan Chattan." |
| MacQuarrie | "An t-Arm Breac Dearg " | {" The army of the chequered red " [tartan]. |
| Matheson . | {" Dail Achadh 'n dà thèarnaidh " | {"The field of the two declivities." (?) |
| Menzies | "Geal 'us Dearg a suas" . | " Up with White and Red." |
| Munro | " Caisteal Foulis 'n a theine " | {"Castle Foulis ablaze ;" referring probably to beacon or signal lights. |
| Stewart (Appin) . | "Creag an Sgairbh " . | {" The Cormorant's Rock," on which is built Castle Stalker. |

# GENERAL WADE'S REPORT ON THE HIGHLANDS, 1724.[1]

May it please Your Majesty,

I N Obedience to Your Majesty's Commands and Instructions under your Royal Sign Manual bearing date the 3rd day of July 1724, Commanding me to go into the Highlands of Scotland, and narrowly to inspect the present Situation of the Highlanders, their Customs, Manners and the State of the Country in regard to the Robberies and Depredations, said to be committed in that part of your Majesty's Dominions; As also to make strict and particular enquiry into the effect of the last Law for Disarming the Highlanders and for securing your Majesty's Loyal and faithful Subjects, represented to be left Naked and Defenceless by paying due obedience thereto; and to inform Your Majesty of all other particulars contained in the said Instructions, and how far the Memorial delivered to Your Majesty by Simon Lord Lovat and his Remarks thereupon are founded on Facts, and the present Practices of those People; And whether the Remedies mentioned therein may properly be applied for preventing the Several Grievances, Abuses, and Violences complained of in the said Memorial. Your Majesty has farther been pleased to Command me to make such Enquirys and endeavour to get such Information, relating to the several particulars above mentioned as may enable me to suggest to your Majesty, such other Remedies as may conduce to the Quiet of your Faithful Subjects and the good Settlement of that part of the Kingdom.

The Day after I received your Majesty's Instructions I proceeded on my Journey, and have Travelled through the greatest and most uncivilized Parts of the Highlands of Scotland; And humbly beg leave to lay before Your Majesty the following Report, which I have collected as well from my own Observations, with all Faithfulness and Impartiality, as from the best Informations I could procure during my Continuance in that part of the Country.

The Highlands are the Mountainous Parts of Scotland, not defined or described by any precise Limits or Boundaries of Counties or Shires but are Tracts of Mountains, in extent of Land, more than one-half of the Kingdom of Scotland; and are for the most part on the Western Ocean, extending from Dumbarton to the North End of the Island of Great Britain, near 200 Miles in length, and from about 40 to 80 Miles in breadth.

---

[1] This is the first of two Reports on the state of the Highlands drawn up by General Wade in the years 1724 and 1727 respectively. Both Reports, together with the "Memorial anent the True State of the Highlands," an extract from which is given at page 31, are printed at length in Colonel James Allardyce's *Historical Papers relating to the Jacobite Period* (New Spalding Club, 1895), vol. i., pp. 131-176.

All the Islands on the West and North-West Seas are called Highlands as well from
their Mountainous Situation, as from the Habits, Customs, Manners and Language of
their Inhabitants. The Lowlands are all that part of Scotland on the South of Forth
and Clyde, and on the East side of the Kingdom from the Firth of Edinburgh to
Caithness near the Orkneys is a Tract of Low Country from 4 to 20 Miles in Breadth.

The Number of Men able to carry Arms in the Highlands (including the Inhabitants of the Isles) is by the nearest Computation about 22,000 Men, of which Number
about 10,000 are Vassals to the Superiors well affected to Your Majesty's Government;
most of the remaining 12,000 have been engaged in Rebellion against Your Majesty,
and are ready, whenever encouraged by their Superiors or Chiefs of Clans, to create
new Troubles and rise in Arms in favour of the Pretender.

Their Notions of Virtue and Vice are very different from the more civilized part
of Mankind. They think it a most Sublime Virtue to pay a Servile and Abject
Obedience to the Commands of their Chieftains, altho' in opposition to their Sovereign
and the Laws of the Kingdom, and to encourage this, their Fidelity, they are treated
by their Chiefs with great Familiarity, they partake with them in their Diversions, and
shake them by the Hand wherever they meet them.

The Virtue next to this, in esteem amongst them, is the love they bear to that
particular Branch of which they are a part, and in a Second Degree to the whole
Clan, or Name, by assisting each other (right or wrong) against any other Clan with
whom they are at Variance, and great Barbarities are often committed by One, to
revenge the Quarrels of Another. They have still a more extensive adherence one to
another as Highlanders in opposition to the People who inhabit the Low Countries,
whom they hold in the utmost Contempt, imagining them inferior to themselves in
Courage, Resolution, and the use of Arms, and accuse them of being Proud, Avaricious,
and Breakers of their Word. They have also a Tradition amongst them that the
Lowlands were in Ancient Times, the Inheritance of their Ancestors, and therefore
believe they have a right to commit Depredations, whenever it is in their power to put
them in Execution.

The Highlanders are divided into Tribes or Clans, under Lairds, or Chieftains (as
they are called in the Laws of Scotland), each Tribe or Clan is subdivided into Little
Branches sprung from the Main Stock who have also Chieftains over them, and from
these are still smaller Branches of Fifty or Sixty Men, who deduce their Original from
them, and on whom they rely as their Protectors and Defenders. The Arms they
make use of in War, are, a Musket, a Broad Sword and Target, a Pistol and a Durk
or Dagger, hanging by their side, with a Powder Horn and Pouch for their Ammunition. They form themselves into Bodies of unequal Numbers according to the strength
of their Clan or Tribe, which is Commanded by their Respective Superior or Chieftain.
When in sight of the Enemy they endeavour to possess themselves of the highest
Ground, believing they descend on them with greater force.

They generally give their fire at a distance, they lay down their Arms on the Ground and make a Vigorous Attack with their Broad Swords, but if repulsed, seldom or never rally again. They dread engaging with the Cavalry and seldom venture to descend from the Mountains when apprehensive of being charged by them.

On sudden Alarms, or when any Chieftain is in distress, they give Notice to their Clans or those in Alliance with them, by sending a Man with what they call the Fiery Cross, which is a Stick in the form of a Cross, burnt at the End, who send it forward to the next Tribe or Clan. They carry with it a written Paper directing them where to Assemble; upon sight of which they leave their Habitation and with great Expedition repair to the place of Rendezvous, with Arms, Ammunition and Meal for their Provision.

I Presume also to Represent to Your Majesty, that the Manners and Customs of the Highlanders, their Way of Living, their Strong Friendships, and Adherence to those of their own Name, Tribe and Family, their blind and Servile Submission to the Commands of their Superiors and Chieftains, and the little Regard they have ever paid to the Laws of the Kingdom, both before and since the Union, are truly set forth in the Lord Lovat's Memorial and other Matters contained in the said Paper, which Your Majesty was pleased to direct should be put into my Hands to peruse and Examine.

The Imposition mentioned in that Memorial commonly called the Black Meal is levyed by the Highlanders on almost all the Low Country bordering thereon. But as it is equally Criminal by the Laws of Scotland to pay this Exaction or to Extort it the Inhabitants to avoid the Penalty of the Laws, agree with the Robbers, or some of their Correspondents in the Lowlands to protect their Horses and Cattle, who are in effect but their Stewards or Factors, and as long as this payment continues, the Depredations cease upon their Lands, otherwise the Collector of this Illegal Imposition is obliged to make good the loss they have sustained. They give regular Receipts for the same Safe Guard Money, and those who refuse to submit to this Imposition are sure of being Plundered, their being no other way to avoid it but by keeping a constant Guard of Armed Men, which, altho' it is sometimes done, is not only illegal, but a more expensive way of securing their property.

The Clans in the Highlands, the most addicted to Rapine and Plunder, are, the Cameron's on the West of the Shire of Inverness, the Mackenzie's and others in the Shire of Ross who were Vassals to the late Earl of Seaforth, the McDonell's of Keppoch, the Broadalbin Men, and the McGregors on the Borders of Argyleshire. They go out in Parties from Ten to Thirty Men, traverse large Tracts of Mountains till they arrive at the Lowlands where they Design to Commit Depredations, which they chuse to do in places distant from the Clans where they Inhabit; They drive the Stolen Cattle in the Night time, and in the Day remain on the Tops of the Mountains or in the Woods (with which the Highlands abound) and take the first occasion to sell them at the Fairs or Markets that are annually held in many parts of the Country.

c

Those who are robbed of their Cattle (or Persons employ'd by them) follow them by the Tract and often recover them from the Robbers by Compounding for a certain sum of Money agreed on, but if the Pursuers are Armed and in Numbers Superior to the Thieves and happen to seize any of them, they are seldom or never prosecuted, the poorer sort being unable to support the charge of Prosecution.

They are likewise under the Apprehension of becoming the Object of their Revenge, by having their Houses and Stacks burnt, their Cattle stolen or hockt, and their Lives at the Mercy of the Tribe or Clan to whom the Banditti belong. The Richer sort (to keep, as they call it good Neighbourhood) generally compound with the Chieftain of the Tribe or Clan, for double Restitution, which he willingly pays to save one of his Clan from Prosecution, and this is repaid him by a Contribution from the Thieves of his Clan, who never refuse the payment of their proportion to save one of their own fraternity. This Composition is seldom paid in Money, but in Cattle stolen from the opposite side of the Country to make reparation to the Person injured.

The Chiefs of some of these Tribes never fail to give Countenance and Protection to those of their own Clan; and tho' they are taken and committed to Prison, by the Plaintiff (who is) better satisfied than if the Criminal was executed, since he must (be) at the Charge and Trouble of a tedious dilatory and expensive Prosecution; and I was assured by one who annually attended the Assizes at Inverness for four Years past, that there had been but one Person Executed there by the Lords of Justiciary and that (as I remember) for Murder, tho' that Place is the Judicature, in Criminal Cases, for the greatest part of the Highlands of Scotland.

There is another Practice used in the Highlands, by which the Cattle stolen are often recovered, which is, by sending Persons to that part of the Country most suspected and making an offer of a Reward (which the Highlanders call Tascal-Money) to any who will discover the Cattle and the Persons who stole them, by the temptation of the Reward and promise of Secrecy, discoveries were often made and Restitution obtained. But to put a stop to a practice they thought an injury to the Tribe, the whole Clan of the Camerons (and others since by their Example) bound themselves by Oath never to take Tascal-Money, nor to inform one against the other. This they take upon a Drawn Durck or Dagger, which they kiss in a solemn manner and the Penalty declared to be due to the said Oath, is, to be stabbed with the same Dagger. This manner of Swearing is much in practice on all other occasions, to bind themselves one to another that they may with more security exercise their Villany, which they imagine less Sinful than the Breach of that Oath, since they commit all sorts of Crimes with impunity, and are so severely punished if forsworn. An instance of this happened in December 1723, when one of the Clan of the Camerons suspected to have taken Tascal-Money, was in the Night time called out of his Hut from his Wife and Children and hanged up near his own door. Another of that Tribe was, for the same Crime (as they call it) kept a Month in the Stocks and afterwards privately made away with.

The Encouragement and Protection given by some of the Chiefs of Clans is reciprocally rewarded by giving them a share of the Plunder, which is sometimes one half or two thirds of what is stolen. They exercise an Arbitrary and Tyrannical power over them; They determine all disputes and differences that happen among their Vassals, and on extraordinary occasions such as the Marriage of a Daughter, the building of a House, or any other pretence for the support of their Chief, or honour of the Name, he Levies a Tax on the Tribe; to which Imposition, if any one refuse to contribute, he is sure of the severest Treatment or at best to be cast out of the Tribe. And it is not to be wonder'd that those who submit to this Servile Slavery, will, when Summoned by their Superiors, follow them into Rebellion.

To remedy these Inconveniences there was an Act of Parliament, passed in the year 1716 for the more effectual securing the Peace of the Highlands in Scotland, by Disarming the Highlanders, which has been so ill executed, that the Clans the most disaffected to Your Majesty's Government remain better Armed than ever, and consequently more in a Capacity not only of committing Robberies and Depredations, but to be used as Tools or Instruments to any Foreign Power or Domestic Incendiaries who may attempt to disturb the Peace of Your Majesty's Reign. By this Act the Collectors for Taxes were empowered to pay for the Arms delivered in, as they were Valued by Persons appointed for that Service in the respective Countries, but as the Government was to support the Charge, they did not scruple to Appraise them at a much higher rate than their real worth, few or none being delivered up except such as were broken and unfit for Service; And I have been informed that from the time of passing that Act, to the time it was put in execution, great Quantities of broken and useless Arms were brought from Holland and delivered up to the Persons appointed to receive the same at exorbitant prices.

The Spaniards who landed at Castle Donnan in the Year 1719 brought with them a great Number of Arms: They were delivered to the Rebellious Highlanders who are still possessed of them, many of which I have seen in my passage through that Country, and I judge them to be the same from their peculiar make, and the fashion of their Locks. These and others now in their Possession by a Moderate Computation are supposed to amount to 5 or 6000, besides those in the possession of the Clans who are in Your Majesty's Interest, provided as they alledge, for their own defence.

The Legislature in Scotland before the Union of the Kingdoms have ever considered the Highlands in a different State from the rest of the Nation, and made peculiar Laws for their Government under the severest Penalties. The Chieftains of Clans were obliged to send their Children or nearest Relations to Edinburgh as Hostages for the good behaviour of their respective Clans, and in default they might by the Law be put to death.

The Clans and Tribes who lived in a State of Anarchy and Confusion (as they seem to be in at this present time) were, by the very Words of the Act of Parliament to be pursued with Fire and Sword, but as the Execution of the Laws relating to the Highlands was under the care of the Privy Council of Scotland (now no longer Subsisting, who by Act of Parliament were obliged to sit the first Day in every Month for that purpose) it often happen'd that Men of great Power in the Highlands were of the said Council, who had no other way of rendering themselves considerable than from their Numbers of Armed Men, and consequently the less Zealous in putting the Laws in Execution against them. The Independent Companies raised by King William not long after the Revolution reduced the Highlanders into better order than at any time they had been in since the Restauration. They were composed of the Natives of the Country, inured to the fatigue of travelling the Mountains, lying on the Hills, wore the same Habit, and spoke the same Language; but for want of being put under proper Regulations, Corruptions were introduced, and some who commanded them, instead of bringing Criminals to Justice (as I am informed) often compounded for the Theft and for a Sum of Money set them at Liberty. They are said also to have defrauded the Government by keeping not above half their Numbers in constant Pay; which, as I humbly conceive, might be the reason Your Majesty caused them to be disbanded.

Your Barracks were afterwards built in different parts of the Highlands, and Parties of the Regular Troops under the Command of Highland Officers, with a Company of 30 Guides (Established to conduct them through the Mountains) was thought an effectual Scheme, as well to prevent the rising of the Highlanders disaffected to Your Majesty's Government, as to hinder the Depredations on your faithful Subjects. It is to be wished that during the Reign of Your Majesty and your Successors, no Insurrections may ever happen to experience whether the Barracks will effectually answer the end proposed; yet I am humbly of opinion; That if the number of Troops they are built to contain, was constantly Quartered in them (whereas there is now in some but 30 Men) and proper Provisions laid in for their support during the Winter Season, they might be of some use to prevent the Insurrections of the Highlanders; Though as I humbly conceive, (having seen them all) that two of the four are not built in as proper Situations as they might have been.

As to the Highland Parties, I have already presumed to represent to Your Majesty the little use they were of in hindering Depredations, and the great sufferings of the Soldiers employed in that Service, upon which your Majesty was Graciously pleased to Countermand them.

I must further beg leave to Report to your Majesty that another great Cause of Disorders in the Highlands, is the want of proper Persons to execute the several Offices of Civil Magistrates, especially in the Shires of Ross, Inverness and some other parts of the Highlands. The Party Quarrels and violent Animosities amongst the Gentlemen (equally well affected to your Majesty's Government) I humbly conceive to be one great Cause of this Defect. Those who were in Arms for your Majesty, who raised a Spirit in the Shire of Inverness and recovered the Town of that Name from the Rebells (their Main Body being then at Perth) Complain, that the Persons employed as Magistrates over them have little Credit or Interest in that Country, and that three of Deputy Sheriffs in those parts were Persons actually in Arms against your Majesty at the time of the late Rebellion which (as I am credibly informed) is true. They likewise complain, that many of the most considerable Gentlemen are left out in the Commissions of Lord Lieutenants, Deputy Lieutenants, Sheriffs, etc. And I take the liberty to observe that the want of acting Justices of the Peace is a great encouragement to the Disorders so frequently committed in that part of the Country, there being but one, residing as an acting Justice for the Space of above a hundred Miles in Compass.

Your Majesty's Commands requiring me to examine into the State and Condition of the late Earl of Seaforth's Estate, engaged me to go to the Castle of Brahan his principal Seat, and other parts of the said Estate, which for the most part is Highland Country, and extends from Brahan to Kintail on the Western Coast, being 36 Miles in length and the most Mountainous part of the Highlands; The whole Isle of Lewis was also a part of the said Earl's Estate. The Tennants before the late Rebellion were reputed the richest of any in the Highlands, but now are become poor by neglecting their business and applying themselves wholly to the use of Arms. The Rents continue to be levied by one Donald Murchieson a Servant of the late Earl's who annually remits (or carries) the same to his Master into France.

The Tennants when in a Condition are also said to have sent him free Gifts in proportion to their several Circumstances but are now a year and a half in Arrear of Rent. The Receipts he gives to the Tennants are, as Deputy Factor to the Commissioners of Forfeited Estates, which pretended Power in the year 1721 he extorted from the Factor appointed by the said Commissioners to Collect those Rents for the use of the Publick, whom he attacked with above 400 Arm'd Men as he was going to enter upon the said Estate; having with him a Body of 30 of Your Majesty's Troops. The last year this Murchieson travell'd in a Public manner to Edinburgh to remit £800 to France for his Master's use, and remained there fourteen days unmolested.

I cannot omit observing to Your Majesty; this National tenderness your Subjects of North Britain have one for the other, is great encouragement to the Rebells and attainted Persons to return home from their Banishment.

Before I conclude this Report, I presume to observe to your Majesty the great Disadvantages Regular Troops are under when they engage with those who Inhabit

Mountainous Situations. The Serennes (*sic*) in France, and Catalans in Spain, have in all times been Instances of this Truth. The Highlands of Scotland are still more impracticable, from the want of Roads, Bridges, and from excessive Rains that almost continually fall in those parts, which by Nature and constant use become habitual to the Natives, but very difficultly supported by the Regular Troops. They are unacquainted with the Passages by which the Mountains are traversed, exposed to frequent Ambuscades, and Shots from the Tops of the Hills, which they return without effect, as it happened at the affair of Glenshiels, where the Rebells lost but one Man in the (*sic*) tho' a Considerable number of Your Majesty's Troops were killed and wounded.

I have endeavoured to Report to your Majesty as true and impartial an Account of the several particulars required by my Instructions, as far as I have been able to Collect them during my short continuance in the Highlands, and, as Your Majesty is pleased to Command me, presume to offer my humble opinion of what I conceive necessary to be done towards establishing Order in those Parts, and reducing the Highlands to a more due Submission to Your Majesty's Government.

## PROPOSAL.

### I.

That Companies of such Highlanders as are well affected to his Majesty's Government be Established, under proper Regulations and Commanded by Officers speaking the Language of the Country, subject to Martial Law and under the Inspection and Orders of the Governors of Fort-William and Inverness, and the Officer Commanding his Majesty's Forces in those Parts.

The Expence of these Companies which may in the whole consist of 250 or at most 300 Men, may be answered by reducing one Man p Troop and Company of the Regular Forces.

### 2.

That the said Companies be employed in Disarming the Highlanders, preventing Depredations, bringing Criminals to Justice, and hinder Rebells and Attainted Persons from inhabiting that part of the Kingdom.

### 3.

That a Redoubte or Barrack be erected at Inverness, as well for preventing the Highlanders descending in the Low Country in time of Rebellion, as for the better Quartering his Majesty's Troops, and keeping them in a Body sufficient to prevent or Subdue Insurrections.

4.

That in order to render the Barrack at Killihnimen of more use than I conceive it to be of at present (from its being situate at too great a distance from Lake Ness) a Redoubte be built at the West End adjoining to it, which with the said Barrack may be able to contain a Batallion of Foot, and a Communication made for their mutual support, the space of ground between one and the other being less than 500 Yards. This appears to be more necessary from the Situation of the Place, which is the most Centrical part of the Highlands, a considerable Pass, equally distant from Fort-William and Inverness, and where a Body of 1000 Men may be drawn together from these Garrisons in twenty-four hours, to suppress any Insurrections of the Highlanders.

5.

That a small Vessel with Oars and Sails be built on the Lake Ness, sufficient to carry a Party of 60 or 80 Soldiers and Provisions for the Garrison, which will be a means to keep the Communication open between that place and Inverness and be a safe and ready way of sending Parties to the Country bordering on the said Lake, which is Navigable for the largest Vessels. It is 24 Miles or more in length, and a Mile or more in breadth, the Country being Mountainous on both sides.

6.

That the Governors, or such as his Majesty is pleased to appoint to Command at Fort-William, Inverness, or Killihnimen, till the Peace of the Highlands is better Established, be required to reside at their respective Stations, and to give an Account of what passes in that Country to the Commander in Chief of the Forces in Scotland, and to such other whom his Majesty is pleased to appoint.

7.

That Inspection be made into the present Condition of the Garrisons and Castles in North Britain, and necessary Repairs made, to secure them from the danger of a Sudden Surprize, and more especially the Castle of Edinburgh, which remains exposed to the same attempt as was made on it in the Year 1715, there being nothing effectually done to it since that time, for the security of that important place, on which depends not only the Safety of the City, but of all that part of the Kingdom.

8.

That a Regiment of Dragoons be ordered to Quarter in the Low Country between Perth and Inverness (when Forrage can be provided for their Support) which will not only hinder the Highlanders descending into that Country from the apprehensions they are under of engaging with Horse, but may be a means to prevent the Landing of small Bodies of Troops that may be sent from Foreign parts to invade that part of the Kingdom, or encourage the Highlanders to Rebellion.

9.

That for the support of the Civil Government proper Persons be nominated for Sheriffs and Deputy Sheriffs in the Highland Counties, and that Justices of the Peace and Constables be Established in proper Places with small Salaries allowed them for the Charge they say they are of necessity at in seizing and sending Criminals to distant Prisons; and that Quarter Sessions be punctually kept at Killihnimen, Ruthven in Badenoch and Fort-William, and if occasion should require at Bernera near the Coast of the Isle of Skye.

10.

That an Act of Parliament be procured effectually to punish the Highlanders inhabiting the most uncivilized parts of the Country, who carry or conceal in their Dwellings, or other Places, Arms contrary to Law; and as the Penalty of a Fine in the former Act has never been (or from their Poverty can never be) levied, it is hoped the Parliament will not Scruple to make it Felony or Transportation for the first Offence.

11.

That an Act of Parliament be procured impowering the Heretors and Freeholders in every County to assess themselves Yearly, not exceeding a definite Sum, to be applied by the Commissioners of the Land Tax and Justices of the Peace for defraying the Charges of apprehending, prosecuting, and Maintaining of Criminals while in Gaol; For, as the Prosecutor is now to defray the Charges it is not to be wondered at that so few of them have been brought to Justice, and so many Malefactors escaped with Impunity.

All which is most humbly Represented and Submitted to
Your Majesty's Royal Consideration.

GEORGE WADE.

*London, 10th December, 1724.*

THE UNDERWRITTEN CLANS OR TRIBES WERE ENGAGED IN THE LATE REBELLION, MOST OF THEM ARE ARMED AND COMMIT DEPREDATIONS.

The Mackenzies and the small Clans vizt., the Meras, McLennans, Murchiesons and the McLeods of North Assynt, the Melays inhabiting the Countries belonging to the late Lord Seaforth, and all the Gentlemen and others of the Name of Mackenzie in the Main Land and Isle of Lewis, in Ross and Sutherland Shires.

The McLeods and others of Glenelg in the Isle of Skye, and the Harris, in the Shire of Inverness.

The McDonels and others of Slate or Skye and North Uist, in the Shire of Inverness.

The McDonels and others of Glengary, Abertarff, and Knoidart, in Inverness-shire.

The McDonels and others of Moidart, Arisaig, Muick, Canna, South Uist, in Inverness and Argyleshires.

The Camerons of Lochiel in Inverness-shire.

The Camerons of Ardnamurchan, Swin and Morvine in Argyleshire, and the other small Tribes in those Countries.

The McDonels of Keppoch and others in that part of Lochaber belonging to Mcintosh of Borlum in Inverness-shire.

The Stewarts of Appine and others in that Country in Argyleshire.

The McLeans in Mull, Rhume, Coll, Morvine, Ardnamurchan and Swinard, in Argyleshire.

The several Clans in that part of Lochaber belonging to the Duke of Gordon, in Inverness-shire, and those in Murray and Banffshires.

The McPhersons in Badenoch in the Shire of Inverness.

The McNeils of Barra in Argyleshire.

The Mcintoshes and other Tribes of that Name in Inverness-shire.

The Robertsons belonging to Strowan in Perthshire.


THE UNDERWRITTEN CLANS BELONG TO SUPERIORS WELL AFFECTED TO HIS MAJESTY.

|  | Men able to bear Arms. |
|---|---|
| The Duke of Argyle . | . 4000 |
| Lord Sutherland and Strathnaver . | . . 1000 |
| *Carry forward* | 5000 |

D

|  | Men able to bear Arms. |
|---|---|
| *Brought forward* | 5000 |
| Lord Lovat, Frazers | 800 |
| The Grants . | 800 |
| The Ross's and Monro's | 700 |
| Forbes of Culloden | 200 |
| Ross of Kilravock . | 300 |
| Sir Archibald Campbell of Clunis | 200 |
|  | 8000 |

#### THE TWO CLANS UNDERWRITTEN, FOR THE MOST PART WENT INTO THE REBELLION IN 1715 WITHOUT THEIR SUPERIORS.

| | |
|---|---|
| The Athol Men . | 2000 |
| The Broadalbin Men | 1000 |
| | 3000 |

#### THE CLANS UNDERWRITTEN WERE IN THE LATE REBELLION AND ARE STILL SUPPOSED TO BE DISAFFECTED TO HIS MAJESTY'S GOVERNMENT.

|  | Men able to bear Arms |
|---|---|
| The Tribes and Clans of the late Lord Seaforth | 3000 |
| Macdonel's of Slate | 1000 |
| Macdonel's of Glengary | 800 |
| Macdonel's of Moidart | 800 |
| Macdonel's of Keppoch | 220 |
| Lochiel (Camerons) | 800 |
| The McLeod's in all . | 1000 |
| Duke of Gordon's followers | 1000 |
| Stewart's of Appine . | 400 |
| Robertson's of Strowan . | 800 |
| Mcintoshe's and Farquharsons | 800 |
| McLeans in the Isle of Skye | 150 |
| Chisholms of Strathglass | 150 |
| McPhersons . . | 220 |
|  | 11,140 |

## ROMAN CATHOLICKS IN THE HIGHLANDS.

The late Earl of Seaforth, but none of his followers except the Lairds Mackenzie of Kilewn, and Mackenzie of Ardloch; the first has power over the Inhabitants of the Isle of Lewis and the latter over those who inhabit near Coigach and Loch Broom, which is in the North part of Seaforth's Country.

Chisholm of Strathglass and his Clan are Roman Catholicks.

Most of Glengary's Tribe are Roman Catholicks but he himself is not.

McDonald of Moidart and many of his Clan are Roman Catholicks.

McLeod of Barra and his Tribe are Roman Catholicks.

The Duke of Gordon and the most considerable of his followers are Roman Catholicks.


LIST OF THE MOST CONSIDERABLE GENTLEMEN WHO ARE WELL AFFECTED TO HIS MAJESTY'S GOVERNMENT WHO INHABIT AND HAVE ESTATES IN THE COUNTIES UNDER MENTIONED.

| | |
|---|---|
| MURRAY | Mr Brodie, Member of Parliament.<br>Mr Ross of Kilravock.<br>Laird of Grant, Member of Parliament.<br>Sir Harry Innes.<br>Mr Duff of Brachan. |
| NAIRN . | Mr Ross, Junior.<br>Mr Brodie of Brodie.<br>Mr Forbes of Culloden, Member of Parliament. |
| INVERNESS | The Laird of Grant.<br>The Lord Lovat.<br>Mr Forbes of Culloden. |
| ROSS | Mr Ross of Kilravock.<br>Colonel Munro, Member of Parliament.<br>General Ross.<br>Mr Munro of Culcairn. |
| CROMARTY | Mr Ross of Kilravock.<br>Sir Wm. Gordon, Member of Parliament. |
| SUTHERLAND . | The Earl of Sutherland. |
| CAITHNESS | The Earl of Caithness.<br>Mr Sinclair of Ulbster. |
| ORKNEY | The Earl of Morton. |

## SCHEME DELIVERED TO THE KING IN APRIL. 1725.

In the Report I had the Honour to lay before his Majesty at my return from the Highlands of Scotland, I took the liberty to represent the present state of that part of his Majesty's Dominions. The Proposals contained in the said Report and those I shall now take the Liberty to mention are, in my humble Opinion, the effectual and practicable Means of reducing the Highlanders to a due obedience to his Majesty's Government.

Experience has shewn that the Measures hitherto taken have proved insufficient to reduce the Highlanders to due obedience to the Laws, and to prevent the Depredations so frequently committed on the Inhabitants of the low Country, which is a great oppression to the well affected (who are entitled to the protection of the Government) but it is of so much more importance to the State itself that the Highlanders should be disarmed, who may (if not timely prevented) prove of dangerous consequence to the Peace of the Kingdom. For, while such a number of Men who are bold, resolute and disaffected, remain in a Capacity of doing Meschief, they are ready Instruments to be employed by any foreign Power, who may attempt to Invade his Majesty's Dominions or excite his Subjects to Rebellion.

The Peace and Tranquility we at present Enjoy under his Majesty's auspicious Reign, is the proper time to apply a remedy to this growing Evil.

If the Highlanders can be dispossessed of their Arms (or reduced to the Necessity of hiding them under ground where they will rust and spoil) it will at the same time prevent the Depredations, and render it very difficult for them to rise in Arms against the Government. For, if Arms should hereafter be brought from Foreign Parts when Designs are carrying on to create new Troubles, it will be hardly possible to disperse them to the Highlanders who are scattered in so large an extent of Country, when the Forts and Barracks are garrisoned with Soldiers in the very Center of the Highlands.

Several Laws have been made to restrain these People, but they have generally failed of Success, as I humbly conceive, either from partiality, negligence or from the private Views of those who were Employed in putting them in Execution ; And the Disarming Act of the first Year of his Majesty's Reign had no other effect than to defraud the Publick of a Considerable Sum of Money and to render the Enemies of the Government more formidable.

It is therefore necessary that an Act of Parliament be procured, Empowering his Majesty (or those he is pleased to appoint) to cause the several Clans to be summoned (one after another) to bring in their Arms by certain Days specified in the said Summons, after which, whoever is found in Arms (except such as are qualified by Law) should be transported to serve as Soldiers in any of His Majesty's

Plantations in America, or Garrisons beyond the Seas, with a Clause making it lawful for his Majesty's Forces to assist the Civil Magistrate, and to reduce them by force of Arms in Case they assemble in Numbers to oppose the Execution of the Act, and also a Clause of Indemnity for the Soldiers who shall happen to kill or wound any of them, as in the Law against Riots and Tumults.

It is absolutely necessary that his Majesty have a power by the said Act to appoint such Persons as he shall think fit (altho' they were not Natives of that part of the Kingdom) to put the Penalties of this Law in Execution, otherwise it will render this Act of Parliament as useless as the former.

I shall now presume to give my humble opinion how the Scheme for Disarming the Highlands may be put in execution.

That three Companies of Highlanders be raised consisting of 60 or 70 Men each, Commanded by Captains.

That three Companies of Highlanders consisting of half that Number be commanded by Lieutenants.

That the Six Companies consisting of about 300 Men be compleated and Armed by the first of June in order to join the Regular Troops at Inverness, when they March to their first Encampment.

That four Battalions of the Forces now in Scotland be in readiness to form a Camp in the Highlands.

That the Regiment Quartered at Fort-William remain there during the Summer, and supply the Barracks of Ruthven and Bernara with Garrisons.

That the Regiment of Foot now ordered to Scotland be Quartered at Innersnait, Stirling, Perth, and the Sea Port Towns on the Eastern Coast.

That the Regiment now Quartered at Berwick be ordered to send five Companies to Edinburgh and Leith to Quarter there during the Summer.

A Detachment of fifty Dragoons may be ordered to attend the Camp, a greater Number not being able to Subsist in the Highlands for want of Forage.

By this Disposition the several Garrisons and Barracks will be supplied with Men, and the Sea Port Towns provided with Soldiers sufficient to Assist the Officers of his Majesty's Customs, so that of the Six Regiments of Foot in Scotland there will remain for the Encampment four Battalions, the Highland Companies, and Fifty Dragoons.

The first Camp is proposed to be formed at or near Castle Brahan, the principal Seat of the late Earl of Seaforth, and the Vassals and Tennants of the said Earl (who even at this time continue in a state of Rebellion) may be first summon'd to deliver up their Arms. And if a promise of an Indemnity was made them for the Rents they have paid to Murchieson for the use of the said Earl, it might probably induce them to submit for the future to become Tennants to his Majesty and pay in their Rents for the use of the Publick. But if they refuse to

Submit to the delivery of their Arms, they may be made Examples to others, by being treated with as much vigour as can be justified by Law, and the Act of Parliament put in Execution against them in its utmost Extent.

When this is effected the Forces may move to the next Clans who are Armed, and so proceed from one to another as long as the Season of the Year will admit the Troops to continue Encamped in the Mountains, and if no unforeseen difficulties happen, it is humbly hoped that all the disaffected Clans to the North of Fort-William and the Lake Ness may be subdued before the end of the Campaign.

That a Sixth Rate Man of War be appointed to attend the Service on the Eastern Coast, to receive on board and carry to Berwick, such of the Highlanders who shall be condemned to Transportation.

That a Quantity of Bisquit be put on board the said Ship and landed at Inverness for the use of the Parties that may be sent into the Mountains.

That Officers and Serjeants of the Regiments in the West Indies be appointed at Inverness or Berwick, to receive such Highlanders as may be sent away for Soldiers.

## PROVISION OF MONEY WILL BE WANTING FOR THE PURPOSES FOLLOWING.

For building a Vessel on the Lake Ness.

For repairing the Fortifications of Edinburgh Castle and Fort-William.

For building two New Forts and Barracks at Inverness and Killihnimen, each sufficient to contain a Batallion of Foot.

For Gratuitys to such Highlanders as shall contribute to facilitate the Execution of the Disarming Scheme, Discover Arms conceal'd or Persons Outlawed or Attainted of High Treason.

For the Maintenance of Prisoners till their Tryal or Transportation.

For the Extraordinary Charge of Encampments, the Carriage of Provisions and Ammunition for the use of the Forces, and other Contingent Charges.

For the Support of the General and Staff Officers to be employed in this Service.

For mending the Roads between the Garrisons and Barracks, for the better Communication of his Majesty's Troops.

It is to be hoped that two Years will be sufficient to put in Execution the several Services abovenamed, and that the Extraordinary Expence to the Government will not exceed Ten thousand pounds for each Year.

# EXTRACT FROM "MEMORIALL ANENT THE TRUE STATE OF THE HIGHLANDS AS TO THEIR CHIEFTENRIES, FOLLOWINGS AND DEPENDANCES BEFORE THE LATE REBELLION" (1745).[1]

\*　　\*　　\*　　\*　　\*　　\*　　\*　　\*　　\*　　\*

I NOW proceed to Narrate the Highland followings and dependances beginning in the South at Argyll-Shire.

CAMPBELLS. In the Irish (Gaelic) tongue Called Clanquin. The Duke of Argyll is their Chieften, and is Named in the Highlands Mack-Callen-More, he can raise out of his own property, Small Vassals, and Kinsmen Lands, 3000 Men. The Earl of Broadalbine more than 1000 and the many Great Barrons such as Auchinbreck, Ardkindloss, Lochnell, etc., etc., at least Another 1000. So that that Clan Could bring to the field above 5000 Men besides a Vast many Barrons and Gentlemen, not only out of Argyll, but out of Dumbarton, Streoling and Perth Shires, and are at present the Richest and Most Numerous Clan in Scotland, their Countreys and Bounds Most Extensive, their Superiorities, Jurisdictions and other Dependances by far the Greatest in the Kingdom, which makes them the familie of Greatest Significancy and power in North Brittain and Always has been So, Since the Declyn of the Douglasses, the totall Fall of the Cummins, and the extinction of the Earl of Ross his Familie.

MACKLEANS.—In Irish called Clan Lein, Sir Hector Macklean is their Chieften and is Called in the Highlands Mackillein, was a very potent Clan About 200 years Agone, and Could have raised above 800 men, but now that the familie of Argyll are possessed of their Chieften's Estate, they will hardly make 500, and even Many of these brought out of the Duke's Lands.

MACKLACHLEN. In Irish Called Clan Lachlen, the Laird of Macklachlen is the Chief, can raise 200 Men,

STEWART OF ASSIN. The Laird of Assin is the Chief, he holds his Lands of the Crown, and can raise 300 Men.

MCDOUGALS OF LORN. In Irish called Clanrickcuil, their Chieften the Laird of Makdougall and is Called in the Highlands Mackcuill Lorn, was a more

---

[1] See page 15, *note*. The authorship of this Memorial has been attributed to Duncan Forbes of Culloden.

potent familie of old but now much Diminished by the Campbells, and Can (I believe) Still bring out 200 Men.

Proceeding Northward by the Coast and Isles.

MACKDONALD OF SLATE. Sir Alexander Mackdonald is their Chief, in Irish Called Mack-Conell simply, by way of Preheminence, he has a very considerable Estate which holds all of the Crown, and lyes in the Isles of Skye and Uist and can bring out 700 Men.

MACKDONALD OF CLANRONALD. In Irish the Chieften is Called Mackick-allen, and in English Captain of Clanronald, he has a very handsome estate, holds most of it of the Crown, which lyes in Moidart, and Arisack, on the Continent, and in the Isles of Uist, Benbecula, Cana, Rum, etc., he brings out 700 Men.

MACKDONALD OF GLENGARY. The Laird of Glengary is their Chief, who in Irish is Called Mackick Alaster, he has a pretty good estate, all holden of the Crown, which lyes in the Countreys of Glengary, and Knoidart, both on the Continent, and Can bring out 500 Men.

MACKDONALD OF KEPOCH. Kepoch is their Chieftain, in Irish is called Mackickvailt, he is not so much as a Propriatar of one furr of Land, but only Tacksmen and tennants, both himself and kinsmen, in most of their possessions, to the Laird of Mackintosh, and the remaining part to the Duke of Gordon, all lying in Lochaber, he can raise and bring out 150 men.

MACKDONALD OF GLENCO. The Laird of Glenco is their Chief, who in Irish is Called Mackickian, he is but a very small propriatar, he holds his lands of Stewart of Apin, and Can raise 150 Men.

These Five Chieftens of Mackdonalds, all Claim a Lineal Descent from Alexander Mackdonald, Earl of Ross, Successor and Representative of Donald of the Isles, but none of them have any Clear Documents to Vouch the Same, So that that great and Aspyring Familie, who wadged frequent wars with our Scots Kings, and who Acted as Sovereigns themselves, and oblidged Most of the Clans to Swear Fealty to them, is now Utterly Extinct, The last Earl having No Sons, neither had he any Near Male relation to Succeed him.

CAMERONS. A very potent Clan in Lochaber, the Laird of Lochiel is their Chief, who is Called in Irish Mackoildin, he has a good Competent estate, but none of it holden of the Crown, The most of it is of the Duke of Argyll, and the remainder of the Duke of Gordon, he can bring out 800 Men of Old there were Severall Small tribes in that Countrey Viz. McMartins, Clanigilivile, and Clanigilouvie, who were always esteemed to be of the Clancattan, but now Call themselves all Camerons and are very faithfull to their Chief.

MACKLEODS. Were Two distinct and both very potent families of Old, Viz. Mackleod of Lews and Mackleod of Harris, both thought to be of Danish Extraction, But the former is Utterly Extinct, and their Lands purchased and possessed by the Mackenzies, The now only Laird of Macleod is their Chieften, and is in Irish Called Mackloit, he has a very Considerable Fortune, all holden of the Crown, lying in Glenelg on the Continent, and in the Isles of Sky and Harris, etc., etc., he can raise and bring out 700 Men.

MACKINNONS.—The Laird of Mackinnon is their Chief, who in Irish is called Mackenoin, holds his Lands of the Crown, both in the Isles of Sky and Mull and Can raise 200 Men.

I pass now again to the South to give Account of the Inland Chieftens beginning again at Argyle Shire and from thence proceeding Northward.

There are Severalls of Qualitie, as well as Gentlemen who are Chieftens, who have the Command of Severall Highlanders in the Countreys of Argyll, Monteith, Dumbarton, Streoling, and Perth Shires, Such as the Duke of Montrose, Earls of Murray and Bute, as also the Macfarlands, Macknails, Macknabs and Macknachtens, etc., etc., whom I freely pass over Since for Some Considerable time they have given No Disturbance by Armaments or Convocations.

DUKE OF PERTH.—Is no Claned familie, although the head of a Considerable Number of Barrons and Gentlemen of the Name of Drummond in the Low Countreys, he is brought in here Allennarly Upon account of his command of about 300 Highlanders in Glenertonie and Neighbourhood.

ROBERTSONS.—The Laird of Strowen is their Chief, they are in the Irish called Clandonachie, his Lands holds of the Crown and lye in Roinach and Brae of Atholl, he can raise on his own Estate about 200 Men: There are near 500 More Robertsons in Atholl who Seldom or Never follow their Said Chief being a part of the following of the Duke of Atholl after Named.

MENZIESES.—Sir Robert Menzies of Weem is the Chieften and is in Irish Called Menernach, he has a very handsome Estate all holden of the Crown, Lying in Apenedull and Roinach, and can raise 500 Men.

STEWART OF CAIRNTULLIE. Is no Chieften but has an handsome Estate in Strathbran and Strathtey, all holden of the Crown, out of which he can raise 200 Men.

CLAN GREGORE.—Are a people very Remarkable for wicked Achievements, that Name has been Severall times Discharged by Act of Parliament, So that they are at present Disguised Under the Severall Names of Campbells, Graham, Murray, and Drummond, etc., and Dispersed thorrow Dumbarton, Streoling and Perthshires, They have No freeholder or Barron Amongst them and few or None that have any heritage, they have no present Chieften, the said Dignitie being just now Electlve and Continues no longer than the Current Expedition and is Detur Digniori, they can raise among them 500 Men and Are rarely Absent from any Great Convocation whatever the Quarrell may be, Since plunder and Booty is their Bussiness.

DUKE OF ATHOLL.—He is no Claned familie, although Chieften and head of a Number of Barrons and Gentlemen of the Name of Murray in the low

E

Countrey, but is deservedly placed here upon the Account of his extensive following of About 3000 Highlanders, a Good Many of them out of his own property, but most of them Upon the Account of Vast Superiorities in Glenalmond, Glenlyon, Balquhidder, Strathtay, Atholl, Bishoprick of Dunkeld, Strathardel and Glenshee.

Crossing the Grampians we come to Marr.

FARQUHARSONS,—The only Claned familie in Marr, or Aberdeenshire, Are the Farquharsons, in Irish Called Claniunla, they Can bring out 500 Men. The Laird of Invercald is their Chief, who has a very handsome estate holden of the Crown, both in Perth and Aberdeen Shires, there Are Severall other Barrons of his Name, that have competent fortunes.

DUKE OF GORDON. Is no Claned familie, Although a Chieften of a Very Considerable and powerfull Name in the Low Countries. besides that he has a great Posse of Gentlemen on horse back in Enzie and Strathboggie, but he is only placed here. upon the Account of his followings of Highlanders in Strathavin and Glenlivet, which will be about 300 Men. His extensive Superiorities and Jurisdictions in the Highlands, Viz., in Badenoch and Lochaber, does not yield him Any followers, the possessions of his own very property, as well as these whole Countreys, follow their Naturall Chieftens, of whom they are Descended. and have no Manner of Regard either to Masters or Superiors.

GRANTS,—A Considerable Name and familie in Strathspey, the Laird of Grant is their Chief, who has an handsome and Large Estate, both in Strathspey and Urquhart, all holden of the Crown except Abernethie, which he holds of the Earl of Murray, He can raise out of Strathspey 700 Men and out of Urquhart 150, he has Severall Barrons of his Name, both in Invernes, Murray, Bamff, and Aberdeen-Shires,

MCINTOSHES. This was one of the most potent Clans in Scotland, when their Residence was at (*sic*) Castle in Lochaber, the Antient Seat of their familie (of which Countrey they are Still Heritable Stewarts) but the Camerons having purchased most of Said estate has much Diminished their power. The Laird of Mackintosh is their Chief. in Irish Called Macintoshuk and in English Commonly termed Captain of Clan Chattan, he can bring out 800 Men, Including the Small Neighbouring families. of Mackgillivray. Mackqueen, Mackbain, etc., etc., who all own themselves his Kinsmen, His Countreys are Brae Lochaber, Badenoch, Strathern and Strathnern. He Still retains a very Competent Estate, he holds Brae Lochabar, Moy and Largs of the Crown, Badenoch of the Duke of Gordon, and Most of his kinsmen hold Strathern and Strathnairn of the Earl of Murray,

MCPHERSONS. Called in Irish Clanvurich, their chief is the Laird of Clunie, he can bring out 300 Men, his whole Lands and all his Kinsmens lands, are holden of the Duke of Gordon and lye in Badenoch.

FRAZERS. Are a Considerable Clan in the Countreys of Aird and Strath-arrigg. Their Chieften is Lord Lovat, in Irish called Mackimmie, has a very

Considerable estate all holden of the Crown, and Can raise 700 Men, he has a good Number of Barrons of his Name, All in Inverness Shire.

GLENMORISTON GRANT. Is no Chieften, neither does he ever follow any, he brings out 100 Men, his lands are holden of the Crown, and does frequently in Armaments join with McDonald of Glengary.

CHISOLMS.—Their Chieftain is Chisholm of Straglass, in Irish Called Inshisolich, holds his Land of the Crown and Can bring out 200 Men.

MCKENZIES.—One of the Most Considerable Clans Under one head (next to the Campbells) in the Nation. The Earl of Seaforth was, and Now Lord Fortrose is, their Chief, in Irish is called Mackkynnich, He out of his Countreys of Kintaile, Lochelsh, Lochbroon, and Lochcaron, on the Continent, and in the Isles of Lews, etc., Can raise 1000 Men which is all he can Command, The Earl of Cromartie with 8 or 9 Barrons of the Name and an Number of Smaller Gentlemen can amongst them raise 1000 More, but are not Much Inclined to follow their Chief, Neither are they in Use, or Very Apt to Armaments in that Countrey of Ross, etc., of late they are much come in to Independancy.

MONROES.—Sir Hary Monroe of Foules is their Chief, his Lands are holden of the Crown, and Can raise 300 Men.    **1358155**

ROSSES.—Lord Ross is their Chief, his Lands hold of the Crown, and Can raise 300 Men.

SUTHERLANDS.—The Earl of Sutherland is their Chief, Can raise 700 Men.

MACKAYS. The Lord Rae is their Chief, His Estate lyes in Strathnaver, and he can raise 500 Men.

SINKLAIRS.—The Earl of Caitness is their Chief, and Could raise 500 Men, but his Estate being Mostly gone, both it and the followings are now in the hands of Sincklairs of Dunbeth and Ulpster, etc.

The whole following brought in one View.

| | | | | | |
|---|---|---|---|---|---|
| Campbells | 3000 | Mackleods | 700 | Mackintoshes . | 800 |
| Mackleans . | 500 | Mackinnons . | 200 | Mackphersons | 300 |
| Macklachlens. | 200 | Duke of Perth | 300 | Frazers . | 700 |
| Stewarts of Apin | 300 | Robertsons . | 200 | Glenmoriston . | 100 |
| Mackdougalls | 200 | Menzieses . . | 300 | Chisolm's | 200 |
| McDonald of Slate . | 700 | Stewart, Garntilly | 200 | Mackenzies | 2000 |
| McDonald, Clanronald . | 700 | Mackgregors . . | 500 | Monroes . | 300 |
| McDonald, Glengary . | 500 | Duke of Atholl . | 3000 | Rosses . | 300 |
| McDonald, Kepoch | 150 | Farquharsons . | 500 | Sutherland | 700 |
| McDonald, Glencoe | 150 | Duke of Gordon . | 300 | Mackays | 500 |
| Camerons . | 800 | Grants . . | 850 | Sincklairs . | 500 |
| First Colum . | 7200 | Second Colum . | 8050 | Third Colum . | 6400 |

In all 21,650 Men.

Ye have Now all the power of the Armed Highlanders att one View which ye may perceive to be above 20,000, A Sufficient force to have Conquered All the rest of the Scottish Nation, if they had a mind, and Could but have agreed how to Divide the Booty, and Consequently a force, that was Capable when United to Disturb the peace of the whole United Island at their pleasure, and Might at last, with but a small Conjunction of foreigners, have endangered the totall overthrow of our happy Constitution.

This was the State of the Nation as to our Scots Highlanders before the Rebellion, but now that the Government, out of their great prudence and wisdom, by many wholsome Laws and Acts of Parliament, have so far Destroyed and eradicate the most of all Dependances by Discharging all obligations, for Hunting, Watching and warding. And Also Discharging all personall Services in Charters, and further taking Away all Wardholdings which in the very Nature imported the Same, Besides the Subjects being Now happily liberate from forfietry in time of Minority and from their being deprived of their wifes portions, as also free'd of the Sadd effects of the hard and oppressive practices, of Recognitions, Single And Life-rent escheats, and All this Most Generously done by his Most Gracious Majesty to the Great Loss and Diminution of his Crown rents.

And further Now Considering that Not only the Smaller Gentrie, but the whole Lowest class of People, have their Chattels and Moveable Effects, as well as their lives, taken out of the power and hands, of all Heritable Jurisdictions Great and Small, and thereby freed them from the terrour of being Subject, to the penalties and Arbitrary Decrees of these Ignorant and Mercenary Judges, and that hereby not only Vassalls, but all within Regallities, Stewartries, etc., are fully liberate from their former Slavery and Dependance, but Now also that all farmers, tennantries, and the very Lowest people are free'd from being bound to pay their Masters any oppressive or Illegal Services, which will not bear being Named in Such.

When all that is Said is Maturely Considered, and the whole body of the people clearly perceive themselves manumitted from a State of Slavery and Misery, and Now made free Denisons of the happy English Constitution; and when once Convinced that it is not in the power of Any Superior, Chieften, or Land-Lord, to oppress (or in the least hurt) them either in their persons or estates, Ye may be sure it will make a very Strange Revolution in their Minds and Sentiments and will determine them as to their future peaceable Deportment.

And if that Villainous practice of Thieving was once totally Suppressed, which forces them to retain the Use of Arms for Self Defence there would never there-after be Use for any, Neither any Convocation be heard of in an Age.

It is with Good Ground Now believed, that of All the Grand list Mentioned More than three fourths of them will vanish, and be laid Aside, particularly the whole Inland Chieftens and Superiors, and that henceforth none of those potentates (of any Denomination) will ever be Capable to bring a Single 100 Men to the field More than their Domestick Servants, Excepting these Naturall Chieftens After-Named, whose followers are Generally all their Kinsmen Descended of their families, and who have no manner of Regard either to Superiors or Landlord but where it Chances to be their own Chieften.

| | | | | | |
|---|---|---|---|---|---|
| Mackleans | . 500 | Mackdonald of Slate | . 700 | Mackdonald, Glenco | 150 |
| Macklachlans | 200 | Mackdonald of Clanranald | 700 | Mackleods | 700 |
| Stewart of Apin | 300 | Mackdonald of Glengary | 500 | Mackinnons | . 200 |
| Camerons, Lochil | . 800 | Mackdonald, Kepoch | . 150 | | |
| First Colum | . 1800 | Second Colum | . 2050 | Third Colum | . 1050 |

In all, 4900 Men.

These families are Now the only people whose Chieftenries and Capacitie of Giving Disturbance Still Subsists, and are not in the least touched or Diminished, by all the Acts and Laws as Yet made. Since they have an Inherent Attractive Virtue, which makes their people follow as Iron Claps to the Loadstone, whereas the whole others in the Generall Grand list was rarely brought out (even before the late good Laws) without Some force and Compultion.

It must be a Work of Some time before these Ignorant and Barbarious people, Can be brought to make the right Use of their Reason, So as to Compare their State with others, if that was once happily done, their Miserable and beggarly Dependance, and blind obedience without Asking Questions, would Soon fall to the Ground.

\* \* \* \* \* \* \* \* \* \* \* \*

# THE DISARMING ACT, 1746.[1]

## 19 GEO. II. C. 39.

*An Act for the more effectual disarming the Highlands in* Scotland ; *and for more effectually securing the Peace of the said Highlands ; and for restraining the Use of the Highland Dress ; and for further indemnifying such Persons as have acted in defence of his Majesty's Person and Government, during the unnatural Rebellion ; and for indemnifying the Judges and other Officers of the Court of Justiciary in* Scotland, *for not performing the Northern Circuit in* May, *One thousand seven hundred and forty six ; and for obliging the Masters and Teachers of Private Schools in* Scotland, *and Chaplains, Tutors and Governors of Children or Youth, to take the Oaths to His Majesty, His Heirs, or Successors, and to register the same.*

Preamble
reciting
the Acts,
1 Geo. I.

WHEREAS by an Act made in the First Year of the Reign of His late Majesty King *George* the First, of Glorious Memory, intituled, *An Act for the more effectual securing the Peace of the Highlands in* Scotland, it was enacted, That from and after the First Day of *November*, which was in the Year of our Lord One thousand seven hundred and sixteen, it should not be lawful for any Person or Persons (except such Persons as are therein mentioned and described) within the Shire of *Dunbartain*, on the North Side of the Water of *Leven, Stirling* on the North Side of the River of *Forth, Perth, Kincardin, Aberdeen, Inverness, Nairn, Cromarty, Argyle, Forfar, Bamff, Sutherland, Caithness, Elgine,* and *Ross,* to have in his or their Custody, Use, or Bear, Broad Sword or Target, Poignard, Whinger, or Durk, Side Pistol, Gun, or other warlike Weapon, otherwise than in the said Act was directed, under certain Penalties appointed by the said Act ; which Act having by Experience

---

[1] This Act received the Royal Assent on August 12, 1746. Its administration was entrusted to Lieut.-General Humphry Bland, Commander of the Forces in North Britain. His execution of this duty is the subject of an interesting paper by Mr A. H. Millar in the *Proceedings of the Society of Antiquaries of Scotland,* March 9, 1896. In 1747 the Heritable Jurisdictions Act was passed, which broke up the feudal power of the great landowners. Some amazing instances of feudal tyranny in the Highlands in the first half of the eighteenth century are noted in Captain Burt's *Letters from the North of Scotland,* vol. ii., p. 246 *et seq.* (Ed. 1876.)

been found not sufficient to attain the Ends therein proposed, was further enforced by an Act made in the Eleventh Year of the Reign of his late Majesty, intituled, *An Act for more effectual disarming the Highlands in that Part of* Great Britain *called* Scotland; *and for the better securing the Peace and Quiet of that Part of the Kingdom:* And whereas the said Act of the Eleventh Year of His late Majesty being, so far as it related to the disarming the Highlands, to continue in Force only during the Term of Seven Years, and from thence to the End of the next Session of Parliament, is now expired: And whereas many Persons within the said Bounds and Shires still continue possessed of great Quantities of Arms, and there, with a great Number of such Persons, have lately raised and carried on a most audacious and wicked Rebellion against His Majesty, in favour of a Popish Pretender, and in Prosecution thereof did, in a traiterous and hostile Manner, march into the Southern Parts of this Kingdom, took Possession of Several Towns, raised Contributions upon the Country, and committed many other Disorders, to the Terror and great Loss of His Majesty's faithful Subjects, until, by the Blessing of God on His Majesty's Arms, they were subdued: Now, for preventing Rebellion, and traiterous Attempts in Time to come, and the other Mischiefs arising from the Possession or Use of Arms, by lawless, wicked, and disaffected Persons inhabiting within the said several Shires and Bounds; be it enacted by the King's most Excellent Majesty, by and with the Advice and Consent of the Lords Spiritual and Temporal, and Commons, in this present Parliament assembled, and by the Authority of the same, That from and after the First Day of *August,* One thousand seven hundred and forty six, it shall be lawful for the respective Lords Lieutenants of the several Shires above recited, and for such other Person or Persons as His Majesty, His Heirs, or Successors shall, by His or Their Sign Manual, from time to time, think fit, to authorise and appoint in that Behalf, to issue or cause to be issued out. Letters of Summons in His Majesty's Name, and under his or their respective Hands and Seals, directed to such Persons within the said several Shires and Bounds, as he or they, from time to time, shall think fit, thereby commanding and requiring all and every Person and Persons therein named, or inhabiting within the particular Limits therein described, to bring in and deliver up, at a certain Day, in such Summons to be prefixed, and at a certain Place therein to be mentioned, all and singular his and their Arms and warlike Weapons, unto such Lord Lieutenant, or other Person or Persons appointed by His Majesty, His Heirs, or Successors, in that Behalf, as aforesaid, for the Use of His Majesty, His Heirs, or Successors, and to be disposed of in such Manner as His Majesty, His Heirs, or Successors shall appoint; and if any Person or Persons, in such Summons mentioned

10 & 11 Geo. I.

Lord Lieutenants, etc., to issue Summons for delivering up of Arms.

by Name, or inhabiting within the Limits therein described, shall, by the Oaths of One or more credible Witness or Witnesses, be convicted of having or bearing any Arms, or warlike Weapons, after the Day prefixed in such Summons, before any One or more of His Majesty's Justices of the Peace for the Shire or Stewartry where such Offender or Offenders shall reside, or be apprehended, or before the Judge Ordinary, or such other Person or Persons as His Majesty, His Heirs, or Successors shall appoint, in Manner herein after directed, every such Person or Persons so convicted shall forfeit *The Penalty.* the Sum of Fifteen Pounds Sterling, and shall be committed to Prison until payment of the said Sum ; and if any Person or Persons, convicted as afore- *On Non-payment of the Penalty, the Persons, if fit, are to serve as Soldiers in America.* said, shall refuse or neglect to make Payment of the foresaid Sum of Fifteen Pounds Sterling, within the Space of One Calendar Month from the Date of such Conviction, it shall and may be lawful to any one or more of His Majesty's Justices of the Peace, or to the Judge Ordinary of the Place where such Offender or Offenders is or are imprisoned, in case he or they shall judge such Offender or Offenders fit to serve His Majesty as a Soldier or Soldiers, to cause him or them to be delivered over (as they are hereby impowered and required to do) to such Officer or Officers belonging to the Forces of His Majesty, His Heirs, or Successors, who shall be appointed from time to time to receive such Men, to serve as Soldiers in any of his Majesty's Forces in *America :* for which Purpose the respective Officers, who shall *Articles of War to be read to them ; and entry thereof to be made, &c.* receive such Men, shall then cause the Articles of War against Mutiny and Desertion to be read to him or them in the Presence of such Justices of the Peace, or Judge Ordinary, who shall so deliver over such Men, who shall cause an Entry or Memorial thereof to be made, together with the Names of the Persons so delivered over, with a Certificate thereof in Writing, under his or their Hands, to be delivered to the Officers appointed to receive such Men ; and from and after reading of the said Articles of War, every Person so delivered over to such Officer, to serve as a Soldier as aforesaid, shall be deemed a listed Soldier to all Intents and Purposes, and shall be subject to the Discipline of War ; and in case of Desertion, shall be punished as a *If unfit, to be im- prisoned for Six Months, and find Bail.* Deserter ; and in case such Offender or Offenders shall not be judged fit to serve his Majesty as aforesaid, then he or they shall be imprisoned for the space of Six Calendar Months, and also until he or they shall give sufficient Security for his or their good Behaviour for the Space of Two Years from the giving thereof.

II. And be it further enacted by the Authority aforesaid, That all Per- sons summoned to deliver up their Arms as aforesaid, who shall, from and *Conceal- ing, etc., of Arms.* after the Time in such Summons prefixed, hide or conceal any Arms, or other warlike Weapons, in any Dwelling-house, Barn, Out-house, Office, or any

other House, or in the Fields, or any other Place whatsoever ; and all
Persons who shall be accessary or privy to the hiding or concealing of such
Arms, and shall be thereof convicted by the Oaths of One or more credible
Witness or Witnesses, before any One or more of His Majesty's Justices of
the Peace, Judge Ordinary, or other Person or Persons authorized by His
Majesty in Manner above mentioned shall be liable to be fined by the said
Justices of the Peace, Judge Ordinary, or other Person authorised by His
Majesty, before whom he or they shall be convicted according to their Discretion, in any Sum not exceeding One hundred Pounds Sterling, nor under The Penalty.
the Sum of fifteen Pounds Sterling, of lawful Money of *Great Britain*, and
shall be committed to Prison until Payment ; and if the Person so convicted,
being a Man, shall refuse or neglect to pay the Fine so imposed, within the On Non-payment the Per-sons, if fit,
Space of One Calendar Month from the Date of the said Conviction, he 
shall, in case he be judged by any One or more Justice or Justices of the to be delivered over to
Peace, or the Judge Ordinary of the Place where such Offender is imprisoned, serve as a
fit to serve His Majesty as a Soldier, be delivered over to serve as a Soldiers in America ;
Soldier in His Majesty's Forces in *America*, in the Manner before directed,
with respect to Persons convicted of having or bearing of Arms ; and in case
such Offender shall not be judged fit to serve His Majesty as aforesaid, then if not fit, to be im-
he shall be imprisoned for the Space of Six Calendar Months, and also until prisoned for Six
he shall give sufficient Security for his good Behaviour, for the Space of Months and find
Two Years from the giving thereof ; and if the Person convicted shall be a Bail.
Woman, she shall, over and above the foresaid Fine, and Imprisonment till
payment, suffer Imprisonment for the Space of Six Calendar Months, within Penalty on Women, if
the *Tolbooth* of the Head Burgh of the Shire or Stewartry within which she convicted.
is convicted.

III. And be it further enacted by the Authority aforesaid, That if, after Arms hidden in
the Day appointed by any Summons for the delivering up of Arms in pursuance any House,
of this Act, any Arms or warlike Weapons, shall be found hidden or con- etc., the Tenant to
cealed in any Dwelling-house, Barn, Out-house, Office, or any other House be deemed and suffer
whatsoever, being the Residence or Habitation of or belonging to any of the as the Concealer,
Persons summoned to deliver up Arms as aforesaid, the Tenant or Possessor etc.
of such Dwelling-house, or of the Dwelling-house to which such Barn, Office,
or Out-house belongs, being thereof convicted in Manner above mentioned,
shall be deemed and taken to be the Haver and Concealer of such Arms,
and being thereof convicted in Manner above mentioned, shall suffer the
Penalties hereby above enacted against Concealers of Arms, unless such Tenant
or Possessor, in whose House, Barn, Out-house, Office, or other House by
them possessed, such Arms shall be found concealed, do give Evidence, by
his or her making Oath, or otherwise to the Satisfaction of the said Justices

F

of the Peace, Judge Ordinary, or other Person authorized by His Majesty, before whom he or she shall be tried, that such Arms were so concealed and hid without his or her Knowledge, Privity, or Connivance.

Second Offence Transportation.

IV. And be it further enacted by the Authority aforesaid, That if any Person who shall have been convicted of any of the above Offences, of bearing, hiding, or concealing Arms, contrary to the Provisions in this Act, shall thereafter presume to commit the like Offence a second Time, that he or she being thereof convicted before any Court of Justiciary, or at the Circuit Courts, shall be liable to be transported to any of His Majesty's Plantations beyond the Seas, there to remain for the Space of Seven Years.

Officers to be appointed by His Majesty.

V. And for the more effectual Execution of this present Act, be it further enacted by the Authority aforesaid, That it shall be lawful to His Majesty, His Heirs, or Successors, by His or Their Sign Manual, from time to time, to authorize and appoint such Persons as he or they shall think proper, to execute all the Powers and Authorities by this Act given to One or more Justice or Justices of the Peace, or to the Judge Ordinary, within their respective Jurisdictions, as to the apprehending, trying, and convicting such Person or Persons who shall be summoned to deliver up their Arms, in pursuance of this Act.

What shall be a sufficient Summons, and legal Notice.

VI. And to the end that every Person or Persons named or concerned in such Summons, may have due Notice thereof, and to prevent all Questions concerning the Legality of such Notice, it is hereby further enacted by the Authority aforesaid, That such Summons, notwithstanding the Generality thereof, be deemed sufficient, if it express the Person or Persons that are commanded to deliver up their Weapons, or the Parishes, or the Lands, Limits, and Boundings of the respective Territories and Places, whereof the Inhabitants are to be disarmed as aforesaid; and that it shall be a sufficient and legal Execution or Notice of the said Summons, if it is affixed on the Door of the Parish Church or Parish Churches of the several Parishes within which the Lands (the Inhabitants whereof are to be disarmed) do lie on any *Sunday*, between the Hours of Ten in the Forenoon, and Two in the Afternoon, Four Days at least before the Day prefixed for the delivering up of the Arms, and on the Market Cross of the Head Burgh of the Shire or Stewartry within which the said Lands lie, Eight Days before the Day appointed for the said Delivery of the Arms; and in case the Person or Persons employed to affix the said Summons on the Doors of the several Parish Churches, or any of them, shall be interrupted, prevented, or forcibly hindered, from affixing the said Summons on the Doors of the said Churches, or any of them, upon Oath thereof made before any of His Majesty's Justices of the Peace, the Summons affixed on the Market Cross of the said Head Burgh of the Shire or Stewartry as aforesaid, shall be deemed and taken to be a sufficient Notice to all the Persons commanded thereby to deliver up their Arms, within the true Intent and Meaning, and for the Purposes of this Act.

VII. And to the end that there may be sufficient Evidence of the Execution, or Notice given of the Summons for disarming the several Persons and Districts, as aforesaid, be it further enacted by the Authority aforesaid, That upon the elapsing of the said several Days to be prefixed for the delivering up Arms, the Person or Persons employed to fix the Summons, as above mentioned, on the Market Cross of the Head Burghs of any Shire or Stewartry, shall, before any One of His Majesty's Justices of the Peace, for the said Shire or Stewartry, make Oath, that he or they did truly execute and give Notice of the same by affixing it as aforesaid; and the Person or Persons employed to affix the said Summons on the Doors of the Parish Church or Parish Churches, shall make Oath in the same Manner, and to the same Effect, or otherwise shall swear that he or they were interrupted, prevented, or forcibly hindered from affixing the said Summons as aforesaid; which Oaths, together with Copies or Duplicates of the Summons, to which they severally relate, shall be delivered to the Sheriff or Steward Clerk of the several Shires or Stewartries, within which the Persons intended to be disarmed do live or reside, who shall enter the same in Books, which he and they is and are hereby required to keep for that Purpose; and the said Books in which the Entries are so made, or Extracts out of the same, under the Hand of the Sheriff or Steward Clerk, shall be deemed and taken to be full and complete Evidence of the Execution of the Summons, in order to the Conviction of the Persons who shall neglect or refuse to comply with the same.

*Evidence of Notice given of the Summons to be made on Oath.*

*Oath, with Duplicates of the Summons, to be delivered to the Sheriff, etc. and to be entered in their Evidence to be good.*

VIII. And be it further enacted by the Authority aforesaid, That if any such Sheriff or Steward Clerk neglect or refuse to make such Entry as is above mentioned, or shall refuse to exhibit the Books containing such Entries, or to give Extracts of the same, being thereto required by any Person or Persons who shall carry on any Prosecutions, in pursuance of this Act, the Clerk so neglecting or refusing shall forfeit his Office, and shall likewise be fined in the Sum of Fifty Pounds Sterling; to be recovered upon a summary Complaint before the Court of Session, for the Use of His Majesty, His Heirs, or Successors.

*Sheriff not making Entry, etc.*

*The Penalty.*

IX. And be it further enacted by the Authority aforesaid, That it shall and may be lawful to and for the Lord Lieutenant of any of the Shires aforesaid, or the Person or Persons authorized by His Majesty, His Heirs, or Successors, as aforesaid, to summon the Person or Persons aforesaid to deliver up his or their Arms, in manner above mentioned, or to and for any One Justice of the

*Lord Lieutenants, etc., to appoint Persons to summon,*

Peace of the respective Shires above mentioned, or to the Judge Ordinary within their respective Jurisdictions, or to such Person or Persons as shall be authorized by His Majesty, His Heirs, or Successors, for trying Offences against this Act, to authorize and appoint such Person or Persons as they *and appre-* shall think fit, to apprehend all such Person or Persons as may be found *hend, etc., such as* within the Limits foresaid, having or wearing any Arms, or warlike Weapons, *shall be found with* contrary to Law, and forthwith to carry him or them to some sure Prison, *Arms.* in order to their being proceeded against according to Law.

X.  And be it further enacted by the Authority aforesaid, That it shall and may be lawful to and for His Majesty, His Heirs, and Successors, by Warrant under His or Their Royal Sign Manual, and also to and for the Lord Lieutenant of any of the Shires aforesaid, or the Person or Persons authorized by His Majesty, to summon the Person or Persons aforesaid to deliver up their Arms, or any One or more Justices of the Peace, by *Search may be* Warrant under his or their Hands, to authorize and appoint any Person or *made for* Persons to enter into any House or Houses, within the Limits aforesaid, *Arms by Day or* either by Day or by Night, and there to search for and to seize all such *Night.* Arms as shall be found contrary to the Direction of this Act.

*Search by* XI.  Provided, That if the above mentioned Search shall be made in *Night to be made in* the Night-Time, that is to say, between Sun setting and Sun rising, it shall *Presence of a Con-* be made in the Presence of a Constable, or of some Person particularly to be *stable, etc.* named for that Purpose in the Warrant for such Search ; and if any Persons, *In case of Opposi-* to the Number of Five or more, shall at any time assemble together to *tion,* obstruct the Execution of any Part of this Act, it shall and may be lawful to and for every Lord Lieutenant, Deputy Lieutenant, or Justice of the Peace where such Assembly shall be ; and also to and for every Peace Officer within any such Shire, Stewartry, City, Burgh, or Place where such Assembly shall be ; and likewise to and for all and every such other Person or Persons, as by His Majesty, His Heirs, or Successors, shall be authorized *the Aid of* and appointed in that Behalf as aforesaid, to require the Aid and Assistance *the King's Forces to* of the Forces of His Majesty, His Heirs, or Successors, by applying to the *be called.* Officer commanding the said Forces (who is hereby authorized, impowered, and commanded to give such Aid and Assistance accordingly) to suppress such unlawful Assembly, in order to the putting this Act in due Execution ; and also to seize, apprehend, and disarm, and they are hereby required to seize, *Offenders* apprehend, and disarm such Persons so assembled together, and forthwith to *to be carried* carry the Persons so apprehended before One or more of His Majesty's *before a Justice.* Justices of the Peace of the Shire or Place where such Persons shall be so apprehended, in order to their being proceeded against, for such their Offences, according to Law ; and if the persons so unlawfully assembled, or any of them, or any other Person or Persons summoned to deliver up his or their Arms in pursuance of this Act, shall happen to be killed, maimed or wounded in the dispersing, seizing, and apprehending, or in the endeavouring to disperse, seize, or apprehend, by reason of their resisting the Persons endeavouring to disperse, seize, and apprehend them ; then all and every such Lord Lieutenant, Deputy Lieutenant, Justice or Justices of the Peace, or any Peace Officer or Officers, and all and every Person or Persons, authorized and appointed by His Majesty, His Heirs, or Successors, in that Behalf, as aforesaid, and all Persons aiding and assisting to him, them, or any of them, shall be freed, discharged, and indemnified, as well against the King's Majesty, His Heirs, and Successors, as against all and every other person and persons of, for, or concerning the killing, maiming, or wounding any such Person or Persons so unlawfully assembled, that shall be so killed, maimed, or wounded as aforesaid. *[margin: Indemnification against Persons killed resisting.]*

XII. And be it further enacted by the Authority aforesaid, That if any Action, Civil or Criminal, shall be brought before any Court whatsoever, against any Person or Persons for what he or they shall lawfully do in pursuance or Execution of this Act, such Court shall allow the Defendant the Benefit of the Discharge and Indemnity above provided, and shall further decern the Pursuer to pay to the Defender the full and real Expences that he shall be put to by such Action or Prosecution. *[margin: Defendant to be allowed the Indemnity, and his Expenses.]*

XIII. Provided nevertheless, and be it enacted by the Authority aforesaid, That no Peers of this Realm, nor their Sons, nor any Members of Parliament, nor any Person or Persons, who, by the Act above recited of the First Year of His late Majesty, were allowed to have or carry Arms, shall by virtue of this Act be liable to be summoned to deliver up their Arms, or warlike Weapons ; nor shall this Act, or the above recited Act, be construed to extend to exclude or hinder any Person, whom his Majesty, His Heirs, or Successors, by Licence under His or Their Sign Manual, shall permit to wear Arms, or who shall be licenced to wear Arms, by any Writing or Writings under the Hand and Seal, or Hands and Seals of any Person or Persons authorized by His Majesty, His Heirs, or Successors, or give such Licence from keeping, bearing, or wearing such Arms, and warlike Weapons, as in such Licence or Licences shall for that Purpose be particularly specified. *[margin: Persons exempted from delivering up their Arms.]*

XIV. And to the end that no Persons may be discouraged from delivering up their Arms, from the Apprehension of the Penalties and Forfeitures which they may have incurred, through their neglecting to comply with the Directions of the said Act of the First Year of His late Majesty's Reign, be it further enacted by the Authority aforesaid, That from and after the Time of affixing any such Summons as aforesaid, no Person or Persons residing within the *[margin: Act 1st Geo. I.]*

Bounds therein mentioned, shall be sued or prosecuted for his or their having,
or having had, bearing, or having borne Arms, at any Time before the
several Days to be prefixed or limited by Summons as aforesaid, for the
respective Persons and Districts to deliver up their Arms; but if any Person
or Persons shall refuse or neglect to deliver up their Arms in Obedience to
such Summons as aforesaid, or shall afterwards be found in Arms, he and
they shall be liable to the Penalties and Forfeitures of the Statute above
recited, as well as to the Penalties of this present Act.

XV. And be it further enacted by the Authority aforesaid, That One
Moiety of the Penalties imposed by this Act with respect to which no other
Provision is made, shall be to the Informer or Informers; and the Other
Moiety shall be at the Disposal of the Justices of the Peace, Judge Ordinary,
or other Person authorized by His Majesty as aforesaid, before whom such
Conviction shall happen, provided the same be applied towards the Expence
incurred in the Execution of this Act.

XVI. And be it further enacted by the Authority aforesaid, That the
above Provisions in this Act shall continue in Force for Seven Years, and
from thence to the End of the next Session of Parliament, and no longer.

XVII. And be it further enacted by the Authority aforesaid, That from
and after the First Day of *August*, One thousand seven hundred and forty
seven, no Man or Boy, within that part of *Great Britain* called *Scotland*,
other than such as shall be employed as Officers and Soldiers in His Majesty's
Forces, shall, on any Pretence whatsoever, wear or put on the Clothes
commonly called *Highland Clothes* (that is to say) the Plaid, Philebeg, or
little Kilt, Trowse, Shoulder Belts, or any Part whatsoever of what peculiarly
belongs to the Highland Garb; and that no Tartan, or party-coloured Plaid
or Stuff shall be used for Great Coats, or for Upper Coats; and if any
such Person shall presume after the said First Day of *August*, to wear or
put on the aforesaid Garments, or any Part of them, every such Person so
offending, being convicted thereof by the Oath of One or more credible
Witness or Witnesses before any Court of Justiciary, or any One or more
Justices of the Peace for the Shire or Stewartry, or Judge Ordinary of
the Place where such Offence shall be committed, shall suffer Imprisonment,
without Bail, during the Space of Six Months, and no longer; and being
convicted for a second Offence before a Court of Justiciary, or at the
Circuits, shall be liable to be transported to any of His Majesty's Plantations
beyond the Seas, there to remain for the Space of Seven Years.

XVIII. And whereas by an Act made in this Session of Parliament,
intituled, *An Act to indemnify such Persons as have acted in Defence of His
Majesty's Person and Government, and for the Preservation of the publick Peace*

*of this Kingdom during the Time of the present unnatural Rebellion, and Sheriffs and others who have suffered Escapes, occasioned thereby, from vexatious Suits and Prosecutions,* it is enacted, That all personal Actions and Suits, Indictments, Informations, and all Molestations, Prosecutions, and Proceedings whatsoever, and Judgments thereupon, if any be, for or by reason of any Matter or Thing advised, commanded, appointed, or done during the Rebellion, until the Thirtieth Day of *April,* in the Year of our Lord One thousand seven hundred and forty six, in order to suppress the said unnatural Rebellion, or for the Preservation of the publick Peace, or for the Service of Safety to the Government, shall be discharged and made void: And whereas it is also reasonable, that Acts done for the publick Service, since the said Thirtieth Day of *April,* though not justifiable by the strict Forms of Law, should be justified by Act of Parliament; be it enacted by the Authority aforesaid, That all personal Actions and Suits, Indictments and Informations, which have been or shall be commenced or prosecuted, and all Molestations, Prosecutions, and Proceedings whatsoever, and Judgments thereupon, if any be, for or by reason of any Act, Matter, or Thing advised, commanded, appointed, or done before the Twenty fifth Day of *July,* in the Year of our Lord One thousand seven hundred and forty six, in order to suppress the said unnatural Rebellion, or for the Preservation of the publick Peace, or for the Safety or Service of the Government, shall be discharged and made void; and that every Person, by whom any such Act, Matter, or Thing shall have been so advised, commanded, appointed, or done for the Purposes aforesaid, or any of them, before the said Five and twentieth Day of *July,* shall be freed, acquitted, and indemnified, as well against the King's Majesty, His Heirs, and Successors, as against all and every other Person and Persons; and that if any Action or Suit hath been or shall be commenced or prosecuted, within that Part of *Great Britain* called *England,* against any Person for any such Act, Matter, or Thing so advised, commanded, appointed, or done for the Purposes aforesaid, or any of them, before the said Twenty fifth Day of *July,* he or she may plead the General Issue, and give this Act and the special Matter in Evidence; and if the Plaintiff or Plaintiffs shall become nonsuit, or forbear further Prosecution, or suffer Discontinuance; or if a Verdict pass against such Plaintiff or Plaintiffs, the Defendant or Defendants shall recover his, her, or their Double Costs, for which he, she, or they shall have the like Remedy, as in Cases where Costs by Law are given to Defendants; and if such Action or Suit hath been or shall be commenced or prosecuted in that Part of *Great Britain* called *Scotland,* the Court, before whom such Action or Suit hath been or shall be commenced or prosecuted, shall allow to the Defender the Benefit of the Discharge and Indemnity above provided, and

All Actions, &c. done for the Service of the Government, to be void, etc.

*England.*

General Issue.

Double Costs.

*Scotland.*

Full Costs. shall further decern the Pursuer to pay to the Defender the full and real Expences that he or she shall be put to by such Action or Suit.

Act 6 Anne. XIX. And whereas by an Act passed in the Sixth Year of Her late Majesty Queen *Anne*, intituled, *An Act for rendering the Union of the Two Kingdoms more entire and complete;* it is, among other Things, enacted, That Circuit Courts shall be holden in that Part of the United Kingdom called *Scotland*, in Manner, and at the Places mentioned in the said Act: And whereas by the late unnatural Rebellion, the Course of Justice in *Scotland* has been so interrupted, as rendered it impracticable to give up and transmit Presentments, in such due Time as Prosecutions might thereupon commence, before the Northern Circuit, to be holden in *May* this present Year, whereby there appeared a Necessity of superseding the said Circuit; be it therefore enacted Judges indemnified for not performing the Circuit Courts. by the Authority aforesaid, That the Judges of the Court of Justiciary, and all and every other Person and Persons therein concerned, are hereby indemnified for their not performing the said Circuit, as by the forecited Act they were obliged to do; any thing in the same Act, or in any other Law or Statute to the contrary notwithstanding.

XX. And whereas a Doubt hath arisen with respect to the Shire of *Dunbartain*, what Part thereof was intended to be disarmed by the First recited Act made in the First Year of His late Majesty King *George*, and intended to be carried into further Execution by the present Act; be it enacted by the Parts of Dunbartain to be disarmed. Authority aforesaid, That such Parts of the said Shire of *Dunbartain* as ly upon the East, West, and North Sides of *Lochlomond*, to the Northward of that Point where the Water of *Leven* runs from *Lochlomond*, are and were intended to be disarmed by the aforesaid Act and are comprehended and subject to the Directions of this Act.

XXI. And whereas it is of great Importance to prevent the rising Generation being educated in disaffected or rebellious Principles, and although sufficient Provision is already made by Law for the due Regulation of the Teachers in the Four Universities, and in the publick Schools authorized by Law in the Royal Burghs and Country Parishes in *Scotland*, it is further necessary, That all Persons who take upon them to officiate as Masters or Teachers in Private Schools, in that Part of *Great Britain* called *Scotland*, should give Evidence of their good Affection to His Majesty's Person and Government; be it therefore enacted by the Authority aforesaid, That from and after the First Day of *November*, in the Year of our Lord One thousand seven hundred and forty six, it shall not be lawful for any Person in Scotland to keep a Private School for Teaching *English*, *Latin*, *Greek*, or any Part of Literature, or to officiate as a Master or Teacher in such School, or any School for Literature, other than those in the Universities, or Established in the respective

Royal Burghs by Publick Authority, or the Parochial Schools settled according to Law, or the Schools maintained by the Society in *Scotland* for propagating Christian Knowledge, or by the General Assemblies of the Church of *Scotland*, or Committees thereof, upon the Bounty granted by His Majesty, until the Situation and Description of such Private Schools be first entered and registered in a Book, which shall be provided and kept for that Purpose by the Clerks of the several Shires, Stewartries, and Burghs in *Scotland*, together with a Certificate from the proper Officer, of every such Master and Teacher having qualified himself, by taking the Oaths appointed by Law to be taken by Persons in Offices of publick Trust in *Scotland;* and every such Master and Teacher of a Private School shall be obliged, and is hereby required, as often as Prayers shall be said in such School, to pray, or cause to be prayed for, in express words, His Majesty, His Heirs, and Successors, by Name, and for all the Royal Family; and if any Person shall, from and after the said First Day of *November,* presume to enter upon, or exercise the Function or Office of a Master or Teacher of any such Private School as shall not have been registered in Manner herein directed, or without having first qualified himself, and caused the Certificate to be registered as above mentioned; or in case he shall neglect to pray for His Majesty by Name, and all the Royal Family, or to cause them to be prayed for as herein directed; or in case he shall resort to, or attend Divine Worship in any Episcopal Meeting-house not allowed by the Law, every Person so offending in any of the Premisses, being thereof lawfully convicted before any Two or more of the Justices of the Peace, or before any other Judge competent of the Place summarily, shall, for the first Offence, suffer Imprisonment for the Space of Six Months; and for the Second, or any subsequent Offence, being thereof lawfully convicted before the Court of Justiciary, or in any of the Circuit Courts, shall be adjudged to be transported, and accordingly shall be transported to some of his Majesty's Plantations in *America* for Life; and in case any Person adjudged to be so transported shall return into, or be found in *Great Britain,* then every such Person shall suffer Imprisonment for Life.

XXII. And be it further enacted by the Authority aforesaid, That if any Parent or Guardian shall put a Child or Children under his care to any Private School that shall not be registered according to the Directions of this Act, or whereof the principal Master or Teacher shall not have registered the Certificate of his having qualified himself as herein directed, every such Parent or Guardian so offending, and being thereof lawfully convicted before any Two or more Justices of Peace, or before any other Judge competent of the Place summarily, shall, for the First Offence be liable to suffer Imprisonment by the Space of Three Months; and for the Second, or any subsequent Offence,

G

*Marginal notes:*

Situation, of Private etc. Schools to be registered; with a Certificate of the Master having qualified himself.

His Majesty, etc., to be prayed for by Name.

Masters not to resort to Episcopal unlicensed Meeting-houses.

The Penalty.

Parents, etc., sending Children to unregistered Schools, etc.

The Penalty.

being thereof lawfully convicted before the Court of Justiciary, or in any of the Circuit Courts, shall suffer Imprisonment for the Space of Two Years from the Date of such Conviction.

XXIII. And whereas by an Act passed in the Parliament of *Scotland*, in the Year of our Lord One thousand six hundred and ninety three, all Chaplains in Families, and Governours and Teachers of Children and Youth, were obliged to take the Oaths of Allegiance and Assurance therein directed ; and there may be some Doubt, whether by the Laws, as they stand at present, they are obliged to take the Oaths appointed to be taken by Persons in Offices of publick Trust in *Scotland:* Therefore be it enacted by the Authority aforesaid, That from and after the First Day of *November*, in the Year of our Lord One thousand seven hundred and forty six, no Person shall exercise the Employment, Function, or Service of a Chaplain, in any Family in that Part of *Great Britain* called *Scotland*, or of a Governor, Tutor, or Teacher of any Child, Children, or Youth, residing in *Scotland*, or in Parts beyond the Seas, without first qualifying himself, by taking the Oaths, appointed by Law to be taken by Persons in Offices of publick Trust, and causing a Certificate of his having done so to be entered or registered in a Book to be kept for that Purpose by the Clerks of the Shires, Stewartries, or Burghs in *Scotland*, where such Persons shall reside ; or in case of any such Governor, Tutor, or Teacher of any such Child, Children, or Youth, acting in Parts beyond the Seas, then in a Book to be kept for that Purpose by the Clerk of the Shire, Stewartry, or Burgh where the Parent or Guardian of such Child, Children, or Youth shall reside. And if any Person, from and after the said First Day of *November*, shall presume to exercise the Employment, Function, or Service of Chaplain, in any Family in *Scotland*, or of a Governor or Teacher of Children or Youth, as aforesaid, without having taken the said Oaths, and caused the Certificate of his having duly taken the same, to be registered, as is above directed ; every Person so offending, being thereof lawfully convicted before any Two or more Justices of Peace, or before any other Judge Competent of the Place summarily, shall for the First Offence, suffer Imprisonment by the Space of Six Months ; and for the Second, or any subsequent Offence, being thereof lawfully convicted before the Court of Justiciary, or in any of the Circuit Courts, shall be adjudged to be banished from *Great Britain* for the Space of Seven Years.

XXIV. Provided always, That it shall be lawful for every Chaplain, School-master, Governour, Tutor, or Teacher of Youth who is of the Communion of the Church of Scotland, instead of the Oath of Abjuration appointed by Law to be taken by Persons in Offices Civil or Military, to take the Oath directed to be taken by Preachers and Expectants in Divinity of the established

*[Marginal notes:]*
Chaplains, etc., in Families, to take the Oaths ;

Certificates to be registered.

The Penalty.

Oath appointed for Chaplains, etc., of the Church of Scotland.

Church of *Scotland*, by an Act passed in the Fifth Year of the Reign of
King *George*, the First, intituled, *An Act for making more effectual the Laws* Act 5
*appointing the Oaths for Security of the Government to be taken by Ministers* Geo. I.
*and Preachers in Churches and Meeting-houses in Scotland;* and a Certificate
of his having taken that Oath shall, to all Intents and Purposes, be as valid
and effectual as the Certificate of his having taken the Oath of Abjuration
above mentioned; and he shall be as much deemed to have qualified himself
according to Law, as if he had taken the Abjuration appointed to be taken
by Persons in Civil Offices.

XXV. And be it further enacted, That from and after the said First Persons
Day of *November*, no Person within *Scotland* shall keep or entertain any Person keeping
or Chaplain in any Family, or as Governor, Tutor, or Teacher of any Child, have not
Children, or Youth, unless the Certificate of such Person's having taken the qualified.
Oaths to His Majesty be duly registered in Manner above directed; and if
any Person shall keep or entertain a Chaplain in his Family, or a Governor,
Tutor, or Teacher of any Child, Children, or Youth under his Care, without
the Certificate of such Chaplain, Governor, Tutor, or Teacher's having respectively qualified himself, by taking the Oaths to His Majesty, being duly
registered in Manner above mentioned, every such Person so offending, being
thereof lawfully convicted before any Two or more of His Majesty's Justices
of Peace, or before any other Judge competent, shall, for the First Offence, The
suffer Imprisonment by the Space of Six Months; and for the Second, or Penalty.
any subsequent Offence, being thereof lawfully convicted before the Court of
Justiciary, or in any of the Circuit Courts in *Scotland*, shall suffer Imprisonment by the Space of Two Years.

XXVI. And for the better preventing any Private Schools from being held Sheriffs,
or maintained, or any Chaplain in any Family, or any Governor, Tutor, or enquire
Teacher of any Children or Youth, from being employed or entertained con- Offences
trary to the Directions of this Act, be it further enacted, That the Sheriffs this Act,
of Shires, and Stewarts of Stewartries, and Magistrates of Burghs in Scotland, etc.
shall be obliged, and are hereby required, from time to time, to make diligent
Enquiry within their respective Jurisdictions, concerning any Offences that shall
be committed against this Act, and cause the same, being the First Offence,
to be prosecuted before themselves; and in case of a Second, or subsequent
Offence, to give Notice thereof, and of the Evidence for proving the same,
to his Majesty's Advocate for the Time being, who is hereby required to
prosecute such Second or subsequent Offences before the Court of Justiciary,
or at the Circuit Courts.

# PART II.

## THE HIGHLAND CAMPAIGNS.

# THE HIGHLAND CAMPAIGNS.

IN the reign of James IV. of Scotland, Don Pedro de Ayala, Spanish Ambassador at the Scottish Court, wrote home to his own sovereigns an appreciative description of the character and accomplishments of the young King of Scots. He notes with special admiration James's knowledge of languages. Not only was he acquainted with Latin, French, German, Flemish, Italian, and Spanish, but, says Don Pedro, "he speaks the language of the savages who live in some parts of Scotland and on the islands."

The language of the Spanish diplomatist fairly represented the feeling with which, in the Middle Ages, the inhabitants of the Highlands were regarded by the average civilised European, and in particular by their Lowland neighbours. To the Scots statesman in the days of the Jameses they were simply so many tribes of marauding barbarians, to be kept in order by whatever means came handiest. Their domestic history is a record of clan feuds and conflicts, often abounding in picturesque incident, but of comparatively little importance in the national history. It is not till the civil wars of the seventeenth century that the Highlanders begin to play an important military part in the general history of the country. We propose to tell briefly the story of the Highland campaigns from the days of Montrose to the end of the Forty-five.

One great battle there is, belonging to the earlier period, which cannot be left unmentioned. In 1411 there took place a Highland insurrection on so large a scale as to be a serious national danger. Donald, Lord of the Isles, had laid claim in right of his wife to the Earldom of Ross, which Euphemia, Countess of Ross, had on becoming a nun resigned in favour of her uncle the Earl of Buchan. The Duke of Albany, Governor of Scotland, refused to entertain the claim, and the Lord of the Isles determined to assert it by force. Aided by some ships from England, he invaded the mainland at the head of an army of 10,000 men. He ravaged the country of Ross, and then marched down through Moray into Aberdeenshire, having declared his intention of burning the town of Aberdeen. To oppose his progress a force was hastily raised under the command of the Earl of Mar, who was supported by many knights and gentlemen of Angus and the Mearns. The armies met on July 24, 1411, at the village of Harlaw, on the Ury, near its junction with the Don. A desperate battle was fought. The Lowland army was greatly outnumbered, but made up in the superiority of its arms and discipline what it lacked in numbers. A decisive defeat was inflicted on the Highlanders. The victory was purchased with terrible loss; nearly every notable family in the north-east country lost one or more of its members. Among the dead were Sir Alexander Ogilvy, the Sheriff of Angus, and his eldest son; Sir James Scrymgeour, Constable of Dundee, Maule of Panmure, Irvine of Drum, and Sir Robert Davidson, Provost of Aberdeen, who had led a force of Aberdeen citizens to the field. The battle was regarded throughout the country as a great national deliverance, only second to Bannockburn. It finally settled the question of the supremacy of the Teuton over the Celt. "The brim battle of the Harlaw" is the subject of one of the finest of our historical ballads.

In the reigns of Queen Mary and James VI. there may be noted the fights at Corrichie (1562), in which the Earl of Huntly was defeated and slain by the Queen and the Earl of Moray; Glenlivat (1594), in which Archibald, seventh Earl of Argyll, was defeated by the Gordons; and Glenfruin (1604), in which he was defeated by the Macgregors.

James Marquess of Montrose, Earle of Kincardine,
Lord Graeme, Baron of Mont dieu, &
Lieutenant Governor and capt: Generall
For the State in the kingdome of Scotland.

# CHAPTER I.

## MONTROSE (1644-1650).

A DETAILED account of the causes which led to the Civil War in the time of Charles I. would be beyond the scope of this work. The ill-advised scheme of establishing Episcopacy in Scotland, which, so far as Scotland was concerned, was the main cause of the troubles, had, even before the Union of the Crowns, been a favourite project of James VI., who was of opinion that "a Scottish Presbytery agreeth as well with a monarchy as God with the devil." So long as the seat of monarchy remained at Edinburgh it was hopeless for any Scots sovereign to force a great religious change upon an unwilling people. The increase of power and independence which came with the accession to the English throne put the King in a very different position. In 1606 the Scottish bishops were restored, with seats in Parliament. In 1618 the famous Five Articles of Perth were passed in a General Assembly held there. By these certain forms of Episcopal worship were introduced. They were harmless enough from the modern point of view, but at the time they aroused deep and bitter feeling throughout the country.[1] An ecclesiastical Court of High Commission was established, and in 1621 the Five Articles were ratified by the Estates, a majority being obtained with the utmost difficulty.

James VI. died in 1625. Charles I. inherited his purposes, but set about their realisation in a stern and resolute temper very different from his father's. What to James had been matter of policy was to Charles matter of conscience. His course of action soon brought matters to a serious crisis. One of his first acts was the resumption, by an act of prerogative, of the Church revenues which had been granted away by the Crown since the Reformation.[2] These were chiefly held by the higher nobility, and the result of the King's act was to create bitter hostility to the Crown on the part of many of the great nobles, and to array them on the side of the popular party in the Church. The King's visit to Scotland in 1633 brought further matter of offence. Serious allegations were made that he had tampered with the constitutional powers of the Estates. The appointment of Laud as Archbishop of Canterbury gave

---

[1] The Five Articles sanctioned—(1) Kneeling at Communion ; (2) administration of Communion to the sick in their own houses ; (3) private baptism ; (4) confirmation of children ; and (5) observance of the festivals of Christmas, Good Friday, Easter, Ascension, and Pentecost.

[2] See, for an account of the exceedingly important transactions with regard to ecclesiastical property at this time, Hill Burton's *History of Scotland*, vol. vi., pp. 75-85.

the King as his chief adviser an ecclesiastical statesman who was little disposed to compromise, and who, as it proved, knew nothing of the temper of the Scottish people. In 1636 the Episcopalian Book of Canons was promulgated by royal authority. In the following year the Service Book was issued. The attempt to enforce its use caused the long-gathering storm to break.

The new liturgy was used for the first time in St. Giles's Cathedral, Edinburgh, on Sunday, July 23, 1637. The riot which took place in the church, of which Jenny Geddes is the traditional heroine, is one of the best known incidents in Scottish history. Similar riots took place all over the country, and these were only the beginning of an agitation which soon became a great national movement. The popular party was known as the Supplicants, and assumed throughout an attitude of scrupulous humility. The Government was obdurate ; the King and his advisers seem to have entirely misjudged the strength and character of the opposition. In the winter of 1637 was formed the committee known as the Tables, which was recognised by the Privy Council as representing the whole body of the Supplicants, and which soon became a power in the State co-ordinate with the Council itself. The Tables were four in number, representing respectively the nobles, the lesser barons, the burghs, and the ministers. Each Table consisted of four persons. A member of the Table of nobility was the young Earl of Montrose.

In February 1638 the National Covenant was signed. This famous document was in the form of a renewal of the Covenant which had been signed in the early days of Protestantism, with additions relative to the new dangers which threatened Church and State. It was scrupulously loyal in its language, but very explicit with regard to the great question of the hour. " We promise and swear," said the signatories, " by the great name of the Lord our God, to continue in the profession and obedience of the said religion ; and that we shall defend the same and resist all those contrary errors and corruptions, according to our vocation, and to the utmost of that power which God hath put into our hands all the days of our life."

The project of renewing the Covenant is commonly attributed to Archibald Johnston of Warriston. It was an admirably devised and entirely successful plan for uniting and organising the anti-prelatical party throughout the kingdom. In the Greyfriars Churchyard at Edinburgh, on February 28, 1638, the Covenant was subscribed by a vast crowd amid a scene of wild enthusiasm. Copies were sent all over the country. Every effort was used to obtain signatures ; both persuasion and coercion were freely employed ; and thousands of names were adhibited. Henceforth the popular party was known by the historic name of Covenanters, and came to be identified not only with the cause of Presbyterianism as against Episcopacy, but with the cause of national independence as against English aggression.

In the summer of 1638 the Marquis of Hamilton came down from London as Commissioner from the King to deal with the Covenanters. He had the widest powers. His confidential instructions were to gain time by every possible means, until the King should be in a position to suppress the Covenanters by force.

The demands of the Covenanters were explicit enough. They included the abolition of the Court of High Commission, the withdrawal of the obnoxious Book of Canons and Liturgy, a free Parliament, and a free General Assembly. It was well understood that Parliament and the Assembly would probably make a clean sweep of Episcopacy, and Hamilton tried in vain to obtain from the Covenanting leaders a guarantee that in the event of their meeting they should not go beyond certain limits. At length, after much temporising, and various journeyings between London and Edinburgh on the part of the High Commissioner, an entire surrender was announced. The Service Book, the Book of Canons, and the High Commission were revoked. A meeting of Assembly was proclaimed for November 21, and Parliament was to be summoned in the following May.

By this time, however, it was clear that sooner or later matters must come to the arbitrament of the sword. The Covenanters were quietly making preparations for war. Early in the year the nucleus of a war-chest was raised by subscription, the list of subscribers being headed by Montrose. Arrangements were made for the collection throughout the country of a "voluntary" contribution, which seems to have been as rigidly exacted as any tax. Large quantities of arms were purchased in Holland. Scots officers trained in the Thirty Years' War were unobtrusively brought over from the Continent. The great stronghold of the Royalist party was in Aberdeenshire, and by far the most powerful of the King's adherents was the "Cock of the North," George, Marquis of Huntly, chief of the great house of Gordon. An attempt was made to gain him over. Colonel Robert Monro, the original of Scott's Dugald Dalgetty, was sent to Strathbogie with tempting offers, including a promise to pay off the Marquis's debts, which amounted to about £100,000 sterling. Huntly's answer uncompromisingly expressed the spirit of Cavalier loyalty. "His family," he said, had risen and stood by the Kings of Scotland, and for his part, if the event proved the ruin of this King, he was resolved to lay his life, honours and estate under the rubbish of the King's ruins."

On November 21, 1638, the General Assembly met in Glasgow Cathedral. The Marquis of Hamilton was present as Commissioner; Alexander Henderson was chosen Moderator, and Johnston of Warriston Clerk of Assembly. The elections had been worked by the Tables so as to produce a thoroughly Covenanting Assembly. Everybody knew what its main business was to be the trial of the bishops. The first few days were occupied in formal and preliminary business. On the seventh day of meeting it was formally decided that the bishops were amenable to the jurisdiction of the Assembly. Thereupon the Commissioner, in the King's name, declared the Assembly dissolved, and on the following day its further meeting was discharged by proclamation under pain of treason.

The Assembly proceeded with its business. The bishops were tried and deposed on various grounds; six of them, together with the two archbishops, were excommunicated. The whole fabric of Episcopacy, Service Book, Book of Canons, Articles of Perth and all, was demolished, and the Episcopal office was declared to be for ever abrogated. The Assembly rose on December 20. "We have now," said the Moderator, "cast down the walls of Jericho; let him that rebuildeth them beware of the curse of Hiel the Bethelite."

The Covenanters had now openly defied the royal authority, and war was inevitable.

The great struggle was to take place in England, but it was in the north of Scotland that the first blow was struck. Aberdeenshire was, as we have seen, the main stronghold of the Royalist party, and there efforts to gain adherents to the Covenant had met with little success. In prospect of a more serious conflict in the south, the Covenanting leaders determined first to get rid of the enemy in their rear, and for this purpose an army of some three or four thousand men was organised under the Earl of Montrose.

James Graham, Earl and afterwards Marquis of Montrose,[1] head of the house of Graham, was at this time a young man of seven-and-twenty. He was a man of unbounded energy and ambition; his mental powers had been trained by education at the University of St. Andrews and by foreign travel; and, as was soon to appear, he possessed in the highest degree the qualities of a leader of irregular troops - personal courage, dash, resourcefulness in emergency, and unfailing constancy in misfortune. Cardinal de Retz said of him that more nearly than any man of his age he resembled one of the heroes of antiquity. He seems to have possessed a marvellous personal magnetism. Patrick Gordon of Ruthven says of him that "he was so affable, so courteous, so benign, as seemed verily to scorne ostentation and the keeping of state, and therefore he quickly made a conquest of the hearts of all his followers, so as when he list he could have led them in a chain to have followed him with cheerfulness in all his enterprises; and I am certainly persuaded that this his gracious, humane, and courteous freedom of behaviour . . . was it that won him so much renowne and enabled him chiefly, in the love of his followers, to go through so great enterprises." His early association with the Covenanters is attributed to his having met with an unexpectedly cold reception from the King on his return from his travels. Be this as it may, we find him in the spring of 1639 at the head of the Covenanting army destined for the North.

Having been joined by General Alexander Leslie, the veteran of the Thirty Years' War, who acted as his military adviser, Montrose marched on Aberdeen. His army was excellently equipped and organised, "weill armed," says Spalding, "both on

---

[1] He was the fifth Earl, and was raised to the rank of Marquis on May 6, 1644.

horse and foot, ilk horseman having five shot at the least, with ane carabine in his hand, two pistols by his sides, and the other two at his saddell toir; the pikemen in their ranks, with pike and sword; the musketeers in their ranks, with musket, musket-staff, bandelier, sword, powder, ball, and match. Ilk company, both on horse and foot, had their captains, lieutenants, ensigns, sergeants, and other officers and commanders, all for the most part in buffle coats and goodly order." [1]

On the approach of the Covenanting army Aberdeen was abandoned by the Marquis of Huntly, and Montrose entered the town peaceably on March 30. At Aberdeen his army was augmented by the accession of 500 Campbells, whom Argyll had sent from the west, and of many Frasers, Keiths, and others, who joined him rather out of hatred to the Gordons than from any love of the Covenant. Leaving a strong garrison in Aberdeen, he marched northward against Huntly. Huntly, however, opened negotiations, and was ultimately induced to come to Aberdeen, where he was made a prisoner and sent to Edinburgh. There the strongest pressure was brought to bear on him to sign the Covenant, but he remained steadfast in his loyalty. "For my own part," said he "I am in your power, and resolved not to leave that foul title of traitor as an inheritance upon my posterity. You may take my head from my shoulders, but not my heart from my sovereign."

The main body of the Covenanting army marched southward in April. In the following month the first blood was drawn in the civil war. A body of some 2000 Covenanters assembled at Turriff on May 13. There they were attacked by a force of the Gordons, with four field-guns. The Covenanters were defeated and driven out of the town. This was the affair known as the "Trot of Turray." The victors marched on Aberdeen, and entered it on May 15. A few days later they disbanded their army. The chiefs remained in Aberdeen until they were driven out by the advent of the Earl Marischal, who entered the town on May 23. Two days later he was joined by Montrose with 4000 men.

After some operations against the castles of some of the Aberdeenshire Royalists, Montrose again retired to the south, and in June Aberdeen was once more occupied by the Royalists under Lord Aboyne. On June 14 they advanced upon Stonehaven. They camped for the night at Muchalls, and on the following day were attacked and defeated by the Earl Marischal and Montrose, who had marched north to meet them. They fell back on Aberdeen. Montrose followed them up, forced the Bridge of Dee, and again entered Aberdeen in triumph. Next day hostilities were brought to an end by the news of the Pacification of Berwick.

While these events were taking place in the north, preparations for war on a much larger scale were going on in the Lowlands. On February 27 the King, determined to reduce his rebellious subjects to obedience, issued the Commission of

---

[1] *Memorials of the Troubles*, vol. i., p. 154.

Array, calling upon the feudal force of England to assemble at York. In Scotland the royal fortresses were seized by the Tables, and an army of over 22,000 men, well organised and equipped, was assembled at Edinburgh. On May 21 it began its march towards the Border under the command of that "little old crooked soldier," Alexander Leslie. The army was accompanied by a contingent of Argyll's Highlanders. These "uncanny trewsmen"—the phrase is Robert Baillie's[1] seem to have been a source of considerable anxiety to their friends. It is curious to note that Highland troops should have made their first appearance on the Borders as the allies of the Covenant.

The two armies never came to blows. The Scots encamped on Duns Law. The King was on the other side of the Tweed. Negotiations were opened, which resulted in the Pacification of Berwick. It was agreed that the royal fortresses were to be restored, and the questions at issue were to be left to the arrangement of a free General Assembly and a free meeting of the Estates.

The Pacification of Berwick merely postponed hostilities. From the first each party accused the other of bad faith. War broke out again in the following summer. In July the Scots army was again assembled for the invasion of England, and on August 28, 1640, the battle of Newburn was fought.

During the next four years there was no important fighting in the north. In Scotland the Covenant was supreme. What restlessness there was among the Aberdeenshire Royalists was suppressed by a force under General Monro. In the summer of 1640 Argyll, acting under a "Commission of Fire and Sword" from the Estates, ravaged the lands of his feudal enemies in the central Highlands and in Angus. It was during this ferocious raid that there took place that destruction of Airlie Castle, which forms the subject of the ballad of the "Bonnie House of Airlie."

The Long Parliament met in November 1640. In the autumn of 1641 the King visited Scotland, and was present at a meeting of the Estates, at which, in outward form, all was harmony; the troubles were brought to an end, and honours and offices were lavished on the Covenanting leaders. On Charles's return to London he found his difficulties with the English Parliament thickening fast. On August 25, 1642, the Royal Standard was raised at Nottingham and the great English Civil War began.

At first things went badly for the Parliamentary cause, and every endeavour was made by its leaders to secure the help of Scotland against the King. In 1643 the Solemn League and Covenant was signed. It was followed by the march of a Scots army into England, again commanded by Sir Alexander Leslie, now Earl of Leven, who had as his major-general his more famous nephew, David Leslie. On July 3, 1644, the combined armies decisively defeated the King at Marston Moor.

[1] The letters of the Rev. Robert Baillie, afterwards Principal of the University of Glasgow, form one of the most valuable sources of information as to the military and political events of the time.

Long before this Montrose had severed his connection with the Covenant, and had cast in his lot with the King. Immediately after the raising of the Royal Standard at Nottingham, Charles had written to him asking for his advice and assistance. Now that the English Parliamentary party had secured the co-operation of the forces of the Covenant, the King was sorely overmatched. If the Scottish army could be compelled to recross the Border, the conditions would be again equalised. Montrose knew the Highlanders thoroughly. They were unaccustomed to discipline ; they owned no allegiance except to their own chiefs ; it was hopeless for any ordinary general to attempt to handle them as a regular army : but Montrose well knew how formidable a force they might be under a leader who could secure their confidence and who knew how to manage them. He believed that he was himself such a leader, and, as the result proved, his belief was entirely justified. He conceived the idea of marching into Scotland with a force which was strong enough to make its way to the Highlands, and which might there form the nucleus of an army to be composed of the loyal clans and certain Irish supports which had been promised by the Earl of Antrim.

Montrose received from the King a commission, dated February 1, 1644, by which he was appointed Lieutenant-General of the royal forces in Scotland. He found himself, however, unable to obtain a body of troops sufficient to force his way to the Highlands as he had designed. He accordingly resolved to find his way through the enemy's country in disguise, a characteristic beginning of the brilliant and daring enterprise which has immortalised his name, and thoroughly in accordance with the character of the leader who was ever ready to stake all upon a single cast.

The companions of his perilous journey were Major, afterwards Sir William, Rollo and Colonel Sibbald. Montrose passed as their servant. On August 22 the party reached the house of Tullibelton, near Dunkeld, which belonged to Montrose's kinsman, Graham of Inchbrakie.

There he lay for some time in hiding, and sent out messengers to collect intelligence as to the state of the royal cause in the country. They returned with the worst news. Under the stern rule of Argyll and the Committee of Estates, the King's adherents had been thoroughly cowed. The enterprise seemed hopeless.

At last news came that the promised Irish succour had landed. Instead of the 10,000 men who were expected, a force of some 1500, commanded by Alastair Macdonald (called Colkitto, " the left-handed,") had reached the Hebrides in July, and had subsequently landed in Knoydart. They had found little support among the western clans. Montrose succeeded in communicating with Colkitto, and directed him to march with all despatch into Atholl. They met at Blair, and there the standard was joined by some 800 of the Atholl men, chiefly Stewarts and Robertsons.

Montrose was now at the head of some 3000 men. Promptitude of action was everything. Argyll, who had assembled a force to attack Colkitto, was approaching from the west. Montrose at once determined to strike a blow at Perth before Argyll could come up. He accordingly marched southward and crossed the Tay.

Perth was defended by a force of 6000 foot and 700 horse, with four guns, the whole commanded by Lord Elcho. Montrose was thus vastly outnumbered; he had neither cavalry nor artillery; and not a few of his men had no better arms than the stones which they picked up on the battle-field.

The armies met on the 1st of September at Tippermuir, between four and five miles to the west of Perth. The right wing of the Covenanters was commanded by Elcho; the left by Sir James Scott, and the centre by the Earl of Tullibardine. Montrose drew up his men three deep, with as long a front as possible. An attack by a party of Elcho's horse, under Lord Drummond, was easily beaten off. Then Montrose's line advanced to the attack. It was made in the traditional Highland manner, which was so often to prove successful against regular troops. The assailants advanced to within short range; then such of them as had muskets fired a volley; then they rushed in and attacked with the broadsword. The peaceable burghers of whom the Covenanting army was largely composed had little chance in a hand-to-hand conflict with savage mountaineers. They broke and fled in utter rout. The Rev. John Robertson, one of the ministers of Perth, describes the sorry plight of some of the citizens who reached the town, "all forefainted and bursted with running, insomuch that nine or ten died that night in town without any wound." "The Provost came into one house," he says, "where there were a number lying panting, and desired them to rise for their own defence: They answered—their hearts were away they would fight no more although they should be killed." The number of killed on the Covenanting side is variously stated; Wishart, Montrose's chaplain and chronicler, gives it as 2000. On the same day Montrose entered Perth as a victor. There he was able to provide his army with clothing, abundance of arms and ammunition, and six pieces of cannon.

At the head of "a pack of naked runagates," as Baillie calls them, Montrose had now defeated an immensely superior force in the field, and had captured one of the chief towns of the kingdom. It was no part of his policy to remain there. After a victory a Highland army always began to melt away, the men returning homewards to secure their plunder and save their harvest. In any case an open town could not be defended against a regular siege by Argyll's army. Elcho had retreated to Aberdeen, and Montrose resolved to follow him up.

He marched northwards through Angus and the Mearns, being joined on the way by the old Earl of Airlie and a considerable force of the Ogilvies and their friends. On reaching the Dee he made no attempt to force the bridge at Aberdeen, but marched up the right bank of the river and forded it at the Mills of Drum. On the night of September 11 he camped at Crathes. On the 13th the Covenanters marched out of Aberdeen to meet him. Their force, which was commanded by Lord

Balfour of Burleigh, consisted of some 2000 foot and 500 horse. Montrose had about 1500 foot and only 44 mounted men. The armies met a little to the west of the city, "between the Craibstane and the Justice Mills," where the Hardgate now runs. After a four hours' engagement the Covenanters broke and fled. Montrose's Irish troops behaved with great spirit in action, but after the battle they seem to have got badly out of hand, and horrible atrocities were committed by them in Aberdeen. "The men that they killed," says Spalding, "they would not suffer to be buried, but tirred (stripped) them of their clothes, syne left their naked bodies lying above the ground. The wife durst not cry or weep at her husband's slaughter before her eyes, nor the mother for the son, nor daughter for the father, which if they were heard then they were presently slain also. Nothing," he says, "was heard but pitiful howling, crying, weeping, mourning through all the streets."[1]

Montrose left Aberdeen on September 16. He had hoped for a large accession of strength in the Gordon country, but found himself disappointed in this, apparently through the personal jealousy of the Marquis of Huntly. With the force at his command he could not meet Argyll's army in the field, so during the following weeks we find him moving rapidly from place to place in the Highlands, on Speyside, in Badenoch, in Atholl, down in Angus, and again up in Aberdeenshire. Argyll had marched northward from Perth on September 14 with a force of some 3000 foot and two regular cavalry regiments, besides ten troops of horse. After following Montrose all over the country he came up with him at Fyvie on October 28. Notwithstanding the great disparity of forces Montrose gave him battle. Argyll was repulsed, and allowed Montrose to retreat into Strathbogie. He himself returned to Edinburgh, "where," says Spalding, "he got but small thanks for his service against Montrose." Thence he withdrew to his castle at Inverary.

Montrose again marched down through Badenoch into the Atholl country. Notwithstanding his military successes his prospects did not seem very cheering. He had not succeeded in raising anything like the force he expected from among the clans, and many of his Lowland officers had left him. Old Lord Airlie and his two sons alone remained faithful throughout. A descent upon the Lowlands was thought of and abandoned. Then was conceived the most daring and brilliant operation of the whole campaign—one of the most daring in all military history. This was to attack Argyll in his own impregnable fortress of Inverary. A blow struck there would shake the Covenanting power to its very foundation, and would gather to the royal standard the many enemies of the well-hated race of Campbell. A forced march in mid-winter over the Argyllshire mountains was only possible to such an army as Montrose's. It was effected with startling rapidity. Montrose passed like a meteor from Blair Atholl along Loch Tay, through Breadalbane and Glenorchy,

---

[1] *Memorials*, vol. ii., p. 407.

I

ravaging the Campbell lands as he went. Argyll fancied himself absolutely secure, believing as he did that Inverary was quite inaccessible to an army from the east. He was rudely undeceived. Early in December some shepherds arrived from the hills with the news that Montrose was close at their heels. Argyll had just time to save his own skin. He escaped by sea to Roseneath. For six weeks, till near the end of January 1645, Montrose's troops pillaged the Campbell country at their pleasure.

His next move was to march northward by Glencoe and Lochaber, with the object of attacking Inverness, which was held by a Covenanting force under Seaforth.[1] By this time he had been joined by many of the western chiefs. At Kilcummin, now Fort Augustus, on January 29 and 30, a bond promising support to the royal cause was subscribed by the chiefs present. Among the signatures appear those of Maclean of Duart, Maclean of Lochbuy, Macdonald of Keppoch, Macdonald younger of Glengarry, the Captain of Clanranald, the Tutor of Struan, the Tutor of Lochiel, the Macgregor, the Macpherson, and Stewart younger of Appin. It was immediately after the signature of this bond that the news reached Kilcummin that Argyll was again on Montrose's track at the head of some 3000 men, partly his own clansmen and partly some of the troops which had been recalled from England. With these he was ravaging Lochaber. Montrose's resolution was at once taken. He made one of his astonishing forced marches over Corryarrack, and down Glen Roy, and on the morning of February 2 swooped on Argyll at Inverlochy.

We have Montrose's own account of this famous march and fight, written to the King the day after the battle[2] : —

"My march was through inaccessible mountains," he says, "where I could have no guides but cowherds, and they scarce acquainted with a place but six miles from their own habitations. If I had been attacked with but one hundred men in some of these passes I must have certainly returned back, for it would have been impossible to force my way, most of the passes being so strait that three men could not march abreast. I was willing to let the world see that Argyle was not the man his Highlandmen believed him to be, and that it was possible to beat him in his own Highlands.

"The difficultest march of all was over the Lochaber mountains, which we at last surmounted, and came upon the back of the enemy when they least expected us, having cut off some scouts we met about four miles from Inverlochy. Our van came within view of them about five o'clock in the afternoon, and we made a halt till our rear was got up, which could not be done till eight at night. The rebels took the alarm and stood to their arms, as well as we, all night, which was moonlight and very clear. There were some few skirmishes between the rebels and us all the night, and with no loss on our side but one man. By break of day I ordered my

[1] Seaforth almost immediately afterwards changed sides ; his signature is appended to the Kilcummin Bond presently to be mentioned.
[2] As to the history of the text of this important letter see Napier's *Memorials of Montrose and his Times*, ii., 179.

men to be ready to fall on upon the first signal, and I understand since, by the prisoners, the rebels did the same. A little after the sun was up both armies met, and the rebels fought for some time with great bravery, the prime of the Campbells giving the first onset, as men that deserved to fight in a better cause. Our men having a nobler cause did wonders, and came immediately to push of pike and dint of sword after their first firing. The rebels ' could not stand it, but after some resistance at first began to run, whom we pursued for nine miles together, making a great slaughter, which I would have hindered if possible, that I might save your Majesty's misled subjects. For well I know your Majesty does not delight in their blood, but in their returning to their duty. There were at least fifteen hundred killed in the battle and the pursuit, among whom there are a great many of the most considerable gentlemen of the name of Campbell, and some of them nearly related to the Earl. I have saved and taken prisoners several of them, that have acknowledged to me their fault and lay all the blame on their chief. Some gentlemen of the Lowlands that had behaved themselves bravely in the battle, when they saw all lost fled into the old castle, and upon their surrender I have treated them honourably and taken their parole never to bear arms against your Majesty. . . . We have of your Majesty's army about two hundred wounded, but I hope few of them dangerously. I can hear but of four killed, and one whom I cannot name to Your Majesty but with grief of mind -Sir Thomas Ogilvy, a son of the Earl of Airlie, of whom I writ to your Majesty in my last. He is not yet dead, but they say he cannot possibly live, and we give him over for dead. Your Majesty never had a truer servant, nor there never was a braver, honester gentleman."

The defeat at Inverlochy was a crushing blow to the Covenanters. The power of the Campbells was humbled to the dust. From the safe refuge of a boat on Loch Fyne Argyll had witnessed the rout of his army and the slaughter of his kinsmen. Montrose thought that he would shortly have Scotland at his feet, and that he would ere long cross the Border at the head of a victorious army. "I am in the fairest hopes," he writes to Charles, "of reducing this kingdom to your Majesty's obedience. And if the measures I have concerted with your other loyal subjects fail me not, which they hardly can, I doubt not before the end of this summer I shall be able to come to your Majesty's assistance with a brave army, which, backed with the justice of your Majesty's cause, will make the rebels in England, as well as in Scotland, feel the just rewards of rebellion. Only give me leave, after I have reduced this country to your Majesty's obedience, and conquered from Dan to Beersheba, to say to your Majesty then, as David's General did to his master, 'Come thou thyself, lest this country be called by my name.'"

Montrose did not rest upon his laurels. After his victory he again marched northward, up what is now the line of the Caledonian Canal. The Covenanting army at

Inverness melted away at his approach. On February 19 he reached Elgin.  Here
he received a welcome accession of strength; he was joined by a force of the Gordons
under Lord Gordon, Huntly's eldest son, and Lord Lewis Gordon.

His object now was to strike at the Lowlands.  The road to the south was blocked
by a force of the troops who had been recalled from England, commanded by General
William Baillie of Letham, an old soldier of Gustavus Adolphus's, and a much more
formidable antagonist than the amateur commanders whom as yet Montrose had had
opposed to him.  There was also a force of some 600 horse under Sir John Hurry,
a soldier of fortune who changed sides four times during the troubles.

From Elgin, Montrose marched by Huntly and Kintore to Stonehaven, plundering
the lands of the north-country Covenanters as he went  Near Fettercairn he came into
touch with Hurry's cavalry, who retreated before him.  Baillie well knew the peculiar
weakness of a Highland army.  He determined to avoid an engagement as long as
possible, knowing that every day of waiting and manœuvring would weaken his enemy
by desertions.  Wishart tells a characteristic story of the two commanders.  The armies
had come face to face with each other at Coupar-Angus, on opposite banks of the Isla.
Neither could cross the river without serious loss if the passage was disputed.  Montrose, in the spirit of old-world chivalry, sent Baillie a challenge by a trumpeter.  He
asked permission to cross the river unopposed, or if the Covenanting general preferred he
might himself cross to Montrose's side, if he would pledge his honour to fight without
further delay.  The old campaigner drily replied "that he would mind his own business
himself, and would fight at his own pleasure, and not at another man's commands."

At last Baillie retired towards Fife, without ever having come to an action.  Montrose
marched westward and occupied Dunkeld.  The way to the south was now open, but
Baillie's Fabian policy had succeeded.  Montrose's army had melted down to some 800
men.  With such a force it was out of the question to invade the Lowlands.  Montrose's
information was that the whole of Baillie's force was now on the west side of the Tay.
He determined to make a dash on Dundee.  Early in the morning of April 3
he started from Dunkeld.  Dundee was reached next day, and occupied with little
resistance.  Montrose, however, had been misinformed as to Baillie's movements, and
he just escaped irreparable disaster.  His men had scattered through the town in quest
of drink and plunder, when news came that Baillie and Hurry, with 3000 foot and 800
horse, were within a mile of the town.  Montrose managed to collect his troops—a
notable example of his personal power of command—and escaped from the east gate
of the town just in time.  Baillie followed close at his heels during the night, hoping to
corner him against the sea at Arbroath.  Montrose, however, doubled back, slipped
round Baillie's rear, crossed the South Esk at Careston Castle at sunrise, and succeeded
in reaching the Grampians.  It was a wonderful achievement: the men had been
marching and fighting for three days and two nights without food or sleep, and were
half dead with hunger and fatigue.  Wishart says that he often "heard officers of

experience and distinction, not in Britain only, but also in Germany and France, prefer this march of Montrose to his most famous victories."

As we have seen, Montrose's army had dwindled to a mere handful. Lord Lewis Gordon, always untrustworthy, had deserted, and had taken many of the Gordons with him. There was nothing to be done but to retire again to the North and endeavour once more to build up an army. Baillie was watching the Highlands from Perth, and Hurry had gone north to Inverness to collect forces for an attack on the Gordons. Lord Gordon had gone home to his own country to raise further levies, and, if possible, to bring back the men who had been carried off by Lord Lewis.

After picking up some recruits in Perthshire, Montrose found his way into the Mar country. There he met Lord Gordon at the head of 1000 foot and 200 horse. He had already been joined by Lord Aboyne, who, with a few horsemen, had escaped from beleaguered Carlisle. By a daring raid on Aberdeen Aboyne secured a much-needed supply of gunpowder. Then it was decided to attack Hurry.

Montrose marched over the hills by the route which is now followed by the road from Cocksbridge to Tomintoul, and then down Strathspey. Hurry advanced from Inverness to meet him. Near Elgin the armies came into touch. Hurry retired on Inverness, closely followed by Montrose. At Inverness the Covenanting army received a large accession of strength, being joined by the Earl of Seaforth, who had again changed sides, the Earl of Sutherland, and a force of the Frasers. This placed Hurry at the head of nearly 4000 men, of whom 400 were cavalry. Montrose's force did not amount to more than 1500 foot and 250 horse, the latter consisting chiefly of the Gordons. Hurry turned upon his enemy, secure of victory. On the evening of May 8 Montrose reached the village of Auldearn, on the road between Forres and Nairn, some two miles east of the latter. Here he was attacked by Hurry on the following morning.

Montrose took up his position along the ridge crowned by the village of Auldearn, at right angles to Hurry's line of advance. The village itself was the centre of his position. It was only occupied by a handful of men, enough to lead the assailants to believe that it was held in force. Alastair Macdonald with 400 Irish was posted on the right, in a position strongly defended by dykes and ditches. Montrose himself was on the left, behind the ridge, with the remainder of the infantry and the whole of the cavalry, the latter under Lord Gordon. Hurry's right wing was commanded by Campbell of Lawers, his left by Captain Drummond; he himself remained in the rear in command of the reserves.

The royal standard had been entrusted to Macdonald, with the object of causing Hurry to believe that Montrose himself was stationed on the right, and if possible of inducing him to make his main attack there. The ruse was successful. Hurry sent the bulk of his force to attack the Irish. Macdonald in an evil moment allowed himself to be drawn from his strong position, and narrowly escaped disaster, though he himself performed Homeric feats of personal prowess. "Some of the pikemen," says Wishart, "by whom he was hard pressed again and again pierced his target with the points of their weapons, which he mowed off with his broadsword by threes and fours at a sweep." News was sent to Montrose that the right wing was routed. Wishart describes what followed. "To prevent a panic among his men at the bad news, with admirable presence of mind he (Montrose) at once called out, 'Come, my Lord Gordon, what are we waiting for? Our friend Macdonald on the right has routed the enemy and is slaughtering the fugitives. Shall we look on idly and let him carry off all the honours of the day?'" With these words he hurled his line upon the enemy. The shock of the Gordons was irresistible. After a brief struggle Hurry's horse wavered, recoiled, wheeled, and fled, leaving their own flanks naked and exposed. Though deserted by the horse, the infantry, being superior in numbers and much better armed, stood their ground bravely until Montrose came to close quarters and forced them to fling down their arms and save themselves by flight." Having thus disposed of Hurry's right wing, Montrose turned upon those who were assailing Macdonald's position. "The horse fled headlong, but the foot, mostly veterans from Ireland, fought on doggedly, and fell man by man almost where they stood." The victory was complete. The Covenanters were pursued for miles with tremendous slaughter. The whole of their colours, baggage, and ammunition were captured by the Royalists.

A week before the battle of Auldearn, Baillie, whom we left at Perth, had broken into the Atholl country, where Blair Castle was held for the King. On hearing of the battle he marched northward, and at Strathbogie was joined by Hurry with the remains of his defeated army. Montrose, weakened by the desertion of many of his Highlanders, was in no haste to fight, and withdrew up Strathspey into Badenoch. Lord Lindsay was collecting a force in Forfarshire with the object of advancing against Montrose from the south. An attempt on Montrose's part to attack him was frustrated by the desertion of the bulk of the Gordon horse. Montrose retired into Strathdon, and took up his position at Corgarff Castle, there to await events.

By the end of June he was once more in a position to fight. Lord Gordon and Colonel Nathaniel Gordon had succeeded in bringing back most of the Gordons, and Alastair Macdonald had brought in more men from the Highland glens. Montrose was at the head of some 2000 men. Baillie, on the other hand, had been seriously weakened by the transfer to Lindsay's force of over 1000 of his best men, in exchange for 400 recruits. He was still in the North, where he had been ordered by the Estates to lay waste Huntly's country.

Montrose accordingly endeavoured to bring Baillie to an engagement at Keith. Baillie, who occupied a strong position there, was not to be drawn. Montrose retired south towards the Don. Baillie had to follow him or leave the road to the Lowlands open. Montrose crossed the Don at Alford and took up his position on a ridge of high ground to the south of the river. There Baillie attacked him on July 2.

The forces were nearly equal in respect of numbers; the Covenanters had rather the best of it in cavalry. Montrose's force was drawn up along the crest of the ridge with the cavalry on the flanks, under Lord Gordon and Aboyne. Part of the force was concealed behind the ridge. Baillie forded the Don about half a mile in front of Montrose's centre, crossed a piece of boggy ground near the river-side, and advanced up the slope of the hill to the attack. He was not waited for. The horse on Montrose's right wing, headed by Lord Gordon and supported by a body of Irish musketeers, charged his cavalry and drove it back in confusion. Then the main body rushed down and fell on with the claymore. The Covenanting infantry made a brave stand, but soon they too broke and fled. Montrose had won another decisive victory. Young Lord Gordon was struck down in the moment of victory by a shot from one of the fugitives. His death was a terrible loss to the army and to the royal cause in Scotland. "Montrose," says Wishart, "could not restrain his grief, but mourned bitterly as for his dearest and only friend."

The victory at Alford cleared Montrose's way to the south. Six days after the battle the Covenanting Parliament met at Stirling and resolved to levy a new army from the Lowland counties. It was to assemble at Perth on July 24. The unlucky Baillie, foreseeing certain disaster, twice tendered his resignation, but it was not accepted, and to make matters worse he was subjected to the control of a military committee whose members could not even agree among themselves.

Montrose in the meantime was receiving great accessions of strength. The news of his victory and the prospect of a descent on the Lowlands brought crowds of clansmen to his standard—Macleans from the west, Macdonalds of Clanranald and Glengarry, Macgregors, Macnabs, Macphersons from Badenoch, Farquharsons from Braemar, and a contingent of Atholl men under Patrick Graham of Inchbrakie. Towards the end of July he marched south from Fordoun, where he had awaited his reinforcements, and appeared in the neighbourhood of Perth. He was still expecting further reinforcements and had no desire to fight a serious battle just yet. A few skirmishes took place, in which the Covenanters always had the worst of it. Early in August he was joined at Dunkeld by a strong force of the Gordons, and by eighty horsemen of the Ogilvies under the brave and ever loyal old Earl of Airlie. All was now ready for the advance into the Lowlands. Montrose marched down through Kinross, descended the vale of the Devon, destroyed Argyll's castle of Castle Campbell near Dollar, and crossed the Forth at the Fords of Frew. On August 14 he reached Kilsyth.

Baillie had to follow him. He crossed the Forth at Stirling Bridge, and on the night of the 14th he camped at Hollinbush, about two and a half miles east of Montrose's position. According to Wishart his force consisted of 6000 foot and 800 horse, while Montrose had 4400 foot and 800 horse. The Covenanting force, however, consisted of hastily raised and untrained levies, mostly Fifeshire men who could with great difficulty be persuaded to serve out of their own shire, and their commander was sorely hampered by the Committee which had been set over him, and which included among its members Argyll, whom Montrose had beaten at Inverlochy, Elcho, whom he had beaten at Tippermuir, and Balfour of Burleigh, whom he had beaten at Aberdeen.

The Committee imagined that Montrose was anxious to avoid an engagement. Exactly the reverse was the case. A Covenanting force of 1500 men had been raised in Clydesdale by the Earl of Lanark; they were approaching from the west, and were now within 12 miles of Kilsyth. Montrose's one object was to fight Baillie before Lanark could come up. He drew up his men in an open meadow a little to the east of Kilsyth. On the morning of the 15th the Covenanters advanced to attack him over rugged ground.

To the north of Montrose's position there was a hill which commanded his left flank. It appeared to the Committee that if this could be occupied they would be in a position to cut off Montrose's expected retreat. They accordingly directed Baillie to move to his right and take possession of the hill. To try to execute a flank movement across the front of an active and determined enemy was simply fatuous, and Baillie knew it, but the Committee insisted on their point. The fatal movement was begun. Montrose saw what was aimed at and despatched a force under Adjutant Gordon to hold the hill. A glen with a burn running through it had to be crossed by the Covenanters. The obvious result happened. The straggling column was charged in flank by the Macleans and Macdonalds and cut in two. Its head was attacked on the hill by Gordon, who was soon strongly reinforced, and was cut to pieces. The rout became general, and the fields were soon covered with terrified fugitives. The pursuit was remorseless and the slaughter frightful; Wishart says that 6000 of the Covenanters perished. Some of their leaders took refuge in Stirling Castle; some escaped by sea; Argyll went on board ship at Queensferry and reached Newcastle.

Kilsyth was Montrose's crowning victory. Baillie had told the Committee that the loss of the day would mean the loss of the kingdom, and he was right. The King's Lieutenant now had Scotland at his feet. The Covenanting leaders fled or submitted; the western levies dispersed to their homes. The imprisoned Royalists were set at liberty. The towns opened their gates; Edinburgh surrendered in the most abject manner. It seemed that the royal authority was completely restored, and Montrose, in the King's name, summoned a meeting of Parliament for October.

His immediate object, however, was to go to the help of the King in England. He had assured Charles that he would soon cross the Border at the head of 20,000 men. He had imagined that the Lowlanders, once freed from the tyranny of Argyll and the Kirk, would flock to his standard, and that he would continue his career of victory till the royal cause was triumphant throughout the island.

He was bitterly undeceived. Mr Gardiner comments with justice on the astonishing absence of all grasp on the concrete facts of politics, which in Montrose was coincident with the most intense realisation of the concrete facts of war.[1] He entirely misjudged the temper of the Lowlands. The sympathies of the common people were all on the side of the Kirk; probably most of them desired nothing more than to be left in peace by both parties to get their harvests in; in any case they hated and feared the Highlander and the Irishman, who had won Montrose's victories. Montrose entirely failed to raise a Lowland army; what recruits he did get were almost all of the upper classes. On the other hand, the army of Kilsyth was rapidly melting away. The clansmen had no fancy to be led south of the Tweed; they were disappointed in not getting the plunder of the Lowland towns; they all found pressing reasons of one kind or another for returning to their homes. The Macdonalds left in a body with Alastair at their head. Montrose marched southward from Bothwell in the beginning of September. Before he reached the Border he found himself in command of a mere handful of men.

In the meantime a formidable antagonist was approaching from the south. David Leslie, at the head of 4000 cavalry, had been detached from the Scottish army before Hereford, and was making for the Border with all possible speed. In the first week of September he crossed the Tweed at Berwick. He continued his march towards Edinburgh, expecting to fight Montrose in the Lothians. When in East Lothian he heard that his enemy was at Kelso. He turned to the west, marched down by Gala Water, and on the night of September 12 encamped at the village of Sunderland.

Montrose was at Selkirk. The greater part of his army was encamped on Philiphaugh, on the north side of the Ettrick. The number of men with him is variously given. According to Mr Gardiner, he had only 500 of his faithful Irish and some 1200 horse, of whom only 150, under Lord Airlie and Nathaniel Gordon, took part in the fight. He was badly served by his cavalry scouts. On the morning of the 13th, favoured by a thick mist, Leslie with his whole force succeeded in surprising the doomed Royalists. With such disparity of force the battle was a mere rout. A brief and gallant stand was made in vain. Montrose and a few others succeeded in saving themselves by flight; most of the men were slain or taken prisoners. The Covenanters butchered their prisoners in cold blood.[2] Among the camp followers were some 300 Irish women, the wives of the soldiers, with their infant children. These shared the fate of their husbands and fathers. Most of the prisoners of rank perished on the scaffold.

The crushing disaster of Philiphaugh ended Montrose's brilliant and fruitless career

---

[1] See the admirable summary of the political situation in the *History of the Great Civil War*, chap. xxxvi.

[2] The contemporary evidence for this statement seems conclusive. It will be found fully reviewed in Napier's *Memoirs of Montrose*, chap. xxviii. Patrick Gordon of Ruthven gives a hideous account of the victors' cruelty. "With the whole baggage and stuff, which was exceeding rich," he says, "there remained none but boys, cooks, and a rabble of rascals, and women with their children in their arms. All those, without commiseration, were cut

K

of victory. Ever since the battle of Naseby (June 14, 1645) the royal cause in England had been hopeless. It was now equally hopeless in Scotland. Montrose escaped to the Highlands, where he attempted in vain to reconstruct an army. In May 1646 the King surrendered himself to the Scots army in England. Shortly afterwards he commanded Montrose to disband his forces. Montrose himself escaped to Norway in September. "His high enterprise had failed," says Mr Gardiner. "No skill of warrior or statesman could deal successfully with a problem the solution of which depended on the one hand upon the wisdom of Charles, and on the other on the discipline of the Gordons and of the Highland clans."

Four years later Montrose again appeared in arms in Scotland. The last act of his drama is brief and tragic. The execution of Charles I. took place on January 30, 1649. The dominant faction in Scotland acknowledged Charles II. as his successor in the kingdom of Scotland, and proceeded to open those negotiations which led to his appearance in Scotland for a brief period in the character of a "Covenanted King." Montrose, filled with grief and rage by the death of his master, was burning with desire to avenge his blood and to restore his son to the crown. Charles, while actually in treaty with the Covenanters, granted to Montrose a commission authorising him to solicit help from the Northern Powers and to effect a descent on Scotland. Montrose landed in Orkney in March 1650 with some 700 men. There he remained some weeks, and was joined by about 800 men from the islands. With this force he crossed into Caithness. A strong force under David Leslie was sent north to meet him. On April 27 he was attacked and defeated at Carbisdale by a detachment under General Archibald Strachan. He escaped wounded from the fight, and a few days later was captured by Macleod of Assynt and handed over to the Covenanting general.

His fate was now sealed. He was sent as a prisoner to Edinburgh. After the battle of Inverlochy the doom of forfeiture and death had been pronounced against him by the Estates, and by the Church he had been "delivered into the hands of the devil." No trial was needed. On May 21, 1650, he was put to death at the Cross of Edinburgh with every circumstance of insult and degradation.

With the justice of his cause we are not here concerned, nor with the vindication of his political conduct. As to the latter, his own point of view is clear enough. "The Covenant which I took," he said to the Covenanting ministers the day before his death, "I own it and adhere to it. Bishops, I care not for them. I never

---

in pieces; whereof there were three hundred women that being natives of Ireland, were the married wives of the Irish. There were many big with child, yet none of them were spared; all were cut in pieces with such savage and inhuman cruelty as neither Turk nor Scythian was ever heard to have done the like. [Here follow some unprintable details.] O impiety, O horrible cruelty, which Heaven doubtless will revenge before this bloody, unjust, and unlawful war be brought to an end!" (*Britane's Distemper*, p. 160). Gordon's narrative is all the more convincing, as he describes in very plain language the cruelty, "filthy lust," "excessive drinking," "godless avarice, merciless oppression, and plundering of the poor labourer," of which some of Montrose's own followers were guilty. But they never did anything approaching this.

intended to advance their interest. But when the King had granted you all your desires, and you were every one sitting under his vine and under his fig-tree, that then you should have taken a party in England by the hand, and entered into a League and Covenant with them against the King, was the thing I judged it my duty to oppose to the yondmost."[1] His military reputation is beyond question. Dr Hill Burton speaks of it depreciatingly, on the ground that "he was defeated on the only occasion when he met face to face with another commander of repute." So he was, when the "other commander of repute" outnumbered him five to one. The story of his campaign speaks for itself. He was one of the greatest commanders of Highland troops that ever lived, and in personal loyalty and bravery he has left an illustrious example to all ages.

The battles of Dunbar and Worcester were followed by the rule of the Commonwealth in Scotland. One more attempt was made for the King in the North. In 1653 a force was raised in the West Highlands by the Earl of Glencairn, who was joined by Glengarry, Lochiel, and Atholl. His idea, apparently, was to emulate the feats of Montrose, but he was not the man to do it. The command of the force was taken over by General Middleton, who arrived from England, having escaped from the Tower. He held a commission as generalissimo of the King's forces in Scotland. An army of 3000 men, under Monk and General Morgan, marched northward against the Royalists. Morgan met and defeated them on the banks of Lochgarry. Lochiel held out in the west for some time, but ultimately submitted.[2] There was no more important warfare in the Highlands for a generation.

---

[1] Narrative of the Rev. Patrick Simson, Napier, p. 787.
[2] For details as to Lochiel's daring and stubborn resistance, see Keltie's *Scottish Highlands*, pp. 296 *et seq.*

# CHAPTER II.

## THE REVOLUTION—KILLIECRANKIE (1689).

THE Revolution of 1688 passed off peacefully in England, but in Scotland, as in Ireland, the new regime only established itself after serious fighting.

The Convention of Estates, which transferred the crown of Scotland from the head of James II. to that of William of Orange, met at Edinburgh on March 14, 1689. King James had left England for ever in December. He had entrusted the charge of his civil affairs in Scotland to the Earl of Balcarres. The charge of his military affairs had been committed to Major-General John Graham of Claverhouse, who had just been raised to the peerage as Viscount Dundee. Claverhouse, who in his youth had served in France and Holland, had during the reigns of Charles II. and James II. been the most active instrument in carrying out the coercive policy of the Scottish Government against the Covenanters, and in that connection has left a name of sinister significance in the history of Scotland. We are now to meet him as the devoted champion of a hopeless cause, and as a commander of Highland forces only second to his great kinsman Montrose.

The Convention began its work surrounded by an atmosphere of violence. No one knew when or how the storm might break. The Castle was held for the King by the Duke of Gordon. The city was full of armed men, Claverhouse's old troopers on the one hand, and on the other the stern and fanatical Cameronians of the West, now eager for vengeance on their old enemies. Dundee was warned that his life and that of Sir George Mackenzie, the "Bloody Mackenzie" of the Covenanters, were in imminent danger. He applied in vain to the Convention for protection. In the Convention itself the King's friends were in a hopeless minority. They accordingly resolved to withdraw to Stirling and there hold a convention by themselves a course which had been authorised by the King. They met for this purpose on March 18, but at the instigation of the Marquis of Atholl they decided to postpone their departure for a day. Dundee, however, declared that he had some fifty troopers mounted and ready to start, and that he would not remain a day longer in Edinburgh. At the head of his troop he rode out under the Netherbow Port, down Leith Wynd, and along the line of road where Princes Street now stands. When he reached the foot of the Castle Rock he halted his troop, climbed the rock, and held an interview with the Duke of Gordon at the postern gate, still visible in the wall. Then he resumed his march towards Stirling.

His departure greatly alarmed the Revolutionary party in the Convention, who well knew that it meant trouble in the North. A party of horse was sent to bring him back.

They overtook him, but returned with their mission unfulfilled. Claverhouse, it was said, assured their commander, Major Buntine, that he would send him back to his masters in a pair of blankets if he attempted to carry out his orders. The fugitives crossed the Forth at Stirling, and Claverhouse safely reached his house at Dudhope near Dundee.

A force of regular troops had been sent from England for the support and protection of the Convention. These consisted of 200 dragoons and some 1100 men of the Scots Dutch Brigade under Major-General Hugh Mackay of Scoury, who reached Edinburgh on March 25. The Convention called out the fencible men in the districts favourable to the Revolution, and sanctioned the formation under Lord Angus of a regiment of the Cameronians. There was much searching of heart among the "wild westland Whigs" as to whether they were free to take service under an uncovenanted King, but the issue of their deliberations was the formation of the famous Cameronian regiment—the 26th Foot which, as we shall see, was soon to give proof of its valour.

Thus protected, the Convention proceeded with its work. On April 4 it passed the memorable resolution which sets forth the delinquencies of King James, and then proceeds to declare that "he hath forefaulted the right to the crown, and the throne is become vacant." On the 11th the Claim of Right was adopted, and William and Mary were declared King and Queen of Scotland. On the same day they were proclaimed at the Cross of Edinburgh.

No attempt was made by the garrison of the Castle to interfere with these proceedings. The Duke of Gordon could scarcely have done so had he wished. His garrison from the first did not exceed 160 men, and it was soon weakened by dissensions and desertions. His only object seems to have been to hold the Castle until it should appear how matters were going in the country. After various summonses the Castle capitulated on June 14.

After his departure from Edinburgh Dundee remained for some time at Dudhope. Ostensibly he was taking no part in public affairs, but he was still surrounded by the troopers with whom he had marched north, and he was in active correspondence with the Highland chiefs, in particular with the redoubtable Ewen Cameron of Locheil. Every Jacobite in Scotland looked to him for leadership, and he was regarded with proportionate alarm by the Whigs. He was cited on March 18 to appear in his place in Parliament, and a few days later was formally summoned to lay down arms, on pain of being dealt with as a traitor. He protested that he was living in peace in his own house, and that he had left the Convention because his life was in danger; in any case, he said, he begged the favour of a delay till after his wife's expected confinement, and was willing to give security not to disturb the peace in the meantime.

On March 30 he was proclaimed a traitor. A force under Mackay was sent to seize him. Dundee and his troopers retreated north into the Gordon country, where he was joined by some sixty horse under Lord Dunfermline. During the next few weeks it is not easy for the purposes of the present work it is not necessary to follow him minutely in his rapid movements about the Highlands. We find him back at Dudhope, having eluded Mackay in the north. Mackay, in the meantime, at the head of some 450 men, had found his way into Deeside. The Master of Forbes met him there with a body of forty horse and some 500 foot, but, says Mackay, "these were so ill armed, and appeared so little like the work, that the General, thanking the Master for his appearance for their Majesty's service, ordered him to dismiss those countrymen with orders to be ready to come together whenever any ennemy party threat'ned their own province."[1] Marching by Strathbogie, Mackay reached and occupied Elgin. There he remained for some time, and communicated with such of the northern chiefs and lairds as were understood to be friendly to the Revolution cause. They were not enthusiastic. "In all the progresses and marches of the General benorth Tay," says Mackay, "he testified to have remarked no true sence of the deliverance which God had sent them except in very few, and that the people in general were disposed to submit to and embrace the party which they judged most like to carry it, their zeal for the preservation of their goods going by them far beyond the consideration of religion and liberty."

In the meantime Dundee had appeared at Inverness, where Macdonald of Keppoch had arranged to meet him with 900 men. The situation which he found there is the subject of a well-known passage in Macaulay; it is more concisely described in Drummond of Balhaldy's *Memoirs of Lochiel.* "He (Dundee) marched directly to Inverness and found Keppoch, who, instead of executing his commission, satt down before that toun, seized the Magistrats, and most wealthy citizens, and obliged them to pay him a sum of mony for their ransome before he consented to dismiss them. His Lordship was extreamly provocked and expostulated the matter with him in very sharp terms. He told him that such courses were extreamly injurious to the King's interest, and that instead of acquiring the character of a patriot, he would be looked upon as a common robber and the enemy of mankind! Keppoch excused himself the best way he could, pretended that the toun was owing him sums equall to what he had received, and in place of conducting my Lord Dundee in the manner he was commissioned, he retreated into his own country."[2] Dundee next retired into Lochaber, leaving Inverness to be occupied by Mackay. Then he made a swoop on the low country. On May 11 he raided Perth at midnight, carried off the lairds of Blair and Pollock as prisoners, and seized a large sum of public money. On the 13th he suddenly appeared before Dundee; Lord Rollo, who was encamped outside the town, had just time to retire within the walls.

[1] Mackay's *Memoirs* (Bannatyne Club, 1833), p. 13.
[2] *Memoirs of Lochiel* (Abbotsford Club, 1842), p. 237.

Dundee then crossed the country by way of Rannoch into Lochaber, where he was received with all honour by Lochiel. Here a great muster of the clans had been arranged from all the West Highlands and the Hebrides gathered Camerons, Macdonalds, Macleods, Macleans, all the hereditary enemies of the Campbells,—it was Montrose's army over again. Dundee's first idea was to make an attempt to discipline them as regular troops, but Lochiel convinced him that it was better to let the Highlander fight in his own way.[1] A vain attempt was made to get King James to come over from Ireland with reinforcements.

In the meantime Mackay at Inverness was trying to recruit *his* army from among the clans, with little success. Some Mackays joined him from the Reay country. He tried to bribe old Lochiel, who, "without opening the letters, brought them to my Lord Dundee and begged that he would be pleased to dictate the answers."

While Dundee was in Lochaber news reached him that Colonel Ramsay, with a force of 1200 men, was coming up from the south through the Atholl country to join Mackay at Ruthven Castle on the Spey, close to Kingussie. Dundee marched to intercept him. Ramsay precipitately retreated towards Perth, and Ruthven Castle was captured and destroyed by the Jacobites. Dundee, after an ineffectual attempt to surprise Mackay, marched up Glenlivat and into Strathdon. After some manœuvring and skirmishing in Aberdeenshire, there came a pause in the campaign as if by mutual consent. Mackay, having left a garrison in Inverness, retired to Edinburgh. He had seen, as Cromwell saw after Dunbar, and as the Government saw in the eighteenth century, that the Highlands could only be permanently kept quiet by the establishment of permanent garrisons among them, and his object now was to induce the authorities to give effect to this view. Dundee in the meantime dismissed the bulk of his men to their homes for the present, and himself made a tour through the districts of some of the more remote clans to secure their support to his master's cause.

It is in the middle of June that the curtain rises on the next act of the drama. The key of the central Highlands was Blair Castle. The Marquis of Atholl had retired to Bath, out of harm's way, on the pretext of his health. Nothing could be done through him. Dundee in vain endeavoured to get Lord John Murray to declare for James. However, Stewart of Ballechin, the Marquis's factor, was a trusty Jacobite, and Dundee solved the difficulty by preparing a commission authorising him to hold the castle for King James in the Marquis's absence, and it was garrisoned accordingly. The clan thus found themselves with a divided allegiance ; most of them ultimately sided with Ballechin and Dundee.

---

[1] Lochiel's views on the subject will be found in the *Memoirs of Lochiel*, pp. 250 *et seq.* They give an interesting account of the old Highland method of warfare. The same volume gives various instances of Dundee's troubles with his unruly army, especially with the incorrigible Keppoch.

Mackay thereupon resolved to march into Atholl and possess himself of Blair at all costs, in the meantime begging Lord John Murray to do all he could to keep the Atholl men from joining Dundee. Mackay's force now consisted of "six battalions of foot . . . with four troops of horse and as many dragoons"—between 3000 and 4000 men in all. He marched from Perth on July 23. On the 27th he reached the Pass of Killiecrankie.

Dundee in the meantime had reassembled his army. Lochiel joined him with 240 men. General Cannon arrived from Ireland at the head of a regiment which had been sent over by King James, "three hundred new-raised, naked, undisciplined Irishmen," Balhaldy calls them. The Macdonalds, Macleans, and other western clans joined in great numbers. There has been much dispute over the number of troops actually engaged under Dundee. It was probably something over 2000.

Dundee reached Blair on the night of July 26 or on the morning of the 27th. As soon as it was heard that Mackay was at the mouth of the Pass a council of war was held. Were they to fight him or not? Some of the old regular officers with the army thought not, the odds were too great. The Highland chiefs, on the other hand, were eager for battle. Lochiel's counsel was emphatic and decided. "Fight immediately," he said, "for our men are in heart; they are so far from being afraid of their enemy that they are eager and keen to engage them, lest they escape their hands, as they have so often done. Though we have few men, they are good, and I can venture to assure your Lordship that not one of them will fail you."

The story of the actual conflict is vividly told by Drummond of Balhaldy[1]:—

"Ane advice so hardy and resolute," says he, "could not miss to please the generous Dundee. His looks seemed to brighten with ane air of delight and satisfaction all the while Locheill was a-speaking. He told his councill that they had heard his sentiments from the mouth of a person who had formed his judgement upon infallible proofs drawn from a long experience, and ane intimate acquaintance with the persons and subject he spoke of. Not one in the company offering to contradict their General, it was unanimously agreed to fight.

"When the news of this vigorous resolution spread through the army, nothing was heard but acclamations of joy, which exceedingly pleased their gallant General; but before the council broke up, Locheill begged to be heard for a few words: 'My Lord,' said he 'I have just now declared, in presence of this honourable company, that I was resolved to give ane implicite obedience to all your Lordship's commands; but I humbly beg leave, in name of these gentlemen, to give the word of command for this ane time. It is the voice of your council, and their orders are that you doe not engage personally. Your Lordship's business is to have an eye on all parts, and

---

[1] The accounts of Killiecrankie vary somewhat as to details. Drummond had probably excellent opportunities of getting first-hand information.

to issue out your commands as you shall think proper; it is ours to execute them with promptitude and courage. On your Lordship depends the fate not only of this little brave army, but also of our King and country. If your Lordship deny us this reasonable demand, for my own part I declare that neither I nor any I am concerned in shall draw a sword on this important occasion, whatever construction shall be putt upon the matter.'

"Locheill was seconded in this by the whole council; but Dundee begged leave to be heard in his turn: 'Gentlemen,' said he, 'as I am absolutely convinced, and have had repeated proofs of your zeal for the King's service and of your affection for me, as his General and your friend, so I am fully sensible that my engageing personally this day may be of some loss if I shall chance to be killed; but I beg leave of you, however, to allow me to give one *Shear-darg* (that is, one harvest day's work) to the King, my master, that I may have ane opportunity of convincing the brave Clans that I can hazard my life in that service as freely as the meanest of them. Ye know their temper, gentlemen, and if they doe not think I have personal courage enough, they will not esteem me hereafter, nor obey my commands with cheerfulness. Allow me this single favour and I promise, upon my honour, never again to risk my person while I have that of commanding you.'

"The council, finding him inflexible, broke up, and the army marched directly towards the Pass of Killychranky, which M'Kay had got clear of some short time before. Att the mouth of the Pass there is a large plain, which extends itself along the banks of the river, on the one side; and on the other there rises a rugged, uneven but not very high mountain.

"M'Kay still drew up his troops as they issued out of that narrow defile on the forsaid plain; and that he might be capable to flank Dundee on both sides in case of ane attack, he ordered his battle all in one line, without any reserves, and drew up his field batallions three men deep only, which made a very long front; for, as I have said already, his army consisted of no less than 3500 foot and two troops of horse. Haveing thus formed his lines, he commanded his troops, that were much fatigued with the quick march they had been obliged to make to prevent being stopt in the Pass, to sitt down upon the ground in the same order they stood, that they might be somewhat refreshed.

"Dundee keept the higher ground, and when his advanced guards came in view of the plain they could discover no enemy; but still as they came nearer they observed them to start to their feet, regiment by regiment, and waite the attack in the order above described. But Dundee never halted till he was within a musquet-shot of them, and posted his army upon the brow of the hill opposite to them; whence, having observed distinctly their order, he was necessitated to change the disposition of his battle, and inlarge his intervals, that he might not be too much out-winged. But before he could effect this the enemy began to play upon him with some field pieces

L

they had brought with them for the siege they intended,[1] and then their whole army fired upon them in platoons, which ran along from line to line for the whole time Dundee took up in disposing of his troops, which he performed in the following order:—

"Sir John M'Lean, then a youth of about eighteen years of age . . . was posted with his battalion on the right; on his left the Irishmen I have mentioned under the command of Collonell Pearson; nixt them the Tutor of Clanranald with his battalion. Glengary with his men were placed nixt to Clanranald's; the few horses he had were posted in the centre, and consisted of Low-country gentlemen and some remains of Dundee's old troop, not exceeding fourty in all, and these very lean and ill-keept. Nixt to them was Locheill; and Sir Donald's[2] battalion on the left of all. Though there were great intervals betwixt the battalions, and a large void space left in the centre, yet Dundee could not possibly stretch his line so as to equall these of the enemy; and, wanting men to fill up the void in the centre, Locheill, who was posted nixt the horse, was not onely obliged to fight M'Kay's own regiment, which stood directly opposite to him, but also had his flank exposed to the fire of Leven's battalion, which they had not men to engage, whereby he thereafter suffered much. But what was hardest of all, he had none of his Clan with him but 240, and even 60 of these were sent as Dundee's advanced guard to take possession of a house from which he justly apprehended the enemy might gall them, if they putt men into it. But there was no helping the matter. Each Clan, whether small or great, had a regiment assigned them, and that too by Locheil's own advice, who attended the Generall while he was makeing his disposition. The designe was to keep up the spirite of emulation in poynt of bravery; for as the Highlanders putt the highest value upon the honour of their familys or Clans, and the renoun and glory acquired by military actions, so the emulation between Clan and Clan inspires them with a certain generous contempt of danger, gives vigour to their hands, and keeness to their courage.

"The afternoon was well advanced before Dundee had gott his army formed into the order I have described. The continual fire of the enemy from the lower ground covered them, by a thick cloud of smoake, from the view of the Highlanders, whereof severals dropping from time to time, and many being wounded, they grew impatient for action. But the sun then shineing full in their faces the Generall would not allow them to engage till it was nearer its decline.

"Locheill as well to divert as to incourage them, fell upon this stratagem. He commanded his men, who, as I have said, were posted in the centre, to make a great shout, which being seconded by those who stood on their right and left, ran quickly through the whole army, and was returned by some of the enemy; but the noise of the cannon and musquets, with the prodigious echoeing of the adjacent hills and rocks, in which there are severall caverns and hollow places, made the Highlanders fancy that

---

[1] Of Blair Castle.                   [2] Sir Donald Macdonald.

their shouts were much brisker and louder than that of the enemy, and Locheill cryed out, 'Gentlemen, take courage. The day is our own. I am the oldest commander in the army, and have allways observed something ominous and fatall in such a dead, hollow, and feeble noise as the enemy made in their shouting. Ours was brisk, lively, and strong, and shews that we have courage, vigour, and strength. Theirs was low, lifeless, and dead, and prognosticates that they are all doomed to dye by our hands this very night!' Though this circumstance may appear triflleing to ane inadvertent reader, yet it is not to be imagined how quickly these words spread through the army, and how wounderfully they were incouraged and animated by them.

"The sun being near its close, Dundee gave the orders for the attack, and commanded that so soon as the M'Leans began to move from the right, that the whole body should, att the same instant of time, advance upon the enemy. It is incredible with what intrepidity the Highlanders endured the enemy's fire; and though it grew more terrible upon their nearer approach, yet they with a wounderfull resolution keept up their own, as they were commanded, till they came up to their very bosoms, and then pourcing it in upon them all att once like one great clap of thounder, they threw away their guns, and fell in pell-mell among the thickest of them with their broad-swords. After this the noise seemed hushed, and the fire ceaseing on both sides, nothing was heard for some few moments but the sullen and hollow clashes of broad-swords, with the dismall groans and crys of dyeing and wounded men.

"Dundee himself was in the centre of the horse, which was commanded by Sir William Wallace of Craigie. The gallant Earl of Dunfermline had formerly that charge, but that very morning, Sir William having presented a commission from King James, that noble Earl calmly resigned, much to the dissatisfaction of Dundee; and from this small incident, it is affirmed, flowed the ruine and disappointment of that undertaking. When they had advanced to the foot of the hill on which they were drawn up, Sir William Wallace, either his courage faileing him, or some unknown accident interposeing, instead of marching forward after the Generall, ordered the horse to wheele about to the left, which not onely occasioned a halt but putt them into confusion. Dundee in the meantime, intent upon the action, and carryed on by the impetuosity of his courage, advanced towards the enemy's horse, which were posted about their artillery in the centre, without observeing what passed behind till he was just entering into the smoak. The brave Earl of Dumfermline and sixteen gentlemen more, not regarding the unaccountable orders of their Collonell, followed their Generall, and observed him, as he was entering into the smoake, turn his horse towards the right, and raiseing himself upon his stirrops, make signes by waving his hatt over his head for the rest to come up. The enemy's horse made but little resistance. They were routed and warmely pursued by those few gentlemen; and as to Wallace and those with him, they did not appear till after the action was over.

"The Highlanders had ane absolute and complete victorey. The pursute was so warm that few of the enemy escaped; nor was it cheap bought to the victors, for they lossed very nearly a third of their number, which did not ammount fully to two thousand men before they engaged."

Dundee was shot down as he was leading the cavalry into action. The handful of horse under Lord Dunfermline, after returning from the pursuit, found him lying on the ground mortally wounded. "The fatall shott," says Drummond, "that occasioned his death, was about two hand's-breadth within his armour, on the lower part of his left side ; from which the gentlemen concluded that he had received it while he raised himself upon his stirrops, and streatched his body in order to hasten up his horse as I have related." He was removed to Blair Castle, where he died a few hours later. His body was buried with all honour in the church of Blair Atholl.[1]

Mackay's army was driven down the Garry in utter rout. "About the middle of the night," says Drummond, "the army returned from the pursute, but the enemy took the opportunity of retreating in the dark, and as they were marching through the Pass, the Atholl men . . . keeping still in a body, attacked them, killed some, and made all the rest prisoners, so that of the troops that M'Kay brought with him the sixth man did not escape. No less than eighteen hundred of them were computed to fall upon the field of battle." In the Highland army some 900 were killed and wounded. Drummond gives a terrible account of the effect of the claymore. "When day returned the Highlanders went out and took a view of the field of battle, where the dreadful effects of their fury appeared in many horrible figures. The enemy lay in heaps allmost in the order they were posted ; but so disfigured with wounds, and so hashed and mangled, that even the victors could not look upon the amazeing proofs of their own agility and strength without surprise and horrour. Many had their heads divided into two halves by one blow ; others had their sculls cutt off above the eares by a back-strock, like a night-cap. Their thick buffe-belts were not sufficient to defend their shoulders from such deep gashes as allmost disclosed their entrails. Several pikes, small-swords, and the like weapons were cutt quite through, and some that wore skull-capes had them so beat into their brains that they died upon the spott."

Mackay, with a small body which he had kept together, made his way to

---

[1] According to some accounts, Dundee died on the field. As to this question, and as to the authenticity of the letter to the King, said to have been dictated by Dundee before his death, see Napier's *Memorials of Dundee*, vol. iii., pp. 650-655, and Appendix No. I.

It was stated in evidence in the subsequent process of forfeiture against Dundee's representatives that "one named Johnston . . . catched the Viscount as he fell from his horse after his being shot, . . . the Viscount then asking the said Johnston how the day went, he answered the day went well for the King meaning King James but that he was sorry for his Lordship; and that the Viscount replied It was the less matter for him seeing the day went well for his Master." The whole proceedings in the process are printed in the *Acts of the Parliaments of Scotland*, vol. ix., Appendix, pp. 52-65.

Drummond Castle. The news of the defeat was brought to Edinburgh by the fugitives, and the Government was panic-stricken. On the other hand, recruits flocked to the victorious army; in a few days its numbers reached 5000 men.

There never was a more fruitless victory. Had Dundee lived he might well have undone the work of the Revolution. The bullet that killed him gave the death-wound to the cause of King James. He was succeeded in the command by Cannon, who at the best was a man of very ordinary abilities, and who was absolutely incapable of commanding a Highland army. An orthodox disciplinarian, he understood neither the peculiarities of the Highland character nor the conditions of Highland warfare. The chiefs began to drop away one by one.

Only one other engagement of any importance took place during the campaign. The newly-raised Cameronian Regiment had been sent north under their young Lieutenant-Colonel, William Cleland. They had garrisoned the town of Dunkeld. On August 18 a party of the Atholl men appeared before the town. These were soon reinforced by the whole of Cannon's army, and on the morning of the 21st they attacked the Cameronians. After a long day of bloody and desperate fighting the Highlanders were repulsed. Disgusted with defeat, and thoroughly distrusting their leader, the clans began to scatter homewards. Cannon took refuge in Mull with the Macleans. The war in Scotland was practically over. In the spring of 1690 a small Jacobite force drew together in Strathspey, under Major-General Buchan, an officer whom James had sent over from Ireland. On April 30 they were attacked in the Haughs of Cromdale by Sir Thomas Livingston, commander of the garrison of Inverness, and easily scattered.

Most of Dundee's officers took service abroad. By the end of 1691 all the Highland chiefs had submitted to the new Government, except the hapless Macdonald of Glencoe. The Massacre of Glencoe, which has left on the Government of the Revolution a stain of blood and treachery never to be effaced, took place on February 13, 1692. The last incident of resistance to the new powers was rather a boyish escapade than a serious act of war. Four young Jacobite officers, who had been taken prisoners at Cromdale, were confined in the fortress of the Bass Rock. One day in June 1691, when most of the garrison were on shore and the remainder were down unloading a collier vessel, the prisoners took possession of the fortress, shut the gates, and turned the guns on their gaolers. They were joined by a number of friends. A French man-of-war supplied them with provisions and stores. They held the Bass for nearly three years, making plundering descents on the neighbouring coast and taking toll of passing ships. In April 1694 they surrendered on honourable terms, and the rule of William and Mary was finally established throughout the British Islands.

# CHAPTER III.

## THE FIFTEEN.

FOR nearly a century after the completion of the Revolution, the adherents of the House of Stuart continued to hope and plot and struggle for the restoration of the fallen dynasty. The complete diplomatic and military history of Jacobitism still remains to be written. In the Stuart Papers at Windsor, in public archives at home and abroad, and in the records of many private families, there is still much material for the elucidation of the strange, pathetic story of the lost cause. All that can be done here is briefly to re-tell the story of the armed attempts which were made on behalf of the Stuarts, so far as they took place in the Highlands of Scotland.

The courage, wisdom, and clemency of William of Orange soon placed the Revolution Government on a secure basis. It was to his great enemy abroad, Louis XIV., that the Jacobites naturally looked for help, and in him they found a zealous and powerful ally.

King James II. died at St. Germains in 1701, and his heritage of misfortune descended to his son, James Francis Edward Stuart, then a boy of twelve, known to his adherents as James III. of England and VIII. of Scotland, to his enemies as the Pretender, and to both parties as the Chevalier de St. George.

All along it was in Scotland that Jacobitism had its strongest footing. As the Jacobites were to find to their cost, the people of England, notwithstanding local ebullitions of Jacobite feeling, were as a whole satisfied with the results of the Revolution ; at all events, they never thought that the restoration of the exiled family was worth a civil war. In Scotland it was different. There the Revolution Settlement was by no means universally popular. The old Cavalier party hated it, of course ; most of the Highland clans hated it because it meant the ascendancy of Argyll ; the Cameronians hated it because it meant an uncovenanted king. The action of the Government in the matter of the Darien project exasperated Scottish national feeling almost to the point of hostilities. The Union of 1707 was carried in the face of a great popular outcry that the honour and independence of the ancient kingdom were being sacrificed at the behest of English politicians. At first it was very far from being a success. Various measures, some excellent in themselves, were imposed on the country in the most unconciliatory manner, as the English way is sometimes apt to be, and the proud and sensitive temper of the Scots was prompt to

JACQUES III.
ROY DE LA GRANDE BRETAGNE.

resent every insult, real or imaginary. The early legislation of the United Parliament was very unpopular north of the Tweed; so was its taxation; still more so was the method of collecting that taxation—by an army of English officials. All this discontent was actively fomented and exploited by Jacobite agents; the repeal of the Union was made a cardinal point in the Jacobite scheme; and throughout the country the feeling was fostered that the "king over the water" was identified with the cause of Scottish nationality and Scottish liberty.

An abortive attempt at an invasion of Scotland in the Jacobite interest was made by Louis in 1708. Early in 1707 Colonel Hooke, the well-known Jacobite agent, came over from France to inquire as to the possibility of a rising against the Government. He stayed at Slains Castle, in Aberdeenshire, as the guest of Lord Errol, and thence communicated with the leading Jacobites throughout the country. The Cameronians were sounded as to their willingness to co-operate. Hooke was given to understand that in the event of a French landing the Scottish Jacobites could raise a force of 25,000 foot and 5000 horse.

Accordingly, in January 1708 a fleet, consisting of five ships of the line, two transports, and twenty-one frigates, was fitted out at Dunkirk under the command of Admiral Fourbin. On board the fleet some 4000 troops were embarked, and the Chevalier himself accompanied the expedition. A British squadron under Sir George Byng was sent to watch Dunkirk, but the French admiral succeeded in getting to sea. The expedition reached the Scottish coast at Montrose, turned south, and anchored off the Isle of May. Byng, however, was on their track. His approaching fleet was sighted by the French on March 14. They at once put to sea. One of their ships was captured, the remainder escaped and returned to France, and so the expedition ended. The Jacobites in Scotland had made no serious preparations for its reception. A few conspirators were put on their trial, nobody was convicted, and the whole thing blew over.

No further attempt at insurrection was made while Queen Anne lived. Towards the end of her reign the hopes of the Jacobites rose high. It was believed that many who willingly accepted the rule of a Stuart princess would not welcome as her successor the petty German sovereign whom the Act of Settlement called to the throne; it was well understood that Anne herself was favourable to her brother's claims; and it was more than guessed that Bolingbroke was on the same side.

Queen Anne died on August 1, 1714. A Tory scheme for proclaiming James her successor collapsed, and George I. was proclaimed king without opposition. The proclamation took place in Edinburgh on August 4. No serious danger was apprehended in Scotland. Some military precautions were taken at Edinburgh Castle and elsewhere, a few rioters were punished, and an eye was kept on such of the great landowners as were known to be disaffected. It was not till the following year that there was to be serious trouble. When it came it was entirely the work of one man.

John Erskine, eleventh Earl of Mar of the Erskine line, has left a name notorious for unprincipled political versatility. The ill-tongued Master of Sinclair speaks of his "dissolute, malicious, meddling spirit." Before the Union he had been Secretary of State for Scotland, and had since been Keeper of the Signet, a Scottish representative peer, and a Privy Councillor. In 1713 he had become one of the Tory Secretaries of State. On Queen Anne's death he did his best to stick to office. He hastened to tender his services and allegiance to the new sovereign. "Your Majesty," he wrote to King George, "shall ever find me as faithful and dutiful a subject and servant as ever any of my family have been to the Crown, or as I have been to my late mistress, the Queen. And I beg your Majesty may be so good not to believe any misrepresentations of me, which nothing but party hatred and my zeal for the interest of the Crown doth occasion; and I hope I may presume to lay claim to your royal favour and protection." In order further to impress on the King the importance of securing his adherence, Mar had obtained from certain of the great Highland chiefs a letter authorising him to assure the Government of their loyalty to His Sacred Majesty King George. "We entreat your Lordship would advise us," the letter proceeds, "how we may best offer our duty to His Majesty upon his coming over to Britain; and on all occasions we will beg to receive your counsel and direction how we may be most useful to his Royal Government." Among those who signed this document were MacLean of that Ilk, Glengarry, Lochiel, Keppoch, Grant of Glenmoriston, and MacPherson of Cluny."[1]

Mar's efforts to retain office were unavailing. He shared the fate of the rest of the Tories, and was dismissed on September 24. From that time forth he seems to have thrown in his lot with the Jacobites, though he remained for some time a courtier of King George.

On August 1, 1715, he attended a levee at Court. On the same or the following day, "in the dress of a private person," and accompanied by Major-General Hamilton, Colonel Hay, and two servants, he went on board a Newcastle collier in the Thames. On reaching Newcastle two or three days later, he hired another vessel and continued his voyage to Scotland. He landed at Elie, in Fifeshire, and was soon joined by some of his Fifeshire friends. On August 17 he was at Kinnoul. On the 18th he crossed the Tay, with forty horse, on his way north; and "next day," says Rae, "he sent letters to all the Jacobites round the country, inviting them to meet him, in haste, at Braemar, where he arrived on Saturday, the 20th of August."

"All the Jacobites round the country" were evidently waiting for the summons. They promptly responded to it. The pretext for the gathering was a great "tinchel," or hunting gathering, to be held at Braemar on August 26. Among those who were present when the day arrived were the Marquis of Huntly, the Marquis of Tullibardine,

---

[1] Both these letters are printed in Rae's *History of the Late Rebellion*, pp. 85, 87.

Seaforth, Glengarry, the Earl Marischal, and a long list of the chief Scottish Jacobites, Lowland as well as Highland.

The result of the meeting was that on September 6, 1715, the standard of King James VIII. was raised at Braemar. There is a well-known tradition to the effect that at the raising of the standard the gilded top of the flagstaff fell to the ground, an omen, in the eyes of the superstitious Highlanders, of the misfortunes which were to overtake the cause.

As soon as the standard of insurrection had been displayed, King James VIII. was proclaimed at Aberdeen, at Dundee, at Montrose, at Perth, at Brechin, and at Inverness; and the Castle of Inverness was seized and garrisoned by Brigadier Mac-Intosh of Borlum. The chiefs called out all their followings. Mar himself appears to have had a little difficulty with his own vassals. There is a well-known letter addressed by him to John Forbes of Inverernan, called "Black Jock," Bailie of the Barony of Kildrummie, which illustrates in a startling manner the tyrannical authority which, even at so recent a date, a great Highland lord exercised over his vassals. It is difficult to realise that the writer was not a mediæval marauder, but a man who had been a Secretary of State to Queen Anne, and who was a well-known figure in the London society which knew Addison and Steele, Bolingbroke and Ormonde.

"INVERCAULD, Sept. 9, at night, 1715.

"JOCKE,—Ye was in the right not to come with the hundred men ye sent up to-night, when I expected four times the number. It is a pretty thing, when all the Highlands of Scotland are now rising upon their King and country's account, as I have accounts from them since they were with me, and the gentlemen of our neighbouring Lowlands expecting us down to join them, that my men should be only refractory. Is not this the thing we are now about which they have been wishing these twenty-six years? And now, when it is come, and the King and country's cause is at stake, will they for ever sit still and see all perish? I have used gentle means too long, and so I shall be forced to put other orders I have in execution. I have sent you enclosed an order for the lordship of Kildrummy, which you are immediately to intimate to all my vassals. If they give ready obedience, it will make some amends, and if not, ye may tell them from me that it will not be in my power to save them (were I willing) from being treated as enemies by those who are ready soon to join me; and they may depend on it that I will be the first to propose and order their being so. Particularly, let my own tenants in Kildrummy know that if they come not forth with their best arms, that I will send a party immediately to burn what they shall miss taking from them. And they may believe this not only a threat, but, by all that's sacred, I'll put it in execution, let my loss be what it will, that it may be an example to others. You are to tell the gentlemen that I'll expect them in their

M

best accoutrements, on horseback, and no excuse to be accepted of. Go about this
with all diligence, and come yourself and let me know your having done so. All this
is not only as ye will be answerable to me, but to your King and country,

" Your assured friend and servant,

" MAR. "

At the same time a manifesto was issued, which, as it contains a very clear and
complete statement of the Jacobite appeal to the country, may here be printed at
length :—

> "*Manifesto by the Noblemen, Gentlemen, and others, who dutifully appear at this
> time in asserting the undoubted rights of their lawful Sovereign, James the
> Eighth, by the Grace of God, King of Scotland, England, France, and Ireland,
> Defender of the Faith, etc.; and for relieving this, his ancient Kingdom,
> from the oppressions and grievances it lies under.*

"His Majesty's right of blood to the crowns of these realms is undoubted, and
has never been disputed or arraigned by the least circumstance or lawful authority.
By the laws of God, by the ancient constitutions, and by the positive unrepealed laws
of the land, we are bound to pay His Majesty the duty of loyal subjects. Nothing
can absolve us from this our duty of subjection and obedience. The laws of God
require our allegiance to our rightful king the laws of the land secure our religion
and other interests; and His Majesty, giving up himself to the support of his Protestant
subjects, puts the means of securing to us our concerns, religious and civil, in our
own hands. Our fundamental constitution has been entirely altered and sunk amidst
the various shocks of unstable faction, while, in searching out new expedients pretended
for our security, it has produced nothing but daily disappointments, and has brought
us and our posterity under a precarious dependence upon foreign councils and interests,
and the power of foreign troops. The late unhappy Union, which was brought about
by the mistaken notions of some and the ruinous and selfish designs of others, has
proved so far from lessening and healing the difference betwixt His Majesty's subjects
of Scotland and England that it has widened and increased them. And it appears
by experience so inconsistent with the rights, privileges, and interests of us, and our
good neighbours and fellow-subjects of England, that the continuance of it must
inevitably ruin us and hurt them ; nor can any way be found out to relieve us, and
restore our ancient and independent constitution, but by the restoring our rightful and
natural king, who has the only undoubted right to reign over us. Neither can we
hope that the party who chiefly contributed to bring us into bondage will at any time
endeavour to work our relief, since it is known how strenuously they opposed, in two
late instances, the efforts that were made by all Scotsmen by themselves, and supported

by the best and wisest of the English, towards so desirable an end, as they will not adventure openly to disown the dissolution of the Union to be. Our substance has been wasted in the late ruinous wars, and we see an unavoidable prospect of having wars continued on us and our posterity so long as the possession of the crown is not in the right line. The hereditary rights of the subjects, though confirmed by conventions and parliaments, are now treated as of no value or force, and past services to the Crown and royal family are now looked upon as grounds of suspicion. A packed-up assembly, who call themselves a British Parliament, have, so far as in them lies, inhumanely murdered their own and our sovereign by promising a good sum of money as the reward of so execrable a crime. They have proscribed, by unaccountable and groundless impeachments and attainders, the worthy patriots of England for their honourable and successful endeavours to restore trade, plenty, and peace to these nations.

"They have broken in upon the sacred laws of both countries by which the liberty of our persons was secured, and they have empowered a foreign prince (who, notwithstanding his expectations of the crown for fifteen years, is still unacquainted with our manners, customs, and language) to make an absolute conquest (if not timely prevented) of the three kingdoms, by investing himself with an unlimited power not only of raising unnecessary forces at home, but also of calling in foreign troops, ready to promote his uncontrollable designs. Nor can we be ever hopeful of its being otherwise, in the way it is at present, for some generations to come. And the sad consequences of these unexampled proceedings have really been so fatal to great numbers of our kinsmen, friends, and fellow-subjects of both kingdoms, that they have been constrained to abandon their country, houses, wives, and children, to give themselves up prisoners, and perhaps victims, to be sacrificed to the pleasure of foreigners, and a few hot-headed men of a restless faction, whom they employ. Our troops abroad, notwithstanding their long and remarkable good services, have been treated, since the peace, with neglect and contempt, and particularly in Holland; and it is not now the officers' long service, merit, and blood they have lost, but money and favour, by which they can obtain justice in their preferments. So that it is evident the safety of His Majesty's person and independency of his kingdoms call loudly for immediate relief and defence.

"The consideration of these unhappy circumstances, with the due regard we have to common justice, the peace and quiet of us and our posterity, and our duty to His Majesty and his commands, are the powerful motives which have engaged us in our present undertaking, which we are firmly and heartily resolved to push to the utmost, and stand by one another to the last extremity, as the only solid and effectual means for putting an end to so dreadful a prospect as by our present situation we have before our eyes; and with faithful hearts true to our rightful king, our country, and our neighbours, we earnestly beseech and expect, as His Majesty commands, the assistance of all our true fellow-subjects to second our attempt, declaring hereby our sincere intentions that we will promote and concur in all lawful means for settling a lasting peace to these lands, under the auspicious government of our native-born rightful sovereign, the direction of our own domestic councils, and the protection of our native forces and troops. That we will in the same manner concur and endeavour to have our laws, liberties, and properties secured by the Parliaments of both kingdoms; that by the wisdom of such Parliaments we will endeavour to have such laws enacted as shall give absolute security to us and future ages for the Protestant religion against all efforts of arbitrary power, popery, and all its other enemies.

"Nor have we any reason to be distrustful of the goodness of God, the truth and purity of our holy religion, or the known excellency of His Majesty's judgment, as not to hope that, in due time, good examples and conversation with our learned divines will remove those prejudices, which we know his education in a Popish country has not riveted in his royal discerning mind; and we are sure, as justice is a virtue in all religions and professions, so the doing of it to him will not lessen his good opinion of ours. That as the King is willing to give his royal indemnity for all that is past, so he will cheerfully concur in passing general acts of oblivion, that our fellow-subjects who have been misled may have a fair opportunity of living with us in the same friendly manner that we design to live with them. That we will use our endeavours for redressing the bad usage of our troops abroad, and bringing the troops at home on the same footing and establishment of pay as those of England. That we will sincerely and heartily go into such measures as shall maintain effectually, and establish a right, firm, and lasting union betwixt His Majesty's ancient kingdom of Scotland and our good neighbours and fellow-subjects of the kingdom of England.

"The peace of these nations being thus settled and we freed from foreign dangers, we will use our endeavours to have the army reduced to the usual number of guards and garrisons; and will concur in such laws and methods as shall relieve us of the heavy taxes and debts now lying upon us, and at the same time, will support the public credit in all its parts. And we hereby faithfully promise and engage that every officer who joins with us in our king and country's cause shall not only enjoy the same post he now does, but shall be advanced and preferred according to his rank and station and the number of men he brings off with him to us. And each foot soldier so joining us shall have twenty shillings sterling, and each trooper or dragoon, who brings horse and accoutrements along with him, £12 sterling gratuity, besides their pay; and in general we shall concur with all our fellow-subjects in such measures as shall make us flourish at home, and be formidable abroad, under our rightful sovereign, and the peaceable harmony of our ancient fundamental constitution, undisturbed by a Pretender's interests and councils from abroad, or a restless faction at home. In so honourable, so good, and just a cause, we do not doubt of the assistance, direction, and blessing of Almighty God, who has so often succoured the royal family of Stuarts, and our country from sinking under oppression." [1]

Long before the raising of the standard at Braemar, the Government had fully appreciated the coming danger, and active measures of precaution were being taken. Parliament voted a reward of £100,000 for the capture of the Pretender. On July 16, the House of Commons voted an Address to the King, urging the necessity of active measures against those concerned in rebellious riots and disorders, and the King in his turn called upon the Parliament to make provision for the defence of the country. The Riot Act, still in force, was passed.

The whole available military force in the country amounted to some 8000 men. Parliament voted a large increase to the army, and the Government proceeded to raise thirteen regiments of dragoons and eight of foot. An Act was also passed empowering the King " to secure and detain such persons as His Majesty shall suspect of conspiring against his person and Government," which had the effect of suspending for six months the Habeas Corpus Act in England, and the corresponding " Act of 1701 " in Scotland. It was also enacted that, should any Crown vassal in Scotland become guilty of high treason, any sub-vassal holding of him should take his place as holding direct from the Crown, and that, on the other hand, should any sub-vassal be implicated in the rebellion, his estate should pass to his immediate superior.  Legislative provision was made for circumventing the well-known plan by which a landowner, who considered it likely that he might himself soon fall within the scope of the law of treason, could provide against a possible forfeiture by conveying his estate to a member of his family ; and the Crown lawyers in Scotland were empowered to call upon any suspected persons to appear and find security for their good conduct. This power was extensively exercised, apparently with the result of forcing a good many waverers to join the standard of rebellion.

In Scotland, active measures were taken spontaneously by the friends of the Hanover succession.  A body, called " The Association of Men of Quality and Substance," was formed at Edinburgh on August 1.  Their Bond of Association sets forth that the subscribers "do, conform to the laudable practice in former times of imminent danger, hereby mutually promise and solemnly engage and oblidge ourselves to stand by and assist one another to the utmost of our power in the support and defence of His Majesty King George, our only rightful sovereign, and of the Protestant succession, now happily established, against all open and secret enemies for the preservation and security of our holy religion, civil liberties, and most excellent constitution both in Church and State." The signatories then undertake to subscribe certain sums of money " for supporting and maintaining of such a

---

[1] An interesting collection of later Jacobite Proclamations is printed in Allardyce's *Historical Papers*, vol. i., pp. 177-194.

number of men to receive orders from His Majesty's Commander-in-Chief for the
time for so many days as the commissioners or managers aftermentioned shall find
the money subscribed for sufficient to maintain ;" and provision is made for the
election by the subscribers of "a competent number of managers . . .
for expending of the money according to the intent of these presents, and for giving
such necessary directions and orders as shall be proper."

At the same time was formed an Association of "those who were willing and
capable to fight in so good a cause, but not able to take the field at their own
charge." Its members bound themselves "that upon the first notice of the Pretender's
landing in any part of Britain, or upon the advice of any insurrection or appearance
of his friends and abettors at home in a hostile manner for the support and assistance
of the said Pretender, they shall assemble and meet together with their best horses
and furniture, whether for foot or horse service according to their abilities ; and to
the best of their power to comply with and obey such orders as they should receive
from the government for the supporting of His Majesty King George, his person
and government, etc."

Both these Associations received zealous support. In Edinburgh a body named
"The Associate Volunteers of Edinburgh" was formed, amounting to some 400 men,
and similar volunteer forces were raised at Glasgow, Dumfries, and in other parts
of the country. The Government, however, was somewhat doubtful as to the ad-
visability of encouraging the formation of armed bodies not subject to military law,
and all this volunteer zeal was somewhat coldly received. It was intimated that
"His Majesty, supposing that the measures the Government had taken for the
security and defence of this part of the nation would prove effectual for that end,
was not willing to put his loving subjects to any further trouble and expense."

The regular forces in Scotland at this time consisted of four reduced regiments
of foot and four regiments of dragoons, in all some 1800 men. These were concentrated at Stirling under the command of Major-General Wightman, an officer who
was to give proof of his capacities for Highland warfare in the affair of Glenshiel
four years later. Then, as always, Stirling was the key of the Highlands, and so
long as it remained in the hands of Government, the Jacobites in the north were
effectually separated from their friends in the south. The force under Wightman was
reinforced by two regiments from England, and the States of Holland were called
upon to send over the contingent of 6000 men with which they had undertaken to
support the British Government in the event of invasion or rebellion. The whole
of the forces in Scotland were placed under the command of the Duke of Argyll,[1]
who was not only a distinguished soldier and statesman, but himself a great Highland chief and the hereditary leader of the Whig cause in the Highlands. He left

---

[1] John, second Duke of Argyll, great-grandson of Montrose's antagonist.

London on September 9, reached Edinburgh on the 14th, and on the 17th arrived at Stirling and took over the command of the army. In response to his request, a battalion of the volunteers, which had been raised in Glasgow, marched to Stirling, and was attached to his command ; and measures were taken for protecting the Western Lowlands against the contingency of a Highland raid.

In the meantime, Mar had collected a considerable force and had begun his march to the south by Moulinearn and Logierait. Some 500 of the Atholl men joined him, under the Marquis of Tullibardine, and by the time he reached Dunkeld his army numbered about 2000. His first object was to seize Perth before it could be occupied by the Hanoverians. He accordingly sent forward Colonel John Hay, brother of Lord Kinnoul, with a detachment of 200 horse. Hay entered Perth on September 14, and there proclaimed King James. Mar himself, with the main body of the army reached Perth on the 28th. In a few days his force amounted to upwards of 5000 men.

The possession of Perth was all-important to the Jacobites. The town itself was a rich source of supply. It commanded some of the most fertile districts in Scotland ; it isolated the Hanoverians in the north ; it enabled the Jacobites to overawe a great part of the Lowlands, and it afforded excellent quarters to the men. There Mar settled down and applied himself to recruiting and raising money. A circular letter was issued requesting, or rather demanding, " loans " from all from whom it seemed likely that they could be extracted. Orders were issued for the collection of the land tax. Loans were demanded from Montrose and other burghs, and a series of proclamations and manifestoes were printed and distributed. Plenty of recruits kept coming in from the north—MacIntoshes, Mackenzies, and Gordons. By the middle of October the force amounted to some 12,000 men.

Mar remained at Perth for more than six weeks. At the end of September James Murray, who had been nominated by the Chevalier his Secretary of State for Scotland, arrived with assurances of speedy assistance from France, and of James's intention shortly to come in person to place himself at the head of his followers. A serious calamity, however, had just befallen the Jacobite cause abroad. Louis XIV. died on September 1, 1715. He had been a faithful and powerful friend to the Stuarts. The Regent Orleans did not continue his policy, but from the beginning cultivated the friendship of the British Government, which meant, of course, the discontinuance of all countenance to the claims of the exiled family. Their adherents could no longer look to France as a base of operations. It appears that they had succeeded in fitting out a considerable fleet at Havre, St. Malo, and other French ports, on board of which were a large quantity of military stores and over 1800 men.[1] These preparations were frustrated by the vigilance of Lord Stair, then British Ambassador at Paris, who

---

[1] Rae, p. 221.

represented to the Regent that to permit the sailing of these vessels would be a breach of the Treaty of Utrecht, and would be regarded by the British Government as an unfriendly act. Orders were accordingly given to the French naval authorities to seize the vessels if they attempted to sail.

The period of inactivity at Perth had the worst effect upon the Highland army. As had been so clearly shown in the campaigns of Montrose and Dundee, a force of Highlanders was only really formidable when kept constantly marching and fighting. Kept idle in camp or quarters, and occupied only in recruiting, raising money, and digging entrenchments, the clansmen soon became discontented and dispirited. The Master of Sinclair in his Memoirs tells us how the time passed. "Mar," he says, "after coming into Perth did nothing' all this while but write; and as if all had depended on his writing, nobody moved in any one thing; there was not a word spoke of fortifying the town, nor the least care taken for sending of powder to any place; we did not want gunsmiths, and yet none of them was employed in mending our old arms. Whoever spoke of those things, which I did often, was giving himself airs, for we lived very well, and as long as meat, drink, and monie was not wanting what was the need of anie more; most of us were going home everie day for our diversion, and to get a fresh supplie of the readie. In that we followed strictly the rule of the gospel, for we never thought of to-morrow. If it escaped any extravagant fellow to say that more troops were coming to join the Duke of Argyle from England or Ireland, he was lookt on as a visionare; or if any seemed to think that these few troops he had would fight, there was no doubt he was a coward, and despaired of our success, which I'm sure they could not have been so positive of in their circumstances but by believing no one would fight against them, which they said confidently; but so soon as men have nothing reasonable to trust to they seldom fail to please themselves with phantoms, and a drowning man catches hold of every straw."[1]

In the meantime the Jacobites in the south of Scotland and in the north of England had risen. Before we proceed to give an account of their operations, there are a few minor events of the war in Scotland which fall to be narrated.

So early as the 8th of September an attempt was made to capture Edinburgh Castle. The enterprise was designed by Lord Drummond, son of the so-called Duke of Perth, and, says Patten,[2] "there were no less than ninety choice men picked out for the enterprise, all gentlemen. They had corrupted one Ainesly, a sergeant, who was afterwards hanged for it, a corporal, and two centinels within the Castle. These were to be ready to assist at a certain place upon the wall near the Sally-port, where, having contrived a scaling-ladder made of ropes, and with pulleys, which being fastened to the top of the wall by the conspirators, the centinel was to draw

---

[1] Memoirs of the Insurrection in Scotland, p. 92.     [2] See p. 100, note.

## MAP TO ILLUSTRATE THE RISING OF 1715.

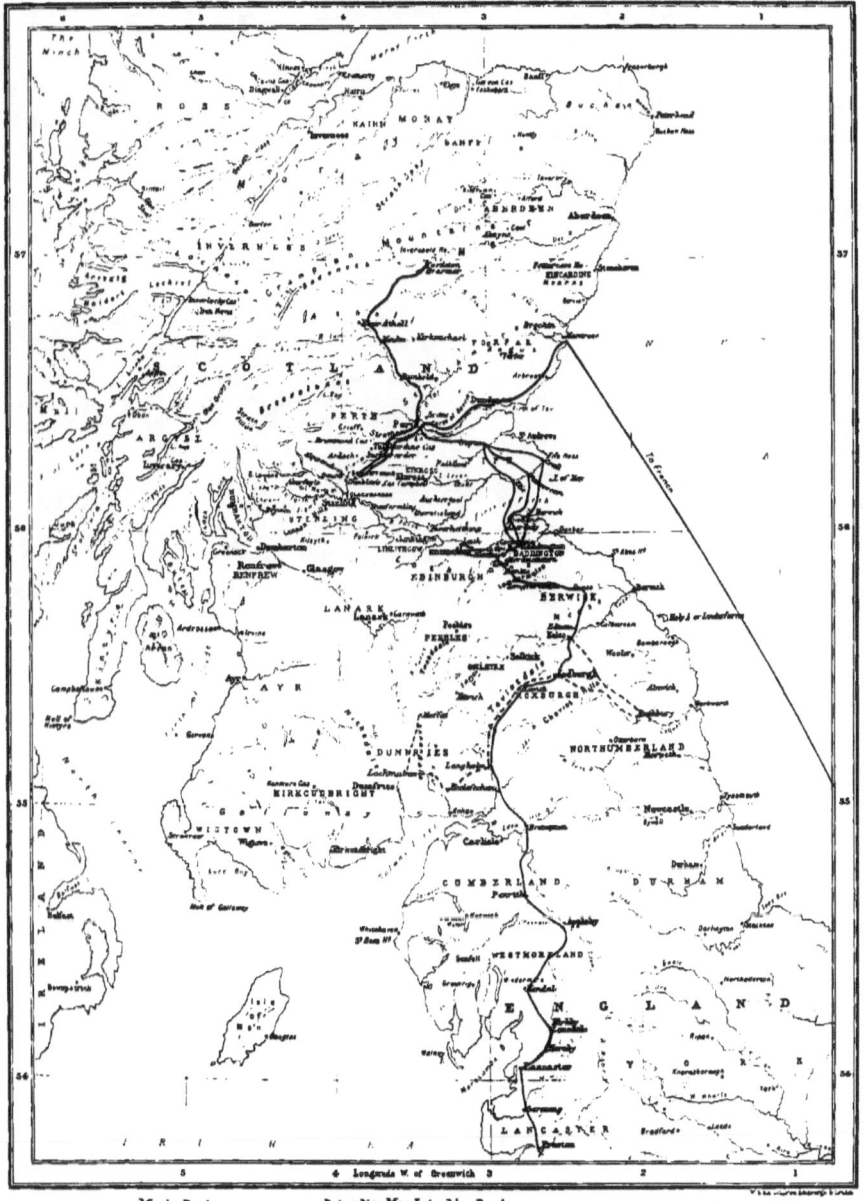

Mar's Route............————Brigadier MacIntosh's Route.........................————
Kenmure's Route.........————Route of the Combined Jacobite Forces into England.————

up with a small rope provided on purpose." A certain Mr Arthur, formerly an officer of the Scots Guards, was concerned in this conspiracy. He communicated the matter to his brother, Dr Arthur, a physician in Edinburgh. "This gentleman," says Rae, "having appeared very melancholy all that day before the attempt was to be made on the thought of the sudden revolution that was at hand, his lady importuned him till she got into the secret, and that evening about 10 o'clock sent a servant with an unsigned letter to My Lord Justice Clerk." The Lord Justice Clerk, Sir Adam Cockburn of Ormiston, at once communicated his intelligence to Colonel Stuart, the Commandant of the Castle. In consequence of this warning the sentries were visited at an earlier hour than usual on the night of the 8th. The treacherous sentinel, finding himself discovered, threw the ladder over the wall and fired upon the conspirators, who fled; the plot was frustrated and the Castle was saved.

A more successful enterprise was carried out by the Master of Sinclair, already mentioned as one of the chroniclers of the insurrection. A large quantity of arms, destined for the forces which were being embodied by the Earl of Sutherland in the north for King George, had been put on board ship at Leith. After sailing, the vessel was compelled by contrary winds to enter the harbour of Burntisland. News of this reached Perth, and it was resolved to make an attempt to seize the prize. Sinclair started for Burntisland at the head of 400 horse, each trooper having a foot soldier mounted behind him. The party reached Burntisland at midnight, took possession of the town, seized the boats in the harbour, and easily captured the vessel. The result of this raid was the capture of over 420 stand of arms.[1]

The Jacobite clans in the West Highlands also showed some activity. On September 17 a body of Macleans, Macdonalds, and Camerons made an ineffectual attempt to seize Fort William. In September the M'Gregors seized the boats on Loch Lomond and proceeded to plunder the lowland shores of the Loch. An expedition was organised against them, consisting of about 100 seamen from the ships of war then lying in the Clyde, supported by volunteers from Paisley, Dumbarton, and the neighbouring towns. Several man-of-war's boats were towed up the Leven by horses, and it was determined to attack the M'Gregors in their stronghold at Inversnaid. Rae gives a somewhat amusing account of how the expedition fared.

"At Night they arriv'd at Luss, where they were join'd by Sir Humphray Colquhoun of Luss, and James Grant of Pluscarden, his Son in Law, followed by 40 or 50 stately Fellows in their short Hose and belted Plaids, arm'd each of 'em with a well fix'd Gun on his Shoulder, a strong handsome Target, with a sharp pointed Steel of above half an Ell in length, screw'd into the Navel of it, on his

---

[1] See Sinclair's *Memoirs*, p. 97 *et seq.*

N

Left Arm; a sturdy Claymore by his Side, and a Pistol or two, with a Durk and Knife on his Belt. Here the whole Company rested all Night; and on the Morrow, being Thursday the 13th, they went on in their Expedition, and about Noon came to Innersnaat, the Place of Danger, where the Pasley Men and those of Dumbarton, and several of the other Companies, to the Number of 100 Men, with the greatest Intrepedity leapt on Shore, got up to the top of the Mountains and stood a considerable Time, beating their Drums all the while, but no Enemy appearing, they went in quest of their Boats, which the Rebels had seiz'd, and having casually lighted on some Ropes, Anchors, and Oars, hid among the Shrubs; at length they found the Boats drawn up a good way on the Land, which they hurled down to the Loch. Such of them as were not damag'd they carry'd off with them, and such as were they sunk or hewed in Pieces. That same Night they returned to Luss, and thence next Day to Dumbarton, from whence they had first set out, bringing along with them the whole Boats they found in their Way, on either side of the Loch, and in the Creeks of the Isles, and moor'd them under the Cannon of the Castle. During this Expedition, the Pinnaces discharging their Pateraroes, and the Men their small Arms, made such a Thundering Noise thro' the multiply'd rebounding Echoes of the vast Mountains on both sides of the Loch, that the M'Gregiours were cow'd and frighted away to the rest of the Rebels, who were encamp'd at Strathphillen, about 16 Miles from the Head of the Loch, where, being all join'd as above, they continued till the 18th of October; about which Time they were also joined by Stuart of Appin with 250 Men, Sir John M'Lean with 400, M'Dougal of Lorn with about 50, and a Part of Broadalbine's Men, in all making up, by the modestest Computation, 2400 Men."

This force marched to Inverary and threatened the Campbell stronghold, but, finding it strongly garrisoned under the Earl of Ilay, the Duke's brother, they withdrew without having effected anything, and ultimately dispersed.

We have now to glance briefly at the rising in the south. On October 11 a party of Jacobites under Lords Kenmure and Carnwath assembled near Lochmaben. On the following day they seized a quantity of arms intended for the use of the militia, which had been deposited in the house of Henderson of Bradeholm. They then marched to Moffat, and on Thursday, October 13, they entered Lochmaben and proclaimed James VIII. On the 14th they marched to Ecclefechan, on the 15th to Langholm, and on the 16th they reached Hawick. On Monday the 17th the party, which only numbered some 180, reached Jedburgh. Next day they marched into England, to Rothbury, where they were joined by the insurgent Jacobites from Northumberland under Lord Derwentwater and Mr Forster a force amounting to some 300 horsemen. The conjoined forces then marched to and occupied Kelso.

The occupation of Stirling by the troops of the Government, and the vigilance of the naval force which now patrolled the Firth of Forth, effectually separated the Jacobites in the south from the main body of the army encamped at Perth. Mar, however, determined to reinforce them with as large a force as possible. Preparations were quietly made for embarking 2500 men under Brigadier MacIntosh of Borlum in boats at Pittenweem, Crail, Elie, and the other small ports along the Fifeshire coast.

At the same time preparations were made at Burntisland as if for some expedition, in order to induce the Government vessels lying in the Firth to concentrate there. On the nights of the 12th and 13th of October the enterprise was carried out. The King's ships succeeded in capturing one boat of the flotilla and in turning back some others, but about 1600 men effected a landing at North Berwick, Aberlady, Gullane, and other places on the coast of East Lothian. As quickly as possible they concentrated at Haddington. Their object was to march southwards in order to join Kenmure's force, but the temptation of a raid on Edinburgh was too great. They were only seventeen miles from the capital, Argyll was at Stirling, thirty-six miles away, and they knew that they could count on many friends among the inhabitants. However, John Campbell, the Lord Provost, acted with the utmost promptitude and decision. He at once called out the City Guards, the trained bands, and the volunteers, told them off to their respective posts for the defence of the city, and sent an urgent express to Argyll at Stirling for a reinforcement of regular troops. Argyll instantly started with 300 dragoons, and 200 foot mounted on country horses, and reached Edinburgh just in time. The Jacobites were at Jock's Lodge when he entered the city. On finding that he was just too late, Brigadier MacIntosh gave up the project of attacking Edinburgh and marched to Leith, where he took possession of the citadel built by Cromwell, blocked the gates, planted the ramparts with cannon from the ships in the harbour, and awaited events.

On the morning of Saturday, October 15, the Duke of Argyll, with a force of regulars, militia, and volunteers, amounting in all to about 1100 men, marched down to Leith and summoned MacIntosh to surrender, declaring that if he were obliged to attack the citadel he would give no quarter. "He received," says Rae, "a resolute answer from a Highland laird called Kinackin, who told the Duke that as to surrendering they laughed at it, and as to bringing cannon and assaulting them, they were ready for him; that they would neither take nor give any quarter with him, and if he thought he was able to force them he might try his hand." Argyll had no guns, the Jacobites were well and strongly posted, and an attempt to carry the citadel by assault must have been attended with tremendous loss. He accordingly retired to Edinburgh to make preparations for a serious attack on the following day. It was obvious that the citadel could not be permanently held by the Jacobites. Accordingly that night about nine o'clock they abandoned it, and taking advantage of the low ebb of the tide, they marched off along the sands eastward in the direction of Musselburgh. About two in the morning they reached Seton House. Before departing they had reported their movements to Mar. The boat which carried their messenger across the Firth had a shot fired after her by the citadel, and so was taken by the Government cruisers for a friend, and allowed to pass untouched.

MacIntosh remained at Seton House for three days, and while there succeeded in obtaining large supplies of cattle, meal, and other provisions. On the 18th letters came from Mar with orders to continue the march towards England. Accordingly, on the morning of the 19th, the Highlanders left Seton. That night they arrived at Longformacus. Immediately after their departure Seton was occupied by a force of dragoons and militia under General Wightman. On the 20th MacIntosh and his men reached Duns. There they remained till the 22nd, when they resumed their march towards Kelso, which they reached on the same evening.

As we have seen, Kelso was by this time occupied by the Jacobite forces under Kenmure, Derwentwater, and Forster. On the approach of the Highlanders a party of horse marched out to meet them at Ednam Bridge "in Compliment to their Conduct and Bravery," and escorted them in triumph into the town.

The total Jacobite force at Kelso now amounted to 1400 foot and 600 horse. On the following day, Sunday October 23, the army attended Divine Service, and a sermon on the text "The right of the first-born is his" (Deuteronomy xxi. 17), was preached by the notorious Robert Patten, who acted as chaplain to the English insurgents, and afterwards turned king's evidence to save his own neck.[1] On Monday King James was proclaimed in the market-place with great ceremony.

The Scottish division of the insurgent army was divided into five troops of horse and six regiments of foot; the English insurgents forming five troops of horse. So long as they remained in Scotland the whole force was commanded by Lord Kenmure. They remained in Kelso to the 27th of October, a fatal delay, as it gave the Government troops in the north of England ample time to make their dispositions.

Much time was lost through the dissension and lack of discipline which throughout were the curse of all the Jacobite enterprises. There was much dissension as to whether the army should cross the Border. The Highlanders were exceedingly unwilling to do so; ultimately the majority yielded to the promise of sixpence a day of regular pay. Some 500 deserted and found their way home as best they could.

Lord Winton proposed that the army should march into the west of Scotland. It was also suggested that an attack should be made on General Carpenter, who was now in the immediate vicinity with a force not exceeding 1000 in number, fatigued by long marches, and consisting, to a large extent, of raw recruits. "But," as Patten says, "there was a fate attended all their councils, for they could never agree to any one thing that tended to their advantage." On October 27 they marched to Jedburgh; there they remained till the 29th, when it was at last definitely resolved to march into

---

[1] His *History of the Late Rebellion* (London 1717) is the main source of information as to the proceedings of the insurgents in England.

England. From Jedburgh they marched to Hawick, and from Hawick to Langholm. At Langholm a party was detached to attack Dumfries. Dumfries could have been easily captured, and its possession, as being the principal town in the south-west of Scotland, would have been of the greatest importance to the cause. However, the leaders of the English Jacobites strongly urged that the whole available force should be sent into England, and the party which was marching against Dumfries was recalled when it had reached Ecclefechan. On October 31 the army crossed the Border and encamped for the night at Brampton, having marched 100 miles in five days. As soon as they entered England Forster took over the command, holding a commission to that effect from Mar.

Penrith was reached on November 2. The *posse comitatus* of Cumberland had been called out by the sheriff, and was assembled near Penrith under Lord Lonsdale and Bishop Nicolson of Carlisle. It amounted to some 14.000 men, but these did not prove very formidable antagonists. "As soon," says Patten, "as a party, who they had sent out for discovery, had seen some of our men coming out of a Lane by the Side of a Wood, and draw up upon the Common or Moor in order, and then advance, and that they had carried an Account of this to their main Body, they broke up their Camp in the utmost Confusion, shifting everyone for themselves as well as they could, as is generally the case of an armed but undisciplined Multitude." None of these warriors received any hurt, except "one man that was shot through the arm." On November 3 the Jacobites reached Appleby, where they remained for two days. On the 5th they marched to Kendal, and on the 6th to Kirkby Lonsdale. On the 7th they entered Lancaster unopposed. In the course of their march they had proclaimed James VIII. in all the principal towns, and had collected the public revenue. Few recruits had joined them; on the other hand, they had suffered from some desertions. For example, Rae mentions that at Appleby "Mr Ainsley, who had joined 'em at Jedburgh, disliking the prospect of their affairs, deserted them with about 16 Tiviot-dale Gentlemen." At Lancaster they succeeded in seizing a quantity of arms which were in the Custom House, a considerable sum of public money, six pieces of cannon, and "some claret and a good quantity of brandy, which was all given to the High-landers to oblige them." Their spiritual wants were ministered to by the Reverend Mr Patten, "the parson of the place excusing himself." They were now in a Jacobite country, and many Lancashire gentlemen joined them, with their servants and friends. "It's true," says Patten, "they were most of them Papists, which made the Scotch Gentlemen and the Highlanders mighty uneasy, very much suspecting the Cause, for they expected all the High-Church Party to have joined them. Indeed," proceeds this estimable divine, "that Party who are never right hearty for the Cause till they are mellow, as they call it, over a bottle or two, began now to show us their blind side; and that it's their just character, that they do not care for venturing their Carcases any farther than the Tavern; there indeed, with their High-Church, and Ormond, they

would make men believe, who do not know them, that they would encounter the
greatest opposition in the World; but after having consulted their Pillows, and the
Fume a little evaporated, it is to be observed of them that they generally become
mighty Tame, and are apt to Look before they Leap, and, with the Snail, if you
touch their Houses, they hide their Heads, shrink back, and pull in their Horns. I
have heard Mr Forster say he was blustered into this Business by such People as
these, but that for the Time to come he would never again believe a drunken Tory."
Considering that this passage was written by as selfish and cowardly a rascal as ever
escaped the gallows, it is not without its humorous aspect.

On the 9th the Jacobite army marched out of Lancaster in pouring rain: on the
same night their horse reached Preston, and the foot on the following day. At Preston
they were in the very centre of English Jacobitism. They were cordially received by
the inhabitants, and were joined by many recruits. It was here, however, that their
final disaster awaited them.

Preston had been occupied by a small force of regular troops, commanded by Sir
Henry Haughton. On the approach of the Jacobites Haughton evacuated the town
and retired to Wigan. His retreat greatly encouraged the insurgents, and made them
imagine that the Government troops would not look them in the face.

They were soon to be undeceived. The troops in Cheshire were commanded by
Major-General Wills. The force under his command and the regiments quartered in
Shropshire, Worcestershire, and Staffordshire were ordered to concentrate at Warrington
on November 10. Wills himself reached Manchester on the 8th; there he heard that
Carpenter was on his way from Durham. On Friday, the 11th, Wills marched to
Wigan with four regiments of dragoons and Preston's foot, the old Cameronian regi-
ment. At Wigan he found the regiments of Pitt and Stanhope, and heard that the
insurgents were still at Preston. He decided to attack them on the following day.

Forster seems to have been extraordinarily ignorant of the movements of his
enemy. Patten says that he relied for his intelligence upon the Lancashire gentlemen.
He seems to have been very badly served, and to have known nothing of Wills's
approach until he was actually before the town.

Wills marched out of Wigan on the morning of Saturday, the 12th, and about
one o'clock arrived at the bridge across the Ribble, just outside Preston. To his
astonishment he found it undefended; Forster having ordered it to be abandoned. He
suspected some stratagem, and thought that probably an ambuscade awaited him in
the deep and narrow lane beyond the bridge. "On these suppositions," says Patten,
"he proceeded with caution, and caused the hedges and fields to be viewed and the
ways laid open for his cavalry to enter. But finding the hedges also clear, he concluded then the enemy was fled, and expected that they had abandoned the town and
all, and would endeavour by their long marches to return to Scotland, tho' he thought
it impossible for them to do it." He found, however, that the insurgents were deter-

mined to defend the town.   MacIntosh was the moving spirit in the defence.   Under
his direction barricades had been thrown up in the streets and mounted with the guns
which had been seized at Lancaster.   "The Earl of Derwentwater," says Patten,
"signally behav'd, having stripp'd into his waistcoat, and encouraged the men by
giving them money to cast up trenches, and animating them to a vigorous defence of
them."   There were four main barriers commanding the chief avenues to the town.
The principal barricade, which protected the approach from Wigan, was commanded
by Brigadier MacIntosh.   As soon as he had inspected the approaches to the town
Wills disposed his troops for the attack.   The main attack was made on MacIntosh
about two in the afternoon.   It was headed by Brigadier Honeywood, one of the
regiments under his command being Preston's foot.   The Government troops, who
had to advance up a narrow street flanked by houses which were filled with the
enemy's men, suffered terrible loss.   Parties, however, were detached to attack these
houses from the lanes behind them, and a number of them were successfully occupied.
Other houses close to the barricade were set on fire, and the insurgents were compelled
to retire further into the town.

The barricade on the Lancaster road was similarly attacked by Brigadier Dormer.
Fighting went on all the afternoon and all night, the troops gradually forcing their
way from house to house and from street to street.   Before daybreak not a few of
the recruits who had joined the Jacobite army made their escape in the direction of
Liverpool by the Fishergate.   This street had been barricaded, but had not been
attacked for want of available troops.

On Sunday the 13th, about mid-day, Carpenter arrived from the north with three
more regiments.   Although senior to Wills, he refused to take over the command
from him, saying that "he had begun the affair so well that he ought to have
the glory of finishing it."   At his suggestion, however, some alterations were made
in the disposition of the troops, and the effective investment of the town was
completed.

The Jacobites were now caught in a trap, and it was evident that the struggle
could only end in one way.   The leaders began to talk of surrender.   The Highlanders were furious when they heard of it.   They "were for sallying out upon the
King's force," says Patten, "and dying, as they called it, like men of honour with
their swords in their hands.   But they were overruled, and were not allowed to stir.
.   .   .   The common men were, one and all, against capitulating, and were terribly
enraged when they were told of it, declaring that they would die fighting, and that
when they could defend their posts no longer they would force their way out and
make a retreat.   .   .   Their madness was such that nothing could quiet them for
a great while.   .   .   .   Many exclaimed against Mr Forster, and had he appeared in
the street he would certainly have been cut to pieces.   But as he did not appear
publickly, yet he had been actually killed in his chamber by Mr Murray had not I

with my hand struck up the pistol with which he fired at him, so that the bullet
went through the wainscot into the wall of the room."

A concise account of the negotiations which took place on the afternoon of the
13th and on the following morning was given by General Wills in his evidence at
the trial of Lord Winton before the House of Lords. "About two o'clock," he
says, "Mr Forster sent out one Mr Oxborough, an Irish Man, offering to lay down
their Arms, and submit themselves, and hoped that I would recommend them to the
King for Mercy; which I refused, and told them I would not treat with Rebels, for
that they had killed several of the King's Subjects, and that they must expect to
undergo the same Fate; upon which he said, that as I was an Officer, and a Man
of Honour, he hoped I would shew Mercy to People who were willing to submit:
Upon which I told them, all I would do for them was, that if they laid down their
Arms, and submitted Prisoners at Discretion, I would prevent the Soldiers from cutting
them to Pieces, till I had further Orders; and that I would give them but one Hour
to consider of it, and sent him back again into the Town to acquaint Forster of it:
Before the Hour was expir'd they sent out Mr Dalzell, Brother to the Earl of Carnwath, and he wanted Terms for the Scotch. My Answer was, that I would not treat
with Rebels, nor give them any other Terms, than what I had before offered them:
Upon which it was desired, that I would grant further Time till Seven a Clock next
Day, to consult the best Method of delivering themselves up. I agreed to grant them
the Time desired, provided that they threw up no new Intrenchments in the Streets,
nor suffer'd any of their People to escape; and that they sent out the Chief of the
English and Scotch, as Hostages for the Performance; and I sent in Colonel Cotten
to bring them out, who brought out the Earl of Derwentwater and Mr MacIntosh.
The next Day, about Seven a Clock, Mr Forster sent out to let me know that they
were willing to give themselves up Prisoners at Discretion, as I had demanded. Mr
MacIntosh being by when the Message was brought, said he could not answer that
the Scotch would surrender in that Manner; for that the Scotch were People of
desperate Fortunes; and that he had been a Soldier himself, and knew what it was
to be a Prisoner at Discretion: Upon which I said, Go back to your People again,
and I will attack the Town; and the Consequence will be, I will not spare one Man
of you. MacIntosh went back, but came running out immediately again, and said that
the Lord Kenmure and the rest of the Noblemen, with his Brother, would surrender
in like Manner with the English."[1]

The troops entered the town in two bodies, meeting in the market-place. The
Jacobite gentlemen and officers were placed under a guard in the inns, and the other
prisoners were confined in the church. The Government troops had lost 146 men killed
and wounded. Of the insurgents, who, during the attack, had been well under cover,

[1] *A Faithful Register of the Late Rebellion,* p. 162 *et seq.*

there were seventeen killed and twenty-five wounded. As great numbers of the insurgents had succeeded in making their escape, the prisoners only amounted to 1497, including Forster, and Lords Derwentwater, Widdrington, Nithsdale, Winton, Kenmure and Nairn. Among the prisoners were several officers who had held commissions in the army. These were tried by court-martial at Preston, and on December 2 four of them were shot. Most of the ordinary prisoners were confined in the castles of Lancaster, Chester, and Liverpool. The noblemen and most of the gentlemen were taken up to London. Their treatment on their arrival there reflects little credit on the authorities. At Highgate they were received by a detachment of the Guards under General Tatton. Here, says Rae, "everyone of 'em had his arms ty'd with a cord coming cross his Back ; and being thus pinion'd, they were not allow'd to hold the reins of the Bridle; but each of 'em had a foot Soldier leading his Horse : And being rang'd into four Divisions, according to the four different Prisons to which they were allotted, and each Division placed between a Party of the Horse Grenadiers and a Platoon of the Foot ; In this Manner General Tatton set out from Highgate about Noon, and proceeded to London thro' innumerable Crowds of Spectators, who all of 'em express'd the utmost Detestation of their rebellious Attempt, by upbraiding them with their Crime, shouting them along in this disgraceful Triumph, and incessantly crying out, King George for ever; no Warming-Pan Bastard : the Mobs in the meantime marched before them beating on a Warming-Pan, while the General's Drums beat a Triumphant March. After this the Noblemen and three or four others were sent to the Tower; Mr Forster, MacIntosh, and about Seventy more, to Newgate, Sixty to the Marshalsea, and Seventy Two to the Fleet."

The 13th of November was a fatal day for the Jacobite cause. The notorious Simon Fraser, afterwards Lord Lovat, who had fled from justice after the atrocious crimes of his youth, had returned to the Highlands and was making a bid for the favour of the Government. He put himself at the head of 300 Frasers, and recalled from the Jacobite army the remainder of his clan, who had joined Mar at Perth. In conjunction with Duncan Forbes of Culloden and Hugh Rose of Kilravock, he planned an attack on Inverness. The available force amounted to about 1300 men. The small Jacobite garrison, however, did not wait to be attacked, but on the night of November 13 evacuated the town and escaped across the Moray Firth. The key of the northern Highlands was again in the hands of the Government.

On the same day the battle of Sheriffmuir was fought.

Mar had remained at Perth since September awaiting events. Recruits had been coming in from the north, Lord Seaforth with his Mackenzies, also Macraes, Chisholms and others. By the beginning of November the force amounted to some 12,000 men, and a movement to the south was determined on.[1] On the 9th a council of war

---

[1] According to Rae, Mar, when he advanced on Dunblane, had "about 10,400 effective men."

O

was held. It was decided that the camp should be struck, and that the army should march to Dunblane. There 3000 men were to be detached "to amuse the King's army at Stirling" by attacking Stirling Bridge and the neighbouring fords. While Argyll thus had his hands full. the main body of the Jacobites was to cross the Forth further up, descend on the Lowlands, and follow MacIntosh into England.

On November 10 Mar marched out of Perth, leaving a garrison, under the command of Colonel Balfour, to hold the town. He reached Auchterarder, nine miles distant, on the same night, and there was joined by General Gordon. On the 11th he "rested . . . to settle the order of battle as well as the order of marching." The Master of Sinclair gives a very vivid picture of the incapacity of the leaders and the lack of discipline of the army. "We marched," he says, "the blind leading the blind, not knowing whither we were going or what we were going to do." Of Mar, he says that "a name and noise was all he sought." On the moor of Auchterarder the army was reviewed. In this review, says Sinclair, "there were squabbles about the posts of our squadrons, and we were never so constant in anything as our being disorderly." [1]

On the morning of Saturday the 12th, General Gordon and Brigadier Ogilvie were ordered to advance and occupy Dunblane. The main body of the army was to follow under General Hamilton, Mar himself, in the meantime, having gone to Drummond Castle to meet Lord Breadalbane. Hamilton had reached Ardoch, when an orderly arrived from Gordon with the news that his advanced guard had come into touch with the enemy. An express was sent off to Mar, who returned with all speed. Gordon was ordered to halt till the main body came up to him. They joined him at Kinbuck, and there the army lay under arms all night. The Master of Sinclair comments with characteristic vigour on the singular lack of military knowledge with which the ground of their bivouac was selected. "I can take it upon me to defy the most ingenious engineer after a month's thinking to contrive a place so fit for the destruction of men, without being in the least capable to help themselves. God knows, had we been attacked by any three regiments of foot posted in the high grounds about they had cut us to pieces." [2]

Argyll had good spies in Perth, and received immediate information of his enemy's intentions. He determined not to wait to be attacked. He ordered the troops at Edinburgh, Glasgow, Kilsyth and Falkirk to join him at Stirling with all possible speed, and to be in readiness to march on the night of the 11th. On the morning of the 12th he crossed the Forth at the head of some 3000 regular troops, consisting of five regiments of dragoons (Portmore's, Evans's, Stair's, Kerr's, and Carpenter's, each 180 strong), and eight regiments of foot (Forfar's, Winton's, Shannon's, Morison's, Montague's, Clayton's, Orrery's, and Edgerton's).

[1] *Memoirs*, p. 203.          [2] *Memoirs*, p. 208, quoted by Hill Burton.

The Glasgow volunteer battalion, 500 strong, were still at Stirling, and were eager to march with the regulars; but, much to their disgust, were left to garrison Stirling, along with the Stirling militia, which, says Rae, "they did with great care and exactness."

On the evening of the 12th, Argyll reached Dunblane, and encamped that night on a rising ground to the east of the town. Next morning he and a party of his officers reconnoitred the Jacobites' position. Mar, as usual, was undecided, and fell back upon his favourite expedient of a council of war. Some of his followers wished to avoid a battle and return to Perth till the spring; but the clansmen at last saw their enemy before them, and were eager to fight. So it was determined to attack Argyll. Argyll drew up his force on the Sheriffmuir in two lines, with three squadrons of dragoons on the right and left of the front line, and six battalions of foot in the centre. The second line was composed of two battalions of foot in the centre, with one squadron of dragoons on either flank, and one squadron was held in reserve behind each wing. The Duke himself commanded on the right, Wightman in the centre, and General Witham on the left. Owing to the nature of the ground, it was impossible for either army to see the whole of the other; the result was that, when the opposing forces came into contact, they were not opposite to each other. Each was out-flanked on the left. It was intended that the Jacobite force should attack in four regularly-formed columns; but when the attack was made, it was just the old disorderly Highland charge. Mar's right wing was composed of the Macdonalds, Macleans, and the Breadalbane men. When the order to attack was received, it is recorded that Sir John Maclean placed himself at the head of his clan and addressed them in these words: "Gentlemen, this is the day we have long wished to see; yonder stands MacCallum More for King George, here stands Maclean for King James. God bless Maclean and King James! Charge, gentlemen." The rush of the clansmen was scarcely checked by the heavy fire with which they were received, and which mortally wounded the young chief of Clanranald. Witham's line was broken to pieces, and forced back on Dunblane, with great slaughter. He did not check his retreat until he had nearly reached Stirling Bridge.

On Argyll's right the fortune of war went otherwise. The left wing of the Jacobites, composed chiefly of Camerons and Stewarts, advanced with great determination. But the regular troops held their ground, and the assailants were, as they advanced, charged in flank by a body of cavalry, under Colonel Cathcart, and were put to flight. Argyll gave them no time to rally, but at once advanced in pursuit. The fugitives immensely outnumbered their pursuers, but Argyll succeeded in keeping them on the run for over two miles, until the river Allan was reached. Mar's right wing did not pursue their beaten opponents very far, but re-formed on an eminence called the Stony Hill of Kippendavie, where, says Rae, "they stood without attempting anything with their swords drawn for near four hours' space."

Here they were found by Argyll when he returned from the pursuit. Argyll expected to be attacked by them, and formed his men accordingly. But "after a while they drew off their rear ranks towards the right, and began to disperse." The Duke, whose troops were by this time dead beat, had no desire to attack them, and accordingly retired into Dunblane. The fugitives of the left wing were, so far as possible, collected there, and there the army lay on their arms all night. The insurgents in the meantime had drawn off towards Auchterarder.

On the following day Argyll returned to Stirling, and two days later Mar re-entered Perth. The losses of the Government troops amounted to 290 officers and men killed, 187 wounded, and 133 taken prisoners—610 in all. Those of the insurgents are estimated at about 800 killed and wounded, and some eighty or ninety prisoners, including Viscount Strathallan and a number of other gentlemen of rank.[1]

Both sides claimed the victory. The day after the battle Colonel Balfour distributed at Perth "An Account of the great and signal Victory obtained over the Duke of Argyll by His Majesty's forces commanded by the Duke of Mar;" and Mar on his return to Perth caused thanksgiving sermons to be preached and a *Te Deum* to be sung. The substantial fruits of victory, however, remained with Argyll. He remained in possession of the field of battle, and had captured fourteen of the Jacobites' colours, six of their guns, and part of their baggage. What was much more important, he had effectively put a stop to Mar's project of marching to the south. For all practical purposes, the back of the rebellion was broken when Mar returned to Perth.

The doubtful issue of the contest is celebrated in one of the most familiar of Scots ballads—

> " There's some say that we wan,
>   Some say that they wan,
>   Some say that nane wan at a', man ;
>   But ae thing I'm sure,
>   That at Sheriffmuir
>   A battle there was which I saw, man ;
>   And we ran, and they ran,
>   And they ran, and we ran,
>   And we ran, and they ran awa', man."

Towards the end of November it appears that Mar approached Argyll with the object of obtaining terms of surrender, but the negotiations came to nothing. Every day now strengthened the hands of the Government and weakened those of the insurgents. Early in November the Dutch auxiliaries had landed in England, and had

---

[1] A nominal list is given by Rae, p. 309.

at once been ordered north. Two of the regiments which had been engaged at Preston were sent to Glasgow, and a train of artillery was shipped at the Tower under orders for Scotland. On the other hand, many of the Highlanders were quietly dispersing, and no news came of the supplies or reinforcements from abroad which the Jacobites hoped for.

The prospects of the Stuart cause were thus darkening down, when news came that James himself had landed in Scotland. He arrived at Peterhead in a French ship on December 22, attended by a retinue of six gentlemen only. News of his landing reached Perth on the 26th, and Mar, accompanied by the Earl Marischal and a number of the Jacobite leaders, set out to meet him. James reached Aberdeen on the 24th and lodged that night at Fetteresso. There he stayed till the 27th, when he was joined by Mar and his companions.

The Prince was detained at Fetteresso for a few days by an attack of ague. There he received the homage of various adherents, and loyal addresses of welcome from the Episcopal clergy of the diocese of Aberdeen and the Jacobite magistrates of Aberdeen. On Monday, January 2, 1716, he resumed his journey by Brechin, Kinnaird, and Glamis. On the 6th he entered Dundee; on Monday the 9th he made his public entry into Perth and reviewed the troops. On the same night he took up his quarters at Scone.

Whatever James's virtues were, they were not those of the successful leader of a desperate insurrection. Sinclair speaks of him as "entirely a stranger to his own affairs, as much as if he had dropt out of another world or from the clouds." Lethargic in mind and body, reserved and melancholy in temperament, he had none of the cheery courage and infectious good-humour which endeared Prince Charlie to his followers. "If he was disappointed in us," says one of them, "we were tenfold more so in him. We saw nothing in him that looked like spirit. He never appeared with cheerfulness and vigour to animate us. Our men began to despise him; some asked if he could speak. His countenance looked extremely heavy. He cared not to come abroad among us soldiers, or to see us handle our arms or do our exercise. Some said the circumstances he found us in dejected him; I am sure the figure he made dejected us; and had he sent us but 5000 men of good troops, and never himself come among us, we had done other things than we have now done."[1] While James remained at Scone he was surrounded by royal state; all the etiquette of a Court was maintained, and various proclamations were solemnly issued in his name. All able-bodied men were called to his standard. A meeting of the Estates was summoned. His coronation was appointed to take place on January 23. However, when that date arrived he was otherwise occupied.

---

[1] *A True Account of the Proceedings at Perth.* By a Rebel. London, 1716. (Attributed to the Master of Sinclair.)

Argyll's reinforcements were arriving from the south, and it was evident that he would soon advance against Perth. It was now the depth of an unusually hard winter; the ground was deeply covered with snow, and the roads were almost impassable. It was decided to throw a further obstacle in the way of Argyll's advance by destroying the villages between Stirling and Perth, so as to deprive the advancing troops of shelter and supplies. An order to this effect under James's sign manual was issued at Scone on January 17. It was carried out by parties of Highlanders. Between the 24th and the 29th Auchterarder, Blackford, Dunning, Muthill, Crieff, and Dalreoch were burnt. An account of the burning of the villages was written at the time by an inhabitant of Auchterarder.[1] He gives a terrible description of the sufferings of the unfortunate people, who were turned out into the bitter winter weather without food or shelter. "It would have pierced a heart in which there remained the very least spark of humanity," he says, "to have heard the mournfull screeches and frightfull cryes of poor women while rocking their infants in cradles upon the snow in the open fields, and looking on their houses, the sanctuaries appointed by God for their protection from the injury of such a season, and their corns, the provision and means of their subsistence, crumbling in a moment into ashes." James, to do him justice, seems to have deeply regretted the necessity of this step. On January 26 he issued a declaration inviting those whose property had been destroyed to lodge claims with a view to compensation, and when he embarked at Montrose he left behind him a letter to the Duke of Argyll with a sum of money for the benefit of the sufferers. Neither letter nor money seemed to have reached their destination.

Argyll's Dutch and English reinforcements reached him before the end of the year, and increased his force to some 9000 men. The artillery, which was expected by sea, was detained at the mouth of the Thames by bad weather. Argyll did not wait for it, but collected from Berwick and from Edinburgh Castle guns enough to make an efficient siege train.

On January 21 Colonel Guest with 200 dragoons was detached from Stirling to reconnoitre the roads leading to Perth, which were deeply covered with snow. On the 24th Argyll himself examined the country as far as Auchterarder. By the 26th the guns from Berwick and most of those from Edinburgh had arrived. Two days were spent in making and repairing gun carriages, and completing other details of equipment. The artillery sent from London reached Leith on the 28th, but Colonel Borgard, the officer in command, hearing that Argyll was already provided with a sufficient train for his expedition, left his guns and stores on board, and with his men marched with all speed to Stirling just in time to join the expedition. All was now ready for the advance. A day's thaw followed by a heavy fall of fresh

---

[1] Printed in the Miscellany of the Maitland Club, vol. iii.

snow had rendered the roads more difficult than ever. But Argyll was determined to proceed at all costs, and accordingly, on Sunday, January 29, he marched out of Stirling and reached Dunblane. Parties were detached to dislodge the Jacobites from Braco Castle, Tullibardine, and the other positions occupied by them. On the 30th the army advanced to Auchterarder, where they bivouacked for the night in the snow.

News of Argyll's imminent advance had reached Perth on the 28th. The general feeling in the Jacobite camp was that Perth should be defended. Preparations were made to resist an attack; the Highlanders to a man were eager for battle. But the leaders had determined that the cause was lost, and that the only thing now to be done was to effect a retreat with the least possible loss. On January 31, about 10 o'clock in the forenoon, the insurgent army marched out of Perth, leaving their guns behind them, crossed the Tay upon the ice, and took the road towards Dundee. On the same day they were followed by James and Mar, the former, Rae tells us, "followed his flying adherents with tears in his eyes, complaining that instead of bringing him to a crown they had brought him to his grave."

On the same day Argyll reached Tullibardine. There he heard of the evacuation of Perth. He at once ordered a detachment of 400 horse and 1000 foot to press on and occupy the town. He himself and General Cadogan rode on with the cavalry and entered Perth about one in the morning of February 1. The foot reached Perth about ten in the following forenoon, and the remainder of the army arrived that evening.

The retreating Jacobites reached Montrose on February 3. On the following day orders were issued to such of the clans as remained together to be ready to march in the evening towards Aberdeen. As the hour appointed for the march approached, James's horses were brought round and his guard was mounted as usual, but he did not appear. He had slipped out on foot and gone to Mar's lodgings. He and Mar reached the shore by a side street. There a boat awaited them, and they went on board a French ship, the *Maria Theresa* of St. Malo, which was ready for them in the harbour. A quarter of an hour afterwards they were joined by about a dozen more of the leaders. The ship hoisted sail and put to sea, and a week later landed them on the French coast near Calais.

The army, thus left to itself, melted rapidly away. The Highlanders scattered in all directions towards their native glens. When the army, now commanded by General Gordon, reached Aberdeen two days later, it amounted to only about 1000 men. Most of the leaders succeeded in effecting their escape by sea either to France or Sweden; the remainder of the men dispersed. Few prisoners were taken; indeed, Argyll does not seem to have been very anxious to make prisoners. He occupied Aberdeen on the 8th. Parties were detached to occupy various houses throughout the Highlands. A few sparks of rebellion smouldered on in the Hebrides, but they were stamped out without difficulty. Argyll's army was distributed among the various

Scottish garrisons. The Duke himself returned to Edinburgh on February 27, and a few days later set out for London. The insurrection was over.

Few prosecutions for rebellion took place in Scotland, the general feeling of the people as well as of the Crown lawyers themselves being adverse to severity. A large number of the prisoners taken at Preston were tried by Commission of Oyer and Terminer at Liverpool, convicted and executed. Further trials and executions took place in London. Many Scots prisoners were removed for trial to Carlisle, a proceeding which excited great indignation in Scotland, being justly regarded as an invasion of the judicial independence of the country. The peers implicated—Nithsdale, Winton, Carnwath, Kenmure, Nairn, Derwentwater, and Widdrington—were impeached before the House of Lords for high treason, and all sentenced to death in the usual horrible terms.[1] Nithsdale escaped from the Tower through his wife's heroism; Winton by his own ingenuity; Kenmure and Derwentwater went to the block. The lives of Carnwath, Nairn, and Widdrington were saved by falling under the general Act of Indemnity passed in 1717, which brought the vengeance of the Government to an end.

---

[1] For a detailed account of these trials see *A Faithful Register of the Late Rebellion.* London, 1718.

# CHAPTER IV.

## GLENSHIEL, 1719.[1]

FOUR years later another attempt was made on behalf of the fallen dynasty. It was more complete and formidable in its preparations than either the attempt of 1715 or that of 1745; but, as it happened, it turned out so complete a failure that it has been almost ignored by most historians.

As has been said, the death of Louis XIV. put an end to the Jacobites' hopes of help from France. After the '15 the Chevalier was compelled to leave Bar-le-Duc, in Lorraine, where he had resided since the Peace of Utrecht. He went first to Avignon, then he crossed the Alps and settled down in the Papal dominions. where he spent the rest of his life. At the same time his French pension of 50,000 crowns was stopped by the Regent.

It was to Sweden that the Jacobites next turned for support. Charles XII. had long projected an invasion of Great Britain, and cordially welcomed them as allies. Baron Gortz, his able and unprincipled Minister, carried on an active correspondence with their leaders, and had projected a descent on Scotland by 12,000 Swedish troops, to be headed by Charles in person, in co-operation with a general Jacobite rising. The scheme, however, proved abortive. The British Government got wind of it; Gyllenborg, the Swedish Minister in London, was arrested, his papers were seized, and the whole project was made public.

In the autumn of 1718 a new chapter in the history of Jacobitism was opened by an offer of assistance from Philip V. of Spain, or rather from his famous Minister, Cardinal Alberoni. During the years 1717 and 1718 the relations between England and Spain had been growing more and more hostile. The military operations of the Spaniards against the Imperial territory in Italy were regarded by the British Government as a breach of the Treaty of Utrecht. Diplomatic remonstrances had proved fruitless, and on August 11 the British squadron in the Mediterranean, under Sir George Byng, attacked the Spanish fleet off Cape Passaro and almost destroyed it. The Spanish ambassador was at once recalled from London; British ships were seized in Spanish ports; British consuls were ordered to leave Spanish territory; and Alberoni

---

[1] I am indebted to the courtesy of the Council of the Scottish History Society for permission to incorporate in this chapter a portion of the Introduction to *The Jacobite Attempt of 1719*, edited by me for the Society in 1895.—ED.

P

determined to strike the British Government in what was believed to be its weakest point by an invasion on behalf of the exiled Stuarts.

The Duke of Ormonde, who had been Captain-General of the British army, and who had fled from impeachment after the accession of George I., and was now openly in the service of the Chevalier, was at this time resident in Paris. Alberoni sent for him to Madrid, and the result of their conferences there was that the Cardinal decided to send an expedition against England, consisting of 5000 men—4000 foot and 1000 troopers with 300 horses, and an ample supply of money, arms, and ammunition for the English Jacobites. Ormonde himself was to command the expedition. He was to land in the west of England, the stronghold of Jacobitism, where it was expected that there would be no difficulty in raising a great army in support of the Stuart cause, and attempt an attack on London. At the same time the young Earl Marischal,[1] who had been out in the '15, and was now in exile at Paris, was to land in the West Highlands and raise the Jacobite clans.

The co-operation of Sweden was also hoped for; but all prospect of this was put an end to by the death of Charles XII., on December 11, 1718, in the trenches before Frederickshall, in Norway. In the meantime James himself was invited to Spain. He left Rome in disguise, and, after a perilous voyage, landed at Rosas, in Catalonia, on March 9, 1719 (N.S.). He proceeded to Madrid, and there was received with royal honours.

The British Government had ample warning of the danger, and prompt measures were taken to meet it. The House of Commons voted the necessary funds; the troops in the west of England were reinforced; and a powerful fleet was fitted out to cruise in the Channel. As the event happened, these precautions were needless. The Spanish fleet put to sea from Cadiz on March 7. On the 29th, near Cape Finisterre, it encountered a terrible storm, which lasted for forty-eight hours. The fleet was scattered to the four winds; horses, guns, stores, and arms had to be thrown overboard. All the ships were more or less crippled, and had to make their way back to Spanish ports as best they could. The project of invading England had to be given up.

The expedition against Scotland, however, was more fortunate. The Earl Marischal sailed from Passage on March 8. Alberoni had given him two frigates and 2000 muskets, with a supply of money and ammunition, and a body of 307 Spanish regular troops to form a nucleus for the army of Highlanders who were expected to flock to James's standard. He also carried letters from Ormonde to a number of the Highland chiefs. James Keith, the Earl's brother, afterwards the famous Marshal Keith, went to France to warn the Jacobite exiles there of what was afoot. He was joined by Clanranald, Lochiel, Seaforth, Tullibardine, Campbell of Glendaruel, and a number of other exiles of the '15. On March 19 they sailed from Havre; they reached the

---

[1] George Keith, tenth and last Earl Marischal.

Lewis on March 24 (O.S.), and found that the Earl Marischal had arrived before them, and that his two frigates were at anchor in the harbour of Stornoway.

Intimation of the intended invasion from Spain had been sent to the leaders of the Jacobite party in the Lowlands, but they had determined that no movement should be made until they were sure that Ormonde had landed. On hearing of the Earl Marischal's arrival, Lockhart of Carnwath sent him a memorial expressing his views as to what ought to be done. The main point emphasised in the memorial is the universal hatred with which the Union was regarded in Scotland, and the importance of making its repeal a chief article of the Jacobite policy. It does not appear that the document ever reached its destination. A catastrophe was very nearly caused by an "unknown fellow" who came to Mr Milnes, tutor to young Macdonald of Glengarry, representing that he was a servant of Lochiel's, that Ormonde's fleet had arrived, and that he had been sent ashore to warn his master's friends to be ready to take up arms. In consequence of this news, which was confirmed by a letter from Lord Stormont, then at his house in Annandale, to the effect that Ormonde's fleet had been seen off the coast, Lords Nairn and Dalhousie prepared to take the field. Lockhart, however, was satisfied that the messenger was either a common swindler or a Government spy, and succeeded in preventing Nairn and Dalhousie from committing themselves. "As for my Lord Stormont's information," says he, "I gave it the less credit when I perceived his Lordship's letter was dated at one in the morning, about which time I knew he was apt to credit any news that pleased him." [1]

Tullibardine, who held a commission as a Lieutenant-General in James's service, took over the command of the troops at Stornoway, the Earl Marischal retaining that of the ships, which had been expressly committed to him by Alberoni. As usual there was much discussion and difference of opinion as to what ought to be done. Ultimately it was decided to cross to the mainland, and on April 13 a landing was effected on the shores of Loch Alsh. On the following day Lord George Murray, Tullibardine's brother, arrived from France. The Jacobite chiefs in the Highlands had been communicated with, and were ready to rise as soon as there was any certain news of the coming of Ormonde's expedition. The Earl Marischal and Brigadier Campbell of Ormidale proposed marching straight to Inverness with the Spaniards and 500 men whom Seaforth undertook to raise, but Tullibardine and Glendaruel insisted on awaiting events.

Several days passed, and there came no news of Ormonde. Tullibardine was with difficulty dissuaded from re-embarking and returning to Spain. This made Marischal resolve to burn his boats. He determined to send the two frigates back to Spain. Tullibardine tried to detain them, but they obeyed Marischal's orders and put to sea, just in time, for within a week after their departure there arrived on the coast a British squadron consisting of five ships: the *Worcester*, 50 guns, *Assistance*, 50,

[1] *Lockhart Papers*, vol. ii, pp. 17-23.

*Dartmouth*, 50, *Enterprise*, 40, and *Flamborough*, 24, under the command of Captain Boyle. The *Assistance* and the *Dartmouth* sailed round the north of Skye and anchored in Loch Kishorn. Boyle with the *Worcester*, *Enterprise*, and *Flamborough* came through Kyle Rhea into Loch Alsh.

The Jacobites had fixed their headquarters at Eilean Donan Castle, the ancient stronghold of the Mackenzies. The castle, now a picturesque ivy-covered ruin, is situated on a little island close to the shore, opposite the village of Dornie, at the point where Loch Alsh branches into Loch Duich and Loch Long. It consists of an ancient and massive keep some fifty feet square, surrounded by court-yards and out-buildings. Here most of the ammunition and provisions of the expedition were stored under the guard of a garrison of forty-five Spaniards, the main body of the troops being encamped on the mainland close to the shore.

On May 10, Boyle with his three ships came up the Loch to Eilean Donan, and sent an officer with a flag of truce to demand the surrender of the Castle. The boat was fired upon and not permitted to land. At eight o'clock in the evening the ships opened fire upon the Castle. The old stone fortress, impregnable in Highland warfare, could not be held under artillery fire, and when a storming party of two boats' crews landed, they met with little resistance. The Spanish garrison were taken prisoners, and afterwards sent round to Leith in the *Flamborough*, and 343 barrels of powder and 52 barrels of musket bullets were captured. The buildings in which the provisions had been stored for the use of the Jacobite camp were set on fire and the Castle was blown up. The *Flamborough* went up Loch Duich in search of another magazine which had been formed near the head of the loch, which on her approach was blown up by the Highlanders.

The invaders were now in a sorry plight. Their retreat by sea was cut off. The coast was vigilantly patrolled by the boats of the British squadron. It was impossible even to cross to Skye. They had lost nearly the whole of their ammunition and provisions, and were in one of the wildest and most desolate parts of Britain, with no base of operations from which it was possible to draw any further supplies. The Government troops in Scotland were being rapidly reinforced from the South. Tullibardine now determined to do what he ought to have done at first, namely, to endeavour to raise a force from among the clans. By this time the fatal news of the dispersal of the Cadiz fleet had reached the Highlands, and naturally recruits were not very plentiful. "Not above a thousand men appeared," says Marshal Keith in his *Memoirs*, "and even those seemed not very fond of the enterprise." On June 5 Lochiel came in with 150 men; on the 7th Seaforth brought in about 500 of his men, and on the 8th arrived a son of Rob Roy's with some 80 more recruits.

In the meantime the garrison of Inverness had been largely reinforced, and on June 5 Major-General Wightman marched from Inverness with a force of about 850 infantry, besides 120 dragoons and some 130 Highlanders, and a battery of four cohorn mortars. He marched to the head of Loch Ness, where he halted for a day, and thence over by Glenmoriston towards Kintail.

It was decided to await Wightman's attack in Glenshiel, the grand and desolate glen which runs inland in a south-easterly direction from the head of Loch Duich, skirting the vast southern slopes of Scour Ouran. The position selected for defence was at the place where the present road crosses the river Shiel by a stone bridge, some five miles above Invershiel.[1] Here a shoulder of the mountain juts into the glen on its northern side, and the glen contracts into a narrow gorge, down which the Shiel, at this point a roaring torrent, runs in a deep rocky channel, between steep declivities covered with heather, bracken, and scattered birches. Above the pass the glen opens out into a little strath. Then, as now, the road ran through the strath on the north side of the river, and entered the pass along a narrow shelf between the river and the hill, from which it was entirely commanded. This position was occupied by the Jacobite forces on July 9. They were joined in the course of the day by about 100 more recruits, and next day by about 100 more.

On the evening of the 9th Lord George Murray, who commanded the outposts, reported that the enemy were encamped within four or five miles, at the head of Loch Clunie.[2] Next morning he reported that they had struck their camp and were marching over the watershed into Glenshiel. As they advanced Murray retired before them, keeping at a distance of about half a mile. About two in the afternoon the armies came in sight of each other, about half a mile apart. Wightman halted and deployed his troops for the attack.

The great natural strength of the Jacobites' position had been increased by hasty fortifications. A barricade had been made across the road, and along the face of the hill on the north side of the river entrenchments had been thrown up. Here the main body was posted, consisting of the Spanish regiment, which now only paraded some 200 strong, under its Colonel, Don Nicolas Bolano, Lochiel with about 150 men, about 150 of "Lidcoat's" and others, 20 volunteers, 40 of Rob Roy's men, 50 of Mac-Kinnon's, and 200 of Lord Seaforth's, commanded by Sir John Mackenzie of Coul. Seaforth himself was on the extreme left, up on the side of Scour Ouran, with 200 of his best men. The hill on the south bank of the river, the right of the position, was occupied by about 150 men under Lord George Murray.[3] Tullibardine com-

---

[1] Wightman, in his despatch of June 11 (*Historical Register*, vol. iv., p. 283), calls the site of the battle the Pass of Strachell, a name which still appears in guide-books, though it is not known in the district. Tullibardine calls it Glenshellbegg. The local Gaelic name is Lub-innis-na-seangan, "The bend of the river at the island of ants."

[2] Wightman gives the name of his camping-ground on the night of the 9th as Strachlony, probably Strathloan, about a mile to the west of where Clunie Inn now stands. This would agree with the distance given by Murray.

[3] These figures, taken from Tullibardine's letter to Mar of June 16, 1719, in the Stuart Papers, make the total Jacobite force about 1120. Lord Carpenter gives the number in action as 1860 (List sent to the Duke of Atholl, July 7, 1719, *Chronicles of the Families of Atholl and Tullibardine*, vol. ii., p. 288). Wightman gives the figures as "1640 Highlanders, besides 300 Spaniards, and a Corps apart of 500 Highlanders, who were posted on a Hill in order to make themselves Masters of our Baggage." His own force amounted, as we have seen, to about 1100. The name "Lidcoat," used in Tullibardine's letter, is evidently a pseudonym; it may mean Glengarry.

manded in the centre, accompanied by Glendaruel. Brigadier MacIntosh of Borlum
was with the Spanish Colonel. The Earl Marischal and Brigadier Campbell were with
Seaforth on the left.

Wightman's right wing was composed of 150 grenadiers under Major Millburn;
Montagu's Regiment, commanded by Lieut.-Colonel Lawrence; a detachment of 50
men under Colonel Harrison; Huffel's Dutch Regiment; and four companies of
Amerongen's. On the flank were 56 of Lord Strathnaver's men under Ensign
Mackay. The whole wing was commanded by Colonel Clayton. The left wing,
which was deployed on the south side of the river, consisted of Clayton's Regiment,
commanded by Lieut.-Colonel Reading, and had on the flank about 80 men of the
Munroes under Munro of Culcairn. The dragoons and the four mortars remained on
the road.

The engagement began between five and six o'clock, when the left wing of the
Hanoverians advanced against Lord George Murray's position on the south of the
river. The position was first shelled by the mortar battery and then attacked by four
platoons of Clayton's with the Munroes. The first attack was repulsed, but the
attacking party was reinforced, and Lord George's men, who were not supported,
were driven from their position, and retreated beyond the burn, which, coming down
from Frioch Corrie, descends towards the Shiel in rear of the ground which they had
occupied. The precipitous banks of the burn effectually checked pursuit. After the
right wing of the Jacobites had been dislodged, Wightman's right began to move up
the hill to attack their left. The detachment commanded by Lord Seaforth was
strongly posted behind a group of rocks on the hillside, and it was against them that
the attack of Montagu and Harrison's troops was directed. Seaforth was reinforced
from the centre by the remainder of his own men under Sir John Mackenzie. Finding
himself hard pressed, Seaforth sent down for further support. Another reinforcement
under Rob Roy went to his aid, but before it reached him the greater part of his
men had given way, and he himself had been severely wounded. Rob Roy's detachment next gave way, and retired towards the mountain. They were followed by
" Lidcoat's " men and others. The whole force of Wightman's attack was now directed
towards the Jacobite centre, against which the fire of the mortar battery had by this
time been turned. The Spanish regulars stood their ground well, but finding that
most of their allies had deserted them, they also at last began to retire up the hill
to the left. The whole of Tullibardine's little army was now in retreat. The retreat
soon became a flight. The victorious Hanoverians pursued their defeated enemies over
the shoulders of Scour Ouran, and only halted as darkness fell, when they had nearly
reached the top of the mountain. Far up the hill there is a corrie which, to this
day, the shepherds call Bealach-na-Spainnteach, "The Spaniards' Pass."

The action had lasted some three hours. The loss of the English troops amounted
to 21 men killed and 121 wounded, officers included. That of the Jacobites is difficult

to estimate; it could not have been great, as Keith thought at the time that not more than 100 men on both sides had been killed or wounded. Besides Seaforth, Lord George Murray was wounded. One English officer was killed, Captain Downes, of Montagu's Regiment. He was buried on the field of battle; his resting-place is still pointed out, on the south side of the river, just above the pass. Local tradition has transformed it into the "Dutch Colonel's Grave." If all tales are true, his ghost still walks the glen o' nights.

On the night after the battle the Jacobite chiefs, seeing that they had neither provisions nor ammunition, and that their few troops had not behaved so as to give much encouragement to try a further action, resolved that the Spaniards should surrender, and that the Highlanders should disperse as best they could. Accordingly next morning the Spanish commander delivered his sword to General Wightman, and "everybody else," says Keith, "took the road he liked best."

A week later Wightman writes to say that he is "taking a tour through all the difficult parts of Seaforth's country to terrify the Rebels by burning the houses of the Guilty and preserving those of the Honest."[1] On June 30 he writes from Inverness, "I have used all possible means to put a Dread upon those who have been more immediately concerned in this late unnatural Rebellion, and by all just accounts am assured the Rebells are totally disperst."[2]

The rising was over. Its leaders, after lurking for a while, with a price on their heads, in Knoydart and in Glengarry's country, effected their escape to the Continent. The Spanish prisoners, 274 in number, were marched to Inverness, and on the 27th they set out for Edinburgh.

"When the Spanish battallion were brought prisoners to Edinburgh," says Lockhart, "the officers, who had the liberty of the town, were used by the loyall party with all the civility and kindness imaginable; but the Government for a long time refused to advance subsistance money to them, by which in a little time they were reduced to great straits, which appeared even in their looks tho' their Spanish pride would not allow them to complain. As I was well acquainted with Don Nicolas who commanded them, I took the liberty to ask him if he wanted money; and finding it was so, I told him it was unkind in him to be thus straitned, when he knew our King, for whose cause he suffer'd, had so many friends in town that would cheirfully assist him; so I immediatly gott him credit for as much money as was necessary for himself and his men, till he gott bills from the Marquis de Beretti-Landi the Spanish ambassadour in Holland, when he thankfully repay'd what was advanced to him."[3] In October the Spaniards were sent home to their own country.

---

[1] *London Gazette,* June 27-30, 1719.
[2] Wightman to Delafaye, Secretary to the Lords Justices, June 30, 1719, Home Office Papers, Record Office, Scotland, Bundle 14, No 60.
[3] *Lockhart Papers,* vol. ii., pp. 23-24.

James and Ormonde were still in Spain, hoping that the enterprise might yet be renewed. Alberoni at first professed his intention of going on with it, but the thing was hopeless. "Cardinal Alberoni," wrote Lord Stair to the British Government on May 24, "still pretends to carry on the enterprise against Great Britain. He has given orders for victualling the ships anew, and for reassembling the troops; but everybody in Spain laughs at that project and, indeed, they do so pretty much in France, except our Jacobites, who have faith enough to believe everything that makes for them, let it be ever so impossible." The fleet would have taken three months to refit, and by this time Alberoni's hands were full of affairs at home. Spain was at war with France. The French army, under the Duke of Berwick, was making rapid progress on the Pyrenean frontier. It was evident that before long the French would be able to dictate terms of peace to Alberoni, and it was certain that one of the conditions of peace would be the departure of James from Spanish territory. Accordingly, it was suggested to him that it might be well that he should return to Italy to meet his bride, Princess Maria Clementina Sobieska,[1] who had just escaped from captivity at Innsbruck. He sailed from Vinaros on the 14th of August, and on the 25th landed at Leghorn.

---

[1] She was the daughter of Prince James Sobieski, and grand-daughter of John Sobieski, King of Poland. When on her way to join her betrothed husband in Italy, she had been arrested at Innsbruck, "a favour of the Emperor to the English Government," as Lord Mahon justly says, "unworthy of them to solicit and base in him to grant."

PRINCE CHARLES EDWARD STUART

# CHAPTER V.

## THE FORTY-FIVE—BEFORE CULLODEN.

A QUARTER of a century elapsed before the sword was again drawn, for the last time, in the cause of the Stuarts. No event in Scottish history has been the subject of deeper or more enduring interest than the rising of 1745. It is full of incidents of personal daring and romantic adventure, and it has all the pathetic interest which attaches to the last struggle of a lost cause. In more ways than one it was, like the Union, the "end of an auld sang." Prince Charlie's departure for France ended the history of old Scotland—the tumultuous and impoverished Scotland of the Middle Ages—"loitering in the rear of civilisation," to use Mr Froude's phrase. Then began the history of modern Scotland, the prosperous agricultural, manufacturing and commercial Scotland in which we live. So vast has been the change that it is not easy to realise that the period which has elapsed between the battle of Culloden and our own day does not exceed the span of two long lives.[1]

After the failure of the Spanish expedition of 1719, James Stuart, as we have seen, returned to Italy. His marriage with Princess Clementina Sobieska, which had already been celebrated by proxy, took place at Montefiascone in September 1719. Two sons were the issue of the marriage, Charles Edward Louis Philip Casimir, born in 1720, and Henry Benedict Maria Thomas, born in 1725. The former was the Prince Charlie of the '45.

Early in life the heir of the lost cause showed that he had inherited not only the personal charm of the Stuarts, but no small share of the valour and capacity of John Sobieski. As a lad of fourteen he gave proof of his courage at the siege of Gaeta. John Walton, the agent of the English Government at Rome, speaks with frank admiration of his bravery and talents. "Everybody," he writes, "says that he will be in time a far more dangerous enemy to the present establishment of the Government of England than ever his father was."[2]

During the years between 1720 and 1740 the history of Jacobitism is that of a succession of fruitless intrigues. Jacobite agents hung about every Court in Europe,

---

[1] For example, in July 1897 there died in Dundee William Robertson, aged ninety-seven, who was in early life a servant to Colonel Alexander Macdonnell of Glengarry. While in that situation he frequently met and conversed with Owen Macdonnell, who had fought at Prestonpans, Falkirk, and Culloden. Owen was then nearing a hundred years old, and was full of stories of the campaign.—*Edinburgh Evening Dispatch*, July 12, 1897.

[2] State Papers, Tuscany, Aug. 7, 1734. Walton's letters are full of information about the Prince's youth. See the extremely interesting early chapters of Mr A. C. Ewald's *Life and Times of Prince Charles Stuart.*

Q

and the little exiled Stuart Court at Rome and Albano was full of busy plotters, hatching projects which came to nothing. In Scotland Lockhart organised a body of "Trustees" to take charge of James's interests. This body was regarded with much jealousy by those who surrounded James in his exile, and appears never to have received his formal authorisation. "They had an opportunity," says Burton, "for quarrelling with the Jacobite clergy, and seem only to have been saved from deeper quarrels with the Court of Albano because neither body could find anything to do or to quarrel about."

In the meantime the Government was taking such measures as seemed best calculated to reduce the Highlands to order and submission. No serious steps were taken to punish those who had taken part in the affair of 1719; it was evidently desired that the whole thing should be allowed to blow over. Two disarming Acts were passed, but were very imperfectly carried into effect. Naturally, they were but obeyed by the clans which were in the interest of the Government. The disaffected clans gave up large quantities of worthless arms; it was said that some were imported from abroad for the purpose—but, as afterwards appeared, they retained an ample supply of efficient weapons. The chief result of the Acts was to deprive the Government of such assistance as they might have received on emergency from the Campbells and other Whig clans.

At the same time was begun the enterprise of opening up the Highlands by the great system of roads which is associated with the name of General Wade. The main roads actually constructed by Wade himself were (1) the great Highland Road, which goes by Dunkeld and Blair Atholl to Inverness, familiar to all travellers by the Highland Railway; (2) a road running from Stirling to Crieff, through Glen Almond, past Loch Tay, and so north to join the Highland road at Dalnacardoch; and (3) a road from Inverness to Fort William, along what is now the line of the Caledonian Canal. This last road was connected with the Highland Road by a branch passing over Corryarrack. As we shall see, this branch was, for military purposes, of more use to the Jacobites than it ever was to the Government.

Since the beginning of the eighteenth century a number of independent Highland companies had been maintained as a kind of police force in the service of the Government. It was Duncan Forbes of Culloden, Lord President of the Court of Session, one of the wisest and most patriotic of Scottish statesmen, who first suggested the idea of utilising the dangerous warlike spirit of the clans by raising Highland regiments for foreign service. The Forty-third Regiment, afterwards the Forty-second, was embodied in Strathtay in May 1740. It inherited from the old independent companies their name of the Black Watch, which it has since made illustrious throughout the world.

In 1739, much against his will, Walpole declared war against Spain. It seemed to the Scottish Jacobites that war with France was inevitable, and that their opportunity was come at last. In the beginning of 1740 some of their leaders met at Edinburgh and framed an "Association" engaging themselves to take arms and venture their lives and fortunes to restore the family of Stuart, provided that the King of France would send over a body of troops to their assistance. This document was signed by Lord Lovat, James Drummond, titular Duke of Perth, Lord Traquair, Sir James Campbell of Auchinbreck, Cameron of Lochiel, John Stuart, brother of Lord Traquair, and Lord John Drummond, and was entrusted to Drummond of Balhaldy to be carried to Rome. The French Court was approached, and was lavish in its promises of aid. Cardinal Tencin, who, on the death of Cardinal Fleury in January 1743, became Prime Minister to Louis XV., was actively friendly to the Stuart cause. John Murray of Broughton, who had now been constituted James's Secretary for Scottish affairs, was sent to Paris to arrange the details of an invasion of Great Britain. It was ultimately arranged that 3000 French troops should be sent to Scotland under the Earl Marischal, while 12,000 under Marshal Saxe were to be landed in England and to march on London. Murray then proceeded to Scotland to prepare the Jacobite clans to support the projected invasion. The troops were assembled at Dunkirk; a fleet was prepared at Brest and Rochefort; and Prince Charles, with his father's permission, came to France to accompany the expedition. "I go, Sire," said he at parting with James, "in search of three crowns, which I doubt not but to have the honour and happiness of laying at your Majesty's feet. If I fail in the attempt your next sight of me shall be in my coffin." "Heaven forbid," answered James, bursting into tears, "that all the crowns of the world should rob me of my son. Be careful of yourself, my dear Prince, for my sake, and I hope for the sake of millions."

Charles reached Paris on January 20, 1744, and the expedition was at once put into motion. The British Government were greatly alarmed, as the greater part of their troops were in Flanders, the fleet was in the Mediterranean, and there were only six ships of the line ready at Spithead. However, the expedition was attended with the usual ill-luck of all Jacobite enterprises. Its fate is thus described by Home in his *History of the Rebellion:* "Orders were immediately given to fit out and man all the ships of war in the different ports of the Channel; never were orders better obeyed, for the French fleet having been driven down the Channel by a strong gale of easterly wind, before they could get up again Sir John Norris with twenty-one ships of the line and a good many frigates arrived in the Downs, where he lay watching the motions of the transports at Dunkirk from the 16th to the 23rd of February. That day an English frigate came into the Downs with the signal for seeing an enemy's fleet flying at her masthead. The English ships unmoored and, having the tide with them, beat down the Channel against a fresh gale of westerly wind; at four in the afternoon the English fleet caught sight of the French ships lying at anchor near Dungeness, but as the tide was spent they also were obliged to come to anchor. While the two fleets were in this position, Marshal Saxe, who with the young Pretender had come to Dunkirk that very day, was embarking his troops as fast as possible. In the evening the wind changed to the east and blew a storm. The French ships, sensible of their inferiority, as soon as it was dark cut their cables and ran down the Channel. During the night all the ships of the English fleet, two excepted, parted their cables and drove. Both the fleets were far enough from Dunkirk, and if the weather had been moderate Marshal Saxe might have reached England before Sir John Norris could have returned to the Downs; but when the storm rose it stopped embarkation, several transports were wrecked, a good many soldiers and seamen perished, and a great quantity of war-like stores was lost; the English fleet returned to the Downs and the French troops were withdrawn from the coast."

This attempt to invade Britain was followed by the formal declaration of war with France. Charles, deeply mortified by the failure of the enterprise, retired to Gravelines, where he lived incognito during the summer of 1744 awaiting events. In the beginning of the following winter he went to Paris, but found the French Government not disposed to renew the attempt at invasion.

The defeat of the British army at Fontenoy in May 1745 at last decided Charles to carry out a project which had long been forming in his mind, namely, to wait no longer for foreign aid, but to come to Scotland himself, to throw himself upon the loyalty of his own people, and with their help to make an attempt to recover the crown of his fathers. Charles's project was not communicated by him to the French Government; whether they knew of it or not they gave it no overt support, but they threw no obstacle in his way. There were then in Paris two merchants of Irish descent, named Ruttledge and Walsh, sons of refugees who had followed the fortunes of James II. They had obtained from the French Government an old man-of-war of 60 guns called the *Elizabeth*, and had also purchased a 16 gun brig, the *Doutelle*, which vessels they had equipped for privateering purposes. These vessels were placed at the disposal of the Prince. He borrowed 180,000 livres from his bankers, pawned his jewels, and procured what arms he could – 1500 muskets, 1800 broad-swords, 20 field guns, and ammunition. These were placed on board the *Elizabeth*.

Charles did not communicate his wild project to his father until he was on the eve of sailing, and it was too late to prevent it. "Let what will happen," he wrote, "the stroke is struck, and I have taken a firm resolution to conquer or to die, and stand my ground as long as I shall have a man remaining with me."

On June 22, 1745, he went on board the *Doutelle* at Nantes, accompanied by the Marquis of Tullibardine, Sir John Macdonald, Æneas Macdonald, Colonel Strickland, Sir Thomas Sheridan, Captain O'Sulivan, George Kelly, Mr Buchanan, and Anthony Walsh, the owner of the ship. On July 4 the *Doutelle* was joined at Belleisle by the *Elizabeth*, and on the 5th the expedition finally set sail for Scotland. Four days after leaving Belleisle the ships were encountered by an English man-of-war, the *Lion*, under Captain Brett, who engaged the *Elizabeth*. After six hours of severe fighting both vessels drew off; the *Elizabeth* being so much damaged that she had to run back into Brest, carrying with her the bulk of the money, arms, and stores which had been provided for the expedition. Charles repeatedly urged Walsh, who was in command of the *Doutelle*, to bear down to the aid of the *Elizabeth*, but Walsh absolutely refused to risk the person of the Prince, kept at a distance from the fight, and after it was over made sail for Scotland. On July 23 the Prince landed on the island of Eriska in the Hebrides.

On the day after the Prince's landing, Alexander Macdonald of Boisdale, brother of Macdonald of Clanranald, came to meet him. When he found upon what errand the Prince and his companions were come to Scotland, "he did all he could," says Æneas Macdonald, "to prevail upon them to return to France without making any attempt to proceed."[1] He pointed out to the Prince the madness of attempting to attack the Government without foreign support, and implored him to abandon his enterprise. Charles was resolute. "If I can only get a hundred good, stout, honest-hearted fellows to join me," he said, "I'll make a trial of what I can do." The result was that Boisdale prevented all Clanranald's men that lived in South Uist and the other islands, to the number of 400 or 500, from joining the insurrection. The Prince, in the meantime, sent a messenger to Sir Andrew Macdonald of Sleat. Æneas Macdonald crossed to the mainland to summon his brother, Macdonald of Kinlochmoidart.

On the 25th Charles himself crossed to Lochnanuagh and landed at Borradale in Arisaig. On the following day young Clanranald, Glenaladale, and a number of other chiefs came in, and messengers were sent out to summon others. The opinion of the chiefs was unanimous that the enterprise was hopeless, and that Charles ought to return, but the Prince's courage and resolution overcame all objections. There was no more zealous Jacobite in Scotland than Cameron of Lochiel, but even he thought that there was not the least prospect of success. He determined not to take arms, but came to Borradale for the purpose of waiting on the Prince. On his way he called at the house of his brother, John Cameron of Fassefern. Home, who had the incident from Fassefern himself, narrates what passed between the brothers. Fassefern asked Lochiel what was the matter that had brought him there at so early an hour? Lochiel told him that the Prince was landed at Borradale and had sent for him. Fassefern asked what troops the Prince had brought with him, what money, what arms. Lochiel answered that he believed the Prince had brought with him neither troops, nor money, nor arms, and, therefore, he was resolved not to be concerned in the affair, and would do his utmost to prevent Charles from making a rash attempt. Fassefern approved his brother's sentiments, and applauded his resolution; advising him at the same time not to go any further on the way to Borradale, but to come into the house and impart his mind to the Prince by letter. "No," said Lochiel, "I ought at

---

[1] Narrative, *Lyon in Mourning.*

least to wait upon him and give my reasons for declining to join him, which admit of no reply." "Brother," said Fassefern, "I know you better than you know yourself. If this Prince once sets his eyes upon you he will make you do whatever he pleases." Fassefern was right. When Lochiel arrived at Borradale he implored Charles to abandon his enterprise and return. When Charles absolutely refused Lochiel then begged him to remain hid where he was till some of his friends should meet together and consult what was best to be done. Charles answered that he was determined to put all to the hazard. "In a few days," said he, "with the few friends I have, I will erect the royal standard, and proclaim to the people of Britain that Charles Stuart has come over to claim the crown of his ancestors, to win it, or to perish in the attempt. Lochiel, who my father has often told me was our firmest friend, may stay at home and learn from the newspapers the fate of his Prince." Lochiel yielded. "No," said he, "I will share the fate of my Prince, and so shall every man over whom nature or fortune hath given me any power."

On Lochiel's decision depended the fate of the insurrection. It seems clear that had he persisted in his refusal to join the Prince very few other chiefs would have done so. As it was, his example was followed by all the Jacobite clans.

It was determined to raise the standard of insurrection on August 19. The *Doutelle*, having discharged her stores, put to sea on the 4th. On the 11th the Prince went by sea to Kinlochmoidart; there he remained to the 17th. In the meantime the first blow had been struck. An English officer named Captain Switenham, when on his way to take command at Fort-William, was taken prisoner on the 14th; and two days later two companies of the Royal Scots, who were on the march from Perth to Fort-William, were attacked on the shores of Loch Lochy by a force under Macdonald of Tiendrish and made prisoners. On the 19th the Prince went from Kinlochmoidart to Glenfinnan, and there the standard of King James VIII. was unfurled by the Marquis of Tullibardine. In the course of the day the standard was joined by Lochiel at the head of seven or eight hundred men, and by Macdonald of Keppoch with about 300. The Prince remained till the 22nd at Kinlochiel, thence he marched by Fassefern, Moy, and Letterfinlay to Invergarry Castle, which he reached on the 26th. There he was joined by Ardshiel with 260 men of the Stewarts of Appin. Murray of Broughton, the Judas of the cause, had joined the Prince on the 18th at Kinlochmoidart. On the 25th he was appointed secretary. On the 26th, at Invergarry, a document was drawn up and signed by all the chiefs present, pledging themselves not to lay down their arms or make peace separately without consent of the whole.

In the meantime the authorities were not idle. To the Government Charles's landing had come as a bolt from the blue. The first rumour of it which had reached them was contained in a letter written by Lord President Forbes to Henry Pelham, the Prime Minister, on August 2.

Sir John Cope, then commanding the troops in Scotland, is described by Home as "one of those ordinary men who are fitter for anything than the chief command in war, especially when opposed, as he was, to a new and uncommon enemy." His incapacity to deal with the terrible emergency with which he was confronted has earned for him an immortality of ridicule, perhaps not altogether deserved. The troops which were at his disposal at the outbreak of the insurrection were thus described by himself at the inquiry into his conduct which subsequently took place. "As much as I can remember on the 2nd of July the troops in Scotland were quartered thus : —

"Gardener's Dragoons at Stirling, Linlithgow, Musselburgh, Kelso, and Coldstream.

"Hamilton's ditto at Haddington, Dunse, and the adjacent Places.

"*N.B.*—Both Regiments at grass.

"Guise's Regiment of Foot at Aberdeen and the Coast-Quarters.

"Five Companies of Lee's at Dumfries, Stranraer, Glasgow, and Stirling.

"Murray's in the Highland Barracks.

"Lascells's at Edinburgh and Leith.

"Two additional Companies of the Royal at Perth.

"Two ditto of the Scotch Fuziliers at Glasgow.

"Two ditto of Lord Semple's at Cupar in Fife.

"Three ditto of Lord John Murray's Highland Regiment at Crieff.

"Lord Loudon's Regiment was beginning to be raised ; and, besides these, there were the standing garrisons of invalids in the Castles.

"*N.B.* — As to the additional Companies of the Royal, Scotch Fuziliers, and Semple's, by reason of the draughts made from them, and the difficulty the officers met with in getting men, I believe, I may safely say, that upon an average they did not exceed 25 Men per Company, and those all new-raised Men. The three additional Companies of Lord John Murray's, I believe, might be pretty near complete ; of these three last I soon after sent one to Inverary, and the other two, which I took with me, mouldered away by desertion upon the March northward."

The first intimation of the Prince's landing reached Cope on August 8. He at once ordered as many troops as could be spared from the garrisons to concentrate at Stirling in readiness for a march into the Highlands. On the 19th he himself left Edinburgh to take command of this force, leaving General Guest at Edinburgh Castle in command of the whole of the troops in the Lowlands. In the meantime the Lord President had gone north to raise the loyal clans for the Government.

Cope left Stirling on the 20th with five companies of Lee's, Murray's Regiment, and two companies of Lord John Murray's Highland Regiment. He halted over the 21st at Crieff to wait for provisions, and there was joined by eight companies of Lascelles's. On the 22nd he resumed his march to Amulree, encountering the utmost difficulties as to transport. Tay Bridge, now Aberfeldy, was reached on the 23rd, Trinifuir on the 24th, Dalnacardoch on the 25th, and Dalwhinnie on the 26th.

At Dalnacardoch he was met by Captain Switenham, who had been released by the insurgents. Switenham informed him that the Prince's force was now some 3000 strong, and that it was his purpose to march over Corryarrack and descend into the Lowlands.

Cope's intention had been to march to Fort Augustus by the Corryarrack road, and his first idea now was to attempt to force the pass, but he was soon satisfied that to attempt to do so in face of a determined enemy would be to court certain destruction. On the morning of the 27th he held a council of war, consisting of all the field-officers and commanders of corps in his army, to consider what ought to be done. The council were unanimously of opinion that an attack upon the pass was out of the question; that to return to Stirling would spread the insurrection by encouraging the disaffected in the north, and would in itself be a dangerous movement; and that to remain where they were would not prevent the enemy from reaching the low country. In these circumstances, it was determined to continue the march northwards to Inverness. This was done, and Inverness was reached on August 29.

The Prince's way to the Lowlands was thus left clear. On the 28th he marched over Corryarrack to Garvemore. It was at first proposed to pursue Cope, but it was considered that he had too long a start, and, accordingly, it was decided to continue the march to the south by Dalwhinnie and Dalnacardoch. Blair Castle was reached on August 31, Dunkeld on September 3, and on the evening of the 4th the Prince entered Perth, and there proclaimed King James VIII. At Perth he was joined by many leading Jacobites, including the titular Duke of Perth, Lord George Murray, Lord Ogilvie, Oliphant of Gask, and the Chevalier Johnstone, well known as one of the historians of the insurrection. Many recruits came in, including 200 of the Robertsons of Struan, and many others from Atholl and the surrounding districts. Something was done to organise the army and to make commissariat arrangements. A sum of £500 was exacted from the city of Perth.[1] Various staff appointments were made. Lord George Murray and the Duke of Perth were appointed lieutenant-generals. The former was not only a devoted Jacobite, but a man of great capacity and of considerable military experience. To him was due no small measure of the success which afterwards attended the Prince's arms.

At Perth information was received that Cope was collecting shipping at Aberdeen in order to convey his troops once more to the south. It was accordingly determined to press on southwards, and, if possible, to anticipate his return by seizing Edinburgh. On the 11th the Prince marched out of Perth, and on the same night reached Dunblane. Next day he marched to Doune, and on the following day crossed the Forth at the Fords of Frew. Linlithgow was reached at six in the morning of Sunday, September 15.

---

[1] The money was much needed. It was said that when he reached Perth the Prince had only a guinea in his pocket.

MAP TO ILLUSTRATE THE RISING OF 1745.

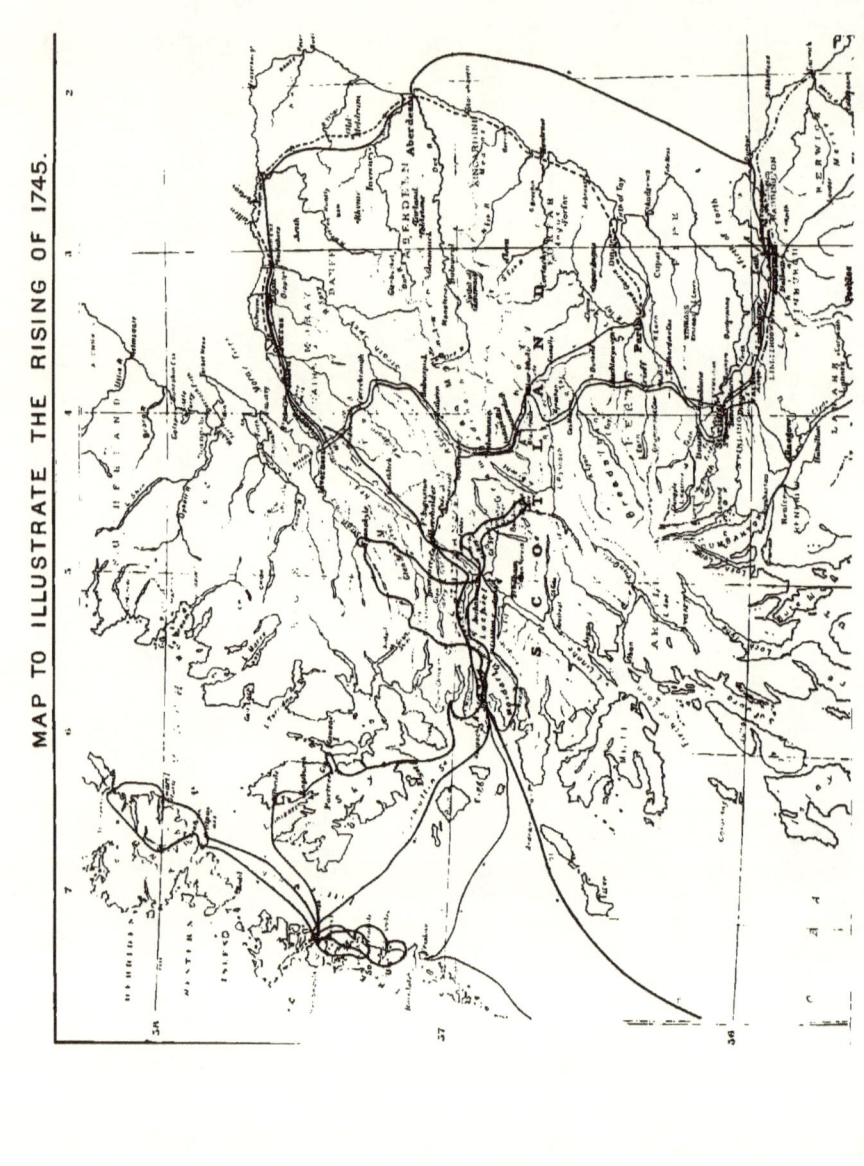

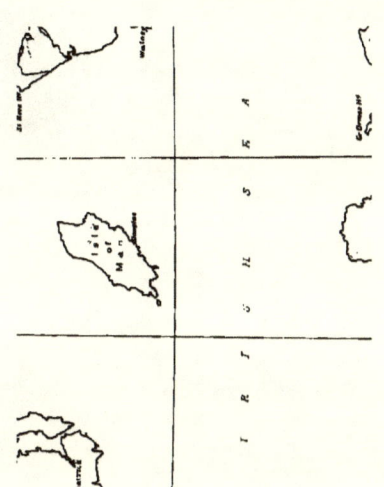

When it became known that Cope had refused battle to the Jacobite army, and that Prince Charles was actually advancing on the Lowlands, the greatest alarm and confusion prevailed in Edinburgh. The Jacobites were almost openly triumphant, while the friends of Government were thrown into the utmost consternation. Edinburgh was almost defenceless, though it was still nominally a fortified city. In those days, it must be remembered, the appearance of the city was very different from that which it now presents. Neither the New Town nor the southern suburbs were then in existence. The city was bounded and defended on the north side by the Nor' Loch, a swampy lake which covered the ground now occupied by Princes Street Gardens; on the west, south, and east it was surrounded by the old Flodden wall, which ran from the West Port out by the Vennel to Heriot's Hospital, thence round by Potterrow to the east end of the Cowgate, then up the hill to the Netherbow Port, which crossed the High Street a little below the Tron Church, and so down to the Nor' Loch, separating the old town of Edinburgh proper from the Canongate, which was then a separate burgh. This wall, which was just a strong park dyke, varying from ten to twenty feet in height, was of little use as a defence in modern warfare. No guns were mounted upon it, indeed there were no platforms upon which guns could be mounted. The wall had no re-entering angles or flanking bastions; in many places houses were built up against it. In some cases these houses were commanded by higher houses opposite to them, and outside the city; a continuous row of such houses ran from the Cowgate to the Netherbow Port. "The condition of the men who might be called upon to defend them," says Home, "was pretty similar to that of the walls." There was a body of civic troops called the Trained Bands, which nominally amounted to sixteen companies of from 80 to 100 each, but these warriors were not likely to prove very formidable in the field. Sir Walter Scott says of them that for many years their officers "had practised no other martial discipline than was implied in a particular mode of flourishing their wine glasses on festive occasions, and it was well understood that if these militia were called on, a number of them were likely enough to declare for Prince Charles, and a much larger proportion would be unwilling to put their persons and properties in danger for either the one or the other side of the cause." Besides these, the only troops available for defence were the men of the Town Guard, the old "Town's Rats," 126 in number, Gardiner's dragoons, who had been left at Stirling, and had retreated before the advancing Jacobites, and Hamilton's dragoons, who were encamped on Leith Links.

Notwithstanding these disadvantages, it was resolved to make some effort to defend the city. A meeting was held, at which it was decided to strengthen the walls as well as time would permit, and to raise a regiment of volunteers. The friends of Government were much encouraged by the arrival of Captain Rogers, aide-de-camp to Cope, who arrived from the north with the news that Cope was going to march his troops from Inverness down to Aberdeen, and bring them south

R

by sea, in time, if possible, to save Edinburgh. Their object, therefore, was to defend the city until his arrival.

On September 6 a petition was presented to the Town Council by about 100 citizens praying that they might be authorised to associate as volunteers for the defence of the city. The number of volunteers rapidly increased, and on September 11, six captains, nominated by the Provost, were appointed to the regiment. On the following day the volunteers assembled in the College yards and were told off into companies, and had arms and accoutrements served out to them. In the meantime, fortifications were added to the walls under the direction of Colin Maclaurin, Professor of Mathematics in the University. The volunteers were instructed with all possible speed in the rudiments of drill, and guns were obtained from the ships at Leith and mounted on the walls.

On Sunday, September 15, it was rumoured that the van of the insurgents had reached Kirkliston. It was now proposed that Hamilton's dragoons should march up from Leith to join Gardiner's at Corstorphine, and that this force, supported by the city volunteers, should give battle to the Highlanders in the open. Lord Provost Stewart offered the services of 90 of the City Guard. Accordingly, orders were issued by General Guest to Hamilton's dragoons to march up to Edinburgh.

What happened on that Sunday morning is graphically described by Scott: "The fire-bell, an ominous and ill-chosen signal, tolled for assembling the volunteers, and so alarming a sound, during the time of Divine service, dispersed those assembled for worship, and brought out a large crowd of the inhabitants to the street. The dragoon regiment appeared equipped for battle. They huzza'd and clashed their swords at sight of the volunteers, their companions in peril, of which neither party were destined that day to see much. But other sounds expelled these warlike greetings from the ears of the civic soldiers. The relatives of the volunteers crowded around them, weeping, protesting, and conjuring them not to expose lives so invaluable to their families to the broadswords of the savage Highlanders. There is nothing of which men in general are more easily persuaded, than of the extreme value of their own lives; nor are they apt to estimate them more lightly when they see they are highly prized by others. A sudden change of opinion took place among the body. In some companies the men said that their officers would not lead them on; in others, the officers said that the privates would not follow them. An attempt to march the corps towards the West Port, which was their destined route for the field of battle, failed. The regiment moved, indeed, but the files grew gradually thinner and thinner as they marched down the Bow and through the Grassmarket, and not above forty-five reached the West Port. A hundred more were collected with some difficulty, but it seems to have been under a tacit condition that the march to Corstorphine should be abandoned, for out of the city not one of them issued. The volunteers were led back to their alarm post and dismissed for the evening, when a few of the most zealous left the town, the defence of which began no longer to be expected, and sought other fields in which to exercise their valour."

"We remember," says Scott, "an instance of a stout Whig and a very worthy man, a writing-master by occupation, who had esconced his bosom beneath a professional cuirass, consisting of two quires of long foolscap writing-paper; and, doubtful that even this defence might be unable to protect his valiant heart from the claymores, amongst which his impulses might carry him, had written on the outside, in his best flourish, 'This is the body of J—— M——, pray give it Christian burial.' Even this hero, prepared as one practised how to die, could not find it in his heart to accompany the devoted battalion further than the door of his own house, which stood conveniently open about the head of the Lawnmarket."

It is all very well for Sir Walter to make fun of these worthy citizens, but probably they acted in the most judicious possible manner. They were not soldiers in any sense; they were entirely unaccustomed to discipline and to the use of arms; had they gone forth to encounter Lochiel's fierce swordsmen they would have been cut to pieces in ten minutes, and their sacrifice would not have averted the capture of the city, or even delayed it by a single day.

On the forenoon of the following day, Monday the 16th, a message was brought from the Jacobite camp by a Writer to the Signet named Alves, who said that he had been taken prisoner by the Jacobites, that he had seen the Duke of Perth, and had received from him a message to the inhabitants of Edinburgh to the effect that if they would admit the Prince peaceably into the city they should be civilly dealt with; if not, they must lay their account with military execution. This increased the alarm of the townsfolk, who now petitioned the Provost to call a meeting to consider what should be done. This the Provost refused to do, as he considered that with the aid of the two regiments of dragoons the defence of the city might still be prolonged. On Tuesday morning the Jacobites advanced to Corstorphine. The dragoons had been drawn up by Colonel Gardiner at Coltbridge to dispute their passage. When the two forces came in sight of each other some "young people well mounted," belonging to the Prince's force, were ordered to ride out and reconnoitre the dragoons. These "young people" rode close up to the dragoons and fired their pistols at them. Then ensued the "Canter of Coltbrig." The dragoons were seized with a general panic, their officers in vain tried to rally them. The men turned their horses' heads and fled in the utmost confusion. Between three and four o'clock in the afternoon they galloped through the fields by the Lang Dykes, where the New Town now stands, in full view of the citizens. They never stopped till they reached Leith; there they only made a short halt. They continued their flight by Musselburgh, and prepared to bivouac for the night in a field near Preston Grange, but a cry was raised that the Highlanders were coming, and these cowardly troopers again fled, and only stopped when they reached Dunbar. Nobody had made any attempt to pursue them.

The city being thus left defenceless, the townsfolk were driven to desperation. A meeting of the Town Council was hastily convened. The Provost sent to request the attendance of the Lord Justice Clerk, the Lord Advocate, and the Solicitor-General, in order that they might assist the Council with their advice; but these functionaries had discreetly left the city when the danger became imminent. Many of the citizens crowded into the Goldsmiths' Hall, where the Town Council were assembled, clamouring for surrender. The meeting was adjourned to the New Church Aisle. While the discussion was proceeding there, a letter addressed to the Lord Provost, Magistrates, and Town Council was handed in at the door. On being opened it was found to be subscribed "CHARLES, P. R." After some discussion the letter was read. It contained a summons to surrender the city; protection was promised to the liberties of the city and to private property; "but," it was continued, "if any opposition be made to us we cannot answer for the consequences, being firmly resolved at any rate to enter the city, and in that case if any of the inhabitants are found in arms against us, they must not expect to be treated as prisoners of war."

When this letter had been read the cry for surrender became louder than ever. It was agreed that a deputation should be sent to wait on the Prince at Gray's Mill, about two miles from Edinburgh, where he was, to request that hostilities should be suspended, in order to give the citizens an opportunity of considering the letter.

The deputation was not long gone when news arrived which entirely altered the aspect of affairs. This was that Cope's transports had arrived from Aberdeen and were lying off Dunbar, where he proposed to disembark his troops and to march immediately to the relief of Edinburgh. Messengers were at once dispatched to recall the deputation, but they were unable to overtake it. Many of the more zealous citizens wished to continue the defence, so as to give Cope time to come up. However, this idea was abandoned, as it was remembered that several magistrates and town councillors were in the power of the Highlanders, who were regarded as mere ruthless savages, and who, it was considered, would, in the event of hostilities being commenced, probably hang them all. About ten o'clock at night the deputies returned with a peremptory answer. "His Royal Highness the Prince Regent," wrote Secretary Murray, "thinks his manifesto and the King his father's declaration, already published, a sufficient capitulation for all His Majesty's subjects to accept of with joy. His present demands are to be received into the city as the son and representative of the King his father, and obeyed as such when there. . . . He expects a positive answer before two o'clock in the morning, otherwise he will think himself obliged to take measures conform." The unlucky bailies could think of nothing better than "to send out deputies once more to beg a suspension of hostilities till nine o'clock in the morning, that the magistrates might have an opportunity of conversing with the citizens, most of whom had gone to bed." A second deputation accordingly started for Gray's Mill about two in the morning in a hackney-coach. The Prince refused to see them or to grant any further delay, and they were briefly ordered to "get them gone."

While these negotiations were going on, the Jacobites, well knowing the value of time, were quietly making preparations to take the city by a *coup de main*. About midnight Cameron of Lochiel ordered his men to get under arms, and very early in the morning a detachment, about 500 strong, started by moonlight from the Borough Muir, guided by Murray of Broughton. They marched round by Hope Park to the Netherbow Port, preserving the strictest silence and keeping well out of sight of the Castle. When they reached the Netherbow, Lochiel placed twenty Camerons on each side of the gate, and hid the rest of his men in St. Mary's Wynd and the adjoining streets. He then sent forward a man in a riding-coat and hunting-cap, who represented himself as the servant of an English officer of dragoons, and asked to be admitted. The guard, however, refused to open the gate, and ordered the man to withdraw, threatening to fire upon him.

Day was now breaking, and Murray proposed that the detachment should retire to St. Leonard's Hill, and there await further orders; but, just as they were about to leave, a piece of good fortune enabled them to effect their purpose. It will be remembered that the second deputation sent out to treat with the Prince went in a hackney-coach. They returned to Edinburgh in the same coach, and were set down in the High Street. The driver had his stables in the Canongate, so, after bringing back the deputation, he had to pass through the Netherbow Port in order to get home. He was known to the man on guard, and accordingly, after some discussion, the gate was opened to let him pass. Lochiel's men instantly rushed in and overpowered, disarmed, and made prisoners of the guard. Parties were at once detached to seize the other gates and the town guard-house. This was quickly and easily done, without bloodshed; "as quietly as one guard relieves another," says Home. This took place about five in the morning, and the citizens were presently awakened by the sound of the pibroch, to find that the Highlanders were masters of Edinburgh.[1]

About ten o'clock the main body of the insurgents, having marched round the south side of Edinburgh, entered the King's Park and halted in the Hunter's Bog. Shortly afterwards Charles himself appeared. A great crowd of people was assembled in the park, one of the spectators being John Home, the historian. He gives a graphic picture of Charles's appearance at the time. "The figure and presence of Charles Stuart were not ill-suited to his lofty pretensions. He was in the prime of

---

[1] Lord Provost Archibald Stewart was brought to trial in 1747 for neglect of duty and misbehaviour in the execution of his office in allowing the city so easily to fall into the hands of the insurgents. The evidence at his trial is a valuable source of information as to what took place.

youth, tall and handsome, of a fair complexion; he had a light-coloured periwig, with his own hair combed over the front; he wore the Highland dress that is, a tartan short-coat without the plaid, a blue bonnet on his head, and on his breast the Star of the Order of St. Andrew." After standing for some time in the park to show himself to the people, Charles mounted his horse and rode to the door of Holyrood. He was ushered into the palace of his fathers by James Hepburn of Keith, one of the most devoted of Jacobites and the model of a high-minded and patriotic Scottish gentleman of the old school.

At mid-day King James VIII. was solemnly proclaimed at the Cross, and the Commission of Regency was read, with the declaration issued at Rome in 1743, and a manifesto in the name of Charles as Prince Regent, dated at Paris, May 16, 1745.

The next two days were spent in Edinburgh. In the meantime Cope had reached Dunbar. The two regiments of dragoons which had fled from Edinburgh had come there on the morning of the 17th, "in a condition not very respectable." The disembarkation of the troops, artillery, and stores was completed on the 18th, and Cope found himself at the head of a force of some 2000 men.[1]

Home had made his way to Dunbar, and by him Cope was furnished with detailed information as to the strength and condition of the Highland army. "He was persuaded," he said, "that the whole number of Highlanders whom he saw within and without the town did not amount to 2000 men; but he was told that several bodies of men from the north were on their way, and expected very soon to join them at Edinburgh. . . . Most of them seemed to be strong, active, and hardy men; many of them were of very ordinary size, and if clothed like our countrymen would, in his opinion, appear inferior to the King's troops. But the Highland garb favoured them much, as it showed their naked limbs, which were strong and muscular: their stern countenances and bushy, uncombed hair gave them a fierce, barbarous, and imposing aspect. As to their arms," he said, "that they had no cannon or artillery of any sort but one small iron gun, which he had seen without a carriage, lying upon a cart drawn by a little Highland horse. That about 1400 of them were armed with firelocks and broadswords; that their firelocks were not similar or uniform, but of all sorts and sizes -muskets, fusees, and fowling-pieces; that some of the rest had firelocks without swords, and some of them swords without firelocks; that many of their swords were not Highland broadswords, but French; that a company or two (about 100 men) had each of them in his hand a shaft of a pitchfork with the blade of a scythe fastened to it, somewhat like the weapon called the Lochaber axe, which the Town Guard soldiers carry. But all of them," he added, "would be soon provided with firelocks, as the arms belonging to the Trained Bands of Edinburgh had fallen into their hands."

---

[1] See p. 136, *note.*

On the 19th of September, Cope left Dunbar, and marched towards Edinburgh. "The people of the country," says Home, "long unaccustomed to war and arms, flocked from all quarters to see an army going to fight a battle in East Lothian." That night Cope encamped in a field to the west of Haddington.

The Jacobite leaders were unanimously resolved to march out and give battle to Cope in the open. On the morning of September 20, the Jacobite camp at Duddingston was struck, and the army commenced its march eastwards. On the same morning Cope resumed his march towards Edinburgh by the high road from Haddington. At Huntington he left the high road, and followed the road passing through St. Germains and Seton until he reached the open ground between Seton and Preston, close to the sea.

From Duddingston the Prince marched to Musselburgh, and there crossed the Esk by the ancient bridge. Lord George Murray, having received intelligence of Cope's whereabouts, considered that it was all-important to attack him if possible from higher ground, and, accordingly, the line of march was inclined to the right. The height near Falside was occupied. The route was then directed downhill towards Tranent, and the army took up its position to the east of that village. The enemies were now within sight of each other, about half a mile apart. Cope had expected to be attacked from the west, but as soon as he saw the enemy appear on his left he changed his front from west to south. On his right were the village of Preston and the wall of Erskine of Grange's park, on his left the village of Seton, in his rear Cockenzie and the sea, in his front the enemy and the town of Tranent. The armies were separated by a piece of impassable boggy ground, which rendered a direct attack impossible.

The Jacobite leaders wished to attack Cope at once, and Lord George Murray sent down an officer to reconnoitre the marsh. He reported that it was impossible to cross it and attack the enemy in front without serious loss. The Jacobites then moved to their left, and took up a position opposite Preston Tower, whereupon Cope resumed his first position, facing Preston, with his right to the sea. Afterwards the Highlanders returned to their former position, and Cope did the same.

Both armies lay on their arms all night. Charles and his officers held a council of war, and resolved to attack at daybreak, across the east end of the marsh.

There was in the Jacobite army a Mr Robert Anderson, son of Anderson of Whitburgh in East Lothian, who knew the ground well, as he had often shot over it. After the council of war had broken up, Anderson came to Hepburn of Keith, and told him that he could undertake to point out the place at which the marsh could be safely crossed by troops, without their being exposed to the enemy's fire. Hepburn sent Anderson to Lord George Murray. Lord George at once saw the importance of the information, and wakened the Prince. It was decided that Anderson's proposal should be adopted. Orders were sent to recall Lord Nairn, who had been detached with 500 men towards Preston, to head off Cope from the Edinburgh road. Before daybreak on the 21st the troops were quietly got under arms, and marched off in column, three deep, under Anderson's guidance. They passed to the east of Ringanhead Farm, across the marsh, and then marched directly north towards the sea until the rear of the column was on firm ground. There they halted, and formed into two lines to the left.

The first line consisted of the Clanranald, Glengarry, and Keppoch Macdonalds, under the Duke of Perth, on the right, and the Macgregors, the Appin Stewarts, and Lochiel's men, under Lord George Murray, on the left. The second line was commanded by Lord Nairn, and consisted of the Atholl men, the Struan Robertsons, the Glencoe Macdonalds, and the Maclachlans. Charles took his place between the lines.

Cope was taken entirely by surprise. As the Highlanders were crossing the marsh they were seen by some of his cavalry pickets, who at once galloped in to give the alarm. When he discovered that he was about to be attacked from the east, he hastily changed his front. His line of battle, as originally arranged, had been as follows : Five companies of Lee's regiment on the right, Murray's regiment on the left, eight companies of Lascelles's regiment and two of Guise's in the centre, two squadrons of Gardiner's dragoons on the right, and two on the left. Apparently there was considerable confusion in taking up the new ground. "The disposition was the same," says Home, "and each regiment in its former place in the line, but the outguards of the foot, not having time to find out the regiments to which they belonged, placed themselves on the right of Lee's five companies, and did not leave sufficient room for the two squadrons of dragoons to form ; so that the squadron which Colonel Gardiner commanded was drawn up behind the other squadron commanded by Lieutenant-Colonel Whitney. The artillery with its guard, which had been on the left and very near the line, was now on the right, a little farther from the line, and in the front of Lieutenant-Colonel Whitney's squadron." [1]

The harvest had just been got in, and the ground between the armies was a wide, level stubble field, without a bush or tree upon it. As the line of the clansmen began to move forward to the sound of the pipes, the field was still covered with a thick mist, but presently the sun rose, the mist lifted, and the opposing forces became clearly visible to each other. "The King's army," says Home, who was an eye-witness, "made a most gallant appearance, both horse and foot, with the sun shining upon their arms." But once again the spectacle was seen of a regular army swept away in a moment by the terrible charge of the claymores.

---

[1] It is very difficult to arrive at any accurate estimate of the number of troops engaged at Prestonpans. Cope's returns were lost, and the figures given by himself at his trial were given from memory. The evidence as to the number of the forces on both sides is very contradictory. It will be found reviewed in the Notes to the Chevalier

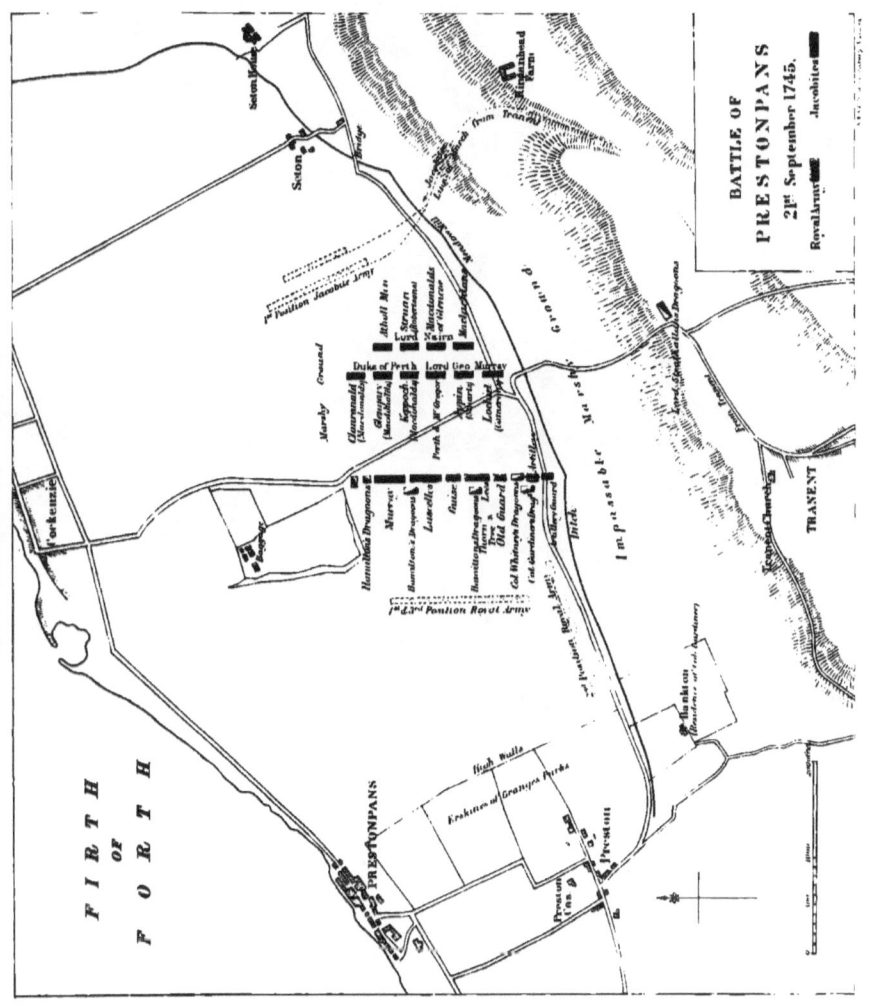

BATTLE OF
PRESTONPANS
21st September 1745.

Royal Army ▬▬▬  Jacobites ▬▬▬

The battle was a mere rout; it did not last five minutes.  Home thus describes the scene : " As the left wing of the rebel army had moved before the right, their line was somewhat oblique, and the Camerons, who were nearest the King's army, came up directly opposite to the cannon, firing at the guard as they advanced. The people employed to work the cannon, who were not gunners [1] or artillerymen, fled instantly.  Colonel Whiteford fired five of the six field-pieces with his own hand, which killed one private man and wounded an officer in Lochiel's regiment.  The line seemed to shake, but the men kept going on at a great pace; Colonel Whitney was ordered to advance with his squadron and attack the rebels before they came up to the cannon : the dragoons moved on, and were very near the cannon when they received some fire which killed several men and wounded Lieutenant-Colonel Whitney.  The squadron immediately wheeled about, rode over the artillery guard, and fled.  The men of the artillery guard, who had given one fire, and that a very indifferent one, dispersed, the Highlanders going on without stopping to

---

Johnstone's *Memoirs* (Ed. 1822), p. 29 *et seq.*  The following are the figures as given by Mr Blaikie (*Itinerary*, pp. 90 and 91), probably as accurate an estimate as can be reached :

| SIR JOHN COPE'S ARMY. | | | THE PRINCE'S ARMY. | |
|---|---|---|---|---|
| EXCLUSIVE OF OFFICERS, SERGEANTS, DRUMS, ETC. | | | Clanranald . | . 200 |
| | | Rank and File. | Lochiel | . 700 |
| Three Squadrons Gardiner's Dragoons (13th H.) . | } | 567 | Keppoch . . | . 300 |
| Three „ Hamilton's „ (14th H.) . | | | Stewart of Appin | . 260 |
| Five Companies Lee's Regiment (44th) . . | . | 291 | Glengarry . | . 400 |
| Murray's Regiment (46th) . . . . . | . | 580 | Glencoe . . | . 120 |
| Eight Companies Lascelles's Regiment (47th) . | } | 570 | Robertson of Struan . | . 200 |
| Two „ Guise's „ (6th) . | | | Duke of Perth . | . 150 |
| Five weak Companies of Highlanders of Lord John | | | Maclachlans . . | . 150 |
| Murray's Regiment (42nd), and Lord Loudon's | | | Lord Nairn . . | . 250 |
| Regiment . . . . . . . . | . | 183 | Grants of Glenmoriston | . 100 |
| Drummond's (Edinburgh) Volunteers . | . | 16 | Cavalry . . . | . 50 |
| | | — | | — |
| | | 2207 | | 2880 |
| Add same proportion of officers, sergeants, drums, | | | Less dismissed by Lochiel, August 30 | . 150 |
| etc., as recorded at Culloden (16 per cent.) . | . | 353 | | — |
| | | — | | 2730 |
| Total | | 2560 | Allowance for desertion by Keppoch's men (Aug. 27), | |
| Six guns and some cohorns (mortars). | | | and a further allowance for leakage owing to de- | |
| They had no gunners ; Lt.-Colonel Whiteford (Marines) | | | sertion, illness, guards, etc., less a few men re- | |
| served the guns with his own hands, and Mr Griffith | | | cruited in Edinburgh . . . . . . | 150 |
| (Commissary) the cohorns. | | | Total | 2580 |

[1] " When Sir John Cope marched with his army to the north, there were no gunners or matrosses to be had in Scotland but one old man who had belonged to the Scots train of artillery before the Union.  This gunner and three old soldiers belonging to the company of invalids in the garrison at the Castle of Edinburgh, Sir John Cope carried along with him to Inverness.  When the troops came to Dunbar, the King's ship that escorted the transports furnished Sir John Cope with some sailors to work the cannon ; but when the Highlanders came on, firing as they advanced, the sailors, the gunner, and the three old invalids ran away, taking the powder flasks with them, so that Colonel Whiteford, who fired five of the field pieces, could not fire the sixth for want of priming.  Sir John Cope had only four field-pieces when he came to Inverness, but he ordered two field-pieces to be taken from the Castle there and added to his train."—Home, p. 113, *note.*

At Prestonpans there were only from ten to fifteen rounds of ammunition per gun.  Evidence of Robert Jack, Cope's Trial.

S

make prisoners. Colonel Gardiner was ordered to advance with his squadron and attack them, disordered as they seemed to be with running over the cannon and the artillery guard. The Colonel advanced at the head of his men, encouraging them to charge; the dragoons followed him a little way; but as soon as the fire of the Highlanders reached them they reeled, fell into confusion, and went off as the other squadron had done. When the dragoons on the right of the King's army gave way, the Highlanders, most of whom had their pieces still loaded, advanced against the foot, firing as they went on. The soldiers, confounded and terrified to see the cannon taken and the dragoons put to flight, gave their fire, it is said, without orders; the companies of the outguard being nearest the enemy, were the first that fired, and the fire went down the line as far as Murray's regiment. The Highlanders threw down their muskets, drew their swords and ran on; the line of foot broke as the fire had been given from right to left; Hamilton's dragoons, seeing what had happened on the right, and receiving some fire at a good distance from the Highlanders advancing to attack them, they immediately wheeled about and fled, leaving the flank of the foot unguarded. The regiment which was next them (Murray's) gave their fire and followed the dragoons. In a very few minutes after the first cannon was fired, the whole army, both horse and foot, were put to flight; none of the soldiers attempted to load their pieces again, and not one bayonet was stained with blood. In this manner the battle of Preston was fought and won by the rebels; the victory was complete, for all the infantry of the King's army were either killed or taken prisoners, except about 170, who escaped by extraordinary swiftness, or early flight."

Colonel Gardiner, who, though severely wounded, had in vain attempted to rally his men, was killed by the stroke of a Lochaber axe. "The panic terror of the English surpasses all imagination," says the Chevalier Johnstone, "they threw down their arms that they might run with more speed, thus depriving themselves by their fears of the only means of arresting the vengeance of the Highlanders. Of so many men in a condition from their numbers to preserve order from the retreat, no one thought of defending himself. Terror had taken entire possession of their minds. I saw a young Highlander about fourteen years of age, scarcely formed, who was presented to the Prince as a prodigy, having killed, it was said, fourteen of the enemy. The Prince asked him if this was true. 'I do not know if I killed them, but I brought fourteen soldiers to the ground with my sword.' Another Highlander brought ten soldiers to the Prince, whom he had made prisoners, driving them before him like a flock of sheep. This Highlander, from a rashness without example, having pursued a party to some distance from the field of battle along the road between the two enclosures, struck down the hindermost with a blow of his sword, calling at the same time 'Down with your arms.' The soldiers, terror-struck, threw down their arms without looking behind them, and the Highlander, with a pistol in one hand and a sword in the other, made them do exactly as he pleased. The rage and despair of these men on seeing themselves made prisoners by a single individual may easily be imagined. These were, however, the same English soldiers who had distinguished themselves at Dettingen and Fontenoy, and who might justly be ranked among the bravest troops of Europe."

The field of battle presented a hideous spectacle, as the killed and wounded had almost all fallen by the edge of the sword. According to Home, the royal troops lost 5 officers and 200 men killed,[1] and 80 officers taken prisoners. The Jacobite loss was 4 officers and 30 men killed, 6 officers and 70 men wounded. Cope's cannon, tents, baggage, and military chest, containing some £2500, were captured. The unlucky general himself, with his principal officers and such of the cavalry as had kept together, fled by Lauder and Coldstream, and next day reached Berwick, where he was received by old Lord Mark Kerr with the famous remark: "Good God! I have seen some battles, heard of many, but never of the first news of defeat being brought by the general officers before."

That night Prince Charles slept at Pinkie House; next day he re-entered Edinburgh in triumph.

After the victory the Highlanders treated their conquered enemies with great forbearance. To the wounded of the royal army they showed a humanity which might well have been imitated by the regulars on a subsequent occasion. They were, however, very active in despoiling the dead. They appropriated wigs, watches, clothes, saddlery, and whatever else they could lay hands on. Their ignorance of civilised life sometimes led them into absurd mistakes, about which some good stories are told. One of the best known of these is that of the Highlander who helped himself to an English officer's watch. Not knowing the nature of a watch, he omitted to wind up his new possession, which, accordingly, stopped during the night. Next day he sold it for a trifle, saying that he was glad to be rid of it, "because she had dee'd in ta nicht-time."

On Monday, September 23, the day after his return to Edinburgh, Prince Charles issued several proclamations. He promised protection to the citizens; he forbade all public rejoicings for his victory, which had been purchased with the shedding of so much British blood and attended with calamity to so many innocent people. He further directed that public worship should be conducted as usual in the city churches. A deputation of the city ministers waited on him to ask whether they would be allowed to offer the usual prayers for King George. The Prince replied that he could not expressly grant them their request without giving the lie to his own pretensions; but, at the same time, he promised that no minister should be called to account for any

---

[1] This is probably under-estimated. Johnstone says 1300, which is out of the question. The real number was probably some 400 or 500.

indiscreet language he might use in the pulpit. Mr M'Vicar, the minister of the West Kirk, managed to compromise matters in his prayers by offering the following petition: " Bless the King! Thou knows what King I mean. May the crown sit long upon his head. And for the man that is come among us to seek an earthly crown, we beseech Thee in mercy to take him to Thyself and give him a crown of glory."

The victory of Prestonpans entirely altered the aspect of Charles's affairs. At first his enterprise had been looked upon, even by his warmest friends, as a piece of Quixotic folly which had no reasonable prospect of success. Now he had beaten the King's troops in a pitched battle, and was master of all Scotland except the Castles of Edinburgh and Stirling and the Highland forts. Now he had to make up his mind what he was going to do next. There were two courses open to him, either to invade England at once, or to stay in Edinburgh for a while to recruit his army and to collect stores, arms, and ammunition. Every day was strengthening the hands of the Government; troops were being recalled from Flanders; 6000 auxiliaries were being sent over by the States of Holland and, as soon appeared, preparations were being made to send a strong force to the north under Marshal Wade. On the other hand, it was considered with justice that the news of Prestonpans would soon bring abundance of re-cruits from the Highlands. It was decided to remain for a few weeks in Edinburgh.

The greatest efforts were made to collect munitions of war. Requisitions were made of stores and public money. A sum of £5000 was levied from the city of Glasgow, and parties were sent out in all directions to beat up recruits. The weeks which followed Prestonpans were the halcyon time of Jacobitism. Prince Charles's followers were flushed with victory and confident of success. The Prince himself kept a royal court at Holyrood, as if he were already at St James's. He spent his days in the camp and the council chamber;[1] in the evenings, says Home, " he received the

---

[1] "The Prince formed a Council which met regularly every morning in his drawing-room. The gentlemen whom he called to it were the Duke of Perth, Lord Lewis Gordon, Lord George Murray, Lord Elcho, Lord Ogilvie, Lord Pitsligo, Lord Nairne, Lochiel, Keppoch, Clanranald, Glencoe, Lochgarry, Ardshiel, Sir Thomas Sheridan, Colonel O'Sullivan, Glenbucket, and Secretary Murray. The Prince, in this Council, used always first to declare what he himself was for, and then he asked everybody's opinion in their turn. There was one-third of the Council whose principles were that kings and princes can never either act or think wrong, so, in consequence, they always confirmed whatever the Prince said. The other two-thirds, who thought that kings and princes thought sometimes like other men, and were not altogether infallible, and that this Prince was no more so than others, and, therefore, begged leave to differ from him when they could give sufficient reasons for their difference of opinion. This very often was no hard matter to do, for as the Prince and his old governor, Sir Thomas Sheridan, were altogether ignorant of the ways and customs of Great Britain, and both much for the doctrine of absolute monarchy, they would very often, had they not been prevented, have fallen into blunders which might have hurt the cause. The Prince could not bear to hear anybody differ in sentiment from him, and took a dislike to everybody that did; for he had a notion of commanding this army as any general does a body of mercenaries, and so let them know only what he pleased, and expected them to obey without enquiring further about the matter. This might have done better had his favourites been people of the country, but, as they were Irish, and had nothing to risk, the people of fashion that had their all at stake, and consequently ought to be supposed capable to give the best advice of which they were capable, thought they had a title to know and be consulted in what was for the good of the cause in which they had so much concern; and if it had not been for their insisting strongly upon it, the Prince, when he found that his sentiments were not always approved of, would have abolished this Council long ere he did."  Lord Elcho's account, cited by Scott, Tales of a Grandfather, chap. lxxix.

ladies who came to his drawing-room; he then supped in public, and generally there was music at supper, and a ball afterwards." His own personal popularity was unbounded. If he had some of the Stuart vices he certainly had a very ample share of the Stuart charm. With his youth, his good looks, his kindness and his courage, he won the goodwill of everyone who saw him. Of course the women were wild about him; not a few of them mounted the White Cockade and gave their jewels and treasured heirlooms to raise a little money for his service. There was a certain Miss Isabella Lumisden, who plainly told her lover, a young artist named Robert Strange, that he need think no more of her unless he joined Prince Charlie. Strange, who afterwards became Sir Robert Strange, the most famous line engraver of his time, joined the Prince's Guards and suffered exile for the cause. He fought at Culloden, and only escaped his pursuers by hiding under his sweetheart's ample hoop. We are indebted to him for a picturesque and detailed account of the battle and the night march which preceded it.[1]

In the meantime, the good folk of Edinburgh were not without a taste of the miseries of war. There was still a small garrison of royal troops in the castle. Shortly after the battle the castle was blockaded by the Highlanders. General Guest, the commandant, demanded that the blockade should be raised forthwith, and informed the Lord Provost that unless communication between the castle and the city were renewed he would open fire upon the city. A night's respite was granted, and the General's communication was laid before Prince Charles. The Prince expostulated upon the unreasonableness of punishing the citizens for what after all was no fault of theirs. The commandant consented to postpone the bombardment till he should receive orders from London. However, on October 1 the Highlanders fired upon a party who were going up the Castle Hill with provisions. Next day the Castle fired upon the houses that covered the Highland guard. The Prince replied by strengthening the blockade, whereupon the cannonade of the city was actually commenced. Throughout the afternoon of October 4 and on the following day fire was maintained from the Half-Moon battery upon the city. Several houses were destroyed, and the citizens were frightened out of their wits. Yielding to their earnest entreaties, the Prince consented to raise the blockade. A very vivid picture of the state of affairs in Edinburgh during the Prince's occupation, and of the conditions under which business was carried on, is given in the diary of Mr John Campbell, then principal cashier of the Royal Bank of Scotland, which was recently printed by the Scottish History Society (*Miscellany*, vol. i., pp. 537-559 *et seq.*).

By the end of October the Prince's army had increased to nearly 6000 men. Many recruits had come from the north under Lord Ogilvie, Gordon of Glenbucket, Lord Pitsligo, Lord Lewis Gordon, Cluny MacPherson, the Marquis of Tullibardine,

---

[1] See p. 153. It is pleasant to note that Strange had his reward; he married Miss Lumisden in 1747.

and others. He had also been joined by the Earls of Kilmarnock and Nithsdale and Lord Kenmure. Two troops of Life Guards, under Lord Elcho and Lord Balmerino, had been organised, and a train of artillery had been formed. By this time Wade was at Newcastle at the head of a powerful force.[1] Charles was eager to fight him without delay, and urged an immediate march into England. His advisers counselled further delay; ultimately a middle course was adopted; it was decided to cross the Border at Carlisle, so as to avoid immediate collision with Wade's army. This would afford an opportunity to the English supporters of the cause to rise, and at the same time would impose upon Wade the necessity of a fatiguing march before he could bring the invaders to an action. On the 31st of October the Prince marched out of Edinburgh, and his army rendezvoused at Dalkeith. It was decided that the march into England should be made in two columns. One, under the Duke of Perth, was to march to Carlisle by the western road, by Peebles and Moffat; the other, commanded by the Prince himself, took the road by Lauder and Kelso. Lord George Murray accompanied the Prince.

The Prince's column reached Lauder on November 3, Kelso on the 4th, and Jedburgh on the 6th. On the 8th he crossed the Esk into England, and on the following day was joined by the western column; the whole army encamped for the night in the villages to the west of Carlisle. On the 10th Carlisle was summoned to surrender. Pattison, the deputy mayor, refused, and preparations were being made for a siege when news arrived that Wade was about to march from Newcastle to relieve Carlisle. The troops were accordingly withdrawn from the trenches, and were marched to Brampton, where they encamped on the 12th. It turned out, however, that Wade was not moving, accordingly the siege of Carlisle was resumed, and on the 15th the town and Castle both surrendered on terms. On the 17th the Prince entered Carlisle, with a hundred pipers playing before him.

A few days after the surrender of Carlisle, a council of war was held to consider the next step. The effective force of the army had been greatly reduced by desertion on the march from Edinburgh, and did not now exceed 4500. There were four possible courses of action: to march to the east and attack Wade; to return to Scotland; to continue the march towards London; or to sit still at Carlisle and see if the English Jacobites would rise, which as yet they showed no sign of doing. The general opinion of the chiefs was that the Prince should return to Edinburgh and carry on a defensive war in Scotland till such time as he was in a condition to attempt invasion. The Prince, however, insisted on continuing the march to the south, and at length the chiefs assented.

The cavalry left Carlisle on November 20, and marched that day to Penrith. On

[1] As to the strength and composition of Wade's force, see Mr Blaikie's *Itinerary*, p. 95. It was estimated at the time at 14,000 foot and 4000 horse, probably an exaggeration.

the following day the Prince followed with the infantry; a garrison of two or three hundred men was left in Carlisle Castle. On the 23rd the Prince marched to Kendal, on the 25th to Lancaster, and on the 26th to Preston, a place of sinister memory to a Jacobite. Here, if anywhere, he might have expected to be joined by many adherents, but a mere handful came, and none of real importance. All along the line of march the invaders had a friendly reception from the gentry, but there were very few indeed who had sufficient belief in Charles's chances of success to peril their lives and fortunes on the result of his enterprise. The common people at first regarded the Highlanders with abject terror, as cannibal savages who ate children, but as they found they had nothing to fear, they came to regard the march as an entertaining show.

Wigan was reached on the 28th, and Manchester on the 29th. Here at last the invaders found active friendship, and obtained both money and recruits. The Chevalier Johnstone, who was attached to the artillery of the Prince's army, gives an amusing account of the capture of Manchester, illustrating at once the adventurous spirit of some of the invaders and the indifference of the inhabitants.

"One of my sergeants, named Dickson, whom I had enlisted from among the prisoners of war at Gladsmuir, a young Scotsman, as brave and intrepid as a lion, and very much attached to my interest, informed me on the 27th, at Preston, that he had been beating up for recruits all day without getting one; and that he was the more chagrined at this, as the other sergeants had had better success. He therefore came to ask my permission to get a day's march ahead of the army, by setting out immediately for Manchester, a very considerable town of England, containing 40,000 inhabitants, in order to make sure of some recruits before the arrival of the army. I reproved him sharply for entertaining so wild and extravagant a project, which exposed him to the danger of being taken and hanged, and I ordered him back to his company. Having much confidence in him, I had given him a horse and entrusted him with my portmanteau, that I might always have it with me. On entering my quarters in the evening, my landlady informed me that my servant had called and taken away my portmanteau and blunderbuss. I immediately bethought myself of his extravagant project, and his situation gave me much uneasiness. But on our arrival at Manchester on the evening of the following day, the 29th, Dickson brought me about 180 recruits, whom he had enlisted for my company.

"He had quitted Preston in the evening with his mistress and my drummer; and having marched all night, he arrived next morning at Manchester, which is about twenty miles distant from Preston, and immediately began to beat up for recruits for 'the yellow-haired laddie.' The populace at first did not interrupt him, conceiving our army to be near the town; but as soon as they knew that it would not arrive till the evening, they surrounded him in a tumultuous manner, with the intention of taking him prisoner, alive or dead. Dickson presented his blunderbuss, which was charged with slugs, threatening to blow out the brains of those who first dared to lay hands on himself or the two who accompanied him ; and by turning round continually, facing in all directions, and behaving like a lion, he soon enlarged the circle which a crowd of people had formed round them. Having continued for some time to manœuvre in this way, those of the inhabitants of Manchester who were attached to the House of Stuart took arms and flew to the assistance of Dickson, to rescue him from the fury of the mob, so that he soon had five or six hundred men to aid him, who dispersed the crowd in a very short time. Dickson now triumphed in his turn ; and putting himself at the head of his followers, he proudly paraded, undisturbed, the whole day with his drummer, enlisting for my company all who offered themselves.

"On presenting me with a list of 180 recruits, I was agreeably surprised to find that the whole amount of his expenses did not exceed three guineas. This adventure of Dickson gave rise to many a joke at the expense of the town of Manchester, from the singular circumstance of its having been taken by a sergeant, a drummer, and a girl. The circumstance may serve to show the enthusiastic courage of our army, and the alarm and terror with which the English were seized." [1]

On December 1 the march was resumed, and on the evening of the 4th the Prince entered Derby.

The invaders were now within 130 miles of London, but it was clear that their position was in the highest degree critical. Wade's army was in the north between them and Scotland ; 10,000 men under the Duke of Cumberland were close to them in Staffordshire, and a third army, some 30,000 strong, commanded by George II. in person, had been organised for the defence of the capital. There had not been the faintest appearance of a movement among the English Jacobites. It was evident that within a few days Charles would have to fight a desperate battle against tremendous odds, a battle in which defeat was almost certain, and in which defeat meant destruction.

The 5th of December was spent in making preparations to fight Cumberland on the following day. In the midst of these preparations a courier arrived from the north with despatches from Lord John Drummond, brother of the Duke of Perth, announcing that he had landed at Montrose with a thousand French troops, who were the forerunners of further reinforcements from France ; and that these had been joined by a large number of Highlanders. On the forenoon of the 5th, a council of war was held and the situation was considered. The Prince was obstinately set on fighting Cumberland, and attempting to cut a way through to London. But the chiefs were unanimously of opinion that the only feasible course was to retreat into Scotland, effect a junction with Lord John Drummond, and await the arrival of succours from France. The Prince reluctantly gave way, and early in

[1] Johnstone's *Memoirs*, p. 48.

the morning of the 6th of December the retreat was commenced. Retracing its steps, the army reached Manchester on the 9th, Preston on the 11th, and Lancaster on the 14th, pursued by Cumberland. Penrith was reached on the 18th. On the evening of that day the rear-guard of the Prince's army, under Lord George Murray, was attacked by a strong body of Cumberland's cavalry close to the village of Clifton. After a sharp skirmish in the moonlight, the pursuers were repulsed. Carlisle was re-entered on the 19th. A garrison of some four hundred men was left to hold the castle ; ten days later they surrendered unconditionally to Cumberland.

On the 20th the army recrossed the Border. The march was continued by Dumfries, Douglas, and Hamilton, and in the afternoon of the 26th of December the Prince entered Glasgow.

Besides the force which had marched into England, a considerable body of men was now in arms for the Prince in Scotland. In Aberdeenshire Lord Lewis Gordon had been raising men and money for the cause ; he had been joined by part of the force which had landed at Montrose with Lord John Drummond. Lord Strathallan was at Perth at the head of another considerable Highland force, and the remainder of Lord John's men joined him there. A number of MacIntoshes, Mackenzies, and Macgregors had also risen, and more recruits had come from Glengarry and Lochiel's country.

In the beginning of December Lord Loudon marched through Stratherrick to relieve Fort Augustus, which was threatened by the Frasers under the Master of Lovat. He captured that old scoundrel. Lord Lovat, who had been playing fast and loose with both sides, and took him as a prisoner to Inverness, whereupon the clan marched under the Master to join the Prince. Lovat shortly afterwards escaped. A force of Macleods and Munroes, under Macleod of Macleod and Munro of Culcairn, was despatched by Loudon into Aberdeenshire to attack Lord Lewis Gordon. Lord Lewis marched to meet them, encountered them at Inverurie on December 23, and put them to flight. He then marched southward to join the Jacobite force at Perth. This brought up the number of men assembled there to over 4000. The fact that this force included a body of French regular troops was of additional advantage to the Jacobites, as the forces of the States of Holland were, by the capitulations of Tournay and Dendermonde, precluded from serving against the King of France or his allies, and the Dutch troops, recently landed in England, were thus prevented from taking part in the campaign.

The Prince remained in Glasgow for a week, and procured from the city a much-needed supply of clothing and other necessaries for his men. It was decided to effect a junction at Stirling with the troops that lay at Perth, and instructions to this effect were sent to Lord John Drummond, who now commanded them. On the 3rd of January, 1746, the Prince's army left Glasgow in two columns ; one, under Charles himself, marching by Kilsyth, the other, under Lord George Murray, by Cumber-

T

nauld. Bannockburn was reached on the 4th, and the Prince took up his quarters at Bannockburn House, the residence of his devoted adherent, Sir Hugh Paterson. There he remained till the 16th. On the 8th the town of Stirling capitulated, and General Blakeney retired to the Castle.

About a fortnight after the evacuation of Edinburgh by the Jacobites, the Government officials had returned to the city. On the 14th of November the city was occupied by Hamilton's and Gardiner's dragoons and Price's and Ligonier's foot. Part of Wade's army had been sent north to strengthen the garrison. The command of this force had been entrusted to General Henry Hawley, a man of savage temper, whose personal courage was greater than his military capacity. He had served as a subaltern at Sheriffmuir, and had a most profound contempt for the Highlanders. He boasted that two regiments of dragoons were sufficient to ride over the whole High-land army, and just before marching from Edinburgh he wrote to Lord President Forbes, "if we were in a condition but to march, we should not mind their numbers."

On January 13, Hawley's advance guard, under Major-General Huske, marched from Edinburgh to Linlithgow. The main body followed on the 15th, and Hawley himself on the 16th. The whole force amounted to nearly 8000 men. On the night of the 16th, they encamped to the north-west of Falkirk; there they were joined by a thousand men from Argyllshire under Colonel John Campbell, afterwards fifth Duke of Argyll.

On the 10th, Prince Charles had commenced the siege of Stirling Castle. On hearing of Hawley's approach, he resolved to meet him half-way, and on the 16th of January encamped on Plean Muir, two miles from Stirling. On the morning of the 17th, he ordered a review of all his troops. It was no sooner over than the troops were formed in column and marched from the field, their destination being kept a profound secret. A small body of horse, under Lord John Drummond, was sent to make a feint along the high road towards Falkirk, through the Torwood, which then extended on both sides of the high road. The rest of the Prince's army went round the south side of the Torwood, and forded the Carron near Dunipace House. They then made for the rising ground to the south-west of Falkirk.

About one o'clock, two officers of the Royal army discovered, by means of a telescope, the advanced guard of the Highland army as it emerged from behind the Torwood. General Hawley had accepted the invitation of the Countess of Kil-marnock, whose husband was with the Prince, to visit Callander House. The Countess appears to have exercised all her powers of fascination in order to make him neglect his duty, with no small success. When the approach of the enemy was perceived, Lieutenant-Colonel Howard, the second in command, was immediately informed of it, and at once went off to Callander House to inform the General. He, however, treated the information very lightly, and said "that the men might put on their accoutrements, but there was no necessity for their being under arms."

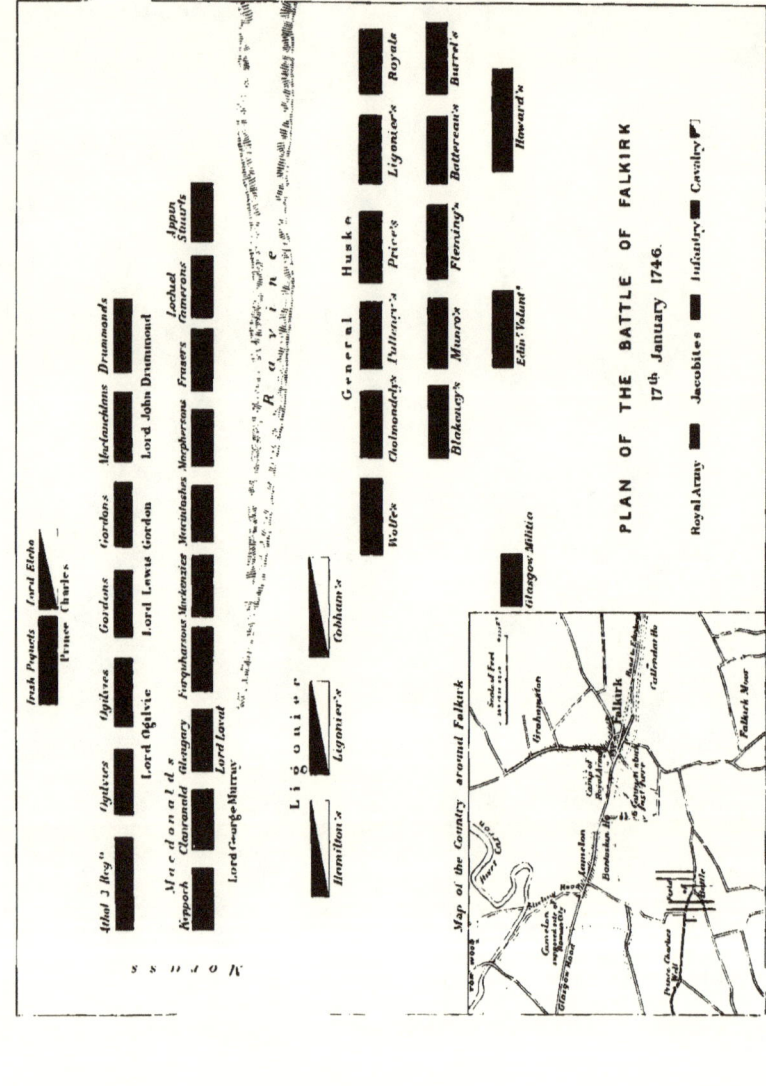

PLAN OF THE BATTLE OF FALKIRK
17th January 1746.

Royal Army  Jacobites  Infantry  Cavalry

The Highland army, marching in two columns, ascended the rising ground to the south of Falkirk, until they looked right down on the King's army. The Macdonalds were at the head of the first column. When the column reached the top of the hill, it halted and formed into line to the left. Patullo, the Prince's muster-master, estimated the strength of the army at Falkirk at 8000 men, besides about 1000 left to continue the blockade of Stirling Castle. The first line consisted of the three Macdonald regiments—Keppoch, Clanranald, and Glengarry ; on their left were the Farquharsons, Mackenzies, Macintoshes, Macphersons, Frasers, Camerons of Lochiel, and on the extreme left the Appin Stewarts. The second line was composed of the three Atholl regiments on the right, the Ogilvies, the Gordons, the Maclauchlans, and the men under Lord John Drummond, who had taken up his position on the left.

The reserve, where Prince Charles took up his position, was composed of the Irish piquets and a small body of horse under Lord Elcho. The first line was commanded by Lord George Murray, the second by Lord John Drummond. The right flank was protected by a morass.

In the absence of General Hawley, the commanding officers formed their regiments in front of their encampment ; and another messenger was despatched to Callander House, from which the General was at last seen galloping in breathless haste without his hat. The army was at once formed in two lines, with a body of reserve. The first line, under General Huske, consisted of a battalion of the Royal Scots, and the regiments of Wolfe, Cholmondeley, Pulteney, Price, and Ligonier. The second line consisted of Barrel's, Blakeney's, Munro's, Battereau's and Fleming's. Howard's regiment, drawn up behind the right of the second line, formed the reserve, and on their left the Edinburgh Volunteers and the Glasgow militia were stationed ; the Argyllshire Highlanders were left to guard the camp. The three regiments of dragoons, Cobham's, Ligonier's, and Hamilton's, commanded by Ligonier, were advanced in extended squadrons in front of the infantry towards its left.

General Hawley at once ordered his cavalry forward to secure the crest of the hill before the Highlanders could reach it, the infantry to follow as rapidly as possible. Just as this advance was ordered the day became overcast, and a storm of wind and rain beat directly in the faces of the soldiers, who were marching up hill with fixed bayonets. The race for the top was gained by the Highlanders, who were formed and ready to receive the dragoons on their arrival, with the great advantage of having the storm of wind and rain from behind, in place of in their faces ; the darkness becoming so great that it was impossible to see to any distance. A deep ravine, extending from the top of the hill, ran due north into the plain, getting deeper and wider in its progress. This ravine separated the left of the Highland army from the right of the Hanoverians.

The dragoons were formed so much to the left and so far in advance, that

Lord George Murray, who commanded the Highland army, believed that they were not supported by infantry, and immediately ordered an attack to be made on them, at the very time that General Hawley had ordered Colonel Ligonier, who commanded the cavalry, to advance against the Highlanders. Such was Hawley's contempt for his opponents that this order was given before his infantry had time to form on the crest of the hill. Lord George, with his sword drawn and his target on his arm, advanced at the head of the Macdonalds of Keppoch till within a few paces of the dragoons, when he gave the orders to fire; this discharge emptied twenty-four saddles, but still the dragoons rushed forward, breaking the Highlanders' line and riding down many of the men. The Highlanders, as usual, threw away their muskets, and fought with their swords, and for a time the conflict consisted of a series of single combats. The Highlanders who had been thrown down in the struggle plunged their dirks into the bellies of the horses. Others seized the riders by their clothes and pulled them to the ground, despatching them with their pistols or dirks, as there was no room to use their swords.

But this fierce struggle did not last long; the dragoons were vanquished, and retreated in great disorder upon their own infantry, spreading terror through their ranks, which broke and fled down the hill, pursued by the Highlanders. In the midst of the retreating mass, General Hawley rode with it towards Falkirk.

All the English army, however, did not retreat. Barrel's regiment stood fast, and was soon joined by parts of two regiments of the first line (Price's and Ligonier's). This body of resolute men moved to their left till they came directly opposite to the Camerons and Stuarts, and began to fire upon them across the ravine. The Highlanders kept their ground and returned the fire; but in this mode of warfare they had no chance with disciplined troops, and after a number had fallen the Highlanders began to retire, still keeping the high ground on their side of the ravine. This success of the Royal troops put a stop to the pursuit, for the Highlanders, hearing so much firing behind them, returned to their former position, expecting to find their second line, but it was not to be found. Some of the men composing it had joined in the pursuit.

Some men, on the other hand, believing that the Hanoverians were getting the best of it, had begun to retreat towards the west, whilst the great mass of the English army was retreating towards the east.

Farquharson of Monaltry, who had command of the Prince's artillery, had not been able to keep up with the rapid march of the army. He was still a mile distant when he heard the firing, and was shortly afterwards met by some two or three hundred of the Highlanders retreating from the field. He compelled them to return with him, leaving his guns behind. Before he arrived, however, Prince Charles and the reserve had advanced to support the Highlanders, and Barrel's regiment, Cobham's dragoons, and the others who had stood with them, were in full retreat towards the camp.

General Hawley, before leaving Falkirk with the remains of his army, ordered his camp to be set on fire, and then retreated towards Linlithgow, leaving an immense quantity of baggage, provisions, and ammunition, besides seven guns which had stuck fast half-way up the hill and had never been brought into action. The battle was all over in twenty minutes. By this time darkness had come on, which was greatly increased by the storm which still raged. The confusion was dreadful, no one seemed to know for some time the result of the action, or where to find either their regiments or officers. Lord Kilmarnock was the first to discover the retreat of the Royal army, but the darkness and disorder were so great that it was impossible to take advantage of the victory, or collect a sufficient number of troops to complete it; so the English army, although harassed by as many Highlanders as could be gathered together, made good its retreat to Linlithgow, where it remained all night. The retreat was continued next day to Edinburgh, where the remains of the army arrived about four o'clock in the afternoon. Prince Charles, with his army, remained at Falkirk all night, and returned next day to his former quarters at Bannockburn.

Home gives the loss of the Royal army at 300 or 400 men; of officers the loss was very severe—Colonel Sir Robert Munro; three Lieutenant-Colonels, Biggar of Munro's regiment, Powell of Cholmondely's, and Whitney of Gardiner's; five captains of Wolfe's and one lieutenant; four captains of Blakeney's and two lieutenants, besides many wounded. Johnstone gives the loss of the Royal army at 600 men killed and 700 prisoners. The loss of the Highlanders is stated at 32 officers and men killed, and 120 wounded.

Throughout the whole of the day which succeeded the battle the weather remained so tempestuous that it was impossible for the victors to pursue their defeated enemies. On the 19th the weather cleared, and an advance on Edinburgh was thought of. It was, however, decided to return to Bannockburn and to proceed with the siege of Stirling Castle. More than a week was spent in siege operations. These were under the charge of a French engineer named Mirabelle de Gordon, who seems to have been a person of singular incapacity. Fire was opened on the castle on January 30, but the besiegers' battery was entirely commanded by the castle guns, and was silenced in less than half-an-hour. In the meantime, the fugitives of Hawley's army had had time to draw together again at Edinburgh, where it was further reinforced by detachments from the army of Marshal Wade. "The army of the enemy," says the Chevalier Johnstone, "in eight or ten days was stronger than it had been before the battle of Falkirk."

Hawley's defeat caused consternation in London. The command of the army in Scotland was transferred to the Duke of Cumberland, who had returned to London after the surrender of Carlisle. He left London on January 25th, and reached Edinburgh on the 30th.

Prince Charles as usual was eager for battle; it was his desire to advance against

Edinburgh at once, and a plan of the expected battle had actually been prepared. But on January 29 a paper signed by Lord George Murray and some of the most influential of the chiefs was laid before him, in which a retreat to the north was advised. This document set forth concisely the position of Charles's military affairs at this time. It was in the following terms :—

" FALKIRK, *29th January*, 1746.

"We think it our duty, in this critical juncture, to lay our opinions in the most respectful manner before your Royal Highness.

"We are certain that a vast number of the soldiers of your Royal Highness's army are gone home since the battle of Falkirk ; and notwithstanding all the endeavours of the commanders of the different corps, they find that this evil is increasing hourly, and not in their power to prevent : and as we are afraid Stirling Castle cannot be taken so soon as was expected, if the enemy should march before it fall into your Royal Highness's hands we can foresee nothing but utter destruction to the few that will remain, considering the inequality of our numbers to that of the enemy. For these reasons, we are humbly of opinion, that there is no way to extricate your Royal Highness and those who remain with you out of the most imminent danger but by retiring immediately to the Highlands, where we can be usefully employed the remainder of the winter by taking and mastering the forts of the north ; and we are morally sure we can keep as many men together as will answer that end, and hinder the enemy from following us in the mountains at this season of the year ; and in spring we doubt not but an army of 10,000 effective Highlanders can be brought together, and follow your Royal Highness wherever you think proper. This will certainly disconcert your enemies, and cannot but be approved of by your Royal Highness's friends both at home and abroad. If a landing should happen in the meantime, the Highlanders would immediately rise, either to join them or to make a powerful diversion elsewhere.

"The hard marches which your army has undergone, the winter season, and now the inclemency of the weather, cannot fail of making this measure approved of by your Royal Highness's allies abroad, as well as your faithful adherents at home. The greatest difficulty that occurs to us is the saving of the artillery, particularly the heavy cannon ; but better some of these were thrown into the river Forth as that your Royal Highness, besides the danger of your own person, should risk the flower of your army, which we apprehend must inevitably be the case if this retreat be not agreed to, and gone about without the loss of one moment ; and we think that it would be the greatest imprudence to risk the whole on so unequal a chance, when there are such hopes of succour from abroad, besides the resources your Royal Highness will have from your faithful and dutiful followers at home. It is but just now we are apprised of the numbers of our own people that are gone off, besides the many sick that are in no condition to fight. And we offer this our opinion with the more freedom that we are persuaded that your Royal Highness can never doubt of the uprightness of our intentions. Nobody is privy to this address to your Royal Highness except your subscribers ; and we beg leave to assure your Royal Highness that it is with great concern and reluctance we find ourselves obliged to declare our sentiments in so dangerous a situation, which nothing could have prevailed with us to have done but the unhappy going off of so many men."[1]

This paper was signed by Lord George Murray, Lochiel, Keppoch, Clanranald, Ardshiel, Lochgary, Scothouse, and Simon Fraser, Master of Lovat.

Charles was deeply mortified by the advice of the chiefs. According to John Hay, who acted occasionally as his secretary, "when the Prince read the paper he struck his head against the wall until he staggered, and exclaimed most violently against Lord George Murray ; his words were, ' Good God ! have I lived to see this.'" Retreat, however, was determined on, and on January 31[2] it was begun, and the army crossed the Fords of Frew. They camped that night at Crieff. On February 1 they left Crieff in two columns, which were to meet at Inverness. One, under Lord George Murray, took the coast road by Perth, Dundee, Montrose, and Aberdeen ; the other, under the Prince, went straight through the mountains by Blair Atholl. On the 16th the Prince reached Moy Hall, the seat of the chief of the MacIntoshes. Lord Loudon, who was at Inverness, formed a plan of surprising and capturing him there. He posted sentries all round the town, with orders that no person was to be allowed to leave it, and in the evening he set out with a force of 1500 men to surprise the castle. Johnstone describes what followed.

"Whilst some English officers were drinking in the house of Mrs Bailly, an inn-keeper in Inverness, and passing the time till the hour of their departure, her daughter, a girl of thirteen or fourteen years of age, who happened to wait on them, paid great attention to their conversation, and, from certain expressions dropped by them, she discovered their designs. As soon as this generous girl was certain as to their intentions, she immediately left the house, escaped from the town, notwithstanding the vigilance of the sentinels, and immediately took the road to Moy, running as fast as she was able, without shoes or stockings, which, to accelerate her progress, she had taken off, in order to inform the Prince of the danger that menaced him. She reached Moy, quite out of breath, before Lord Loudon ; and the Prince, with difficulty, escaped in his robe-de-chambre, night-cap, and slippers to the neighbouring mountains, where he passed the night in concealment. This dear girl, to whom the Prince owed his life, was in great danger of losing her own, from her excessive fatigue on this occasion ;

---

[1] Home, Appendix No. 39, p. 352.
[2] There is some conflict of evidence as to these dates ; those in the text are taken from the Chevalier Johnstone's narrative.

but the care and attentions she experienced restored her to life, and her health was at length re-established. The Prince, having no suspicion of such a daring attempt, had very few people with him in the Castle of Moy.

"As soon as the girl had spread the alarm, the blacksmith of the village of Moy presented himself to the Prince, and assured His Royal Highness that he had no occasion to leave the castle, as he would answer for it, with his head, that Lord Loudon and his troops would be obliged to return faster than they came. The Prince had not sufficient confidence in his assurances to neglect seeking his safety by flight to the neighbouring mountains. However, the blacksmith, for his own satisfaction, put his project in execution. He instantly assembled a dozen of his companions, and advanced with them about a quarter of a league from the castle, on the road to Inverness. There he laid an ambuscade, posting six of his companions on each side of the highway, to wait the arrival of the detachment of Lord Loudon, enjoining them not to fire till he should tell them, and then not to fire together, but one after another. When the head of the detachment of Lord Loudon was opposite the twelve men, about eleven o'clock in the evening, the blacksmith called out with a loud voice, 'Here come the villains, who intend carrying off our Prince; fire, my lads; do not spare them; give no quarter!' In an instant muskets were discharged from each side of the road, and the detachment, seeing their project had taken wind, began to fly in the greatest disorder, imagining that our whole army was lying in wait for them. Such was their terror and consternation that they did not stop till they reached Inverness. In this manner did a common blacksmith, with twelve of his companions, put Lord Loudon and fifteen hundred regular troops to flight. The fifer of his lordship, who happened to be at the head of the detachment, was killed by the first discharge, and the detachment did not wait for a second."

On February 18 the Prince's men entered Inverness. On his approach Loudon evacuated the town and crossed to the Black Isle. Two days later the garrison, which had been left in the castle, surrendered. On the 19th the Prince, who had taken up his quarters at Culloden House, was joined by Lord George Murray.

Inverness remained the headquarters of the Jacobite army till the end, which was now less than two months distant.

In March a force under Brigadier Stapleton was detached to attack Fort Augustus and Fort William. Fort Augustus surrendered on the 5th, but the garrison at Fort William made good their resistance, and the siege was abandoned on April 4. Loudon's force was pursued into Sutherland and dispersed by the Duke of Perth. Loudon himself, with Lord President Forbes, retired to Skye. Lord George Murray raided the Atholl country, and on March 17 surprised and captured the houses occupied by Government troops. He laid siege to his own brother's house, Blair Castle, which was occupied by a force under Sir Andrew Agnew. The siege was abandoned on April 2 on the approach of a relieving force.

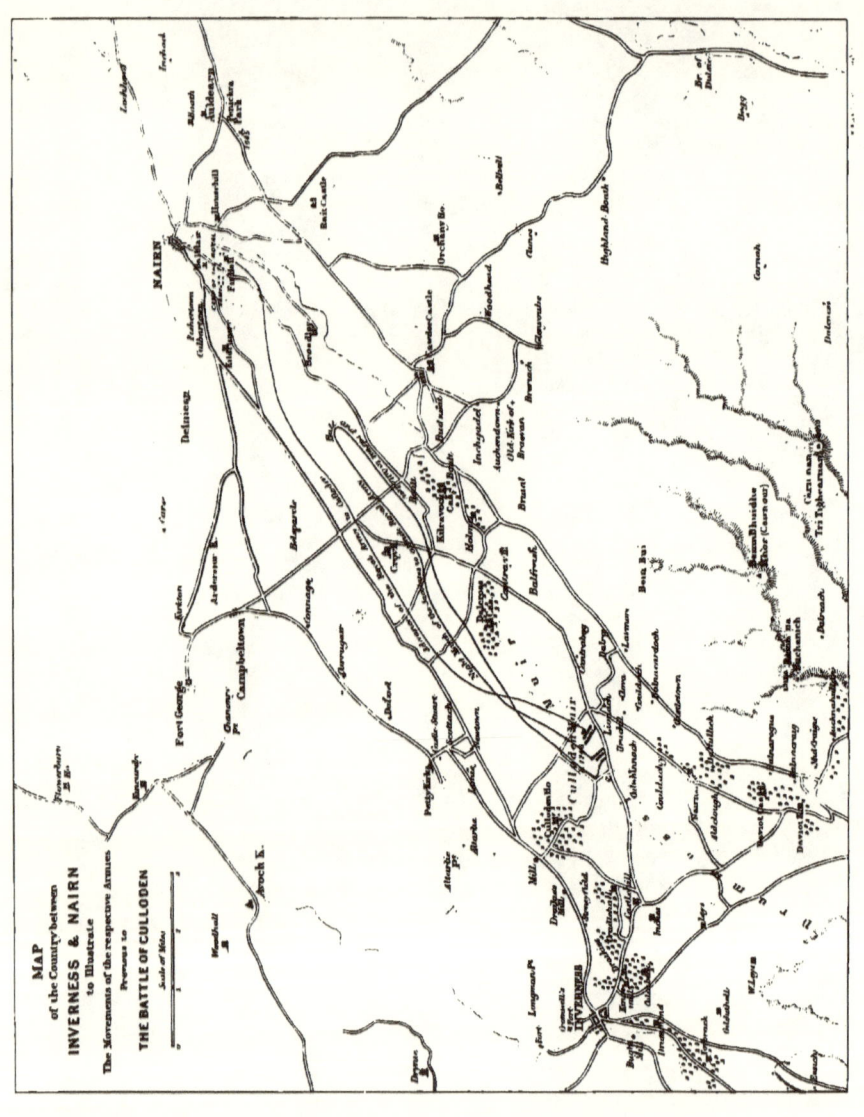

MAP
of the Country between
INVERNESS & NAIRN
to Illustrate
The Movements of the respective Armies
Previous to
THE BATTLE OF CULLODEN
Scale of Miles

About the middle of March the Prince visited Elgin and Gordon Castle.
In the meantime the enemy was approaching from the south. Cumberland, as we have seen, arrived in Edinburgh on the 30th of January, and at once commenced his march to the north. He reached Perth on February 6. On the 8th a force of Hessians, amounting to 5000 infantry and 500 Hussars, under the Prince of Hesse Cassel, landed at Leith. These were ordered to occupy Perth, Stirling, and Bannockburn. On the 20th Cumberland resumed his march northward; he entered Aberdeen on the 27th. On March 12 the first movement towards Inverness was made. General Bland was sent to occupy Inverurie and Old Meldrum; he reached Strathbogie on the 17th. On the 26th six battalions and two cavalry regiments were at Strathbogie, and three battalions and four guns at Old Meldrum. Cumberland himself left Aberdeen on April 8, marching by Old Meldrum and Banff, concentrated his forces at Cullen on the 11th, and crossed the Spey on the 12th; he reached Nairn on the 14th.[1]

We have now reached the opening of the last act of the tragic drama. On the day on which Cumberland reached Nairn, the Prince took up his quarters at Culloden House. The men bivouacked on the heath; the Prince himself stayed up all night. In the morning the army was drawn up on Culloden Moor in order of battle, but no enemy appeared. Lord Elcho was sent to reconnoitre Cumberland's camp. He returned with the report that it was the Duke's birthday, and that the English troops were engaged in celebrating the occasion. The Prince called a council of war, and it was decided that an attempt should be made to surprise Cumberland by a night march, and to attack his camp at early dawn.

Reference has already been made to the presence of Sir Robert Strange as a volunteer with the Prince's army. He took part in the night march and the battle which followed, and has left a concise and graphic account of what he saw. He had been occupied in engraving notes for the Jacobite exchequer when news reached Inverness that Cumberland had passed the Spey. "The town was in a general alarm and even confusion," says Strange: "nothing was heard but the noise of bagpipes, beating of drums, and clash of arms. The field of Culloden was on the following day to be the general rendezvous, and every individual betook himself to his corps.

"The next morning I went betimes to the secretary's office and delivered over the whole of my charge, together with the notes I had been entrusted with. . . . My companions were, in general, glad to see me, and, joking, asked me when they were to have any of my money. I replied that, if they gave a good account of the Duke, I hoped his treasury-chest would supply us.

"The army was now mustering upon the field, it being the 14th; but, unfortunately, we had not been joined by a considerable number of our men, who were actually upon

---

[1] The army advanced from Aberdeen to Cullen in four divisions, by different roads. The routes of the marching columns and the cantonment lists of the troops quartered in Aberdeen are printed in Allardyce's *Historical Papers*, vol. i. pp. 299-303.

U

their march from different parts of the country, and would have been up in the course of a few days. The whole of the Macphersons, a considerable body of the Frasers, some few of the Macintoshes, in general all the Mackenzies, and several other bodies of men who had been raised in the more northern counties, had all received repeated expresses, and were hastening to join the army. In this situation, divested as it were of part of our numbers, we hourly expected the Duke. He had come on to Nairn on the 14th, and was there halting. There was even no appearance of his moving, the 15th being his birthday. In the afternoon of that day the Prince had summoned a council of war to be held upon the field, and had proposed a plan of a march under cloud of night to attack the Duke's army by surprise, and to force his camp. This plan was worthy even of any of the greatest heroes of antiquity, and met with general approbation, particularly amongst the clans. The council remained long in deliberating in what manner it was to be conducted. Two essential things, secrecy and expedition, were the great objects to be observed. There was only one road to Nairn, which was the high road, and this being covered in many places with villages, it was essential to avoid it, to prevent any information being carried to the Duke's army. The next alternative, and indeed the only one, was to attempt a way along the foot of a ridge of mountains which fronted the sea, but had scarcely been ever trode by human foot, and was known by the name of the Moor Road. It would have brought us in upon that part of the enemy's camp from which they could apprehend no danger. It lengthened indeed the road, which, in the sequel, and from the shortness of the night, proved our misfortune.

" Before the council broke up, every regiment as it were had his place assigned him in the order of the march. The van was commanded by Lord George Murray, who, with about one-third of the army, was to have passed the water of Nairn about two miles distant from the town, and who, unexpected by the enemy, was to have invested the Duke's quarters and to have made him prisoner. The remaining two-thirds, commanded by the Duke of Perth and Lord John Drummond, were to have attacked them from the plain, which, in all probability, would have been carried sword in hand. It is to be remarked that the same army had been already surprised at Falkirk.

" Night coming on and not sooner could the army begin its march, to prevent the country people from being alarmed, or any intelligence being carried to the enemy part of our numbers, weak as we were, was under a necessity of being left on the field, in order to save appearances and light up fires, as had been done the preceding evening, and to prevent stragglers, if any there were, forming unnecessary conjectures. The night was favourable to our wishes, but, alas! such a road was never travelled ; the men in general were frequently up to the ankles, and the horses in many places extricated themselves with difficulty. In this manner were we retarded almost the whole of the night ; notwithstanding of which, an uncommon spirit supported itself throughout the army.

"It was now the 16th of April, when day began to break about four in the morning. It was indeed a dreadful knell to us, being as yet above four long miles from Nairn; nor did we know what sort of road we had yet to encounter. Appearances became serious, each was whispering to his neighbour, and, so far as countenances could be descried, disappointment was evidently marked. During this critical moment of suspense, what was to be done? A halt took place; a council was called as soon as the general officers could be got together. The morning was fine, and the day was ushering in apace; it required but little time to deliberate, and, finding it impossible to attack the Duke by surprise, it was judged expedient, for the safety of the army, to give up the enterprise and return to the field of Culloden. Thus were our hopes disappointed. We saw, as it were before us the glorious prize, but we durst not encounter it, for there is almost a moral certainty that we should have been cut off to a man. The enemy was early in motion, must have seen us at a considerable distance, and received us upon the points of their bayonets.

"We now turned about to the left, and as soon as we conveniently could, got into the high road. The Prince, attended by his followers and a few of his body-guards, went on towards Culloden. Thus did the shortness of the night, attended with a most harassing march, prevent a plan from being carried into execution which was as morally certain of success as it would have been glorious to the youth who projected it. For it is a known truth that the enemy had no idea of the intended attack, and that the first information they received was after their army had begun to move; and it was even communicated to them from their own vanguard, who had learnt it upon their march. We had got but a few miles upon the road when a number of the guards, finding themselves overpowered with fatigue, and ready every instant to drop from our saddles, came to a resolution of stopping; we were shown into an open barn, where we threw ourselves down upon some straw, tying our horses to our ankles, and the people assuring us that in case of any danger they should awake us. They were, indeed, as good as their promise, for we had slumbered here but a short time before a woman gave us the alarm that the Duke's horse were in sight. We that instant mounted, and as soon as we got upon the high road the vanguard, as yet at some distance, were approaching. We now made the best of our way; but, before ascending to the field, we found the Prince had been there some time, and was actually at that moment engaged in holding a council of war, deliberating whether we should give battle to the Duke, or, circumstanced as the army was, retire and wait the arrival of our reinforcements. The former was determined on."

The Highlanders had reached their camping ground on Culloden Moor about five o'clock in the morning of the 16th, dead beat with hunger and fatigue. Most of the men lay down to sleep; not a few made their way into Inverness to look for food. The Prince returned to Culloden House; some bread and whisky were, with difficulty, procured for him, and he lay down to sleep. He had not slept more than two hours when he was awakened by the news that Cumberland was on the march from Nairn.

It was now about eight o'clock in the morning. Orders were hurriedly sent to recall the men who had gone to Inverness, and the army was paraded to await Cumberland's attack. According to Patullo's statement,[1] the number on the roll of the Prince's army at this time was about 8000. Several parties, however, had been detached upon different expeditions, and were not come back; and a very large number of men were so exhausted by fatigue, hunger, and want of sleep that it was not possible to bring 5000 to the field. Proposals were made to retire across the river Nairn, and avoid fighting at so great a disadvantage. But Sir Thomas Sheridan and others of the Prince's advisers, "hoping no doubt for a miracle," says Patullo, insisted upon fighting Cumberland at once, and the army was accordingly drawn up in the order of battle. The Prince's army was drawn up in two lines: the Atholl brigade was on the right of the first line, on their left stood Lochiel's Camerons, the Appin Stewarts, the Frasers, the MacIntoshes, the Maclauchlans and Macleans, John Roy Stewart's regiment, the Farquharsons, and on the left of all, the three Macdonald regiments Clanranald, Keppoch, and Glengarry. The Macphersons were absent; when the battle was fought they were on the march from Badenoch. Lord George Murray commanded on the right, and Lord John Drummond on the left.[2] The second line, which was commanded by General Stapleton, consisted of the regiments under Lord Ogilvie, Lord Lewis Gordon, Glenbucket, the Duke of Perth, and Lord John Drummond; on the left were the Irish piquets. On the right of the first line was a troop of Horse-Guards, on the left of the second line a troop of Fitzjames's Horse. The reserve, which was commanded by Lord Kilmarnock, consisted of his regiment of foot-guards, with the remains of Lord Pitsligo's and Lord Strathallan's Horse. Charles himself, escorted by Lord Balmerino's troop of Horse-Guards and Colonel Shea's troop of Fitzjames's Horse, remained on a small eminence in rear of the right of the second line. The right of the position was protected by the walls of a large enclosure.

About twelve o'clock, Cumberland's approaching army appeared at a distance of about two miles and a half. When the Duke perceived that the Prince's army was prepared to give him battle, he halted and deployed his troops for action.

The Duke's force amounted to about 8800 men. His first line consisted of six regiments of infantry: on the right were the Royal Scots (St. Clair's), on their left Cholmondeley's, Price's, the Scots Fusiliers (Campbell's), Munro's, and Barrel's. The second line consisted of Howard's, Fleming's, Ligonier's, Bligh's, Sempill's, and Wolfe's. In the reserve were Blakeney's, Battereau's, and Pulteney's. The Duke of Kingston's Light Horse and a squadron of Cobham's dragoons were placed on the

---

[1] Home, Appendix No. 30, p. 332.
[2] The authorities differ in some details as to the disposition of the troops on both sides: Home's account is followed in the text.

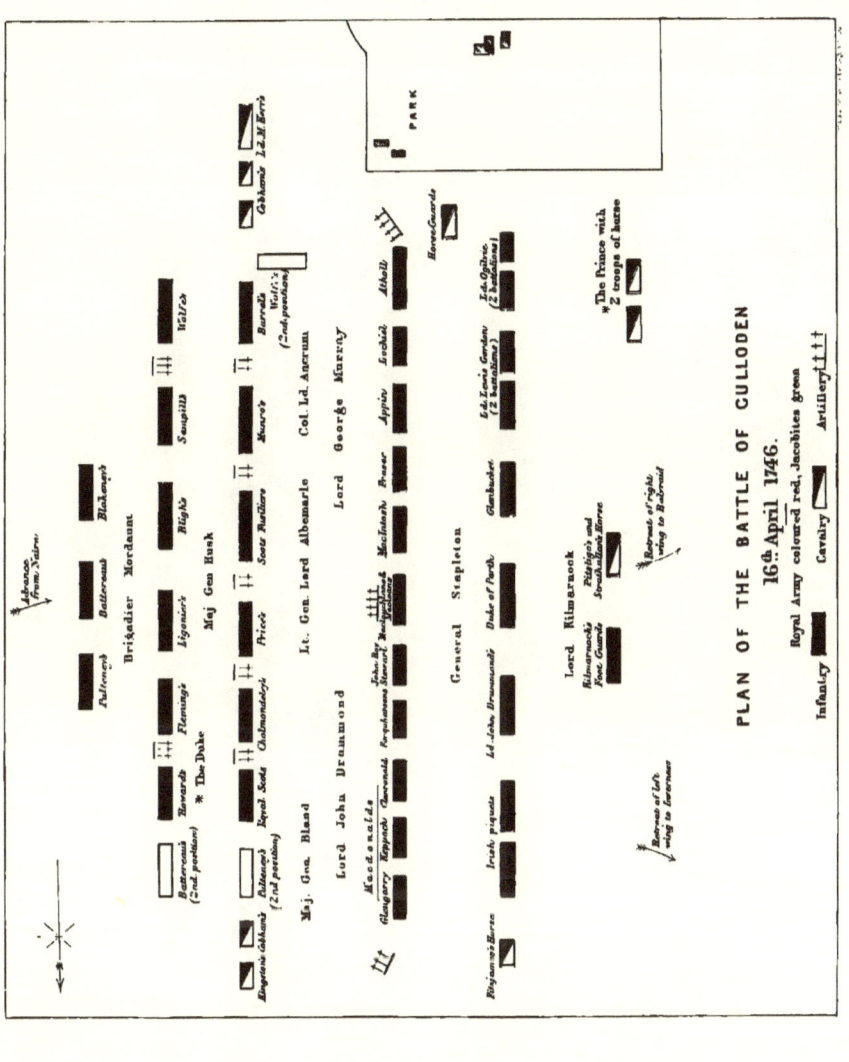

PLAN OF THE BATTLE OF CULLODEN
16th April 1746.

Royal Army coloured red, Jacobites green

right of the first line; Lord Mark Kerr's regiment of dragoons and two squadrons of Cobham's on the left. In this order the army advanced to within six hundred paces of the enemy. Two six-pounders were placed between each regiment of the front line, six more guns were with the second line. The ground was so soft in some places that during the advance some of the artillery horses stuck, but the guns were extricated by means of drag-ropes. As soon as firm ground was reached, artillery fire was opened. It was now about one o'clock. The fire was returned by the artillery of the Jacobites, who had a few guns posted on their flanks and in their centre. The Royal artillery, which was commanded by Lieutenant-Colonel Belford, was well served, and did terrible execution. The guns of the Jacobites, on the other hand, served as they were by untrained gunners, had little effect; they were laid high, and their shot passed harmlessly over the heads of the Royal troops.

The artillery duel lasted nearly an hour. While it continued, Cumberland made some changes in the disposition of his army. Wolfe's regiment, which stood on the left of the second line, was moved up to the left of the first line and then wheeled to the right (*en potence*, as it was called), so as to flank the Jacobite attack. At the same time, Pulteney's regiment was brought up from the reserve to the right of the first line, and Battereau's to the right of the second. The Duke then placed himself between the first and second lines, in front of Howard's regiment. Charles, with the group of officers who surrounded him, at length attracted the notice of Cumberland's artillery, and became a mark for its fire. One of his servants was killed; he himself had a narrow escape.

The Highlanders, waiting impatiently for the order to charge, were now beginning to get out of hand. Charles sent an order to Lord George Murray to advance, but the order was never received, as the officer who carried it was killed on his way by a cannon ball. Lochiel spoke to Lord George, and represented to him the necessity of attacking immediately. As they were speaking, the MacIntoshes broke out of the centre of the line, and advanced against the regiment opposite to them. A general advance was then ordered. The clansmen rushed forward with a shout through a storm of grape and musketry. As they passed Wolfe's regiment, it poured its fire into their right flank, but they rushed on undaunted and attacked Barrel's and Munro's. Both battalions broke; two guns were captured; it looked for a moment as if Prestonpans were to be repeated. But the second line stood firm. Sempill's regiment, which received the brunt of the attack, was drawn up as to receive cavalry—three deep, the front rank kneeling, the second bending forward, the third standing upright. The Highland attack, now broken and disordered, was received with a tremendous fire; the assailants fell in heaps in front of the bayonets; at last the survivors retreated in confusion. Bligh's regiment was equally successful in repelling the attack of the centre. On the left the attack of the Jacobites was comparatively feeble. There is a well-known story to the effect that the Macdonalds refused to take part in the fight, because they felt their honour insulted by being placed on the left of the line.[1] It is said that the Duke of Perth entreated them in vain to advance, and told them that if they behaved with their usual valour they would make a right of the left, and he would call himself Macdonald; and that Keppoch rushed forward calling on them to follow him, and exclaiming, "My God! have the children of my tribe forsaken me?" Be this as it may, they never crossed swords with the enemy, and, when the right and centre of the Prince's army retreated, they joined in the flight.

The whole affair was over in twenty-five minutes. When the first line of the Highlanders gave way, the Royal army did not pursue immediately. The infantry were ordered to remain in position and dress their ranks. The pursuit was begun by the cavalry on Cumberland's right flank, who were gallantly checked by the Irish. At last a general advance was ordered; the Jacobite army broke up into groups, and their retreat became a flight. The greater part fled towards Badenoch and the hills, the remainder towards Inverness. The Royal cavalry pursued the fugitives for miles, and did great execution.[2]

It is said that while the left of the Jacobite line was yet unbroken, Lord Elcho begged the Prince to head a charge in person and retrieve the fortune of the day. Had he done so, the result would merely have been to add to the slaughter. Cumberland's victory was complete. The insurgents lost about 1000 killed and wounded, and the whole of their cannon and baggage. The loss of the victors was reckoned at 310, including four officers killed and fourteen wounded.

Charles fled along the side of Loch Ness, and in the evening reached Gortleg,[3] where he met Lord Lovat. Such of the fugitives as had kept together reached Ruthven on the 18th; there they received a message from the Prince to seek their own safety, and dispersed as best they could.

---

[1] As to this story, see Johnstone's *Memoirs*, p. 144, *note*.

[2] The print here reproduced represents various successive phases of the battle as if occurring simultaneously; thus in the centre the Highlanders are shown charging, while on the flanks the Royal cavalry are advancing for the pursuit. On the left of the picture Kerr's and Cobham's dragoons are forcing their way through the enclosure on the Jacobites' right, the walls of which had previously been broken down to admit their passage. The descriptive letterpress appended to the picture differs in some details from Home.

[3] Now called Gorthlick.

The BATTLE of CULLODEN, April 16. 1746.

# CHAPTER VI.

## THE FORTY-FIVE –AFTER CULLODEN.

KING GEORGE'S forces, twice defeated in the field by the insurgents, were now at last victorious, and their victory was followed by such cruelties and atrocities as never have disgraced a British army. It may be admitted at once that, from the point of view of the Government, severity, even great severity, was justifiable. Militant Jacobitism had to be stamped out once for all, and the military clan system had to be broken up. It was quite out of the question that the north of Scotland should be left in such a condition as to make another rising possible. It may be admitted also that the antecedents and training of the Duke of Cumberland were very different from those of a British General. What there is to say in his defence has been temperately said by Mr Hill Burton.

"To believe that this victory was followed by much cruelty, it is not necessary to believe that the cruelty was wanton. We may be assured, from the Duke of Cumberland's character, that he was led by a sense of duty. But that duty led him to severity. He was a soldier, according to the German notions of a soldier, and a rebel province was a community to be subjected to martial law. Many of the insurgents, attempting to escape or hide themselves, when detected by well-known peculiarities, were put to death by the soldiery, who, even when they made a mistake and slew the wrong man, could not easily be punished. The Duke, brought up in the German military school, seems to have been unable to distinguish between a rebellion suppressed in constitutional Britain, where all men are supposed to be innocent but those proved to be guilty, and a revolted German province, where every accorded grace to the unfortunate people proceeds from the will of the conqueror. Thus there was a propensity to subject all the northern districts to something too closely resembling military law or license."

It may also be admitted that some stories have received general credence without much examination of the evidence on which they rest, but, after all palliations have been conceded and after all exaggerations have been deducted, there remains an amply authenticated residue of hideous charges against the Duke, his officers, and his army. Bishop Forbes made it his business to collect evidence with regard to these atrocities, and the numerous documents relating to them which are included in the *Lyon in Mourning*, and have recently been given to the world for the first time at full length, present a sickening record of infamous outrage and devilish cruelty. We give two

specimen documents, with Bishop Forbes's notes. Their unstudied language presents
a more vivid picture of the terrible reality than could be given by any modern para-
phrase. Some facts may be exaggerated, but it will be seen that the writers have
been careful to avoid groundless statements. When it is recollected that the deeds
narrated took place in the Highlands of Scotland in modern times, and were perpe-
trated by regular troops under the command of English officers, it will be well
understood why the name of the Butcher Cumberland is still mentioned in the North
with loathing and horror.

The first document is a narrative written by Mr Francis Stewart, son of Bailie John
Stewart of Inverness, and communicated by him to Bishop Forbes on October 4, 1748.[1]

"To recollect and enumerate all the hardships endured and cruelties committed
in and about Inverness, on and after the 16th of April 1746, is what I cannot pretend
to do; and I am certain many things were done that very few, if any, can give any
account of. The following facts you have, as I either saw them myself or was
informed of them by others :—

"It is a fact undeniable, and known almost to everybody, that upon Friday, the
18th of April, which was the 2nd day after the battle, a party was regularly detached
to put to death all the wounded men that were found in and about the field of battle.
That such men were accordingly put to death is also undeniable, for it is declared by
creditable people who were eye-witnesses to that most miserable and bloody scene. I
myself was told by William Rose, who was then greeve to my Lord President, that
12 wounded men were carried out of his house and shot in a hollow, which is within
very short distance of the place of action. William Rose's wife told this fact to creditable people, from whom I had it more circumstantially. She said that the party came
to her house, and told the wounded men to get up, that they might bring them to
surgeons to get their wounds dress't. Upon which, she said, the poor men, whom
she thought in so miserable a way that it was impossible they could stir, made a shift
to get up; and she said they went along with the party with an air of cheerfulness
and joy, being full of the thought that their wounds were to be dressed. But, she
said, when the party had brought them the length of the hollow above mentioned,
which is at a very short distance from her house, she being then within the house,
heard the firing of several guns, and coming out immediately to know the cause, saw
all those brought out of her house, under the pretence of being carried to surgeons,
were dead men.

"Upon the same day the party was detached to put to death all the wounded men
in and about the field of battle. There was another party detached, under the command of Collonell Cockeen, to bring in the Lady McIntosh, prisoner, from her house
at Moy. Tho' Cockeen himself was reckoned a most discreet, civile man, yet he

<hr/>

[1] *Lyon in Mourning,* vol. ii., pp. 188-191.

found it impossible to restrain the barbarity of many of his party, who, straggling before, spared neither sex nor age they met with; so that the lady has told many that she herself counted above 14 dead bodies of men, women, and children 'twixt Moy and Inverness. There is one woman still alive who is a sufficient document of the barbarity of Cockeen's party; for she, after receiving many cuts of swords on the face and many stabbs of bayonets in other parts of her body, was left for dead on the highway. However, it has pleased Providence that she still lives to set forth to the world the monstrous cruelty of those miscreants, by a face quite deformed, and many other conspicuous marks of their barbarity.

"I had almost forgot to tell you of a most monstrous act of cruelty committed by the party before mentioned, which was detached to the field of action that is, the burning of a house near the field, in which there were about 18 wounded men. This fact is well vouched by many creditable people. I myself heard one, Mrs Taylor, a wright's wife at Inverness, tell that she went up the day thereafter to the field to search for the body of a brother-in-law of hers who was killed, and that she saw in the rubish the bodies of severals of those that had been scorched to death in a most miserable, mangled way.

"The cruelties committed the day of the action are so many that I cannot pretend at all to enumerate them. That no quarter was given is a thing certain. There is one instance of this that I cannot ommitt. A very honest old gentleman, of the name of McLeod, was pursued by two of the Light Horse from the place of action to the hill near Inverness called the Barnhill; and when he came there, and found it impossible to save his life any further by flight, he went on his knees and beg'd quarters of the two that pursued him, but both of them refused his request, and shot him through the head. Several of the inhabitants of Inverness were witnesses to this fact. There was another poor man shot by a soldier at the door of one Widow McLean, who lives in the Bridge Street of Inverness, as he was making his way for the Bridge. There was a most monstrous act committed in the house of one Widow Davidson in the afternoon after the action. A gentleman, falling sick in town, took a room at her house, being a retired place. He was in a violent fever the day of the action, and unable to make his escape when he was told the Prince and his army were defeat. Several soldiers coming up in the afternoon to this Widow Davidson's, the maid of the house told them there was a rebell above stairs, upon which they went immediately, rushed into the room wherein the poor gentleman lay, and cut his throat from ear to ear. This I was told by an honest woman, a neighbour of Mrs Davidson's, who went to the room and saw the gentleman after his throat was cut.

"The proceedings after His Royal Highness came in to town were, I'm certain, unprecedented. Many gentlemen were taken and confined amongst the common prisoners without any reason given them for their being so used, and after being confined they were for some time denied the use of both bedding and provisions, so

X

that some of them have not to this day recovered the cold they contracted and the
bad usage they met with at that time. The women of Inverness did not escape His
Royal Highness his notice. Severals of them were made prisoners and confined to
the common guard, amongst whom was the Lady Dowager Mackintosh, who was confined for the space of 14 days, and contracted so violent a cold during that time that
she had almost died of it. The usage the prisoners in general met with was so monstrous that I am certain there are few, if any, histories can parallel the like of it. The
allowance of provision for gentle and simple was ½ pound meal each per day, and very
often not so much watter given them as won'd help them to swallow it. I myself
have gone often by the prison at that melancholy time, when I heard the prisoners
crying for watter in the most pitifull manner. Many died at that time of their wounds,
that were never dressed nor look't to, in the utmost agony ; and as none of the inhabitants durst take the least concern in them, dead or alive, I have several times seen
3 or 4 dead bodies in a day carried out of the prisons by the beggars, and brought,
all naked, through the streets to be buried in the churchyard.

"*N.B.* The original of the above, in the handwriting of Mr Francis Stewart, is
to be found among my papers. The said Mr Stewart is betwixt nineteen and twenty
years of age, and is a modest, sober, sensible youth.
                                            "ROBERT FORBES, A.M."

The next document is a narrative written by the Rev. James Hay of Inverness
and sent by him to Bishop Forbes in May 1749.[1]

"One of the dragoons who came first into Inverness after the battle of Culloden
oblidged a servant maid to hold his horse in a closs, and then he followed two Low
Country men into a house, where he hash'd them with his broad sword to death. The
maid heard their lamentable cryes, and when he came out he was all blood. Poor
men ! they had no arms.

"At the same time some of these dragoons found a gentleman who was highly
distressed with a fever, not able to stur from his bed, and there they cut his throat.
He and the other two were some time unburied, for none durst venture to do it.
Ther was a poor beggar killed on the street.

"The prisoners were in a most miserable condition, being stripped of their cloaths
when taken. They were sent to prisons, and some had not wherewith to cover their
nakedness. No regard had to the cryes of the wounded, or to the groans of the
dying. No surgeon allow'd to apply proper remedies for their care or recovery, and
when any of these were in the same unhappy circumstances their instruments were
taken from them that they might give no relief. It was reckon'd highly criminal and
very dangerous to give them anything, even water. The servant maids had more than
common courage. They did (men and boys being allowed to go to the prisoners, but

---

[1] *Lyon in Mourning*, vol. ii., pp. 298-308.

the guards were discharged upon their peril to let any of them out), all that was possible for them, tho' they were sure of maletreatment. And Anna M'Kaye,[1] a poor woman descended of very honest substantiall people in the Isle of Sky, who had her house and effects of a considerable value burnt, as was attested by the best in that island, made it her chief bussiness to get for and carry to the prisoners every thing that possibly she could; so that she was justly called the prisoners' nurse. When Mr Nairn made his escape, sad and dismall was the treatment she met with. Poor woman! what small effects she had got (she being in town sometime before) was taken from her, and she was carried to the guard among a house full of sogars, and the orders were that she should not be allowed to sitt or ly down, and in that condition she was keept for three days and three nights. The common language she was intertained with she will not nor cannot express. She was at five court martialls, had many promises and many threatenings, such as scourging to tell who had a hand in Mr Nairn's escape. She was keept seven weeks thereafter in common prison, and contracted a swelling in her legs that she'll never get the better of.

"Murdoch M'Raw was taken in or near Fort Augustus, who had no concern in the Highland army. (He was nearest relation to the chieftain of that name.) Being sent prisoner to Inverness, where he was not above one hour when he was hang'd at the Cross on the Apple tree. The only thing they alledg'd against him, that he was a spy, which he positively deny'd, and when they put the rope about his neck, he, believing they did it for diversion, said, 'You have gone far enough, if this be jest.' He was keept hanging there naked a night and the most of two days. He appeared all the time as if had been sleeping, his mouth and eyes being shut closs, a very uncommon thing in those who die such a death. Sometimes they . . and whiped the dead body for their diversion.

"Eavan M'Kay was taken in the Highlands by a whig teacher with letters in French or cyphers, and was sent into town, where he was most barbarously and inhumanly treated. Being asked from whom he had and to whom he was going with the letters, to which he giving no answer got five hundred lashes, being ty'd to a stake, and then sent to prison again. Some days after he got five hundred more, and they threatn'd to whip him to death if he would not discover what they wanted. None durst go nigh him while in the pit with any necessary; and when they threw down a pound of meal, which was all the allowance given to any one of the prisoners, it was found untouch'd, he being sickly, full of sores, and most barbarously struck by one of the sogars with the butt of his gun in the breast, of which he complain'd while he

---

[1] "See f. 1124, where this story is more minutely told. The agreement or sameness of circumstances in the narratives of Mr Hay and Mr Stewart is the more remarkable, as I never allowed Mr Hay to know that I had got anything from Mr Stewart, who went from Leith to London and from London to Carolina, so that Mr Hay and he had no opportunity of comparing notes together—an undeniable proof of the truth of the facts. I take the same fact from ten different hands if I can have it from so many.—Robert Forbes, A.M."

lived. At last he was carryed to the Tolbooth. One there said to him that he was a great fool not to discover what he knew, to which he gave a noble return: 'You are the fool. It signifies nothing what they can do to me (Let them do the worst) in respect of what could be done to those from whom I had and to whom I was going with the letters. Their deaths would be great loss, but mine will be none.' His father and he had considerable effects, and all were taken, and the poor father was begging in the town that very time, but durst not say that he was his son. A charitable person, when he died, sent word that if they would allow his body one hour to lie unburied a coffin and grave cloaths would be got, but that was refused. Being carryed to the grave by two or three beggars, a sogar went and thrust his bayonet several times into the body, to try (as he said) if the rebell was dead.

"Jo. Fraser, then present provost, was taken from denner by an officer and musquetiers to Cumberland's stable, where he was ordered to clean it. He said he never cleand his own. He was oblidged to gett men to do it, and there stay for some hours untill they had done.

"Provest Hosack, with the majestrates, having gone to the levie to pay their complements, hearing orders given to shut the ports that no rebell might escape, and that the meeting house should be burnd and the man who preachd in it, said he hoped they would mix mercy with judgment. Upon which they said: 'D——n you puppie, do you pretend to dictate here?' They orderd him to be kickd down stairs. Accordingly he was tossd to the stair head from one to another, and there one of a considerable character gave him a toss that he never touchd the stair untill he was at the foot of the first flate of it. These two gentlemen were ill rewarded,[1] for none could be more attached to the Government than they were. But they had compassion on the distress'd and oppress'd, which was then ane unpardonable crime of the deepest dye. When the orders about the meeting house were given by Halley, Husk said that it should be taken down and the timber given for the ovens, which was done.

"It's not possible to find out the certainty of the poysoned bread. I was told by a person of credite, that a woman in great want saw them burying bread, which afterwards she took a part of, and she and her two children did eat of it, and all the three were dead within 24 hours. One of C——d's sogars said there were some wagons with poysoned bread, and ane gentleman belonging to his army told the same, for he would not, he said, midle with there bread. This is all I can learn about it.

"A gentleman who was long prisoner in Inverness told me that he saw an officer, winter '46, when it was excessively cold and the fireing so scarce that the inhabitants had the greatest difficulty to get any at the greatest price, when the prisoners many times were crying that they would sterve with cold, give half a

---

[1] "Lucky indeed! for I had it from one of Inverness that lists of the disaffected were made up, but this treatment prevented any information of the kind. Robert Forbes, A.M."

crown to the sogars to go in a very cold night and extinguish the prisoner's fire and light, which they did accordingly. All the officers of Blackney's regement, except three, were extremely cruel, but none exceeded Captain Dunlope, who occasioned the prisoners much misery; he being Blackney's adviser, who being a man of a timorous disposition,[1] was affraid to leave undone what he, Dunlope, thought proper to be done. Collonell Leightown was like an infernall fiand when Mr Nairn made his escape, and was one of poor Anna M'Kayes greatest persecuteors, who sometimes offerd her severall guineas, and promised to do great things for her if she would tell who assisted Mr Nairn, and who were in the knowledge of his escapeing. At other times he threatnd her in a terrible manner with severall punishments, particularly scourgeing. But all proved in vain.

" When an account was given that there were many wounded in houses on the field of batle the orders given were that the houses should be burnt and all within them, and if any offerd to come out that they should be shot. Its impossible to know what number suffer'd. There were three tennants' houses and all their office houses. The first that ventur'd to go near that place saw most shocking sights, some of their bodies boiling and others lying with the marks of their ruffels, which when they touched they went into ashes.[2]

" Orders were given on the Fryday to ane officer, Hobbie, or such a name, that he should go to the field of batle and cause carry there all the wounded in the neighbouring houses at a miles distance, some more, some less, and kill them upon the field, which orders were obeyed accordingly. When these orders were given at the levie, an officer who was well pleased told it to his comrades. One of them replyd, ' D- -n him who had taken that order.' He could not do ane inhumane thing, tho no mercy should be shewn to the rebels.

" An officer was heard more than once say that he saw that day seventy-two killed, or, as he termed it, knocked in the head. He was a young captain.

" An officer upon his return from seeing the field of batle told he saw a beautiful young man[3] quite naked and mortally wounded, who begged of him that

---

[1] "Not only so, but likewise of a most peevish, tyrannical disposition, to my certain knowledge and experience, of which I may come to give some instances when I have more leisure.—Robert Forbes, A.M."

[2] "I well remember that Mr Frances Stuart in conversing with me upon these dismal matters, mentioned this circumstance of the ruffels and their turning into ashes when touched.—Robert Forbes, A.M."

[3] "Upon reading this paragraph I plainly saw that MacDonald of Bellfinlay behoved to be the person meant in it, and, therefore, I waited upon Bellfinlay in the Canongate (he being still confined with the sore leg), at 12 o'clock on Tuesday, May 23rd, 1749, when I read in his hearing the above paragraph, and asked him particular questions about all the circumstances contained in it, to which he gave me plain and distinct answers. Bellfinlay said that he himself behoved certainly to be the wounded person meant in the said paragraph, but that it was not literally true that he (Bellfinlay) desired the officer (Hamilton) positively to shoot him, for that he earnestly begged Hamilton *to have pity upon him or to dispatch him.* To which Hamilton answered, ' Be not afraid. I don't believe the sogers will shoot you.' To this Bellfinlay replied, ' How can I expect that they will spare me more than those whom they are now dispatching?' But Bellfinlay mentioned not seventeen or any particular number. Then it was that Hamilton gave Bellfinlay a cordial dram (as Bellfinlay himself termed it), and interposed for his preservation. After this Bellfinlay

he might shoot him, which shockd the officer who said, ' God forbid, how can you imagine that ? '   He replyed that he had seen seventeen shot by an officer and those who were orderd by him.   The officer gave him a dram, which he greedily took, and no wonder, and put (him) like a sack upon a horse and carryed to an house where there were wounded redcoats, who were most disagreeable neighbours to him.   From that he was carryed to an hospitall, and thereafter to Anna M'Kays house where there were very poor intertainment, but she did all she possibly could for him.   By her care he was preserved, and is now healthy and strong.

  " When the redcoats wounds were dressed by ane surgeon one of the P———'s men begged he might dress him ; to which he replyed that he would willingly do it, but it was to no purpose for he would be shott the morrow, which made the poor distress'd crawl¹ in the night on his fours an incredible distance, by which means he escaped.

  " Its most surprising, and never can be accounted for how the wounded, quite naked, and without any kind of nourishment, lived so long in the open fields, the season being very cold.   One instance is most remarkable of one² who was disabled in both legs, and sadly wounded in many other places, particularly a sogar struck him on the face with the butt of his gun which dung out his eye.   When the generall massacre was he lay as if dead, and on the Saturday an officer viewing the field cryed were there any of them in life, to which he answered.   The officer gave him half crown, and ordered him to be carryed to an house, where the red-coats mockd and ridiculed him, surprised to see such a sad spectacle, gave him halfpenny at parting.   But the inhumane, ungenerous, most barbarous canibells rob'd him of all he got.   After staying some dayes there he was carryd to his friends, and is now going on crutches.

    .        .        .        .        .        .

  " A young gentleman of distinction, mortally wounded, lying on the ground, was enquired at by Cumberland to who he belongd.   To which he replyd, To the Prince.

---

was put upon a horse 'not like a sack, but astraddle, and was carried to a tenant's house in the neighbourhood where there were wounded redcoats, etc.   From this house he was taken next day in a cart, and on his way to In-verness he fell in with Robert Nairn in another cart, and both of them were thus driven to the door of the Church in Inverness, where there were many prisoners confined.   But the sentry would not allow them access, telling that his orders were ' to allow access to no person whatsomever.'   Then they were driven ,being still quite naked) to the hospital, where the nurse receivcd them with great tenderness, making a bed for them near the fire, as she looked upon them to be of Cumberland's army ; but next day when the surgeons came their round and took a note of their names, then the nurse became very surly and ill-natured, and repented of her kindness to them.   The surgeons re-ported them to some principal officer, who immediately gave orders to remove them out of the hospital (where they had been only one night), and one, Captain Sinclair, of General Ruth's regiment, who had been in the hospital before them.   All the three were carried to a cellar below Anne Mackay's house, and orders given to take the blankets from them which they had gotten in the hospital.   In three weeks Sinclair was removed to a room, having only a slight flesh wound.  Robert Forbes, A.M."

  ¹ " This I have before heard of by report, and that this particular instance happened on the field of battle, from which the poor wounded man crawled by favour of the dark night.  Robert Forbes, A.M."

  ² " Here, no doubt, is meant the singular instance of John (Alexander) Fraser. . . . . Robert Forbes, A.M."

Then he orderd one of his great men to shoot him, which he refused to do; and then another, who said he would not nor could not do it. Then he applyd to a common sogar, who obeyd him.

"No doubt you have heard of a woman in the Highlands when in labour of child, with 9 or 10 women. A party acquainted their commander of it, who orderd that the house should be burnt, with all who were in it. This, when told by a Collonel, who was there, but had not the command, cryed and shed tears that such a barbarous action should be committed by any who were called Christians.

"McGillavry of Delcrombie, who was not engag'd with the Prince, being at two miles distance from the field of battle without any arms, was attacked by dragoons, who oblidged him to cast of all his cloaths and give them to them, to prevent their dismounting, his cloaths being too good for them to part with, and then they shot him dead. If they had had but swords and he one, he would have given 2 or 3 of them enough of it.

"The men of Glenmoristown and Urquhart were advised to go to Inverness and deliver up their arms, upon solemn promises that they should return safe with protection, which incourag'd also those who were not ingag'd to go. How soon they went there they were put into a church, keept there closs prisoners for a few dayes, and then put into ships for London. The few that liv'd with their sad treatment were sent to the Plantations. To whom the breach of this promise is owing lyes a secret betwixt the mercifull generall[1] and beloved knight,[2] for the one asserted he had allowance to do so, and the other refused, so that every body will be in a strait which of these good men's words they can doubt of.

"The horses, cowes and calfs, ewes and lambs, goats and kids, were taken out of my Lord Lovat's country, the Aird and Glenmazerin, and keept sterving and crying, which was not agreeable to hear or see. The common treatment they mett with was a stroak from the sogers, with D—— n your soul, you rebells! These poor creatures deserv'd to suffer, being highly criminall; and if any of them were sent with the great flocks from the Highlands, they (like the ill-gotten penny) infected and consumed all their kind in England, and no wonder, for many innocent persons were deprived of their all.

"Six or seven weeks after the battle of Culloden, the party commanded by Major Lockart in Glenmoriston shot two old and one young man, a son of one of the former, when they were harrowing, and expecting no harm.

"Grant of Daldrigan, who took no concern with the Highland army, was ordered by Lockart (his house being surrounded by sogars) to gather his own and all the cattle

---

[1] "Here, no doubt, Mr Hay means the Duke of Cumberland."
[2] "Here Mr Hay certainly means the Laird of Grant, who is highly blamed in this particular affair.— Robert Forbes, A.M."

in one part of the country while Lockart was herrying and burning the other part, which being impossible for him to do against the time that Lockart came back, he ordered him to be bound in hand and foot, erecting a gallows, stript him naked, and would not allow his nakedness to be coverd, and carried him to the foot of the gallows with the three corps of the men they had killed the day before, like sacks across on three horses, and hung the three bodies by the feet in the gallows, and they at the same time would have killed Daldrigan had not Captain Grant, in Lowden's regiment, prevented it. They would hardly allow his wife time to take her rings of her fingers, but were going to cutt of her fingers, having stript her of her cloaths, her house and effects being burnt. And in the braes of Glenmoriston a party there ravishd a gentle-woman big with child, and tenants' wives, and left them on the ground after they were ravishd by all the party. And Lockhart, on his way to Strathglass, shot a man widing a water, with the Whig teacher's protection in his hand to shew him, without speaking one word. And the whole party ravishd there a woman big with child, and left her on the ground almost dead. All these are certain facts which may be depended upon, being known by a person of good credite.

"Campbell, an officer of militia, who was a chamberlain to Seaforth, with a party went to Fraser of Kilbokies, who was not with the Highland army, and burnt all his houses and effects they could not take with them, and took 13 score of catle, with many horses of the best kind. His loss was valued at 10,000 merks. And his wife being brought to bed 14 dayes before, they fore'd her to fly with a daughter in fever to the open fields, where they lay that whole night, being very cold. For severall days they killed man, wife, and child many miles from the field of batle. At 5 miles distance ane honest poor woman on the day of batle, who was brought to bed Sunday before, flying with her infant, was attacked by 4 dragoons, who gave her seven wounds in the head thro one plaid, which was eight fold and one in the arm. Then one of them took the infant by the thigh, threw it about his hand, and at last to the ground. Her husband, at the same time, was chased into a moss so far that one of the horse could not come out, where his rider shott him. The young infant who was so roughly maletreat is a fine boy, and the mother recovered and is living.

"Three days after the batle, at 4 miles distance, the sogers most barbarously cut a woman in many places of her body, particularly in the face.

"I am promised some more facts in few dayes, but I did not incline to lose the opportunity of this bearer.

"Tho the running naked[1] be commonly reported, I have not got an account of the certainty. I beg you may let me know when this comes to your hands."

---

[1] "This refers to a story I have heard frequently reported viz, that the soldiers' wives and other women in the camp at Fort Augustus should quite naked have run races, sometimes on foot and sometimes mounted astraddle on Highland shelties, for the entertainment of Cumberland and his officers. See *Scots Magazine* for June 1746, p. 288, 1st col. Robert Forbes, A.M."

Cumberland's comment on the deeds of his soldiers is quoted by Lord Mahon : "I am sorry to leave this country in the condition it is in," he wrote to the Duke of Newcastle on July 17, 1746, "for all the good that we have done has been a little blood-letting, which has only weakened the madness, but not cured it ; and I tremble for fear that this vile spot may still be the ruin of this island and of our family."[1]

While the north of the island was thus given up to military rapine, the lawyers were reaping a harvest of death in the south. Cumberland, it is recorded, pressed for the "utmost severity." An Act had been passed suspending the law which required bills for high treason to be found in the counties where the crime was committed ; under it the Scottish prisoners were removed for trial to England. The trials went on for months. In London Colonel Townley and eight others belonging to the Manchester regiment were hanged on Kennington Common. There were 382 prisoners in Carlisle Castle when the Commission there was opened on August 12 ; most of these were permitted to draw lots for one out of each twenty who was to be tried on the capital charge ; the others were banished by their own consent. Bills were found against 127 altogether ; of these over thirty suffered the extreme punishment of treason. The total number of executions in England was nearly eighty. Charles Radcliffe, brother of the Earl of Derwentwater, was executed upon his former sentence, now thirty years old. Lords Cromarty, Kilmarnock, and Balmerino were tried by their peers and convicted ; Kilmarnock and Balmerino were beheaded. Lovat was impeached, and it was in his trial that Secretary Murray made his memorable appearance in the witness-box. Lovat was condemned and executed ; perhaps none of the victims deserved less pity.

In the meantime Prince Charles, a proscribed fugitive, was being hunted through the north-western Highlands with a price of £30,000 on his head. As we have seen, he reached Gortleg on the evening of Culloden. Next morning he arrived at Invergarry Castle. Four days later, after a weary journey on foot over the hills, he reached Borradale on Lochnanuagh. There he remained for five days. On April 26 he sailed for the Hebrides in an open boat, which had been procured by Donald Macleod of Gualtergill. The party consisted of the Prince, O'Sullivan, Captain Felix O'Neil, Allan Macdonald, Donald Macleod, and Edward Burke, who had guided the Prince from Culloden, with a crew of seven boatmen. After a stormy and perilous voyage they landed at Rossinish in Benbecula. There they remained two days. On the evening of the 29th they again put to sea, and next morning reached Scalpa. From Scalpa Donald Macleod was sent to Stornoway to endeavour to hire a vessel in which the fugitives might leave the country. He succeeded in doing so, and communicated his success to the Prince, who with the rest of the party crossed to Harris and proceeded towards Stornoway on foot. The people of Stornoway, however, had got wind of the purpose for which the hired ship was wanted, and, fearing to compromise themselves,

---

[1] *History of England*, vol. iii., p. 311.

had refused to allow her to depart. There was nothing to be done but to turn south again. On the morning of May 6 the party sailed from Arnish, intending to return to Scalpa. By this time the coast was being watched by the King's ships. Four men-of-war were sighted, and the fugitives put into the desolate Isle of Iffurt. They reached Scalpa again on the 10th. On the 11th they landed in Loch Uskavagh. Next day they walked to Coradale in South Uist.

At Coradale the Prince remained concealed in a forester's cottage for more than three weeks. Here he was comparatively safe. He was visited by Clanranald, Boisdale, and others of his friends, and was able to amuse himself with shooting. Government troops were, however, being landed in the Hebrides in large numbers, and it was evident that the Prince's place of refuge would soon become too dangerous. On June 6 he sailed to the Island of Ouia or Wiay. He was now closely surrounded; parties of regulars and militia were scouring the island in search of him, and he heard constantly of the near neighbourhood of his enemies. On June 10 he went from Ouia to Rossinish, accompanied by O'Neil. From Rossinish he went by boat to Uishness Point—near which he spent the night in a cave--thence to Ciliestella (Kyle Stuley), and on the 15th landed in Loch Boisdale.

From the 15th to the 20th of June the Prince remained in hiding on the shores of Loch Boisdale, sleeping in the open fields at night. On the 21st, accompanied by O'Neil, he reached a hut near Ormaclett, the residence of Clanranald in Benbecula. It was here that he met Flora Macdonald.

Flora Macdonald was the daughter of Macdonald of Milton in South Uist, whose widow had married Captain Hugh Macdonald of Armadale, who was in command of one of the militia companies now on duty in the island. O'Neil had previously met her at Ormaclett. He succeeded in inducing her to render an essential service to the Prince. His position in the Hebrides was becoming every hour more dangerous. Failing a passage abroad his hope of safety lay in getting over to Skye, but every ferry was closely guarded, and no one was permitted to leave the island without a pass.

Miss Macdonald undertook to conduct the Prince to Skye. She procured from her step-father a pass for herself, a man-servant, and her maid, who was described in the pass as Betty Burke, and whom Captain Macdonald, in a letter to his wife, described as an "Irish girl" and "a good spinster." Betty Burke was none other than the Prince himself. Miss Macdonald hired a six-oared boat to convey the party across the Minch. On June 27 she met the Prince at his hiding-place, about eight miles from Ormaclett. On the evening of the following day they put to sea. The party consisted of Flora, her servant Neil MacEachan, the Prince, disguised in women's clothes as Betty Burke,[1] and four boatmen. Next morning they reached the

---

[1] A piece of the dress which the Prince wore as Betty Burke, and a piece of his apron-string, are preserved inside the binding of one of the MS. volumes of the *Lyon in Mourning* in the Advocates' Library, Edinburgh.

point of Waternish in Skye, where they were fired upon by a party of Macleod militia. Crossing Loch Snizort they landed at Kilbride, close to Monkstat, the seat of Sir Alexander Macdonald. Sir Alexander was with Cumberland at Inverness, but Flora knew that the sympathies of his wife, Lady Margaret Macdonald, a daughter of the Earl of Eglinton, were on the Prince's side, and she accordingly proceeded to Monkstat to inform Lady Margaret of their arrival, leaving the Prince with the boat. Macdonald of Kingsburgh, Sir Alexander's factor, was in the house, and Lady Margaret took him into her confidence. It was determined that the Prince should be conducted to Portree, and thence taken over to Raasay, and that in the meantime he should be entertained at Kingsburgh's house.

The *Lyon in Mourning* contains an exceedingly dramatic account of Betty Burke's entertainment at Kingsburgh.

"When the Prince came to Kingsburgh's house (Sunday, June 29) it was be-tween ten and eleven at night; and Mrs MacDonald, not expecting to see her husband that night, was making ready to go to bed. One of her servant maids came and told her that Kingsburgh was come home, and had brought some company with him. 'What company?' says Mrs MacDonald, 'Milton's daughter, I believe,' says the maid, 'and some company with her.' 'Milton's daughter,' replies Mrs MacDonald, 'is very welcome to come here with any company she pleases to bring. But you'll give my service to her, and tell her to make free with anything in the house; for I am very sleepy, and cannot see her this night.' In a little her own daughter came and told her in a surprize, 'O mother, my father has brought in a very odd, muckle, ill-shaken-up wife as ever I saw! I never saw the like of her, and he has gone into the hall with her.' She had scarce done with telling her tale when Kingsburgh came and desired his lady to fasten on her bucklings again, and to get some supper for him and the company he had brought with him. 'Pray, goodman,' says she, 'what company is this you have brought with you?' 'Why, goodwife,' said he, 'you shall know that in due time; only make haste and get some supper in the meantime.' Mrs MacDonald desired her daughter to go and fetch her the keys she had left in the hall. When the daughter came to the door of the hall she started back, ran to her mother, and told her she could not go in for the keys, for the muckle woman was walking up and down in the hall, and she was so frightened at seeing her that she could not have the courage to enter. Mrs MacDonald went herself to get the keys, and I heard her more than once declare that, upon looking in at the door, she had not the courage to go forward. 'For,' said she, 'I saw such an odd muckle trallup of a carlin, making lang wide steps through the hall, that I could not like her appear-ance at all.' Mrs MacDonald called Kingsburgh, and very seriously begged to know what a lang, odd hussie was this he had brought to the house, for that she was so frighted at the sight of her that she could not go into the hall for her keys. 'Did you never see a woman before,' said he, 'goodwife? What frights you at seeing a

woman? Pray, make haste, and get us some supper.' Kingsburgh would not go for
the keys, and therefore his lady behov'd to go for them. When she entered the hall
the Prince happen'd to be sitting; but immediately he arose, went forward, and saluted
Mrs MacDonald, who, feeling a long stiff beard, trembled to think that this behoved
to be some distressed nobleman or gentleman in disguise, for she never dream'd it to
be the Prince, though all along she had been seized with a dread she could not account
for from the moment she had heard that Kingsburgh had brought company with him.
She very soon made out of the hall with her keys, never saying one word. Immediately she importun'd Kingsburgh to tell her who the person was, for that she was sure
by the salute that it was some distressed gentleman. Kingsburgh smiled at the mention
of the bearded kiss, and said: 'Why, my dear, it is the Prince. You have the honour
to have him in your house.' 'The Prince!' cried she. 'O Lord, we are a' ruin'd
and undone for ever! We will a' be hang'd now!' 'Hout, goodwife,' says the honest
stout soul, 'we will die but ance; and if we are hanged for this, I am sure we die
in a good cause. Pray, make no delay; go, get some supper. Fetch what is readiest.
You have eggs and butter and cheese in the house; get them as quickly as possible.'
'Eggs and butter and cheese!' says Mrs MacDonald; 'what a supper is that for a
Prince?' 'O goodwife,' said he, 'little do you know how this good Prince has been
living for some time past. These, I can assure you, will be a feast to him. Besides,
it would be unwise to be dressing a formal supper, because this would serve to raise
the curiosity of the servants, and they would be making their observations. The less
ceremony and work the better. Make haste, and see that you come to supper.' 'I
come to supper!' says Mrs MacDonald; 'how can I come to supper? I know not
how to behave before Majesty.' 'You must come,' says Kingsburgh, 'for he will not
eat a bit till he see you at the table; and you will find it no difficult matter to behave
before him, so obliging and easy is he in his conversation.'

"The Prince ate of our roasted eggs, some collops, plenty of bread and butter,
etc., and (to use the words of Mrs MacDonald) 'the deal a drap did he want in's
weam of twa bottles of sma beer. God do him good o't; for, well I wat, he had my
blessing to gae down wi't.' After he had made a plentiful supper, he called for a
dram; and when the bottle of brandy was brought, he said he would fill the glass
for himself, 'for,' said he, 'I have learn'd in my skulking to take a hearty dram.'
He filled up a bumper, and drank it off to the happiness and prosperity of his land-
lord and landlady. Then taking a crack'd and broken pipe out of his poutch, wrapt
about with thread, he asked Kingsburgh if he could furnish him with some tobacco,
for that he had learn'd likewise to smoke in his wanderings. Kingsburgh took from
him the broken pipe and laid it carefully up with the brogs, and gave him a new
clean pipe and plenty of tobacco.

"The Prince and Kingsburgh turn'd very familiar and merry together, and when
the Prince spoke to Kingsburgh, he for the most part laid his hand upon Kingsburgh's

knee and used several kind and obliging expressions in his conversation with the happy landlord. Kingsburgh remarked what a lucky thing it was that he happened to be at Mougstot (Sir Alexander MacDonald's house), and that it was all a matter of chance that he was there, for he had no design of being there that day. And then he asked the Prince what he would have done if he had not been at Mougstot. The Prince replied, 'Why, sir, you could not avoid being at Mougstot this day, for Providence ordered you to be there upon my account.' Kingsburgh became so merry and jocose that, putting up his hand to the Prince's face, he turned off his head-dress, which was a very odd clout of a mutch or toy, upon which Mrs MacDonald hasted out of the room and brought a clean nightcap for him." [1]

Next morning Charles left the house, still in his female attire. After he was well out of sight of the house, he changed into a Highland dress with which he had been supplied by Kingsburgh, he then bade his host farewell, and proceeded on foot towards Portree, conducted by a guide. Flora Macdonald on horseback took another road towards the same destination. At Portree he was met by Donald Roy Macdonald, who had procured a boat and rowers to convey him to Raasay. On the morning of July 1, after bidding farewell to Flora, he crossed the Sound of Raasay, and landed in that island. Shortly afterwards Flora was taken prisoner by the Government troops and suffered a year's captivity for the assistance which she rendered to the Prince. In 1750 she married the son of Macdonald of Kingsburgh, with whom she afterwards emigrated to America.

The remainder of Charles's wanderings may be briefly summarised. July 1. At Glam in Raasay. 2nd. At Nicolson's Rock near Scorobreck. 4th. At Elgol. 5th. Landed in Loch Nevis. 8th. Pursued by the troops up Loch Nevis. 10th. Arrived at Borradale, and remained there till joined by Glenaladale on the 15th. 17th. At Corrybeincabir. 18th. On the mountains Scoorvuy and Fruighvein. 19th. On the mountain Mamnyncallum in the Brae of Loch Arkaig. 20th. At Corrienagaull in sight of the enemy's camps. 21st. At Corriscorridill, close to two camps, soldiers in sight often. 22nd. At Glensheil. 23rd. On the hills between Glenmoriston and Strathglass. 24th. In a cave at Coiraghoth in the Braes of Glenmoriston with the "Glenmoriston men." These were a party of eight men who had been concerned in the insurrection, and had taken refuge in this cave. The Prince was conducted to their retreat by Glenaladale, "they knowing nothing at all of his royal highness, only suspecting that a young man they were told was in company might be young Clanranald. . . . Accordingly his royal highness set out, and

---

[1] This well-known account is taken from "Remarks, etc., and Particular Sayings of some who were concerned in the Prince's preservation," *Lyon in Mourning*, vol. i., p. 108 *et seq.* The *Lyon in Mourning* is the great source of original information with regard to the Prince's wanderings. The story of his adventures is fully and picturesquely told by Chambers,—*History of the Rebellion*, chapters xxvi., xxvii., and xxviii.; and his footsteps have been minutely traced by Mr W. B. Blaikie in his *Itinerary*. The route given in the text is that contained in the former editions of this work, with some additions and corrections, for which the editor is indebted to Mr Blaikie's book.

by the time appointed came to the place and meeting with these few friends, who
upon sight knew his royal highness, having formerly served in his army, they conducted him to the grotto, where he was refreshed with such cheer as the exigency
of the time afforded ; and making a bed for him, his royal highness was lulled
asleep with the sweet murmurs of the finest purling stream that could be, running
by his bedside, within the grotto, in which romantic habitation his royal highness
pass'd three days, at the end of which he was so well refreshed that he thought
himself able to encounter any hardships.

  " Having time in that space to provide some necessaries and to gather intelligence
about the enemy's motions, they removed on the 2nd of August (July 28 ?) into a
place within two miles of them, called Coirmheadhain, where they took up their
habitation in a grotto no less romantic than the former. After taking some refresh-
ment, they placed their sentries and made up a bed for his royal highness in a
closet shaped out by nature, and seemingly designed by her for the reception of
his royal highness." (Journal in Captain Alexander Macdonald's handwriting, *Lyon in
Mourning*, vol. i., p. 343.)

  August 2. Reached the Braes of Strathglass. 5th. At Glencannich. 6th and
7th. At Ben Acharain. 9th. At Fasnakyle. 12th. On the Braes of Glenmoriston.
14th. In Glengarry. 15th. On the Brae of Achnasual. 16th to 21st. At Loch Arkaig.
22nd. At Torvault. About this time was nearly taken prisoner by a party under
Grant of Knockando, but escaped to the top of Mullintagart. 28th. Set out for
Badenoch to meet Lochiel. 29th. Arrived at Corrineuir. 30th. Came to Mellaneuir,
where he met Lochiel, and two days afterwards was joined by Cluny.

  September 2nd. Went to Uiskchilra. 5th. Went to " Cluny's Cage " in the face
of the mountain Letternilichk, a spur of Ben Alder. (" The day after Clunie arrived
he thought it time to remove from Mellaneuir, and took the Prince about two
miles farther into Benalder, to a little sheil called Uiskchibra, where the hut or
bothie was superlatively bad and smoky ; yet His Royal Highness put up with
everything. Here he remained for two or three nights, and then removed to a
very romantic habitation, made for him by Clunie, two miles further into Benalder,
called the Cage ; which was a great curiosity and can scarcely be described to
perfection. It was situated in the face of a very rough, high and rocky mountain
called Letternilichk, still a part of Benalder, full of great stones and crevices, and
some scattered wood interspersed. The habitation called the Cage, in the face of
that mountain, was within a small thick bush of wood. There were first some rows
of trees laid down in order to level a floor for the habitation ; and as the place
was steep, this raised the lower side to an equal height with the other ; and these
trees in the way of joists or planks were levelled with earth and gravel. There
were betwixt the trees, growing naturally on their own roots, some stakes fixed in
the earth, which with the trees were interwoven with ropes, made of heath and

birch twigs, up to the top of the Cage, it being of a round or rather oval shape; and the whole thatched and covered over with fog. This whole fabric hung, as it were, by a large tree, which reclined from the one end all along the roof to the other, and which gave it the name of the Cage, and by chance there happened to be two stones at a small distance from one another, in the side next the precipice, resembling the pillars of a chimney, where the fire was placed. The smoke had its vent out here, all along the face of the rock, which was so much of the same colour, that one could discover no difference in the clearest day. The Cage was no larger than to contain six or seven persons; four of whom were frequently employed playing at cards, one idle looking on, one baking, and another firing bread and cooking. Here His Royal Highness remained till the 13th of September."— Cluny's Account of Lochiel and himself after the Battle of Culloden. Home, Appendix No. 46). September 13. Heard of the arrival of two French ships in Lochnanuagh and set out for the coast. 14th. Reached Corvoy. 15th. Before daylight, got through Glenroy. 16th. Reached Achnacarie. 17th. Reached Glencamger. 19th. Reached Borradale where the ships were, and went on board. 20th. Early in the morning sailed for France.

Charles landed at Roscoff near Morlaix in Brittany on September 29. About his subsequent career perhaps the less said the better. On his father's death in 1766 he succeeded to the phantom crown. He died at Rome in January 1788, a broken and disappointed old man; and with him perished the last hope of the House of Stuart. His brother Henry, Cardinal York, lived till 1807. But Jacobitism as a political cause may be said to have definitely come to an end on April 24, 1788, when, at a meeting of nonjuring bishops at Aberdeen, it was resolved that King George III. should be prayed for in the services of the church.

Indeed, the cause had all along been condemned to failure. A counter revolution might have taken place at the death of Queen Anne, but scarcely later. The true issue was not between one dynasty and another, it was between the old claim of Divine right and the Parliamentary settlement of the Crown. Charles's real enemy was the Bill of Rights. The ultimate issue of such a contest could not be doubtful. To-day the old doctrine is as obsolete as the Ptolemaic astronomy. How obsolete it is may be curiously illustrated. The heir of line of the House of Stuart, who, by the strict theory of Divine right is now the rightful sovereign of these realms, is the Bavarian princess who represents Princess Henrietta, Duchess of Orleans, youngest daughter of Charles I.[1]

---

[1] The descent is as follows:—Charles I.; Princess Henrietta (1644-70), who married Philip, Duke of Orleans, brother of Louis XIV.; her daughter, Anne Mary (1669-1728), who married Victor Amadeus, Duke of Savoy and King of Sardinia; her son, Charles Emmanuel III. (1701-73), King of Sardinia; his son, Victor Amadeus III. (1726-96), King of Sardinia; his son, Victor Emmanuel I. (1759-1824), King of Sardinia; his daughter, Mary (1792-1840), who married Francis, Duke of Modena; her son, Ferdinand (1821-49), who married Elizabeth of Austria; his daughter, Maria Teresa (*b.* 1849), who in 1868 married Prince Louis of Bavaria. Her son, Prince Rupert, was born at Munich, May 18, 1869.

Probably not one British subject in a thousand has so much as heard her name.

Political causes have their day, but loyalty, courage, and self-sacrifice do not go out of fashion. So long as history is read the White Cockade will remain the symbol of heroic daring and heroic suffering, and men of all parties will think with sympathy and with pride of those who gave up all for the lost cause. Lord Macaulay, the most uncompromising of Whigs, has nobly expressed this feeling. The present sketch may fitly be ended by his *Epitaph on a Jacobite:*—

> To my true king I offered free from stain
> Courage and faith; vain faith, and courage vain.
> For him I threw lands, honours, wealth away,
> And one dear hope, that was more prized than they.
> For him I languished in a foreign clime,
> Grey-haired with sorrow in my manhood's prime;
> Heard on Lavernia Scargill's whispering trees,
> And pined by Arno for my lovelier Tees;
> Beheld each night my home in fevered sleep,
> Each morning started from the dream to weep;
> Till God, who saw me tried too sorely, gave
> The resting-place I asked—an early grave.
> Oh thou, whom chance leads to this nameless stone,
> From that proud country which was once mine own,
> By those white cliffs I never more must see,
> By that dear language which I spake like thee,
> Forget all feuds, and shed one English tear
> O'er English dust. A broken heart lies here.

# LIST OF BOOKS.

The following is a list of some of the more convenient books of reference relating to the Highland campaigns :—

Hill Burton's History of Scotland, chaps. lxxii., lxxiii., lxxv., lxxxii., lxxxix., xcii.

Robert Chambers's History of the Rebellions in Scotland and History of the Rebellion of 1745-46.

Browne's History of the Highlands. 4 vols. Glasgow, 1836.

Keltie's History of the Scottish Highlands. 2 vols. Edinburgh and London, 1877.

Mark Napier's Memorials of Montrose, 2 vols., Maitland Club, 1848; Memoirs of Montrose, 2 vols., Edinburgh, 1856; and Memorials of Dundee, 3 vols., Edinburgh, 1859-62. (Napier reviews the whole of the original authorities, and despite their violent partisanship his books remain the standard works on Montrose and Dundee.)

Chronicles of the Atholl and Tullibardine Families. Collected and arranged by John, seventh Duke of Atholl, K.T. 4 vols. Edinburgh, privately printed, 1896.

Gardiner's History of the Great Civil War, chaps. xxvi., xxx., xxxiii., xxxvi. (Montrose's campaign).

Baillie's Letters and Journals. Edited by David Laing. 3 vols. Edinburgh, 1841-42.

Wishart's Deeds of Montrose. Edited by the Rev. Alex. D. Murdoch and H. F. Morland Simpson. Edinburgh, 1893.

Spalding's Memorials of the Troubles in Scotland, etc. 2 vols. Spalding Club, 1850.

Patrick Gordon of Ruthven's Britane's Distemper. Spalding Club, 1844.

Macaulay's History of England, chap. xiii. (Dundee's campaign).

Philip's Grameid. Edited by the Rev. Alex. D. Murdoch. Scottish History Society, 1888.

Drummond's Memoirs of Sir Ewen Cameron of Locheill. Abbotsford Club, 1842.

Lieut.-General Hugh Mackay's Memoirs of the War in Scotland and Ireland, MDCLXXXIX.-MDCXCI. Bannatyne Club, 1833.

The Lockhart Papers. 2 vols. London, 1817.

The Culloden Papers. London, 1815.

Lord Mahon's History of England from the Peace of Utrecht to the Peace of Versailles, chaps. v., vi., x., xxvii., xxviii., xxix. (1715, 1719, 1745. The chapters relating to the '45 were printed separately as "The Forty-five." London, 1851.)

z

Rae's History of the Late Rebellion. Dumfries, 1718.

Patten's History of the Late Rebellion. London, 1717.

The Master of Sinclair's Memoirs of the Insurrection in Scotland in 1715. Notes by Sir Walter Scott. Abbotsford Club, 1858.

A Faithful Register of the late Rebellion. London, 1718. (Trials of Prisoners.)

A Collection of Original Letters, etc., relating to the Rebellion, 1715. Edinburgh, 1730.

The Jacobite Attempt of 1719. Edited by W. K. Dickson. Scottish History Society, 1895.

Home's History of the Rebellion in 1745. London, 1802.

The Chevalier de Johnstone's Memoirs of the Rebellion in 1745 and 1746. London, 1820.

Maxwell of Kirkconnell's Narrative of Charles Prince of Wales' Expedition to Scotland. Maitland Club, 1841.

Trial of Lord Provost Stewart. Edinburgh, 1747.

Report of the Proceedings of the Board of General Officers on the Conduct of Lt.-Gen. Sir John Cope. London, 1749.

A List of Persons concerned in the Rebellion, 1745-46. With a Preface by Lord Rosebery, and Annotations by the Rev. Walter Macleod. Scottish History Society, 1890.

Dennistoun's Memoirs of Sir Robert Strange and Andrew Lumisden. 2 vols. London, 1855.

Mrs Thomson's Memoirs of the Jacobites. 3 vols. London, 1845.

Ewald's Life and Times of Prince Charles Stuart. London, 1883.

Jesse's Memoirs of the Pretenders and their Adherents. 2 vols. London, 1845.

Klose's Memoirs of Prince Charles Stuart. 2 vols. London, 1845.

Historical Papers relating to the Jacobite Period. Edited by Colonel James Allardyce. 2 vols. New Spalding Club, 1895-96.

March of the Highland Army in the Years 1745-46. (Order-book kept by Captain James Stuart of Lord Ogilvie's Regiment. Contains daily Orders from Oct. 10, 1745, to April 12, 1746.) Miscellany of the Spalding Club, 1841, vol. i., pp. 275-343.

The Lyon in Mourning. Edited by Henry Paton. 3 vols. Scottish History Society, 1895-96.

Itinerary of Prince Charles Edward Stuart. Supplement to The Lyon in Mourning, compiled by W. B. Blaikie. Scottish History Society, 1897. (An invaluable manual. Contains a full bibliography of the authorities for the history of the '45.)

Memorials of John Murray of Broughton. Edited by Robert Fitzroy Bell. Scottish History Society, 1898.

Sir John Cope and the Rebellion of 1745. By the late General Sir Robert Cadell, K.C.B., Edinburgh: William Blackwood & Sons, 1898.

# INDEX.

PRINTED BY W. AND A. K. JOHNSTON, EDINBURGH AND LONDON.

www.ingramcontent.com/pod-product-compliance
Lightning Source LLC
Chambersburg PA
CBHW020606030726

47497CB00007B/2114